Penguin Books
The Story of a Non-Marrying Man
and Other Stories

Doris Lessing was born in 1919 and spent her childhood on a large farm in Southern Rhodesia. In 1949 she arrived in England with very little money and the manuscript of her first novel, *The Grass is Singing*, which was at once accepted.

This was followed by a volume of short stories, *This Was the Old Chief's Country* (1951) and then by *Martha Quest* (1952), the first of the 'Children of Violence' novels; the others in the series were *A Proper Marriage* (1954), *A Ripple from the Storm* (1958), *Landlocked* (1965) and *The Four-Gated City* (1969). Her other works include *Five* (1953: winner of the Somerset Maugham Award for 1954), *Going Home* (1957), *The Golden Notebook* (1962: winner of the Medici Prize), *Briefing for a Descent into Hell* (1971), *The Summer Before the Dark* (1973), *Memoirs of a Survivor* (1975), *To Room Nineteen* (1978), and *The Temptation of Jack Orkney* (1978). The novels already published in her visionary cycle, *Canopus in Argos*, are: *Shikasta* (1979), *The Marriages between Zones Three, Four and Five* (1980), *the Sirian Experiments* (1981), *The Making of the Representative for Planet 8* (1982), and *The Sentimental Agents in the Volyen Empire* (1983).

In 1982 Doris Lessing was awarded the Austrian State Prize for Literature and The Shakespeare Prize.

Man

Doris Lessing

The Story of a
Non-Marrying Man
and Other Stories

Penguin Books

Penguin Books Ltd, Harmondsworth, Middlesex, England
Viking Penguin Inc., 40 West 23rd Street, New York, New York 10010, U.S.A.
Penguin Books Australia Ltd, Ringwood, Victoria, Australia
Penguin Books Canada Ltd, 2801 John Street, Markham, Ontario, Canada L3R 1B4
Penguin Books (N.Z.) Ltd, 182–190 Wairau Road, Auckland 10, New Zealand

This collection first published by Jonathan Cape 1972
Published in Penguin Books 1975
Reprinted 1976, 1977, 1979, 1980, 1982, 1985

Set, printed and bound in Great Britain by
Cox & Wyman Ltd, Reading
Set in Intertype Plantin

Contents

For Jenny, with my love

The Story of a Non-Marrying Man

and Other Stories

Out of the Fountain

I could begin, There was once a man called Ephraim who lived in ... but for me this story begins with a fog. Fog in Paris delayed a flight to London by a couple of hours, and so a group of travellers sat around a table drinking coffee and entertaining each other.

A woman from Texas joked that a week before she had thrown coins into the fountain in Rome for luck – and had been dogged by minor ill-fortune ever since. A Canadian said he had spent far too much money on a holiday and at the same fountain three days ago had been tempted to lift coins out with a magnet when no one was looking. Someone said that in a Berlin theatre last night there had been a scene where a girl flung money all about the stage in a magnificently scornful gesture. Which led us on to where money is trampled on, burned, flung about or otherwise ritually scorned; which is odd, since such gestures never take place in life. Not at all, said a matron from New York – she had seen with her own eyes some Flower Children burning money on a sidewalk to show their contempt for it; but for her part what it showed was that they must have rich parents. (This dates the story, or at least the fog.)

All the same, considering the role money plays in all our lives, it *is* odd how often authors cause characters to insult dollar bills, roubles, pound notes. Which enables audience, readers, to go home, or to shut the book, feeling cleansed of the stuff? Above it?

Whereas we are told that in less surly days sultans on feast days flung gold coins into crowds happy to scramble for it; that kings caused showers of gold to descend on loved ministers; and that if jewels fell in showers from the sky no one would dream of asking suspicious questions.

The nearest any one of us could remember to this kingly stuff was a certain newspaper mogul in London who would reward a promising young journalist for an article which he (the mogul) liked, with an envelope stuffed full of five pound notes sent around by special messenger – but this kind of thing is only too open to unkind interpretation; and the amount of ill-feeling aroused in the bosoms of fellow journalists, and the terror in that of the recipient for fear the thing might be talked about, is probably why we stage such scenes as it were in reverse, and why, on the edge of a magic fountain, we slide in a single coin, like a love letter into an envelope during an affair which one's better sense entirely deplores. Sympathetic magic – but a small magic, a mini-magic, a most furtive summoning of the Gods of Gold. And, if a hand rose from the fountain to throw us coins and jewels, it is more than likely that, schooled as we are by recent literature, we'd sneer and throw them back in its teeth – so to speak.

And now a man who had not spoken at all said that he knew of a case where jewels had been flung into the dust of a public square in Italy. No one had thrown them back. He took from his pocket a wallet, and from the wallet a fold of paper such as jewellers use, and on the paper lay a single spark or gleam of light. It was a slice of milk-and-rainbow opal. Yes, he said, he had been there. He had picked up the fragment and kept it. It wasn't valuable, of course. He would tell us the story if he thought there was time, but for some reason it was a tale so precious to him that he didn't want to bungle it through having to hurry. Here there was another swirl of silkily gleaming fog beyond the glass of the restaurant wall, and another announcement of unavoidable delay.

So he told the story. One day someone will introduce me to a young man called Nikki (perhaps, or what you will) who was born during the Second World War in Italy. His father was a hero, and his mother now the wife of the Ambassador to . . . Or perhaps in a bus, or at a dinner party, there will be a girl who has a pearl hanging around her neck on a chain, and when asked about it she will say: Imagine, my mother was given this pearl by a man who was practically a stranger, and when she gave it to me she said . . . Something like that will happen: and then this story will have a different beginning, not a fog at all . . .

There was a man called Ephraim who lived in Johannesburg. His father was to do with diamonds, as had been his father. The family were immigrants. This is still true of all people from Johannesburg, a city a century old. Ephraim was a middle son, not brilliant or stupid, not good or bad. He was nothing in particular. His brothers became diamond merchants, but Ephraim was not cut out for anything immediately obvious, and so at last he was apprenticed to an uncle to learn the trade of diamond-cutting.

To cut a diamond perfectly is an act like a samurai's sword-thrust, or a master archer's centred arrow. When an important diamond is shaped a man may spend a week, or even weeks, studying it, accumulating powers of attention, memory, intuition, till he has reached that moment when he finally knows that a tap, no more, at just *that* point of tension in the stone will split it exactly *so*.

While Ephraim learned to do this, he lived at home in a Johannesburg suburb; and his brothers and sisters married and had families. He was the son who took his time about getting married, and about whom the family first joked, saying that he was choosy; and then they remained silent when others talked of him with that edge on their voices, irritated, a little malicious, even frightened, which is caused by those men and women who refuse to fulfil the ordinary purposes of nature. The kind ones said he was a good son, working nicely under his uncle Ben, and living respectably at home, and on Sunday nights playing poker with bachelor friends. He was twenty-five, then thirty, thirty-five, forty. His parents became old and died, and he lived alone in the family house. People stopped noticing him. Nothing was expected of him.

Then a senior person became ill, and Ephraim was asked to fly in his stead to Alexandria for a special job. A certain rich merchant of Alexandria had purchased an uncut diamond as a present for his daughter, who was to be married shortly. He wished only the best for the diamond. Ephraim, revealed by this happening as one of the world's master diamond-cutters, flew to Egypt, spent some days in communion with the stone in a quiet room in the merchant's house, and then caused it to fall apart into three lovely pieces. These were for a ring and earrings.

Now he should have flown home again; but the merchant asked him to dinner. An odd chance that – unusual. Not many people got inside that rich closed world. But perhaps the merchant had become infected by the week of rising tension while Ephraim became one with the diamond in a quiet room.

At dinner Ephraim met the girl for whom the jewels were destined.

And now – but what can be said about the fortnight that followed? Certainly not that Ephraim, the little artisan from Johannesburg, fell in love with Mihrène, daughter of a modern merchant prince. Nothing so simple. And that the affair had about it a quality out of the ordinary was shown by the reaction of the merchant himself, Mihrène's conventional papa.

Conventional, commonplace, banal – these are the words for the members of the set, or class, to which Mihrène Kantannis belonged. In all the cities about the Mediterranean they live in a scattered community, very rich, but tastefully so, following international fashions, approving Paris when they should and London when they should, making trips to New York or Rome, summering on whichever shore they have chosen, by a kind of group instinct, to be the right one for the year, and sharing comfortably tolerant opinions. They were people, are people, with nothing remarkable about them but their wealth, and the enchanting Mihrène, whom Ephraim first saw in a mist of white embroidered muslin standing by a fountain, was a girl neither more pretty nor more gifted than, let's say, a dozen that evening in Alexandria, a thousand or so in Egypt, hundreds of thousands in the countries round about, all of which produce so plentifully her particular type – her beautiful type: small-boned, black-haired, black-eyed, apricot-skinned, lithe.

She had lived for twenty years in this atmosphere of well-chosen luxury; loved and bickered with her mother and her sisters; respected her papa; and was intending to marry Paulo, a young man from South America with whom she would continue to live exactly the same kind of life, only in Buenos Aires.

For her it was an ordinary evening, a family dinner at which a friend of Papa's was present. She did not know about the diamonds: they were to be a surprise. She was wearing last year's dress and a choker of false pearls: that season it was smart to wear 'costume' pearls, and to leave one's real pearls in a box on one's dressing-table.

Ephraim, son of jewellers, saw the false pearls around that neck and suffered.

Why, though? Johannesburg is full of pretty girls. But he had not travelled much, and Johannesburg, rough, built on gold, as it were breathing by the power of gold, a city waxing and waning with the fortunes of gold (as befits this story), may be exciting, violent, vibrant, but it has no mystery, nothing for the imagination, no invisible dimensions. Whereas Alexandria . . . This house, for instance, with its discreetly blank outer walls that might conceal anything, crime, or the hidden court of an exiled king, held inner gardens and fountains, and Mihrène, dressed appropriately in moonwhite and who . . . well, perhaps she wasn't entirely at her best that evening. There were those who said she had an ugly laugh. Sometimes the family joked that it was lucky she would never have to earn a living. At one point during dinner, perhaps feeling that she ought to contribute to the entertainment, she told a rather flat and slightly bitchy story about a friend. She was certainly bored, yawned once or twice, and did not try too hard to hide the yawns. The diamond-cutter from Johannesburg gazed at her, forgot to eat, and asked twice why she wore false pearls in a voice rough with complaint. He was gauche, she decided – and forgot him.

He did not return home, but wired for money. He had never spent any, and so had a great deal available for the single perfect pearl which he spent days looking for, and which he found at last in a back room in Cairo, where he sat bargaining over coffee cups for some days with an old Persian dealer who knew as much about gems as he did, and who would not trade in anything but the best.

With this jewel he arrived at the house of Mihrène's father, and when he was seated in a room opening on to an inner court where jasmine clothed a wall, and lily pads a pool, he asked permission to give the pearl to the young girl.

It had been strange that Papa had invited this tradesman to dinner. It was strange that now Papa did not get angry. He was shrewd: it was his life to be shrewd. There was no nuance of commercial implication in a glance, a tone of voice, a turn of phrase, that he was not certain to assess rightly. Opposite this fabulously rich man into whose house only the rich came as guests, sat a little diamond-cutter who proposed to give his daughter a small fortune in the shape of a pearl, and who wanted nothing in return for it.

They drank coffee, and then they drank whisky, and they talked of the world's jewels and of the forthcoming wedding, until for the second time Ephraim was asked to dinner.

At dinner Mihrène sat opposite the elderly gentleman (he was forty-five or so) who was Papa's business friend, and was ordinarily polite: then slightly more polite, because of a look from Papa. The party was Mihrène, her father, her fiancé Paulo, and Ephraim. The mother and sisters were visiting elsewhere. Nothing happened during the meal. The young couple were rather inattentive to the older pair. At the end, Ephraim took a screw of paper from his pocket, and emptied from it a single perfect pearl that had a gleam like the flesh of a rose, or of a twenty-year-old girl. This pearl he offered to Mihrène, with the remark that she oughtn't to wear false pearls. Again it was harshly inflected; a complaint, or a reproach for imperfect perfection.

The pearl lay on white damask in candlelight. Into the light above the pearl was thrust the face of Ephraim, whose features she could reconstruct from the last time she had seen him a couple of weeks before only with the greatest of difficulty.

It was, of course, an extraordinary moment. But not dramatic – no, it lacked that high apex of decisiveness as when Ephraim tapped a diamond, or an archer lets loose his bow. Mihrène looked at her father for an explanation. So, of course, did her fiancé. Her father did not look confused, or embarrassed, so much as that he wore the air of somebody standing on one side because here is a situation which he has never professed himself competent to judge. And Mihrène had probably never before in her life been left free to make a decision.

She picked up the pearl from the damask, and let it lie in her palm. She, her fiancé, and her father, looked at the pearl whose value they were all well equipped to assess, and Ephraim looked sternly at the girl. Then she lifted long, feathery black lashes and looked at him – in inquiry? An appeal to be let off? His eyes were judging, disappointed; they said what his words had said: Why are you content with the second-rate?

Preposterous . . .

Impossible . . .

Finally Mihrène gave the slightest shrug of shoulders, tonight covered in pink organza, and said to Ephraim, 'Thank you, thank you very much.'

They rose from the table. The four drank coffee on the terrace over which rose a wildly evocative Alexandrian moon, two nights away from the full, a moon quite unlike any that might shine over strident Johannesburg. Mihrène let the pearl lie on her palm and reflect moonrays, while from time to time her black eyes engaged with Ephraim's – but what colour his were had never been, would never be, of interest to anyone – and, there was no doubt of it, he was like someone warning, or reminding, or even threatening.

Next day he went back to Johannesburg, and on Mihrène's dressing-table lay a small silver box in which was a single perfect pearl.

She was to marry in three weeks.

Immediately the incident became in the family: 'That crazy little Jew who fell for Mihrène . . .' Her acceptance of the pearl was talked of as an act of delicacy on her part, of kindness. 'Mihrène was so kind to the poor old thing . . .' Thus they smoothed over what had happened, made acceptable an incident which could have no place in their life, their thinking. But they knew, of course, and most particularly did Mihrène know, that something else had happened.

When she refused to marry Paulo, quite prettily and nicely, Papa and Mamma Kantannis made ritual remarks about her folly, her ingratitude, and so forth, but in engagements like these no hearts are expected to be broken, for the marriages are like the arranged marriages of dynasties. If she did not marry Paulo, she would marry someone like him – and she was very young.

They remarked that she had not been herself since the affair of the pearl. Papa said to himself that he would see to it no more fly-by-nights. arrived at his dinner-table. They arranged for Mihrène a visit to cousins in Istanbul.

Meanwhile in Johannesburg a diamond-cutter worked at his trade, cutting diamonds for engagement rings, dress rings, tie pins, necklaces, bracelets. He imagined a flat bowl of crystal, which glittered like diamonds, in which were massed roses. But the roses were all white, shades of white. He saw roses which were cold marble white, white verging on coffee colour, greenish white, like the wings of certain butterflies, white that blushed, a creamy white, white that was nearly beige, white that was almost yellow. He imagined a hundred shades of white in rose shapes. These he pressed together, filled a crystal dish with them and gave them to – Mihrène? It is possible that already he scarcely thought of her. He imagined how he would collect stones in shades of white, and create a perfect jewel, bracelet, necklet, or crescent for the hair, and present this jewel to – Mihrène? Does it matter whom it was for? He bought opals, like mist held behind glass on which lights moved and faded, like milk where fire lay buried, like the congealed breath of a girl on a frosty night. He bought pearls, each one separately, each one perfect. He bought fragments of mother-of-pearl. He bought moonstones like clouded diamonds. He even bought lumps of glass that someone had shaped to reflect light perfectly. He bought white jade and crystals and collected chips of diamond to make the suppressed fires in pearl and opal flash out in reply to their glittering frost. These jewels he had in folded flat paper, and they were kept first in a small cigarette box, and then were transferred to a larger box that had been for throat lozenges, and then to an even larger box that had held cigars. He played with these gems, dreamed over them, arranged them in his mind in a thousand ways. Sometimes he remembered an exquisite girl dressed in moonmist: the memory was becoming more and more like a sentimental post-card or an old-fashioned calendar.

In Istanbul Mihrène married, without her family's approval, a young Italian engineer whom normally she would never have met. Her uncle was engaged in reconstructing a certain yacht; the engineer was in the uncle's office to discuss the reconstruction when Mihrène came in. It was she who made the first move: it would have to be. He was twenty-seven, with nothing but his salary, and no particular prospects. His name was Carlos. He was political. That is, precisely, he was revolutionary, a conspirator. Politics did not enter the world of Mihrène. Or rather, it could be said that such families *are* politics, politics in their aspect of wealth, but this becomes evident only when deals are made that are so vast that they have international cachet, and repute, like the alliances or rifts between countries.

Carlos called Mihrène 'a white goose' when she tried to impress him with her seriousness. He called her 'a little rich bitch'. He made a favour of taking her to meetings where desper-ately serious young men and women discussed the forthcoming war – the year was 1939. It was an affair absolutely within the traditions of such romances: her family were bound to think she was throwing herself away; he and his friends on the whole con-sidered that it was he who was conferring the benefits.

To give herself courage in her determination to be worthy of this young hero, she would open a tiny silver box where a pearl lay on silk, and say to herself: *He* thought I was worth some-thing . . .

She married her Carlos in the week Paulo married a girl from a French dynasty. Mihrène went to Rome and lived in a small villa without servants, and with nothing to fall back on but the memory of a nondescript elderly man who had sat opposite her throughout two long, dull dinners and who had given her a pearl as if he were giving her a lesson. She thought that in all her life no one else had ever demanded anything of her, ever asked anything, ever taken her seriously.

The war began. In Buenos Aires the bride who had taken her place lived in luxury. Mihrène, a poor housewife, saw her husband who was a conspirator against the fascist Mussolini become a conscript in Mussolini's armies, then saw him go away to fight, while she waited for the birth of her first child.

The war swallowed her. When she was heard of again, her hero was dead, and her first child was dead, and her second, conceived on Carlos's final leave, was due to be born in a couple of months. She was in a small town in the centre of Italy with no resources at all but her pride: she had sworn she would not earn the approval of her parents on any terms but her own. The family she had married into had suffered badly: she had a room in the house of an aunt.

The Germans were retreating through Italy: after them chased the victorious armies of the Allies ... but that sounds like an official war history.

To try again: over a peninsula that was shattered, ruinous, starved by war, two armies of men foreign to the natives of the place were in movement; one in retreat up towards the body of Europe, the other following it. There were places where these opposing bodies were geographically so intermingled that only uniforms distinguished them. Both armies were warm, well clothed, well fed, supplied with alcohol and cigarettes. The native inhabitants had no heat, no warm clothes, little food, no cigarettes. They had, however, a great deal of alcohol.

In one army was a man called Ephraim who, being elderly, was not a combatant, but part of the machinery which supplied it with food and goods. He was a sergeant, and as unremarkable in the army as he was in civilian life. For the four years he had been a soldier, for the most part in North Africa, he had pursued a private interest, or obsession, which was, when he arrived anywhere at all, to seek out the people and places that could add yet another fragment of iridescent or gleaming substance to the mass which he carried around in a flat tin in his pack.

The men he served with found him and his preoccupation mildly humorous. He was not disliked or liked enough to make a target for that concentration of unease caused by people who alarm others. They did not laugh at him, or call him madman. Perhaps he was more like that dog who is a regiment's pet. Once he mislaid his tin of loot and a couple of men went into a moderate danger to get it back: sometimes a comrade would bring him a bit of something or other picked up in a bazaar – amber, an amulet, a jade. He advised them how to make bargains; he went on expeditions with them to buy stones for wives and girls back home.

He was in Italy that week when – *everything disintegrated.* Anyone who has been in, or near, war (which means, by now, everyone, or at least everyone in Europe and Asia) knows that time – a week, days, sometimes hours – when everything falls apart, when all forms of order dissolve, including those which mark the difference between enemy and enemy.

During this time old scores of all kinds are settled. It is when unpopular officers get killed by 'accident'. It is when a man who has an antipathy for another will kill him, or beat him up. A man who wants a woman will rape her, if she is around, or rape another in her stead if she is not. Women get raped; and those who want to be will make sure they are where the raping is. A woman who hates another will harm her. In short, it is a time of anarchy, of looting, of arson and destruction for destruction's sake. There are those who believe that this time out of ordinary order is the reason for war, its hidden justification, its purpose and law, another pattern behind the one we see. Afterwards there are no records of what has happened. There is no one to keep records: everyone is engaged in participating, or in protecting himself.

Ephraim was in a small town near Florence when his war reached that phase. There was a certain corporal, also from Johannesburg, who always had a glitter in his look when they talked of Ephraim's tin full of jewels. On an evening when every human being in the place was hunter or hunted, manoeuvred for advantage, or followed scents of gain, this man, in civilian life a store-keeper, looked across a room at Ephraim and grinned.

Ephraim knew what to expect. Everyone knew what to expect – at such moments much older knowledges come to the surface together with old instincts. Ephraim quietly left a schoolroom for that week converted into a mess, and went out into the early dark of streets emptied by fear, where walls still shook and dust fell in clouds because of near gunfire. But it was also very quiet. Terror's cold nausea silences, places invisible hands across mouths . . . The occasional person hurrying through those streets kept his eyes in front, and his mouth tight. Two such people meeting did not look at each other except for a moment when their eyes violently encountered in a hard clash of inquiry. Behind every shutter or pane or door people stood, or sat or crouched, waiting for the time out of order to end, and guns and sharp instruments stood near their hands.

Through these streets went Ephraim. The Corporal had not seen him go, but by now would certainly have found the scent. At any moment he would catch up with Ephraim who carried in his hand a flat tin, and who as he walked looked into holes in walls and in pavements, peered into a church half filled with rubble, investigated torn earth where bomb fragments had fallen and even looked up into the branches of trees as he passed and at the plants growing at doorways. Finally, as he passed a fountain clogged with debris, he knelt for a moment and slid his tin down into the mud. He walked away, fast, not looking back to see if he had been seen, and around the corner of the church he met Corporal Van der Merwe. As Ephraim came up to his enemy he held out empty hands and stood still. The Corporal was a big man and twenty years younger. Van der Merwe gave him a frowning look, indicative of his powers of shrewd assessment, rather like Mihrène's father's look when he heard how this little nonentity proposed to give his daughter a valuable pearl for no reason at all, and when Ephraim saw it, he at once raised his hands above his head like a prisoner surrendering, while Van der Merwe frisked him. There was a moment when Ephraim might very well have been killed: it hung in the balance. But down the street a rabble of soldiers were looting pictures and valuables from another church, and Van der Merwe, his attention caught by them, simply watched Ephraim walk away, and then ran off himself to join the looters.

By the time that season of anarchy had finished, Ephraim was a couple of hundred miles north. Six months later, in a town ten miles from the one where he had nearly been murdered by a man once again his military subordinate (but that incident had disappeared, had become buried in the foreign texture of another time, or dimension), Ephraim asked for an evening's leave and travelled as he could to V—, where he imagined, perhaps, that he would walk through deserted streets to a rubble-filled fountain and beside this fountain would kneel, and slide his hand into dirty water to retrieve his treasure.

But the square was full of people, and though this was not a time when a café served more than a cup of bad coffee or water flavoured with chemicals, the two cafés had people in them who were half starved but already inhabiting the forms of ordinary life. They served, of course, unlimited quantities of cheap wine. Everyone was drunken, or tipsy. In a wine country, when there is no food, wine becomes a kind of food, craved like food. Ephraim walked past the fountain and saw that the water was filthy, too dirty to let anyone see what was in it, or whether it had been cleared of rubble, and, with the rubble, his treasure.

He sat on the pavement under a torn awning, by a cracked wood table, and ordered coffee. He was the only soldier there; or at least, the only uniform. The main tide of soldiery was washing back and forth to one side of this little town. Uniforms meant barter, meant food, clothing, cigarettes. In a moment half a dozen little boys were at his elbow offering him girls. Women of all ages were sauntering past or making themselves visible, or trying to catch his eye, since the female population of the town were for the most part in that condition for which in our debased time we have the shorthand term: being prepared to sell themselves for a cigarette. Old women, old men, cripples, all kinds of person, stretched in front of him hands displaying various more or less useless objects – lighters, watches, old buckles or bottles or brooches – hoping to get chocolate or food in return. Ephraim sat on, sad with himself because he had not brought eggs or tinned stuffs or chocolate. He had not thought of it. He sat while hungry people with sharp faces that glittered with a winy fever pressed about him and the bodies of a dozen or so women arranged themselves in this or that pose for his inspection. He felt sick. He was almost ready to go away and forget his tin full of gems. Then a tired-looking woman in a much-washed print dress lifted high in front because of pregnancy came to sit at his table. He thought she was there to sell herself, and hardly looked at her, unable to bear it that a pregnant woman was brought to such a pass.

She said: 'Don't you remember me?'

And now he searched her face, and she searched his. He looked for Mihrène; and she tried to see in him what it was that changed her life, to find what it was that that pearl embodied which she carried with her in a bit of cloth sewn into her slip.

They sat trying to exchange news; but these two people had so little in common they could not even say: And how is so and so? What has happened to him, or to her?

The hungry inhabitants of the town withdrew a little way, because this soldier had become a person, a man who was a friend of Mihrène, who was their friend.

The two were there for a couple of hours. They were on the whole more embarrassed than anything. It was clear to both by now that whatever events had taken place between them, momentous or not (they were not equipped to say), these events were in some realm or on a level where their daylight selves were strangers. It was certainly not the point that she, the unforgettable girl of Alexandria, had become a rather drab young woman waiting to give birth in a war-shattered town; not the point that for her he had carried with him for four years of war a treasury of gems, some precious, some mildly valuable, some worthless, bits of substance with one thing in common: their value related to some other good which had had, arbitrarily and for a short time, the name *Mihrène*.

It had become intolerable to sit there, over coffee made of burned grain, while all round great hungry eyes focused on him, the soldier, who had come so cruelly to their starving town with empty hands. He had soon to leave. He had reached this town on the back boards of a peasant's cart, there being no other transport; and if he did not get another lift of the same kind, he would have to walk ten miles before midnight.

Over the square was rising a famished watery moon, unlike the moons of his own city, unlike the wild moons of Egypt. At last he simply got up and walked to the edge of the evil-smelling fountain. He kneeled down on its edge, plunged in his hand, encountered all sorts of slimy things, probably dead rats or cats or even bits of dead people, and after some groping, felt the familiar shape of his tin. He pulled it out, wiped it dry on some old newspaper that had blown there, went back to the table, sat down, opened the tin. Pearls are fed on light and air. Opals don't like being shut away from light which makes their depths come alive. But no water had got in, and he emptied the glittering, gleaming heap on to the cracked wood of the table top.

All round pressed the hungry people who looked at the gems and thought of food.

She took from her breast a bit of cloth and untwisted her pearl. She held it out to him.

'I never sold it,' she said.

And now he looked at her – sternly, as he had done before.

She said, in the pretty English of those who have learned it from governesses: 'I have sometimes needed food, I've been hungry, you know! I've had no servants . . .'

He looked at her. Oh, how she knew that look, how she had studied it in memory! Irritation, annoyance, grief. All these, but above all disappointment. And more than these, a warning, or reminder. It said, she felt: Silly white goose! Rich little bitch! Poor little nothing! Why do you always get it wrong? Why are you stupid? What is a pearl compared with what it stands for? If you are hungry and need money, sell it, of course!

She sat in that sudden stillness that says a person is fighting not to weep. Her beautiful eyes brimmed. Then she said stubbornly: 'I'll never sell it. Never!'

As for him he was muttering: I should have brought food. I was a dummkopf. What's the use of these things . . .

But in the hungry eyes around him he read that they were thinking how even in times of famine there are always men and women who have food hidden away to be bought by gold or jewels.

'Take them,' he said to the children, to the women, to the old people.

They did not understand him, did not believe him.

He said again: 'Go on. Take them!'

No one moved. Then he stood up and began flinging into the air pearls, opals, moonstones, gems of all kinds, to fall as they would. For a few moments there was a mad scene of people bobbing and scrambling, and the square emptied as people raced back to the corners they lived in with what they had picked up out of the dust. It was not yet time for the myth to start, the story of how a soldier had walked into the town, and inexplicably pulled treasure out of the fountain which he flung into the air like a king or a sultan – treasure that was ambiguous and fertile like a king's, since one man might pick up the glitter of a diamond that later turned out to be worthless glass, and another be left with a smallish pearl that had nevertheless been so carefully chosen it was worth months of food, or even a house or small farm.

'I must go,' said Ephraim to his companion.

She inclined her head in farewell, as to an acquaintance re-encountered. She watched a greying, dumpy little man walk away past a fountain, past a church, then out of sight.

Later that night she took out the pearl and held it in her hand. If she sold it, she would remain comfortably independent of her own family. Here, in the circle of the family of her dead husband, she would marry again, another engineer or civil servant: she would be worth marrying, even as a widow with a child. Of course if she returned to her own family, she would also remarry, as a rich young widow with a small child from that dreadful war, luckily now over.

Such thoughts went through her head: at last she thought that it didn't make any difference what she did. Whatever function Ephraim's intervention had performed in her life was over when she refused to marry Paulo, had married Carlos, had come to Italy and given birth to two children, one dead from an unimportant children's disease that had been fatal only because of the quality of war-food, war-warmth. She had been wrenched out of her pattern, had been stamped, or claimed, by the pearl – by something else. Nothing she could do now would put her back where she had been. It did not matter whether she stayed in Italy or returned to the circles she had been born in.

As for Ephraim, he went back to Johannesburg when the war finished, and continued to cut diamonds and to play poker on Sunday nights.

This story ended more or less with the calling of the flight number. As we went to the tarmac where illuminated wisps of fog still lingered, the lady from Texas asked the man who had told the story if perhaps he was Ephraim?

'No,' said Dr Rosen, a man of sixty or so from Johannesburg, a brisk, well-dressed man with nothing much to notice about him – like most of the world's citizens.

No, he was most emphatically not Ephraim.

Then how did he know all this? Perhaps he was there?

Yes, he was there. But if he was to tell us how he came to be a hundred miles from where he should have been, in that chaotic, horrible week – it was horrible, horrible! – and in civvies, then that story would be even longer than the one he had already told us.

Couldn't he tell us *why* he was there?

Perhaps he was after that tin of Ephraim's too! We could think so if we liked. It would be excusable of us to think so. There was a fortune in that tin, and everyone in the regiment knew it.

He was a friend of Ephraim's then? He knew Ephraim?

Yes, he could say that. He had known Ephraim for, let's see, nearly fifty years. Yes, he thought he could say he was Ephraim's friend.

In the aircraft Dr Rosen sat reading, with nothing more to tell us.

But one day I'll meet a young man called Nikki, or Raffele; or a girl wearing a single pearl around her neck on a gold chain; or perhaps a middle-aged woman who says she thinks pearls are unlucky, she would never touch them herself: a man once gave her younger sister a pearl and it ruined her entire life. Something like that will happen, and this story will have a different shape.

An Unposted Love Letter

Yes, I saw the look your wife's face put on when I said, 'I have so many husbands, I don't need a husband.' She did not exchange a look with you, but that was because she did not need to – later when you got home she said, 'What an affected thing to say!' and you replied, 'Don't forget she is an actress.' You said this meaning exactly what I would mean if I had said it, I'm certain of that. And perhaps she heard it like that, I do hope so *because I know what you are* and if your wife does not hear what you say then this is a smallness on your part that I don't forgive you. If I can live alone, and out of fastidiousness, then you must have a wife as good as you are. My husbands, the men who set light to my soul (yes, I know how your wife would smile if I used that phrase), are worthy of you ... I know that I am giving myself away now, confessing how much that look on your wife's face hurt. *Didn't she know that even then I was playing my part?* Oh no, after all, I don't forgive you your wife, no I don't.

If I said, 'I don't need a husband, I have so many lovers,' then of course everyone at the dinner-table would have laughed in just such a way: it would have been the rather banal 'outrageousness' expected of me. An ageing star, the fading beauty ... 'I have so many lovers' – pathetic, and brave too. Yes, that remark would have been too apt, too smooth, right for just any 'beautiful but fading' actress. But not right for me, no, because after all, I am not just any actress, I am Victoria Carrington, and I know exactly what is due to me and from me. I know what is fitting (not for *me*, that is not important) but for what I stand for. Do you imagine I couldn't have said it differently – like this, for instance: 'I am an artist and therefore androgynous.' Or: 'I have created inside myself Man who plays opposite to my Woman.'

Or: 'I have objectified in myself the male components of my soul and it is from this source that I create.' Oh, I'm not stupid, not ignorant, I know the different dialects of our time and even how to use them. But imagine if I had said any of these things last night! It would have been a false note, you would all have been uncomfortable, irritated, and afterwards you would have said: 'Actresses shouldn't try to be intelligent.' (Not you, the others.) Probably they don't believe it, not really, that an actress must be stupid, but their sense of discrepancy, of discordance, would have expressed itself in such a way. Whereas their silence when I said, 'I don't need a husband, I have so many husbands,' was right, for it was *the remark right for me* – it was more than 'affected', or 'outrageous' – *it was making a claim that they had to recognize.*

That word 'affected', have you ever really thought why it is applied to actresses? (You have of course, I'm no foreign country to you, I felt that, but it gives me pleasure to talk to you like this.) The other afternoon I went to see Irma Painter in her new play, and afterwards I went back to congratulate her (for she had heard, of course, that I was in the auditorium and would have felt insulted if I hadn't gone – I'm different, I hate it when people feel obliged to come back). We were sitting in her dressing-room and I was looking at her face as she wiped the make-up off. We are about the same age, and we have both been acting since the year ... I recognized her face as mine, we have the same face, and I understood that it is the face of every real actress. No, it is not 'mask-like', my face, her face. Rather, it is that our basic face is so worn down to its essentials because of its permanent readiness to take other guises, become other people, it is almost like something hung up on the wall of a dressing-room ready to take down and use. Our face is – it has a scrubbed, honest, bare look, like a deal table, or a wooden floor. It has modesty, a humility, our face, as time wears on, wearing out of her, out of me, our 'personality', our 'individuality'.

I looked at her face (we are called rivals, we are both called 'great' actresses) and I suddenly wanted to pay homage to it, since I knew what that scoured plain look cost her – what it costs me, who have played a thousand beautiful women, to keep my features sober and decent under the painted shell of my make-up, ready for other souls to use.

At a party, all dressed up, when I'm a 'person', then I try to disguise the essential plainness and anonymity of my features by holding together the 'beauty' I am known for, creating it out of my own and other people's memories. Of course it is almost gone now, nearly all gone the sharp, sweet, poignant face that so many men loved (not knowing it was not me, it was only what was given to me to consume slowly for the scrubbed face I must use for work). While I sat last night opposite you and your wife, she so pretty and *human*, her prettiness no mask, but expressing every shade of what she felt, and you being yourself only, I was conscious of how I looked. I could see my very white flesh that is guttering down away from its 'beauty'; I could see my smile that even now has moments of its 'piercing sweetness'; I could see my eyes, 'dewy and shadowed', even now ... but I also knew that everyone there, even if they were not aware of it, was conscious of that hard, honest, workaday face that lies ready for use under this ruin, and it is the discrepancy between that working face and the 'personality' of the famous actress that makes everything I do and say affected, that makes it inevitable and right that I should say, 'I don't want a husband, I have so many husbands.' And I tell you, if I had said nothing, not one word, the whole evening, the result would have been the same: 'How affected she is, but of course she *is* an actress.'

Yet it was the exact truth, what I said: I no longer have lovers, I have husbands, and that has been true ever since ...

That is why I am writing this letter to you; this letter is a sort of homage, giving you your due in my life. Or perhaps, simply, I cannot tonight stand the loneliness of my role (my role in life).

When I was a girl it seemed that every man I met, or even heard of, or whose picture I saw in the paper, was my lover. I took him as my lover, *because it was my right*. He may never have heard of me, he might have thought me hideous (and I wasn't very attractive as a girl – my kind of looks, striking, white-fleshed, red-haired, needed maturity, as a girl I was a milk-faced, scarlet-haired creature whose features were all at odds with each other, I was pretty only when made up for the stage) ... he may have found me positively repulsive, but I took him. Yes, at that time I had lovers in imagination, but none in reality. No man in the flesh could be as good as what I could invent, no real lips, hands, could affect me as those that I created, like God. And this remained true when I married my first husband, and then my second, for I loved neither of them, and I didn't know what the word meant for years. Until, to be precise, I was thirty-two and got very ill that year. No one knew why, or how, but *I* knew it was because I did not get a big part I wanted badly. So I got ill from disappointment, but now I see how right it was I didn't get the part. I was too old – if I had played her, the charming ingenuous girl (which is how I saw myself then, God forgive me), I would have had to play her for three or four years, because the play ran for ever, and I would have been too vain to stop. And then what? I would have been nearly forty, too old for charming girls, and then, like so many actresses who have not burned the charming girl out of themselves, cauterized that wound with a pin like styptic, I would have found myself playing smaller and smaller parts, and then I would have become a 'character' actress, and then ...

Instead, I lay very ill, not wanting to get better, ill with frustration, I thought, but really with the weight of years I did not know how to consume, how to include in how I saw myself, and then I fell in love with my doctor, inevitable I see now, but then a miracle, for that was the first time, and the reason I said the word 'love' to myself, just as if I had not been married twice, and had a score of men in my imagination, was because *I could not manipulate him*, for the first time a man remained himself, I could not make him move as I wanted, and I did not know his lips and hands. No, I had to wait for *him* to decide, to move, and when he did become my lover I was like a young girl, awkward, I could only wait for his actions to spring mine.

He loved me, certainly, but not as I loved him, and in due course he left me. I wished I could die, but it was then I understood, with gratitude, what had happened – I played, for the first time, a woman, as distinct from that fatal creature 'a charming girl', as distinct from 'the heroine' – and I and everyone else knew that I had moved into a new dimension of myself, I was born again, and only I knew it was out of love for that man, my first husband (so I called him, though everyone else saw him as my doctor with whom I rather amusingly had had an affair).

For he was my first husband. He changed me and my whole life. After him, in my frenzy of lonely unhappiness, I believed I could return to what I had been before he had married me, and I would take men to bed (in reality now, just as I had, before, in imagination), but it was no longer possible, it did not work, for I had been possessed by a man, the Man had created in me himself, had left himself in me, and so I could never again use a man, possess one, manipulate him, make him do what I wanted.

For a long time it was as if I was dead, empty, sterile. (That is, *I* was, my work was at its peak.) I had no lovers, in fact or in imagination, and it was like being a nun or a virgin.

Strange it was, that at the age of thirty-five it was then for the first time I felt virgin, chaste, untouched. I was absolutely alone. The men who wanted me, courted me, it was as if they moved and smiled and stretched out their hands through a glass wall which was my absolute inviolability. Was this how I should have felt when I was a girl? Yes, I believe that's it – that at thirty-five I was a girl for the first time. Surely this is how ordinary 'normal' girls feel? – they carry a circle of chastity around with them through which the one man, the hero, must break? But it was not so with me, I was never a chaste girl, not until I had known what it was to remain still, waiting for the man to set me in motion in answer to him.

A long time went by, and I began to feel I would soon be an old woman. I was without love, and I would not be a good artist, not really, the touch of the man who loved me was fading off me, *had* faded, there was something lacking in my work, it was beginning to be mechanical.

And so I resigned myself. I could no longer choose a man; and no man chose me. So I said, 'Very well then, there is nothing to be done about the shape of fate: my truth is that I have been loved once, and now that is the end, and I must let myself sink towards a certain dryness, a coldness of intelligence – yes, you will soon develop into an upright, red-headed, very intelligent lady (though, of course, affected!) whose green eyes flash the sober fires of humorous comprehension. All the rest is over for you, now accept it and be done and do as well as you can the work you are given.

And then one night . . .

What? All that happened outwardly was that I sat opposite a man at a dinner party in a restaurant, and we talked and laughed as people do who meet each other casually at a dinner-table. But afterwards I went home with my soul on fire. I was on fire, being consumed . . . And what a miracle it was to me, being able to say, not: That is an attractive man, I want him, I shall have him, but: My house is on fire, that was the man, yes, it was he again, there he was, he has set light to my soul.

I simply let myself suffer for him, knowing he was worth it *because* I suffered – it had come to this, my soul had become its own gauge, its own measure of what was good: I knew what *he* was because of how my work was afterwards.

I knew him better than his wife did, or could (she was there too, a nice woman in such beautiful pearls) – I know him better than he does himself. I sat opposite him all evening. What was there to notice? An ageing actress, pretty still, beautifully dressed (that winter I had a beautiful violet suit with mink cuffs) sitting opposite a charming man – handsome, intelligent and so on. One can use these adjectives of half the men one meets. But somewhere in him, in his being, something matched something in me, he had come into me, he had set me in motion. I remember looking down the table at his wife and thinking: Yes, my dear, but your husband is also my husband, for he walked into me and made himself at home in me, and because of him I shall act again from the depths of myself, I am sure of it, and I'm sure it will be the best work I can do. Though I won't know until tomorrow night, on the stage.

For instance, there was one night when I stood on the stage and stretched up my slender white arms to the audience and (that is how they saw it, what *I* saw were two white-caked, raddled-with-cold arms that were, moreover, rather flabby) and I knew that I was, that night, nothing but an amateur. I stood there on the stage, *as a woman* holding out my pretty arms, it was Victoria Carrington saying: Look how poignantly I hold out my arms don't you long to have them around you, my slender white arms, look how beautiful, how enticing Victoria is! And then, in my dressing-room afterwards I was ashamed, it was years since I had stood on the stage with nothing between me, the woman, and the audience – not since I was a green girl had I acted so – why, then, tonight?

I thought, and I understood. The afternoon before a man (a producer from America, but *that* doesn't matter) had come to see me in my dressing-room and after he left I thought: Yes, there it is again, I know that sensation, that means he has set the forces in motion and so I can expect my work to show it ... It showed it, with a vengeance! Well, and so that taught me to discriminate, I learned I must be careful, must allow no second-rate man to come near me. And so put up barriers, strengthened around me the circle of cold, of impersonality, that should always lie between me and people, between me and the auditorium; I made a cool, bare space no man could enter, could break across, unless his power, his magic, was very strong, the true complement to mine.

Very seldom now do I feel my self alight, on fire, touched awake, created again by – what?

I live alone now. No, *you* would never be able to imagine how. For I knew when I saw you this evening that you exist, you are, only in relation to other people, you are always giving out to your work, your wife, friends, children, your wife has the face of a woman who gives, who is confident that what she gives will be received. Yes, I understand all that, I know how it would be living with you, I *know* you.

After we had all separated, and I had watched you drive off with your wife, I came home and ... no, it would be no use telling you, after all. (Or anyone, except, perhaps, my colleague and rival Irma Painter!) But what if I said to you – but no, there are certain disciplines which no one can understand but those who use them.

So I will translate into your language, I'll translate the truth so that it has the *affected*, almost embarrassing, exaggerated ring that goes with the actress Victoria Carrington, and I'll tell you how when I came home after meeting you my whole body was wrenched with anguish, and I lay on the floor sweating and shaking as if I had bad malaria, it was like knives of deprivation going through me, for, meeting you, it was being reminded again what it would be like to be with a man, really with him, so that the rhythm of every day, every night, carried us both like the waves of a sea.

Everything I am most proud of seemed nothing at all – what I have worked to achieve, what I *have* achieved, even the very core of what I am, the inner sensitive balance that exists like a sort of self-invented super instrument, or a fantastically receptive and cherished animal – this creation of myself, which every day becomes more involved, sensitive, and delicate, seemed absurd, paltry, spinsterish, a shameful excuse for cowardice. And my life, which so contents me because of its balance, its order, its steadily growing fastidiousness, seemed eccentrically solitary. Every particle of my being screamed out, wanting, needing – I was like an addict deprived of his drug.

I picked myself off the floor, I bathed myself, I looked after myself like an invalid or like a – yes, like a pregnant woman. These extraordinary fertilizations happen so seldom now that I cherish them, waste nothing of them, and I both long for and dread them. Every time it is like being killed, like being torn open while I am forced to remember what it is I voluntarily do without.

Every time it happens I swear I can never let it happen again, the pain is too terrible. What a flower, what a fire, what a miracle it would be if, instead of smiling (the 'sweetly piercing' smile of my dying beauty), instead of accepting, submitting, I should turn to you and say . . .

But I shall not, and so something very rare (something much more beautiful than your wife could ever give you, or any of the day-by-day wives could imagine) will never come into being.

Instead . . . I sit and consume my pain, I sit and hold it, I sit and clench my teeth and . . .

It is dark, it is very early in the morning, the light in my room is a transparent grey, like the ghost of water or of air, there are no lights in the windows I see from my own. I sit in my bed, and watch the shadows of the tree moving on the brick wall of the garden, and I contain pain and . . .

Oh my dear one, my dear one, I am a tent under which you lie, I am the sky across which you fly like a bird, I am . . .

My soul is a room, a great room, a hall – it is empty, waiting. Sometimes a fly buzzes across it, bringing summer mornings in another continent, sometimes a child laughs in it, and it is like the generations chiming together, child, youth, and old woman as one being. Sometimes you walk into it and I shut my eyes because of the sweet recognition in me of what you are, I feel what you are as if I stood near a tree and put my hand on its breathing trunk.

I am a pool of water in which fantastic creatures move, in which you play, a young boy, your brown skin glistening, and the water moves over your limbs like hands, my hands, that will never touch you, my hands that tomorrow night, in a pool of listening silence, will stretch up towards the thousand people in the auditorium, creating love for them from the consumed pain of my denial.

I am a room in which an old man sits, smiling, as he has smiled for fifty centuries, you, whose bearded loins created me.

I am a world into which you breathed life, have smiled life, have made me. I am, with you, what creates, every moment, a thousand animalcules, the creatures of our dispensation, and every one we have both touched with our hands and let go into space like free birds.

I am a great space that enlarges, that grows, that spreads with the steady lightening of the human soul, and in the space, squatting in the corner, is a thing, an object, a dark, slow, coiled, amorphous heaviness, embodied sleep, a cold stupid sleep, a heaviness like the dark in a stale room – this thing stirs in its sleep where it squats in my soul, and I put all my muscles, all my force, into defeating it. For this was what I was born for, this is what I am, to fight embodied sleep, putting around it a confining girdle of light, of intelligence, so that it cannot spread its slow stain of ugliness over the trees, over the stars, over you.

It is as if, since you turned towards me and smiled, letting light go through me again, it is as if a King had taken a Queen's hand and set her on his throne: a King and his Queen, hand in hand on top of my mountain sit smiling at ease in their country.

The morning is coming on the brick wall, the shadow of the tree has gone, and I think of how today I will walk out on to the stage, surrounded by the cool circle of my chastity, the circle of my discipline, and how I will raise my face (the flower face of my girlhood) and how I will raise my arms from which will flow the warmth you have given me.

And so, my dear one, turn now to your wife, and take her head on to your shoulder, and both sleep sweetly in the sleep of your love. I release you to go to your joys without me. I leave you to your love. I leave you to your life.

A Year in Regent's Park

Last year was out of ordinary from the start – just like every other year. What start, January? But January is a mid-month, in the middle of cold, snow, dark. Above all, dark. In January nothing starts but the new calendar, which says that the down-swing of our part of the earth towards the long light of summer has already begun, is already stimulating the plants, changing their responses. I would make the beginning back in autumn, when I 'found myself possessor' – I put it like that because some-one else is now in possession – of a wild, very long, narrow garden, between mellow brick walls. There was an old pear tree in the middle, and at its end a small wood of recently sprung trees, sycamores, an elder, an ash. This treasure of space was twenty minutes' strolling time from Marble Arch, on a canal. The garden had to be prepared for planting. By luck I found a boy, up from the country to try his fortune in London, who hated all work in the world but digging. He chose to live in half a room which he curtained with blankets, carpeted with newspapers, then matting, and wall-papered with his poems and pictures. He was, of course, in the old romantic tradition of the adventurous young, challenging a big city, but he saw himself and the world as newly hatched, let's say a year before, when he became twenty and discovered that he was free and probably a hippy. He lived on baked beans and friendship, and when he needed money, dug people's gardens. Together we stripped off the top layer of this potential garden, which was all builder's rubble, cans, bottles, broken glass. Under this was London clay. It is a substance you hear enough about; indeed, London's history seems made of it. But when you actually come on tons of the stuff, yards deep, heavy, wet, impervious, without a worm or a root in it, it is so airless and unused, you wonder how London ever came to be all gardens and woodland. I could not believe my gardening book, which said that clay is perfect potential soil for plants. I, friends, and the boy from the country, made shapes of the stuff, and thought it was a pity none of us was a sculptor – but that wasn't going to turn the clay into working earth. At last, we marked out flowerbeds, and turned over the clay in large clods, the weeds and grass still on them. The place looked like a ploughed field before the cultivators move in. But even before the first frosts, the soil between the flinty-sided miniature boulders was showing the beginning of a marriage between rotting grass and clay fragments. It had rained. It was raining. As London does, it rained. Going out to inspect the clods, each so heavy I could only pick one up at a time, I found they had softened their harsh contours somewhat, but I couldn't break them by flinging them down or bashing them with a spade. They looked eternal. Steps led up from the under-earth – the flat was a basement flat – and standing at eye-level to the garden, it all looked like a First World War film: trenches full of water, wet mats of the year's leaf, enormous clods, rotting weeds, bare trunks and dripping branches. All, everything, wet, bare, raw.

That was December. Around Christmas, after several heavy frosts, I went up to see how things went on, kicked one of the clods – and it crumbled. The boy from the country who, being not a farming boy but a country-town boy, and who therefore had not believed the book either, saying the garden needed a bulldozer, came on my telephone call, and about an hour of the lightest work with a hoe transformed the heaving scene into neat areas of tilth mixed with dead grass. Not really dead, of course, but ready to come to life with the spring. But now we had faith in the book, and we turned the roots upwards to be killed by the frost. This happened. Each piece of stalk or root filled with wet, and then swelled as it froze, and burst like water-mains in severe cold. Long before spring the earth lay broken and tamed, all the really hard work done, not by the spade, or the hoe, or even the worms, but by the frost. The thing is, I knew Africa, or a part of it, and there you can never forget the power of sun, wind, rain.

But in gentler England you do forget, as if the north-slanting sun must have less power than a sun overhead, as if nature itself is less drastic in her workings. You can forget it, that is, until you see what a handful of weeks of weather can do to smash a seventy-by-twenty-foot bit of wilderness into conformity.

It rained in January, and in February it did not stop. If I set one foot off the top of the steps that came up from the flat, I sank in clay to my ankle. The light was strained through cold cloud, but it was strong enough to drag the snowdrops up into it. I walked in Regent's Park along paths framed with black glistening twigs which were swelling, ready to burst: the shape of spring, next year's promise, is exposed from the moment the leaves fall. The park was all grey water, sodden grass, black trees, and the water-fowl had to contend for crumbs and crusts with the gulls that had come inland from a stormy sea. In March it rained, and was dull. Usually by March more than snowdrops and crocuses are showing from snow or mud; and already the paths are loaded with people staking claims in the spring. But it was a bad month. My new garden was calling forth derisory remarks from friends who were not gardeners and who did not know what a month's warmth can do for water-filled trenches, bare walls, sodden earth. April wasn't doing anything like what the poet meant when he said, 'Oh, to be in England' – certainly he would have returned at once to his beloved Italy. April was not the beginning of spring, but the continuation of winter. It was wet, wet, wet, and cold, and it all went on the same day after day. And in the park, where I walked daily, only the lengthening evenings talked of spring, for in spite of crocuses everywhere, the buds seemed frozen on the bushes and trees. It would never end. I don't know how they bear it in northern countries, like Sweden or Russia. It is like being shut inside a caul of ice, when the winter lengthens itself so.

And it was so wet. If you took one step off the paths you squelched. No air, you knew, could possibly remain in that sponge. There was so much water everywhere, tons of it hanging in the air over our heads, tons falling every day, lakes underfoot.

Suddenly there were some days of summer. No, not spring.

Last year was without spring. In no other country that I know is it possible for things to change so fast. And when one state holds, then the one just past seems impossible. In the garden, from which baths of steam flew up to join the by now summerlike clouds, bluebells, hyacinths, crocuses and narcissus had sprung up, and if you turned the earth, the worms were energetically at work. Weeks of growth were being concentrated into each day; nature did overtime to catch up; and if things had gone on like that, we would have been precipitated straight into full summer, with fruit blossom and spring flowers flying past as in a speeded up film but no, suddenly, we were in a cold drought. And it went on for weeks. A cold sunless drought, a dry dull cold, with sometimes a cold, withdrawn sun. In the garden the water sank fast in the newly turned, loose earth, and you could walk easily over the clay. The pear tree hung on the edge of blossom, but did not flower. The trees at the bottom of the garden had a look of green about them, but it was like the smear of moss on soil soaked and soaked again. When I turned a spade of earth, the worms were sluggish. The birds, dodging plentiful cats, snapped off each new blade of grass as it appeared, and slashed the crocuses with their beaks. In the park, the black boughs had frills of leaf on them, but walking along the shores you could see the ducks and the geese sitting on their eggs on leafless islands. The waters were still tenanted by adult birds, who converged towards their providers on the lakes' edges, and climbed up on the banks with their coloured beaks open, hissing and demanding. Soon, off the little islands would tumble nestfuls of baby birds, who would learn from the parents to follow the stiffly moving shapes along the banks with their expectations for bread. But not yet. And the blossoms were not yet. Everything was in check in that no-spring of last year when first it rained without sun, and then held a chilly drought for weeks. Yet we knew that spring must have arrived, must be here. Slowly, the chestnut avenue unfurled shrill green from each stiff twig's end. The catkins were dangling on branches inhibited from bursting into leaf. The roses had been pruned almost to the earth, but very late. The fine hair-lines of the willow branches trailing into the water had become yellow-

green instead of wintry yellow-grey. And everywhere, on haw-
thorn and cherry, on plum and currant and with beam and
apple, the buds of that year's flowering stood arrested among leaf
buds. The park's gardeners bent heavily-sweatered over
flowerbeds that had a cold dusty look, and the grass wore thin
and showed the soil, as often happens in late summer after
drought, but not often so early in the year. The evenings had
already nearly reached their midsummer length – for just as
spring stands outlined in black buds on empty branches in Nov-
ember, so the lengthening evenings of April, May, then June,
spread summer light everywhere when the earth is still gripped
with cold, and you are clutching at summer before it has begun,
marking Midsummer Day as a turn towards the dark of winter
before the winter has been warmed from the soil. The earth is
tilted forward, dipped completely into light, light that urges on
blossom, leaf, grass, light which is more powerful for growth
even than warmth. The avenues are filled with strolling people
until nine and after; the theatre is open; the swings in the children's playgrounds are never still. England's myriads of expert
gardeners visit the rose gardens to match those paragons with the
inhabitants of their own gardens – but last year found that the
cold was still holding the roses, tightening their veins and arteries,
and giving the long reddening shoots the pinched look of a
person short of blood. And it all went on and on, the dry cold,
just as, earlier, the wet winter had extended itself, and the park
seemed like a sponge that could never dry.

And then, the year having swallowed spring whole, the sun and
rain came together and all at once, the whole park burst into flower,
as did the pear tree in my garden, and the laburnum over the wall.

In each year, there is always a week which is the essence of
spring, all violent growth, bloom and scent, just as there is one
week which is quintessential autumn, the air full of flying tinted
leaves.

But last year, trees whose flowering is usually separated by
their different natures flowered at the same time; the cherries,
currants, hawthorns, lilacs and damask roses were out with bluebells, tulips, stocks, and there were so many different kinds of

blossom that it seemed as if there must be hundreds of species of flowering tree instead of a couple of dozen. We walked over new grass under trees crammed with pink, with ivory, with greenish-white flower; we walked beside lakes where crowds of ducklings and goslings swam beside their parents, minute balls like thistle-down tossing violently with every wind-ripple, and threatened all the time by the oars from rowing boats launched into the waters by spring and all summer at the same time, with flying, rolling, showering clouds, and lovers lay everywhere over the grass, rummaging and ravishing, while the squirrels leaped about like kittens after cotton reels, up and down the trunks of the chestnut trees that had belatedly achieved their proper summer shape, pyramidal green with pink and white candles. The squirrels were as fat as house-cats, fed full from the litter baskets, and their friends' offerings. From all the streets around the park, and from much further afield, came people with bread, biscuits, cake, each with a look of private, smiling pleasure. One woman who had, not the usual few bread slices or stale cake, but a carrier-bag full of food, confided to me as she stood surrounded by hundreds of pigeons, sparrows, geese, ducks, swans, thrushes, that her children had recently grown up and left home and her husband and herself were sparse eaters. Yet years of cooking for uncritically ravenous teenagers and their friends had got her used to providing and catering. She had found herself ordering much more food than an elderly couple could ever eat; she suppressed urges to create new and wonderful dishes. But she had found the solution. Each time the need gripped her to give a dinner party for twelve, or an informal party for fifty, she filled a bag and took a bus to Regent's Park where, on the edge of the bird-decorated waters, she went on until her supplies ran out and her need to feed others was done. The birds, having swum or flown along the banks beside her until they were sure she had no more food, turned their attention to the next likely provisioner, or floated and bobbed and circled to the admiration of humans who all around the shores were bound to be exclaiming: 'Oh, if only I could be a duck on a hot day like this, right in all that cool water!' – while these same waterfowl might quite reasonably be expected to be muttering: 'If only I could be a human, with naked skin for the wind to blow on and the water to touch, and not a bird encased in feathers in such a way, that nothing but my poor feet can ever feel the air or water . . .' At any rate, these birds certainly have a fine sense of themselves, their function, their place. Accustomed to seeing them on the water, or tucked into neat shapes drowsing on the grass around the verges, I imagined that that was where they always stayed. But not so, as I discovered one very early morning when I got up at five to have – or so I imagined – the park to myself. There were five or six people already there, strolling about, talking, or at least acknowledging each other, in the cameraderie of those who feel themselves to be out of the ordinary. Meanwhile, the geese and ducks were all over the grass, and under the trees, where in the day they are never seen. Mother ducks and geese, each surrounded by their blobs of coloured down, were introducing these offspring to the land world, as distinct from the water world they inhabited when the park was busy. Greylag geese stood under the Japanese plums. Black swans were under the hawthorns. A squirrel came to investigate a duckling that was disconsolately alone under an arch of climbing rose. It was not six in the morning, but it seemed as if things had been busy for hours – as probably they had, now the nights were so short, and hardly dark at all from a bird's point of view, who probably can't tell the difference between dusk, dawn, or the shimmering dark of a summer's midnight. While people still slept, or were crawling out of bed, there was the liveliest of intimate occasions in the park, which the birds and animals had more or less to themselves.

The park changed as the gardeners arrived and the people walked through on their way to offices. The water-birds decided to resume their correct places on the lakes – there is no other way to describe the way they do it, the mother birds calling their broods to them, and returning along the paths to the water's edge to leave the grass and paths and trees for humans. Again the waters were loaded with ducks and geese plain and coloured, dignified or as glossily extravagant as the dramatically painted and varnished wooden ducks from toyshops. It is exactly in the same way that the front of a theatre full of stage managers, assistants prompters, directors, empties for a performance as the public come in. There was the land part of the park, with the usual sparrows and pigeons, and there the lakes so crowded it seemed there could not be room for one more bird – yet all the eggs were still not hatched on the islands which now were filled with green, so that the patiently sitting birds could no longer be seen through the binoculars of London's bird-watchers. And every day, while the earlier-hatched broods became gawky and lumpish attempts after the elegant finish of their parents, freshly hatched birds scattered over the water.

On an arm of the lake where a bridge crossed over, a water-hen was sitting in full view of everybody. The water is very shallow there. A couple of yards from shore, the water-hens had made a nest in the water of piled dead sticks. But not all the sticks were dead. One had rooted and was in leaf, a little green flag above the black-and-white shape of the moorhen who sat a few feet from the bridge. There she crouched, looking at the people who looked at her. All day and half the night, when the park was open to the public, they stopped to observe her. They did more than look. On the twiggy mattress that extended all around her, were bits of food thrown by admirers. But these offerings caused the poor moorhens much trouble, because particularly the sparrows, sometimes thrushes and blackbirds, even ducks and other non-related moorhens, came to poke about in the twigs for food. The moorhen – male or female, it seemed they took it in turns to sit – had to keep rising in a hissing clatter of annoyance, to frighten them off. Or the mate who was swimming about, to fetch morsels of food for the sitting bird, came fussing up to warn off trespassers, but still the sparrows kept darting in to grab what they could, and fly off. Even the big swans came circling, so that the little moorhens looked like miniatures beside the white giants. Much worse than bread was thrown. All the lake under and around the bridge became laden with cans, bits of paper and plastic, and this debris lay bobbing or sagging on water which already, after only a few days of the powerful new summer, was beginning to smell. Now the summer was really here, and the park crowded, grass and paths were always littered, and the water smelled worse every day. Particularly where the moorhens were. That sitting of moorhen eggs must have been the most public in moorhen history. Yet they had chosen the site, had built the nest. And they went on with their work of warming the eggs, till it was done. Admirers loitered on the bridge through the last days, to shield the birds from possible vandals and to prevent cans being aimed at the birds themselves, and also to catch, if possible, the moment when a moorhen chick took to the water. I am sure there were those who did see this, for the attention was assiduous. I missed it, but one hot afternoon when the bridge was more than usually crowded, I saw a minute dark-coloured chick floating near the nest, with a parent energetically foraging near it for bits of food. The sitting bird lifted itself off the twig mattress to stretch her muscles in a great yawn of wing, and there was a glimpse of white under her: an unhatched egg, and some shell. There was another chick there too, disinclined to join its sibling on the water. The swimming parent fetched slimy morsels for the one on the nest. He, or she, took the fragments and pushed them into the chick's gape. The swimming chick was crammed by the swimming parent. It looked as if the swimming bird was trying to make the water-borne chick venture farther from the nest. It kept heading off, in the energetic purposeful way of moorhens, and swinging around to see if the little chick had followed. But the chick had scrambled back to the nest, and disappeared under the sitting bird. The swimming bird went off quite a distance, and got on to the bank by itself. On the bridge was a threesome, a tall pretty girl with a young man on either side. They had been watching the moorhens. She said: 'Oh, I know, he's gone off to see his mistress, and she is going to have to feed her babies herself.' 'How do you know?' asked one young man. The other laughed, very irritated. He walked off. The girl followed him, looking anxious. The young man who had said 'How do you know?' followed them both, hurrying.

All afternoon, the birds took turns on the nest, one swimming and fetching food for the other, and from time to time a chick climbed down off the great logs of the timber platform he had been hatched on, and bobbed and rocked on the waves. Meanwhile, all the surface of the lake around the nest was full of every kind of swimming bird, adult, half-grown, and just hatched. In such a throng, that one minute moorchick was an item, precious only to the guardian parents.

Moorhens are strict-looking, tailored, black-and-white birds among the fanciful ducks, the black swans with their red sealing-wax bills. They have a look of modest purpose, of duty, of restraint. And then one comes up out of the water to join birds crowding for thrown bread, and the exposed feet are a shock, being large, whity-green, scaly, reptilian, as if they had belonged to half-bird, half-lizard ancestors, and have descended unaltered down the chains of evolution while the birds modified above water into the handy, tidy moorhen shape – a land shape, it is easy to think. Yet the moorhen is more water-bird than any duck or goose. If you stand feeding a crowd of birds, and there are gulls there, they will swoop in and past, having caught bits of bread from the air as if these were leaping fish – the gulls will get everything, if you aren't taking care of the others. A tall goose will stand delicately taking pieces from your fingers, like a well-mannered person, then turn to slash savagely another competing goose with its beak: after the gulls, the geese provide for themselves best. The ducks, apparently clumsy and waddling, are quick to snatch bits when the geese miss. But to try and feed the moorhens – for which, sentimentally, I have a fancy – is harder than to feed shyer deer in a zoo when the big ones have decided they are going to get what is going. First, the moorhens have to get up on the bank on those clumsy water-feet. And then their movements are slower than the other birds'; the moorhens are poking about after the bits when the others have swallowed them and are already crowding in for more. Yet, in the water, there is nothing quicker and neater.

That long public sitting succeeded, at last, in adding only one moorchick to the park's population. One afternoon there were two parents and two chicks, busy with each other and their nest among the crowds of birds; next afternoon there were two moorhens and one bobbing dark fluffball.

But the nest was there, with bits of bread still stuck in the twigs. And there it stayed all summer, and all autumn, and although the green fell off, or was pecked off the sentinel twig, nest and twig are there now, in winter – so perhaps in the coming spring the same or another pair of moorhens will bring up another family, in spite of the staring ill-mannered people and their ill-judged offerings, and their cans and their plastic and their smell. But the twig platform will certainly have to be refurnished, for as soon as the moorhen family had left it, it was found most convenient by the other fowl to sit on, and play around; and the twig that had rooted and stood up was a good perch for water-venturing sparrows. There never were so many sparrows as last year: you could mark the season's increase in population by the contrast between the young birds' tight shape and shiny fresh-painted look, and their duller shabbier parents. Where did they all hatch? Apart from those of the water-birds, and a shallow fibre nest that was exposed, when autumn came and stripped the chestnut avenue, woven on twigs not much higher above the path than a tall man's head, so that the sitting bird in its completely concealing clump of leaves must have been inches above the walking people – apart from these, I saw no nests save one on the ground, among bluebells and geraniums and clumps of hosta. The bird was sleekly brown, and watching me, not over-anxiously, as I watched her from the path a yard or so away. She sat with her warm eggs pressed to her spread claws by her breast, and saw possible enemies pass and repass all day, for the days it took her to get the chicks out into the light. Yet, like the moorhen, she had chosen that exposed place to sit, near a path, just behind the Open Air Theatre. Perhaps, like the foxes that are coming in from the country, which hunts and poisons and traps them, to the suburbs, where they live off town refuse, some birds are coming to terms with us, our noise, and our mess, in ways we don't yet see? Perhaps they even like us? And not only people – a few yards from the sitting brown bird was a place where somebody was putting out food for stray cats. There were saucers of old and new food, and milk, and water, bits of sandwich and biscuit, under the damask roses all the summer, and the cats came to this food, and did not attack the sitting bird – who, perhaps, used this food when the cats were not there? It is possible that she put up with the amplified voices and music from the theatre because of its restaurant, not more than a few seconds' flight away, just the right distance for a quick crumb-gathering before the eggs had time to chill. There must have been many other nests in that thick little wood where the theatre is, and many birds calling that patch of the park theirs. Certainly, each year's production of *A Midsummer Night's Dream*, good, bad or indifferent, offers marvellous moments that are not in the stage directions, when an owl hoots for Oberon, or swallows swoop over Titania's and Bottom's heads, or, while a moon stands up over the trees, making the stage seem small and insignificant, starlings loop and swirl past on their last flight before roosting. And all the time, while plays are being rehearsed and acted, the birds are building, sitting, feeding their young, and the fact that they choose this, the noisiest part of the park, surely says something about the way they view us. Or don't see us, don't regard us at all, except perhaps in association with food scraps? There's nothing odder than what is ignored, not seen, not noticed. Perhaps those moorhens chose that spot, the most public there is, because the water is the right depth there, and nothing else mattered; and they were not aware of their audience on the bridge except as a noisy frieze which emitted lumps of food and other objects.

The park holds dozens of self-contained dramas, human and animal, in the space of an eye-sweep. On a Sunday afternoon, in July, when the drought had held and held, and the bushes under the tree-cover were wilting because what showers had fallen were not heavy enough to penetrate the thick leaf-layers, the park was full, and coachloads of people from everywhere were visiting the zoo. There were queues at the zoo gates hundreds of yards long, and inside the zoo it was like a fair. There is a path down the west side of the zoo. It is tree-shaded. A bank rises sharply to the fields used for football and cricket. Being summer, and Sunday, it was cricket time, and four separate games were in progress, each with its circle of reserve players, friends, wives, children, and casual watchers. This world, the world of Sunday cricket, was absolutely self-absorbed, and each game ignored the other three. On the slopes under the trees were lovers, twined two by two. At the end where the Mappin Terraces are, four young people lay asleep. They were tourists, and looked German, or perhaps Scandinavian. They all four had long hair. The two girls had long dresses, the young men fringed leather. They owned four rucksacks and four guitars. Most likely they had been up talking, singing and dancing all night, or perhaps had not the money to pay for a night's sleep. Now they slept in each other's arms all day without moving. Quite possibly they never knew that cricket was being so devotedly played so close, and that while they slept the zoo filled and emptied again. From the slope where they were you can see nicely into the children's zoo, and across to the elephants' house. You can see, too, the goats and bears of the terraces. Some people who had given up the effort of getting into the zoo sat on the slopes near the four sleepers, talking a lot, not trying to be quiet, and they watched the elephants showing off, poor beasts, in return for their little house and the trench-enclosed space they have to live in. A woman arrived with a plastic bag and sat on a bench, with her back to the lovers and the sleeping young people, and fed sparrows and pigeons, frowning with the concentration of the effort needed to let the *poor* sparrows (who were so small) get as much food as the (unfairly) large pigeons. And a little girl in the children's zoo clutched at a donkey no higher than she was, and cried out: 'It's getting wet, oh the donkey's getting wet!' True enough, here came a small sample of the long-awaited rain. Not much. A brief sparkling drench. No one stopped doing anything. The cricketers played on. The woman frowned and fussed over the unfairness of nature. The lovers loved. The four sleeping young people did not so much as turn over, but a passing youth tiptoed up and covered the guitars with the girls' long skirts. And the little girl wept because of the poor donkey who was getting wet and apparently liking it, for it was kicking and hee-hawing. Where was her mamma? Where, her papa? She was alone with her donkey and her grief. And the rain pelted down and stopped, having done no good and no harm to anything. It was weeks before some real rain arrived and saved the brown scuffing grass; weeks before that moment of high summer which was nothing to do with gardener's calendar, or even the length of the days, shortening fast again, again the same number of hours as in the long-forgotten no-spring. But it is a moment whose quality is over-lushness, heaviness, fullness, plenty. All the trees are crammed and blowsy with leaf. They sag and loll and drag. The willows trail too long in the water, and then they look as if someone has gone around each one in a boat with shears, chopping the fronds to just such a length, like human hair trimmed around a pudding-basin. The ducks and geese who have been delicately, languidly, nibbling bits of leaf, and floating in and out through the trailing green curtains, now tread water and strive upwards on their wings to nip off bits of leaf. Perhaps it is the birds who have eaten the low branches away to an exact height all around? There are so many of them now, the chicks all having grown up, that everywhere you look are herds of geese, flocks of ducks, the big swans, moorhens. Surely the park can't possibly sustain so many? What will happen to them all? Will they be allotted to other less bird-populated parks, each bird conditioned from chickhood to regard every human being in sight as a moving bread-fountain? Meanwhile, the rowing boats and the sailing boats have to manoeuvre through crowds of waterfowl, the sparrows are in flocks, the roses teem and mass, everything is at the full of its provision, its lushness. The hub of the park now is not the chestnut avenue, and the so English herbaceous border, but the long Italianate walk that has the fountain and the tall poplars at one end, the formal black-and-gold gates at the other, and roses lining it all the way. A summer avenue, asking for deep blue skies and heat, just as the chestnut avenue, and the hawthorns, the plums, cherries and currants, are for spring, or for autumn.

The summer gardeners all seem to be youngsters working with bare torsos, or bare feet. They cool off by standing in the fountain's spray as the wind switches it about. 'They say' that the hippies have decided this work, summer gardening, is good for them, us, society. One evening I heard these sentiments offered to one gardening girl by another:

'There aren't any hang-ups here, you can do your own thing, but you've got to pull your weight, that's fair enough.'

There is a different relationship between these summer amateur gardeners and the park's visitors, and between the visitors and the familiar older gardeners, these last being more proprietary. I remember an exchange with one, several springs ago, on an occasion when it had snowed, the sun had come out, and friends had rung to say that the crocuses were particularly fine. Out I went to the park and found that the new crocuses, white, purple, gold, stood everywhere in the snow. Each patch had been finely netted with black cotton to stop the birds eating them. I was bending over to see how the netting was done – a tricky and irritating job, surely? – when I saw that a uniformed gardener had emerged from his watchman's hut and was standing over me.

'And what may you be doing?'

'I am looking at your crocuses.'

'They are not my crocuses. They are public property.'

'Oh, good.'

'And I am paid to watch them.'

'You mean to tell me that you are standing in that unheated wooden hut in all this cold and snow just to guard the crocuses?'

'You could say that.'

'Isn't this cotton any use, then?'

'Cotton is effective against bird thieves. I am not saying anything about human thieves.'

'But I wasn't going to eat your crocuses!'

'I am only doing my job.'

'Your job is, as it were, to be a crocus-watcher?'

'Yes, madam, and it always has been and my father before me. When I was a little lad I knew the work I wanted to do and I've done it ever since.'

Not thus the youngsters, much less suspicious characters, understanding quite well how respectable citizens may envy them their jobs.

There was this incident when the geraniums had flowered

once, and needed to be picked over to induce a second flowering. There were banks of them, covered with dead flower. I myself had resisted the temptation to nip over the railings and dead-head the lot: another had not resisted. With a look of defiant guilt, an elderly man was crouching in the geraniums, hard at work. Leaning on his spade, watching him, was a summer gardener, a long-haired, barefooted, naked-chested youth.

'What's he doing that for?' said he to me.

'He can't stand that there won't be a second flowering,' I said. 'I can understand it. I've just dead-headed all mine in my own garden.'

'All I've got room for is herbs in a pot.'

The elderly man, seeing us watching him, talking about him, probably about to report his crime, looked guiltier than ever. But he furiously continued his work, a man of principle defying society for duty.

On a single impulse, I and the gardener parted and went in different directions; we were not able to bear causing him such transports of moral determination.

But, of course, he was quite in the right: when all the other banks of geraniums were brown and flowerless, the bank he had picked over was as brilliant as in spring.

By now it had rained, and had rained well, and just as it was hard to remember the long cold wet of the early year in the cold drought, and the cold drought in the dry heat, now the long dryness had vanished out of memory, for it was a real English summer, all fitfully showery, fitfully cool and hot. Yet it was autumn; the over-fullness of everything said it must be. A strong breeze sent leaves spinning down, and the smell of the stagnant parts of the lakes was truly horrible, making you wonder about the philosophy of the park-keepers – it was against their principles to clear away the smelly rubbish? They couldn't afford a man in a boat once a week to take it away? Or they had faith in the power of nature to heal everything?

In my garden, last year's wasteland – so very soon to be left behind – the roses, the thyme, geranium, clematis, were all strongly flowering, and butterflies crowded over lemon balm and hyssop. The pear tree was full of small tasteless pears. The tree was too old. It could produce masses of blossom, but couldn't carry the work through to good fruit. At every movement of the air, down thumped the pears. All the little boys from the Council flats came jumping over the walls to snatch up the pears, which they needed to throw at each other, not to eat. When invited to come in and pick them, great sullenness and resentment resulted, because the point was to raid the big rich gardens along the canal, into which hundreds of gardenless people looked down from the flats, to raid them, dart away with the spoils, and then raid again, coming in under the noses of furious householders.

One afternoon I was in a bus beside the park, and the wind was strong, and all the air was full of flying leaves. This was the moment, the week of real autumn. Rushing at once to the park, I just caught it. Everything was yellow, gold, brown, orange, heaps of treasure lay tidily packed ready to be burned, the wind crammed the air with coloured leafage. It was cooling – the Northern hemisphere, I mean, not the park, which of course had been hot, cold and in between ever since the year had started running true to form, some time in July. The leaves were blown into the lakes, and sank to make streams of bubbles in which the birds dived and played. All around the moorhens' battered nest lay a starry patterning of plane leaves in green and gold. You could see how, if this were wilderness, land would form here in this shallow place, in a season or two; how this arm of the lake would become swamp, and then, in a dry season, new earth, and the water would retreat. All the smelly backwaters were being covered over with thick soft layers of leaf, the plastic, the tins, the papers vanishing, as, no doubt, the park-keepers had counted on happening when autumn came.

I walked from one end of the park to the other, then back and around and across, the squirrels racing and chasing, and the birds swimming along the banks beside me in case this shape might be a food-giving shape, and this food shape might have decided to distribute largess around the next bend and was being mean now because of future plenty. There were many fewer birds. The great families bred that year off the islands had gone, and the population was normal again, couples and individuals sedately self-sufficient.

Only a week later, that perfection of autumn was over, and stripped boughs were showing the shape of next spring. Yet, visiting Sweden, where snow had come early and lay everywhere, then leaving it to fly home again, w.. ' flying from winter into autumn, a journey back in time in one afternoon. The aircraft did not land when it should have done, owing to some hitch or other, and, luckily for us, had to go about in a wide sweep over London. I had not before flown so low, with no cloud to hide the city. It was all woodland and lakes and parks and gardens, and a highly coloured autumn still, with loads of russet and gold on the trees. All the ugly bits of London you imagine nothing could disguise were concealed by this habit of tree and garden.

In the park, though, from the ground, the trees looked very tall, very bare, and wet. The lakes were grey and solid. When the birds came fast across to see if there was food, they left arrow shapes on the water spreading slowly, and absolutely regular, till they dissolved into the shores: there were no boats out now, for these had been drawn up and lay overturned in rows along the banks, waiting for spring.

And the dark had come down.

The park in winter is very different from high, crammed, noisy summer. A long damp path in early twilight . . . it is not much more than three in the afternoon. Two gentlemen in trim dark suits and tidy, slightly bald heads, little frills of hair on their collars – a reminiscence of the eighteenth century or a claim on contemporary fashion, who knows? – two civil servants from the offices in the Nash terraces walk quietly by, their hands behind their backs, beside the water. They talk in voices so low you think it must be official secrets that they have come out to discuss in privacy.

The beds are dug and turned. New stacks of leaf are made every day as the old ones burn, scenting the air with guilt, not pleasure, for now you have to remember pollution. But the roses are all there still, blobs of colour on tall stems. All the stages of the year are visible at once, for each plant has on it all brightly tinted hips, then dead roses, which are brown dust rose-shaped, then the roses themselves, though each has frost-burn crimping the outer petals. Hips, dead roses, fresh blooms – and masses of buds, doomed never to come to flower, for the frosts will get them if the pruner doesn't: Pink Parfait and Ginger Rogers, Summer Holiday and Joseph's Coat, are shortly to be slashed into anonymity.

For it will be the dead of the year very soon now, soon it will be the shortest day.

I sit on a bench in the avenue where in summer the poplars and fountain make Italy on a blue day, but now browny-grey clouds are driving hard across from the north-east. Crowds of sparrows materialize as I arrive, all hungry expectation, but I've been forgetful, I haven't so much as a biscuit. They sit on the bench, my shoe, the bench's back, rather hunched, the wind tugging their feathers out of shape. The seagulls are in too, so the sea must be rough today, or perhaps there is an oil slick.

Up against the sunset, today a dramatic one, gold, red, and packed dark clouds, birds slowly rotate, like jagged debris after a whirlwind. They look like rooks, but that's not possible, they must be more gulls. But it is nice to imagine them rooks, just as, on the walk home, the plane trees, all bent one way by the wind, seem, with their dappled trunks, like deer ready to spring together towards the northern gates.

Mrs Fortescue

That autumn he became conscious all at once of a lot of things he had never thought about before.

Himself, for a start . . .

His parents . . . whom he found he disliked, because they told lies. He discovered this when he tried to communicate to them something of his new state of mind and they pretended not to know what he meant.

His sister who, far from being his friend and ally, 'like two peas in a pod' – as people had been saying for years – seemed positively to hate him.

And Mrs Fortescue.

Jane, seventeen, had left school and went out every night. Fred, sixteen, loutish schoolboy, lay in bed and listened for her to come home, kept company by her imaginary twin self, invented by him at the end of the summer. The tenderness of this lovely girl redeemed him from his shame, his squalor, his misery. Meanwhile, the parents ignorantly slept, not caring about the frightful battles their son was fighting with himself not six yards off. Sometimes Jane came home first; sometimes Mrs Fortescue. Fred listened to her going up over his head, and thought how strange he had never thought about her before, knew nothing about her.

The Danderlea family lived in a small flat over the off-licence that Mr and Mrs Danderlea had been managing for Sanko and Duke for twenty years. Above the shop, from where rose, day and night, a sickly reek of beer and spirits they could never escape from, was the kitchen and the lounge. This layer of the house (it had been one once) was felt as an insulating barrier against the smell, which nevertheless reached up into the bedrooms above.

Two bedrooms – the mother and father in one; while for years brother and sister had shared a room, until recently Mr Danderlea put up a partition making two tiny boxes, giving at least the illusion of privacy for the boy and the girl.

On the top floor, the two rooms were occupied by Mrs Fortescue, and had been since before the Danderleas came. Ever since the boy could remember, grumbling went on that Mrs Fortescue had the high part of the house where the liquor smell did not rise; though she, if remarks to this effect reached her, claimed that on hot nights she could not sleep for the smell. But on the whole relations were good. The Danderleas' energies were claimed by buying and selling liquor, while Mrs Fortescue went out a lot. Sometimes other old women came to visit her, and an old man, small, shrunken and polite, came to see her most evenings, very late indeed, often well after twelve.

Mrs Fortescue seldom went out during the day, but left every evening at about six, wearing furs: a pale shaggy coat in winter, and in summer a stole over a costume. She always had a small hat on, with a veil that was drawn tight over her face and held with a bunch of flowers where the fur began. The furs changed often: Fred remembered half a dozen blond fur coats, and a good many little animals biting their tails or dangling bright bead eyes and empty paws. From behind the veil, the dark, made-up eyes of Mrs Fortescue had glimmered at him for years; and her small old reddened mouth had smiled.

One evening he postponed his homework, and slipped out past the shop where his parents were both at work, and took a short walk that led him to Oxford Street. The exulting, fearful loneliness that surged through his blood with every heart-beat, making every stamp of shadow a reminder of death, each gleam of light a promise of his extraordinary future, drove him around and around the streets muttering to himself, brought tears to his eyes, or snatches of song to his lips which he had to suppress. For a while he knew himself to be crazy, and supposed he must have been all his life (he could no longer remember himself before this autumn); this was a secret he intended to keep for himself and the tender creature who shared the stuffy box he spent his nights in. Turning a corner that probably (he would not have been able to say) he had already turned several times before that evening, he saw a woman walking ahead of him in a great fur coat that shone under the street lights, a small veiled hat, and tiny sharp feet that took tripping steps towards Soho. Recognizing Mrs Fortescue, a friend, he ran forward to greet her, relieved that this frightening trap of streets was to be shared. Seeing him, she first gave him a smile never offered him before by a woman; then looked prim and annoyed; then nodded at him briskly and said as she always did: 'Well, Fred, and how are things with you?' He walked a few steps with her, said he had to do his homework, heard her old woman's voice say: 'That's right, son, you must work, your mum and dad are right, a bright boy like you, it would be a shame to let it go to waste' – and watched her move on, across Oxford Street, into the narrow streets beyond.

He turned and saw Bill Bates coming towards him from the hardware shop, just closing. Bill was grinning, and he said: 'What, wouldn't she have you then?'

'It's Mrs Fortescue,' said Fred, entering a new world between one breath and the next, just because of the tone of Bill's voice.

'She's not a bad old tart,' said Bill. 'Bet she wasn't pleased to see you when she's on the job.'

'Oh, I don't know,' said Fred, trying out a new man-of-the-world voice for the first time, 'she lives over us, doesn't she?' (Bill must know this, everyone must know it, he thought, feeling sick.) 'I was just saying hullo, that's all.' It came off, he saw, for now Bill nodded and said: 'I'm off to the pictures, want to come?'

'Got to do homework,' said Fred, bitter.

'Then you've got to do it then, haven't you?' said Bill reasonably, going on his way.

Fred went home in a seethe of shame. How could his parents share their house with an old tart (whore, prostitute – but these were the only words he knew), how could they treat her like an ordinary decent person, even better (he understood, listening to them in his mind's ear, that their voices to her held something not far from respect) – how could they put up with it? Justice insisted that they had not chosen her as a tenant, she was the company's tenant, but at least they should have told Sanko and Duke so that she could be evicted and . . .

Although it seemed as if his adventure through the streets had been as long as a night, he found when he got in that it wasn't yet eight.

He went up to his box and set out his schoolbooks. Through the ceiling-board he could hear his sister moving. There being no door between the rooms, he went out to the landing, through his parents' room (his sister had to creep past the sleeping pair when she came in late) and into hers. She stood in a black slip before the glass, making up her face. 'Do you mind?' she said daintily. 'Can't you knock?' He muttered something, and felt a smile come on his face, aggressive and aggrieved, that seemed to switch on automatically these days if he saw his sister even at a distance. He sat on the edge of her bed. 'Do you *mind*?' she said again, moving away from him some black underwear. She slipped over her still puppy-fatted white shoulders a new dressing-gown in cherry-red and buttoned it up primly before continuing to work lipstick on to her mouth.

'Where are you going?'

'To the pictures, if you've got no objection,' she clipped out, in this new, jaunty voice that she had acquired when she left school, and which, he knew, she used as a weapon against all men. *But why against him?* He sat, feeling the ugly grin which was probably painted on his face, for he couldn't remove it, and he looked at the pretty girl with her new hair-do putting thick black rings around her eyes, and he thought of how they had been two peas in a pod. *In the summer* . . . yes, that is how it seemed to him now; through a year's-long summer of visits to friends, the park, the zoo, the pictures, they had been friends, allies, then the dark came down suddenly and in the dark had been born this cool, flip girl who hated him.

'Who are you going with?'

'Jem Taylor, if you don't have any objection,' she said.

'Why should I have any objection, I just asked.'

'What you don't know won't hurt you,' she said, very pleased with herself because of her ease in this way of talking. He recognized his recent achievement in the exchange with Bill as the same step forward as she was making, with this tone or style; and out of a quite uncustomary feeling of equality with her asked: 'How is old Jem, I haven't seen him lately.'

'Oh Fred, I'm *late*.' This bad temper meant she had finished her face and wanted to put on her dress, which she would not do in front of him.

Silly cow, he thought, grinning and thinking of her alter ego, the girl of his nights, does she think I don't know what she looks like in a slip, or nothing? Because of what went on behind the partition, in the dark, he banged his fist on it, laughing, and she whipped about and said: 'Oh Fred, you drive me crazy, you really do.' This being something from their brother-and-sister past, admitting intimacy, even the possibility of real equality, she checked herself, put on a sweet contained smile, and said: 'If you don't *mind*, Fred, I want to get dressed.'

He went out, remembering only as he got through the parents' room and saw his mother's feathered mules by the bed, that he had wanted to talk about Mrs Fortescue. He realized his absurdity, because of course his sister would pretend she didn't understand what he meant ... His fixed smile of shame changed into one of savagery as he thought: Well, Jem, you're not going to get anything out of her but *do you mind* and *have you any objection* and *please yourself*, I know that much about my sweet sister ... In his room he could not work, even after his sister had left, slamming three doors and making so much racket with her heels that the parents shouted at her from the shop. He was thinking of Mrs Fortescue. But she was old. She had always been old, as long as he could remember. And the old women who came up to see her in the afternoons, were they whores (tarts, prostitutes, *bad women*) too? And where did she, they, do it? And who was the smelly old man who came so late nearly every night?

He sat with the waves of liquor-smell from the ground floor arising past him, thinking of the sourish smell of the old man, and of the scented smell of the old women, feeling short-breathed because of the stuffy reek of this room and associating it (because of certain memories from his nights) with the reek from Mrs Fortescue's room which he could positively smell from where he sat, so strongly did he create it.

Bill must be wrong: she couldn't possibly be on the game still, who would want an old thing like that?

The family had a meal every night when the shop closed. It was usually about ten thirty when they sat down. Tonight there was some boiled bacon, and baked beans. Fred brought out casually: 'I saw Mrs Fortescue going off to work when I was out.' He waited the results of this cheek, this effrontery, watching his parents' faces. They did not even exchange glances. His mother pushed tinted bronze hair back with a hand that had a stain of grease on it, and said: 'Poor old girl, I expect she's pleased about the Act, when you get down to it, in the winter it must have been bad sometimes.' The words *the Act* hit Fred's outraged sense of propriety anew; he had to work them out; thinking that his parents did not even apologize for the years of corruption. Now his father said – his face was inflamed, he must have been taking nips from the glass under the counter – 'Once or twice, when I saw her on Frith Street before the Act I felt sorry for her. But I suppose she got used to it.'

'It must be nicer this way,' said Mrs Danderlea, pushing the crusting remains of the baked beans towards her husband.

He scooped them out of the dish with the edge of his fried bread, and she said: 'What's wrong with the spoon?'

'What's wrong with the bread,' he returned, with an unconvincing whisky glare, which she ignored.

'Where's her place, then?' asked Fred, casual, having worked out that she must have one.

'Over that new club in Parton Street. The rent's gone up again, so Mr Spencer told me, and there's the telephone she needs now – well, I don't know how much you can believe of what *he* says, but he's said often enough that without him helping her out she'd do better at almost anything else.'

'Not a word he says,' said Mr Danderlea, pushing out his dome of a stomach as he sat back, replete. 'He told me he was doorman for the Greystock Hotel in Knightsbridge – well, it turns out all this time he's been doorman for that strip-tease joint along the street from her new place, and that's where he's been for years, because it was a night-club before it was strip-tease.'

'Well, there's no point in that, is there?' said Mrs Danderlea, pouring second cups. 'I mean, why tell fibs about it, I mean everyone knows, don't they?'

Fred again pushed down protest: that, yes, Mr Spencer (Mrs Fortescue's 'regular', but he had never understood what they had meant by the ugly word before) was right to lie; he wished his parents would lie even now; anything rather than this casual back-and-forth chat about this horror, years-old, and right over their heads, part of their lives.

He ducked down his face and shovelled beans into it fast, knowing it was scarlet, and wanting a reason for it.

'You'll get heart-burn, gobbling like that,' said his mother, as he had expected.

'I've got to finish my homework,' he said, and bolted, shaking his head at the cup of tea she was pushing over at him.

He sat in his room until his parents went to bed, marking off the routine of the house from his new knowledge. After an expected interval Mrs Fortescue came in, he could hear her moving about, taking her time about everything. Water ran, for a long time. He now understood that this sound, water running into and then out of a basin, was something he had heard at this hour all his life. He sat listening with the ashamed, fixed grin on his face. Then his sister came in; he could hear her sharp sigh of relief as she flumped on the bed and bent over to take off her shoes. He nearly called out, 'Good night, Jane,' but thought better of it. Yet all through the summer they had whispered and giggled through the partition.

Mr Spencer, Mrs Fortescue's regular, came up the stairs. He heard their voices together; listened to them as he undressed and went to bed; as he lay wakeful; as he at last went off to sleep.

Next evening he waited until Mrs Fortescue went out, and followed her, careful she didn't see him. She walked fast and efficient, like a woman on her way to the office. Why then the fur coat, the veil, the make-up? Of course, it was habit, because of all the years on the pavement; for it was a sure thing she didn't wear that outfit to receive customers in her place. But it turned out that he was wrong. Along the last hundred yards before her door, she slowed her pace, took a couple of quick glances left and right for the police, then looked at a large elderly man coming towards her. This man swung around, joined her, and they went side by side into her doorway, the whole operation so quick, so smooth, that even if there had been a policeman, all he could have seen was a woman meeting someone she had expected to meet.

Fred then went home. Jane had dressed for her evening. He followed her too. She walked fast, not looking at people, her smart new coat flaring jade, emerald, dark-green, as she moved through varying depths of light, her black puffy hair gleaming. She went into the Underground. He followed her down the escalators, and on to the platform, at not much more than arm's distance, but quite safe because of her self-absorption. She stood on the edge of the platform, staring across the rails at a big advertisement. It was a very large, dark-brown, gleaming revolver holster, with a revolver in it, attached to a belt for bullets; but instead of bullets each loop had a lipstick, in all the pink-orange-scarlet-crimson shades it was possible to imagine lipstick in. Fred stood just behind his sister, and examined her sharp little face examining the advertisement and choosing which lipstick she would buy. She smiled – nothing like the appealing shame-faced smile that was stuck, for ever it seemed, on Fred's face, but a calm, triumphant smile. The train came streaming in, obscuring the advertisement. The doors slid open, receiving his sister, who did not look around. He stood close against the window, looking at her calm little face, willing her to look at him. But the train rushed her off again, and she would never know he had been there.

He went home, the ferment of his craziness breaking through his lips in an incredulous raw mutter: a revolver, a bloody revolver . . . His parents were at supper, taking in food, swilling in tea, like pigs, pigs, pigs, he thought, shovelling down his own supper to be rid of it. Then he said, 'I left a book in the shop, Dad, I want to get it,' and went down dark stairs through the sickly rising fumes. In a drawer under the till was a revolver which had been there for years, against the day when burglars would break in and Mr (or Mrs) Danderlea would frighten them off with it. Many of Fred's dreams had been spun around that weapon. But it was broken somewhere in its black-gleaming interior. He carefully hid it under his sweater, and went up, to knock on his parents' door. They were already in bed, a large double bed at which, because of this hideous world he was now a citizen of, he was afraid to look. Two old people, with sagging faces and bulging mottled fleshy shoulders lay side by side, looking at him. 'I want to leave something for Jane,' he said, turning his gaze away from them. He laid the revolver on Jane's pillow, arranging half a dozen lipsticks of various colours as if they were bullets coming out of it.

He went back to the shop. Under the counter stood the bottle of Black and White beside the glass stained sour with his father's tippling. He made sure the bottle was still half full before turning the lights out and settling down to wait. Not for long. When he heard the key in the lock he set the door open wide so Mrs Fortescue must see him.

'Why, Fred, whatever are you doing?'

'I noticed Dad left the light on, so I came down.' Frowning with efficiency, he looked for a place to put the whisky bottle, while he rinsed the dirtied glass. Then casual, struck by a thought, he offered: 'Like a drink, Mrs Fortescue?' In the dim light she focused, with difficulty, on the bottle. 'I never touch the stuff, dear . . .' Bending his face down past hers, to adjust a wine bottle, he caught the liquor on her breath, and understood the vagueness of her good nature.

'Well all right, dear,' she went on, 'just a little one to keep you company. You're like your Dad, you know that?'

'Is that so?' He came out of the shop with the bottle under his arm, shutting the door behind him and locking it. The stairs glimmered dark. 'Many's the time he's offered me a nip on a cold night, though not when your mother could see.' She added a short triumphant titter, resting her weight on the stair-rail as if testing it.

'Let's go up,' he said insinuatingly, knowing he would get his way, because it had been so easy this far. He was shocked it was so easy. She should have said: 'What are you doing out of bed at this time?' Or: 'A boy of your age, drinking, what next!'

She obediently went up ahead of him, pulling herself up.

The small room she went into, vaguely smiling her invitation that he should follow, was crammed with furniture and objects, all of which had the same soft glossiness of her clothes, which she now went to the next room to remove. He sat on an oyster-coloured satin sofa, looked at bluish brocade curtains, a cabinet full of china figures, thick creamy rugs, pink cushions, pink-tinted walls. A table in a corner held photographs. Of her, so he understood, progressing logically back from those he could rec-ognize to those that were inconceivable. The earliest was of a girl with yellow collar-bone-length curls, on which perched a top hat. She wore a spangled bodice, in pink; pink satin pants, long black-lace stockings, white gloves, and was roguishly pointing a walking stick at the audience – at him, Fred. 'Like a bloody gun,' he thought, feeling the shameful derisive grin come on to his face. He heard the door shut behind him, but did not turn, wondering what he would see: he never had seen her, he realized, without hat, veil, furs. She said, pottering about behind his shoul-der: 'Yes, that's me when I was a Gaiety Girl, a nice outfit, wasn't it?'

'Gaiety Girl?' he said, protesting, and she admitted: 'Well, that was before your time, wasn't it?'

The monstrousness of this second 'wasn't it' made it easy for him to turn and look: she was bending over a cupboard, her back to him. It was a back whose shape was concealed by thick, soft, cherry-red, with a tufted pattern of whirls and waves. She stood up and faced him, displaying, without a trace of consciousness at the horror of the fact, his sister's dressing-gown. She carried glasses and a jug of water to the central table that was planted in a deep-pink rug, and said: 'I hope you don't mind my getting into something comfortable, but we aren't strangers.' She sat op-posite, having pushed the glasses towards him, as a reminder that the bottle was still in his hand. He poured the yellow, smelling liquid, watching her face to see when he must stop. But her face showed nothing, so he filled her tumbler half full. 'Just a splash, dear . . .' He splashed, and she lifted the glass and held it, in the vague tired way that went with her face, which, now that for the first time in his life he could really look at it, was an old shrunken face, with small black eyes deep in their sockets, and a small mouth pouting out of a tired mesh of lines. This old, rather kind face, at which he tried not to stare, was like a mask held between the cherry-red gown over a body whose shape was slim and young; and the hair, beautifully tinted a tactful silvery-blond and waving softly into the hollows of an ancient neck.

'My sister's got a dressing-gown like that.'

'It's pretty, isn't it? They've got them in at Richard's, down the street, I expect she got hers there too, did she?'

'I don't know.'

'Well, the proof of the pudding's in the eating, isn't it?'

At this remark, which reminded him of nothing so much as his parents' idiotic pattering exchange at supper-time, when they were torpid before sleep, he felt the ridiculous smile leave his face. He was full of anger, but no longer of shame.

'Give me a cigarette, dear,' she went on, 'I'm too tired to get up.'

'I don't smoke.'

'If you could reach me my handbag.'

He handed her a large crocodile bag, that she had left by the photographs. 'I have nice things, don't I?' she agreed with his unspoken comment on it. 'Well, I always say, I always have nice things, whatever else . . . I never have anything cheap or nasty, my things are always nice . . . Baby Batsby taught me that, never have anything cheap or nasty, he used to say. He used to take me on his yacht, you know, to Cannes and Nice. He was my friend for three years, and he taught me about having beautiful things.'

'Baby Batsby?'

'That was before your time, I expect, but he was in all the papers once, every week of the year. He was a great spender, you know, generous.'

'Is that a fact?'

'I've always been lucky that way, my friends were always generous. Take Mr Spencer now, he never lets me want for anything, only yesterday he said: Your curtains are getting a bit passé, I'll get you some new ones. And mark my words, he will, he's as good as his word.'

He saw that the whisky, coming on top of whatever she'd had earlier, was finishing her off. She sat blinking smeared eyes at him; and her cigarette, secured between thumb and forefinger six inches from her mouth, shed ash on her cherry-red gown. She took a gulp from the glass, and nearly set it down on air: Fred reached forward just in time.

'Mr Spencer's a good man, you know,' she told the air about a foot from her unfocused gaze.

'Is he?'

'We're just old friends now, you know. We're both getting on a bit. Not that I don't let him have a bit of a slap and a tickle sometimes to keep him happy, though I'm not interested, not really.'

Trying to insert the end of the cigarette between her lips, she missed, and jammed the butt against her cheek. She leaned forward and stubbed it out. Sat back – with dignity. Stared at Fred, screwed up her eyes to see him, failed, offered the stranger in her room a social smile.

This smile trembled into a wrinkled pout, as she said: 'Take Mr Spencer now, he's a good spender, I'd never say he wasn't, but but but . . .' She fumbled at the packet of cigarettes and he hastened to extract one for her and to light it. '*But*. Yes. Well, he may think I'm past it, but I'm not, and don't you think it. There's a good thirty years between us, do you know that?'

'Thirty years,' said Fred, politely, his smile now fixed by a cold determined loathing.

'What do you think, dear? He always makes out we're the same age, now he's past it, but – well, look at that then if you don't believe me.' She pointed her scarlet-tipped and shaking left hand at the table with the photographs. 'Yes, that one, just look at it, it's only from last summer.' Fred leaned forward and lifted towards him the image of her just indicated which, though she was sitting opposite him in the flesh, must prove her victory over Mr Spencer. She wore a full-skirted, tightly belted, tightly bodiced striped dress, from which her ageing bare arms hung down by her sides, and her old neck and face rose shameless under the beautiful gleaming hair.

'Well, it stands to reason, doesn't it,' she said. 'Well, what do you think then?'

'When's Mr Spencer coming?' he asked.

'I'm not expecting him tonight, he's working. I admire him, I really do, holding down that job, three, four in the morning sometimes, and it's no joke, those layabouts you get at those places and it's always Mr Spencer who has to fix them up with what they fancy, or get rid of them if they make trouble, and he's not a big man, and he's not young any more, I don't know how he does it. But he's got tact. Tact. Yes, I often say to him, you've got tact, I say, it'll take a man anywhere.' Her glass was empty, and she was looking at it.

The news that Mr Spencer was not expected did not surprise Fred; he had known it, because of his secret brutal confidence born when she had said: 'I never touch the stuff, dear.'

He now got up, went behind her, stood a moment steeling himself, because the embarrassed shame-faced grin had come back on to his face, weakening his purpose – then put two hands firmly under her armpits, lifted her and supported her.

She at first struggled to remain sitting, but let herself be lifted. 'Time for by-byes?' she said. But as he began to push her, still supporting her, towards the bedroom, she said, suddenly coherent: 'But Fred, it's Fred, Fred, it's Fred . . .' She twisted out of his grip, fell two steps back, and was stopped by the door to the bedroom. There she spread her two legs under the cherry gown, to hold her trembling weight, swayed, caught at Fred, held tight, and said: 'But it's *Fred*.'

'Why should you care,' he said, cold, grinning.

'But I don't work here, dear, you know that – no, let me go. For he had put two great schoolboy hands on her shoulders.

He felt the shoulder tense, and then grow small and tender in his palms.

'You're like your father, you're the spitting image of your father, did you know that?'

He opened the door with his left hand; then spun her around by pushing at her left shoulder as she faced him; then, putting both hands under her armpits from behind, marched her into the bedroom, while she tittered.

The bedroom was mostly pink. Pink silk bedspread. Pink walls. A doll in a pink flounced skirt lolled against the pillow, its chin tucked into a white fichu over which it stared at the opposite wall where an eighteenth-century girl held a white rose to her lips. Fred pushed Mrs Fortescue over dark-red carpet, till her knees met the bed. He lifted her, and dropped her on it, neatly moving the doll aside with one hand before she could crush it.

She lay eyes closed, limp, breathing fast, her mouth slightly open. The black furrows beside the mouth were crooked; the eyelids shone blue in wells of black.

'Turn the lights out,' she implored.

He turned out the pink-shaded lamp fixed to the headboard. She fumbled at her clothes. He stripped off his trousers, his underpants, pushed her hands aside, found silk in the opening of the gown that glowed cherry-red in the light from the next room. He stripped the silk pants off her so that her legs flew up, then flumped down. She was inert. Then her expertise revived in her, or at least in her tired hands, and he achieved the goal of his hot imaginings of these ugly autumn nights in one shattering spasm that filled him with no less hatred. Her old body stirred feebly under him, and he heard her irregular breathing. He sprang off her in a leap, tugged back pants, trousers. Then he switched on the light. She lay, eyes closed, her face blurred with woe, the upper part of her body nestled into the soft glossy cherry stuff, the white legs spread open, bare. She made an attempt to rouse herself, cover herself. He leaned over her, teeth bared in a hating grin, forcing her hands away from her body. They fell limp on the stained silk spread. Now he stripped off the gown, roughly, as if she were the doll. She whimpered, she tittered, she protested. He watched, with pleasure, tears welling out of the pits of dark and trickling down her mascara-stained face. She lay naked among the folds of cherry colour. He looks at the greyish crinkles around the armpits, the small flat breasts, the loose stomach; then at the triangle of black hair where white hairs sprouted. She was attempting to fold her legs over each other. He forced them apart, muttering: 'Look at yourself, look at yourself, then!' – while he held in his nausea which was being fed by the miasmic smell that he had known must be the air of this room.

'Filthy old whore, disgusting, that's what you are, disgusting!' He let his grasp slacken on her thighs, saw red marks come up on them as the legs flew together and she wriggled and burrowed to get under the cherry-red gown.

She sat up, holding the gown around her. Pink gown, pink coverlet, pink walls, pink pink pink everywhere. And a dark-red carpet. He felt as if the room were built of flesh.

She was looking straight up at him.

'That wasn't very nice, was it?'

He fell back a step, feeling his own face go hot. That was how his mother corrected him: *That isn't very nice, dear*, in a long-suffering, reproachful voice exactly like Mrs Fortescue's.

'That wasn't at all nice, Fred, it wasn't nice at all. I don't know what can have got into you!'

Without looking at him, she let her feet down over the edge of the bed. He could see them trembling. She was peering over and down to fit them into pink-feathered mules.

He noted that he was feeling a need to help her fit her pathetic feet into the fancy mules. He fled. Down the stairs into his room, and face down on to his bed. Through the ceiling-board an inch from his ear he could hear his sister move. Up he jumped again, out of his box, and through his parents' room which he hated so much he behaved as if it were a vacuum, and simply not there.

His sister was lying coiled on her bed, in her cherry-pink gown, painting her nails coral.

'Very clever, I don't think,' she said.

He looked for the gun: it was on her dressing-table, in a litter of lipsticks.

He took up the gun and pointed it down at that woman his sister in her terrifying intimacy of warm pink.

'Stupid,' she said.

'That's right.'

She went on doing her nails.

'Stupid, stupid, stupid,' she said.

'That's right.'

'Then why? – oh do stop it, put that thing down.'

He put it down.

'If you don't mind, I want to get into bed.'

He said nothing, and she looked up at him. It was a long, hollow, upwards look that she had taken from an advertisement, probably, or a film. But then the look changed, and she was Jane. She had seen something in him.

His face was changed? His voice had changed? *He* had changed?

Triumph warmed his backbone; he smiled. He had regained his sister, he had made a step forward and come level with her again.

'Please yourself,' he said, and went to the door.

'Ta-ta, good night, mind the bugs don't bite,' said she, in a ritual of their childhood – of last year.

'Oh, be your age,' he said. He went through the loathsome dark of his parents' bedroom without thinking more than: Poor old things, they can't help it.

Side Benefits of an Honourable Profession

Or rather, perhaps, a condition of, the mud which nurtures? Flowers, of course – but that isn't the point. No, definitely not an effluent, a by-product. Accurate as well as charitable to see it all as a kind of compost, the rich mad muck which feeds those disciplined performances, exactly the same night after night that we see and marvel at and which might even cause us to exclaim – if we haven't entirely lost that naïvety which I, for one, maintain the theatre needs as dreams need sleep, and could not exist without for one moment: how *can* he/she bear to be someone else so entirely and devotedly every blessed night and two afternoons a week for hours at a stretch! Even with intervals for orange juice or Scotch. Possibly for months at a time. If the play finds favour, as they say.

Those two, for instance: household names, or at least in those households (one per cent of the population) which prefer to give room to these rather than to the more vigorous performers, football players, or horses or dogs – those two, having rehearsed for a month a play which called for a slow progress towards a bed, made of the bed itself a stage for – not at all for the guilt-ridden and eventually murderous lusts which the play incorporated, but for innocence.

It was an innocence so immaculate that words like mud and compost perhaps need looking at again. If, that is, we do not want to examine innocence.

It so happened – and no chance either, I feel – that both he (we'll call him John) and she (Mary will do) were involved during the period of rehearsal with some pretty savage moments in their private lives. He was in trouble with his marriage; and she, having been divorced, had reached that point with a possible new husband when she must decide whether to marry him or not. On the whole she felt not. At any rate, it wasn't at all that either could look forward, after a day of rehearsing passions not their own, to loving tranquillity. Far from it, and on the contrary, both returned to scenes, reproaches and torments not very different – and they even said so, with that appropriate good trouper's laugh used by actors to dismiss their private lives when engaged on their real business – from those they were developing during rehearsals. Well, one night Mary *found* herself, when everybody had left the darkened theatre, backstage and by the great bed which was such a feature of the play. It was made up, but for economy's sake not more than was essential. She sat by the bed on the little stool which was also part of the set and found herself shedding a tear, though for what she could not have said (her words when describing the experience). Through blurred vision she saw a figure approaching from the dressing-rooms: no ghost or burglar, but the handsome John, whose feet, or at least some impulse, had brought him here, also in the belief that the building was deserted. No need, she said, for words. He sat on the companion stool on the other side of the bed. He offered her a cigarette. Between them stretched the crumpled sheet on which they had spent at least four hours that day of steady, grindingly repetitive rehearsal locked in each other's arms, apparently in the extremes of passion. They left half an hour later, without even the casual theatre kiss that by custom they would have offered each other on parting. Next evening, and without arranging it, they met again. For a week these two rolled, morning and after-noon and some evenings, in torments of simulated lust and its associated emotions, and at night met, chaste and tender, for a half-hour before returning to their tumultuous private lives. They were too shy, as she explained, to touch each other. As in a first love, the lighting of a cigarette, the accidental meeting of a hand, were exquisitely painful – indeed, more than enough. That nightly half-hour was filled with restoring breaths of air from lost horizons. Finally their *affaire* (so she always pronounced it) culminated in a kiss so delicate, so exquisite, that its poetry was enough to decide her not to marry her possible husband, and him to leave his wife. No, that kiss was not on the *first night*, but after the dress rehearsal. The first night being successfully accomplished in the usual ritual crescendo of shared tension, flowers, champagne, congratulations and the theatre, emptying backstage into darkness as it had an hour ago in front, the two *found themselves*, on their way out, by the bed – a slight detour and a temporary shedding of their first-night guests being necessary. Looking at the pillow-case, which should have been put on fresh for the just-completed performance, she noted a smear of lipstick – hers, from the dress rehearsal. 'Really,' she said, irritably, 'I do think they might have remembered to put on a clean pillow-case for the first night.' 'I quite agree,' he said, cool, and with precisely the same degree of professional irritation at incompetence; 'that lipstick must have been visible from half-way up the stalls.' With which they kissed each other, comradely and brisk, as is customary, said good night, and parted, she to reaffirm to her lover that no, she would not marry him, and he to disagree with his wife who was saying that really, as responsible and adult people, they should try again.

Or take that well-known playwright, now dead, whose dissatisfaction with his wives was not so much proclaimed – they were all damned fine women he told the newspapers – as demonstrated by the fact that he dismissed them one after another, usually about four years after marrying them. He was on his sixth wife when she met, by chance, wives five and four, and confessed that things were not as they ought to be. Remarks were made that caused them to contact previous wives. Six women, five ex-wives and the present incumbent, met one afternoon – not, they said, in any spirit of anger, but from a scientific desire for psychological clarity. In each of this man's plays (we will call him John) appeared a woman, sometimes in a leading part, sometimes not, who was wise, witty, warm, tender, beautiful and all-forgiving, the last quality being the most valuable, in life if not theatrically, as each of these women had discovered. They were all actresses and all had played this woman, presented under different names, in different clothes and in different epochs. The first wife had played her in his first-performed play as a suburban schoolteacher; the current wife had played her, evolved into full flower, four years ago in the shape of an Italian princess. They all had the same experience, an uneasiness which developed even during those first rapturous days of an at-last-discovered perfect love, that made them feel – and all of them said they had felt it – as if they were not themselves, as if, in life, they were being forced into a role, and even, as one of them put it, as if there were always a third person present – a ghost. The ghost, of course, of the stage woman. And each one had experienced that moment when, betrayed, wounded, knifed to the heart by reality, their John had shouted (and with such conviction of betrayal that there was nothing at all to be said): Why don't you behave like—? You aren't like *her* at all!' – using the name for whichever incarnation of his 'she' that *she* had in fact played. And this was the moment when, giving her a look of disgusted dismissal, he had gone off into his study to begin the new play which would incorporate, in minor or major part, the new version of this woman who must continually be re-created in art since she did not exist in life. Which play, when it was put on, would infallibly lead to her – the present wife's – divorce. Because, although she did not know it, was still perhaps a half-tried girl waiting for her big chance, the new wife was already blue-printed, summoned. And from that moment about a week after the rehearsals started, when she approached the great man shyly, her beautiful eyes shining with the effort it was costing her, and said, 'I must say this, I really must, forgive me, but thank you for letting me play this beautiful part in your beautiful play,' nothing was more certain than that he would marry her, and then divorce her the moment he finally understood that she was after all, only Mary, who might sulk, complain or cry just like any woman.

Or take the case of Mary X – this time a female writer. It was when she was well on her career that her husband pointed out, and with rancour, that in almost everything she wrote occurred the same figure, male, though that was *not* the point, because he was for all practical purposes sexless, being a slight, wry clown or harlequin figure, on whose face was printed the same grimace whatever he was actually doing, whether playing the flute, dancing or being – apparently – a normal person, a smile that could not be distinguished from the contractions of the muscles which indicated pain or sorrow. Once having understood the truth of her husband's accusation, she searched through every word she had ever written. Sure enough, there he was, right from the beginning, even in those apprentice pieces written decades before and now filed away. The point was, who was he? Where did he come from? Her father? No. Her brothers? No. Her husband? Certainly not, nothing of the Petrouchka about him, and besides, the demon lover (her husband's name for him) had predated the husband by years. Her sons? She sincerely hoped not. Her mother then? – since such figures from the underworld are no respecters of sex. No. Who? Who, possibly? No one. There was nobody she could think of, no matter how far back she went in her childhood, who could possibly have stood in for or inspired this ambiguously enticing wraith. But she did know, in the present, one, two, perhaps three of him. Pursuing this discovery, she made the new one that while until the performance of her first play, twelve years ago now, she had not met once, not once, any person, male or female, who incarnated the sad clown, since then and starting with the actor who had played the part (nicknamed Pierrot by the company even before her play was known by them) – briefly a friend before he had faded, as befitted his character, into a wry offstage existence on the fringes of her life – she had known several; she was never without him. The fact was, then, that the making flesh and blood of her – but her *what*? fantasy? a figure from her night-dreams? – on stage had had the power to bring him finally towards her? Well if so, it is not a thought a sensible person could enjoy. Particularly not a writer. She contents herself, when meeting a man who turns that unmistakable face towards her, with saying to herself, never to her husband who so strangely and obdurately resents this rival who could never be one, *Here he is again*, and with the secret contraction of the heart, the laugh that is half a shudder, which are the tributes we pay to the dark of our natures.

But to return to the light, the easily understood, with a man whom I once knew who claimed that his tragedy was that while loving women he was unable. He was always in our company, and taking us out, and being seen in public with us, but, when it came to the point – there it was, he said. Very well then. He was shooting a big film. During the course of this, it was necessary, he said, to make a screen test of the leading actor for another film, also to be shot by him, in which he, the actor, might again play the leading role. Reasonable enough – it was a very different film in which a handsome alcoholic eighteenth-century rake would endeavour, but fail, to rape a beautiful village girl in circumstances which would force her to become his mistress. In the film which was currently being shot, he was playing a lusty working-class youth before whom women fell like cut grass. The scene was set for the test. In came the actor, transmogrified out of overalls and a cloth cap into aristocratic elegances. It was about ten in the morning. The scene to be shot was the moment of the gentleman's failure with the lady – her lack of refinement and probably unwashed condition were responsible, the script suggested. Usually half a morning would have done for such a test. But for the whole of that day, hour after hour after hour, the studio with its armies of hands, lighting experts, camera crews, make-up women, watched the mad director with the marvellous politeness of their most necessary discipline, while *he* watched the handsome hero attempt and fail, attempt and fail, and attempt and fail and fail, again and again, to have the beautiful and scornful girl. The great expanse of the harshly lit studio, the small area of especially focused lights, the four-poster bed, and at least three hundred people standing about, if they were not actually assisting, forced to watch while the lusty young man who for weeks and weeks had been light-heartedly romping his way through at least a dozen women in one film, was reduced to public impotence for the benefit of another. Again and again. And again.

When it was all over, but not until five minutes before the trade-union rules made it inevitable that the camera crews must go home to tea and their wives, the mad director said, addressing the by now exhausted young man: 'Well, that'll do I think. But actually, love, I do think that X (another actor) would probably be better in this particular role. You are too earthy darling, let's face it. He's more subtle.'

Or the famous screen actress, American, well known for her fastidiousness about what she plays. Much dreaded is that moment when, surrounded by lawyers, agents, a husband and protectors of all kinds, she hands back a script with: 'As it stands, it really is not for me – if we may suggest some changes . . .?'

What, then, is for her? She has played, for some decades now, women in every kind of desperate situation, ex-jailbirds, betrayed lovers, doomed invalids, sorrowing mothers. But what can be the common denominator which causes her to say: Yes, this is for me? I once knew a man who worked, on a very humble level, in films she was starring in. What was she like, I wanted to know. It was offered that she was businesslike, adamant in her choices of co-stars, would not be photographed without the exact density of a piece of gauze being specified by lawyers, in triplicate, for certain revealing shots; that she could never be shot in such a way that her nose, not her best point, could emphasize itself . . . Yes, but what is she *like*? Good God, said he, you must have seen her in a hundred films.

She lives, has lived, a life of improbable probity, married to the same man, with never a breath of scandal; remains a lady who insists on maintaining what she describes as the high standards of Hollywood.

Not long ago, I heard, she turned down a part which would have involved her battering to death her husband (in such a way that it could look as if someone else had done it) so that she could benefit from his will. That was, she claimed, nothing but unmotivated nasty-mindedness. Soon afterwards she was pleased to play a part where she battered to death – but openly, as it were nobly – a lawyer lover who had tricked her out of a fortune.

Fairly straightforward really, daylight stuff still, as is this . . .

A certain English gentleman, a sort of semi-lord, being a middle son (he refers to himself with a rather tetchy refusal to conform to current prejudices as well-connected) lives in a large country-house but alone, as his wife died shortly after their marriage. Alone, that is, except for his manservant. Failing to re-marry, the usual rumours gathered about him and his way of life, dark tastes of all kinds were hinted at, and the women who had not succeeded in marrying him allowed it to be understood that it was their discovery of his secret which had cooled their pur-suit.

He had been a widower for more than a decade when he was taken to what he called 'a show'. He did not care for the theatre at all. There he saw Mary Griffiths, a woman who had been married twice but who had announced to everyone and even to the Press that she did not intend to marry, she chose freedom.

She was an attractive blonde woman, her stage personality formed in the fifties to the formula of that time – casual, loud-mouthed, frank – and, as she insisted, as common as dirt. She took pains to conceal her middle-class origin – a handicap when she first started to act. She took care to play parts suited to this formula – mostly sad dishevelled girls doomed to disharmony. 'A lost ugly duckling with moments of swan,' as one critic put it. *A jolie laide* said another, thus enabling Mary to describe herself as more laid than jolly, and to reap bouble benefit, when people protested the joke was not new, by claiming: 'Well, I've never had an education – I've never pretended I did – have I then?'

What the gentleman saw in her struck his friends into incred-ulity, and her into laughter, and then thought. She was the re-incarnation, he said, of his grandmother, the best horsewoman in the country, the bravest woman he had ever known – and, but of course, a great lady.

Mary wondered for a while whether to take riding lessons, in case some play or film producer saw in her what her still un-known admirer saw, but decided against it. They were intro-duced, and he began to court her – the only word for it. She was living at the time with a fashionable dress-designer, and it was hard to say which of the two, Mary or her lover ('boy-friend'), got more excitement from the ritual. John sent her flowers, formally charming notes, left visiting cards, took her to tea, drove her into the country in his Bentley – or rather, sat with her in the back seat while the manservant drove – took her to dinner. From each excursion Mary returned to mourn with her dress-designer the sad lack of romance in modern life, and more than once they lay wrapped tearfully in each other's arms, because of the poetry their relationship lacked and must now always lack (there being a time and a place for everything) because for them flowers, formal notes, drives and long intimate dinners were simply impossible, out of key. Their fate had been to meet before a fitting-room mirror, to quarrel half an hour later, and to start living together a week after. Surely, they both wondered, it was not possible that gentleman John could be working up to a proposal of marriage? As Mary put it: 'I know he's nuts, but he's not completely gone – me, his wife, he must be joking.'

About six months went by of a patient courtship conducted to rules invisible to Mary, but which she respected. Why not? As she said, she'd have time to fit in a dozen of such relationships concurrently, apart from acting in one play and rehearsing for another and keeping her boy-friend happy. What did those people *do* with themselves in those days, she asked, putting that time at about a hundred years back while waiting for the moment of truth? Then, at last, John told her that he had decided she was the woman for him.

'You are the woman for him?' inquired her dress-designer.

'That's what he said – I swear it.'

Mary was then invited, and for the first time, to week-end at his house. Her lover made her some dinner dresses, romantic rather than frank, and the two of them considered her day clothes, since both felt strongly that she should be properly dressed for the occasion. But as at the time she was wearing very short skirts, if she wore skirts at all, and she was not prepared completely to lose her character, a trouser suit was concocted that was chiefly mink, which, worn with mink boots, made her look like a moon Eskimo.

Mary discovered that for the week-end there would be three people in the house: herself, gentleman John and the manservant. She found the house charming. It fitted her like a glove, she insisted to disbelieving friends. In the afternoon she was taken for a drive, the manservant driving, drank sherry in the library before dinner, the manservant acting as butler, and ate a long and formal dinner, the manservant handing the dishes he had previously chosen. Then, intrigued to the point of hysteria, as she afterwards said, Mary waited for what surely must be a dishonourable proposal.

At eleven fifty-five John leaned his handsome person towards her and said: 'My dear, you must understand what my feelings towards you are, but before I could ask any woman to share my life, there is something I must do. If you like, you can call it a test.'

Mary was willing for the test.

John then nodded at the servant who went out of the room and came back a moment later wheeling a tall black coffin, upright. It had wheels at the feet end, for manoeuvrability. This coffin was steered, upright, in front of a tall mirror. The servant, in his impeccable black clothes, stood as it were to attention, at one side of it. John, with a smiling nod of encouragement at Mary, went to the coffin, and stood inside it, his hands crossed on his breast, gazing into the mirror. Inside the black coffin, black-clothed John; beside it, the black-clothed servant.

Mary said afterwards that she was bothered because no gesture or pose that occurred to her seemed to be appropriate. So she rubbed out her cigarette, folded her hands in her lap, and remained silent, smiling. At the end of a long five minutes, her John stepped down from the coffin and nodded at the servant, who wheeled it away. He leaned intimately towards her.

'Brandy?' he inquired.

'Just a little, please.'

Nothing more was said about the coffin. Soon after, he escorted her to her room. There, but outside it, he kissed her. 'And not bad either,' she said, describing the moment, 'Not – bad – at all!' He said that she had passed every test, and with her permission he would like to ask her to marry him. She said she would think it over, and he kissed her hand and hoped that she would sleep well.

Still thinking it over, she returned next day to London, driven by the manservant, who offered not one word about the midnight ceremony. She had decided that she would be damned if she would ask him questions, but she cracked, and so found that the ceremony of the coffin took place every night of her John's life at midnight. 'It's not every woman,' said the servant, 'who goes along with it. Some I've seen come and go who didn't take it as you did, madam.'

Mary consulted with her lover, who designed her a bridal gown, inspired, he said, by a fifteenth-century French court dress – too way out for current fashions, but he had been dying to make use of the ideas it provoked.

The dress ready, Mary wrote to John saying that he could have his answer, but he must come around to the dressing-room after the performance one night. If she could forgive him, he replied, he would not actually watch the performance again, one show a year was really enough for him, though it went without saying, he hoped, that he respected her profession.

When he arrived at the dressing-room door, he was made to wait. At last the dresser admitted him. He did not immediately know where to look – Mary was not there, it seemed, and since he had never been in an actress's dressing-room before, or, for that matter, backstage at all, the little room with its efficient mirrors, the cold strong working light, the surgical-looking appliances on the dressing-table, the clinical jars and bottles, were hostile to him. There stood the dresser, a small, devoted, grey figure, hands folded, her face saying nothing, in front of something that looked like – yes, she stood aside and there it was, a long black coffin, and in it, stretched out, dressed in the white wedding gown, eyes closed, hands folded around flowers, flowers all around her, lay his love Mary, dressed for a wedding ceremony, but most adamantly dead.

'As dead as blasted Ophelia,' as she said, when describing the scene to her friends and her lover in their favourite restaurant later that night.

He stared, stiffened, and went white – all this from the dresser, because, as Mary said, she was damned if she was going to open her eyes and spoil the performance. He then bowed, and went silently out, taking his dismissal like a gentleman.

The dress became a starry item in the designer's next collection, but by then he and Mary were no longer together. Discussing it in the friendly matter-of-fact way imposed on them by their style, or mode, they agreed there was something quite unassimilable about that wedding dress. Either she should put the bloody thing on and go to a registry office and be done with it, or they should call the thing off, with no hard feelings.

The dress then, prêt-à-porter, ready-to-wear, boutiqued, internationalized, led a thousand brides to the altar and the registrar's table.

Still quite straightforward – or, at least, understandable. But now enters the dark – or, at least, the tale turns slightly to the moonlit side.

Mary had the dress hanging up in her cupboard for some months. She could not wear it, it was not her style, but she did not want, for some reason, to part with it. At last she wore it for a fancy-dress party, and became, for one night, a fifteenth-century court lady.

At the party were stage and film directors, as well as the cooks, dress-designers, hairdressers and pop stars who were the lions of the current fashionable scene. A director who had seen Mary a dozen times in her usual kind of role on stage or on television, saw her now in a new light. A man with a fine nose for what was next, he wanted to make a large full-blooded film of a nineteenth-century novel whose heroine was a headstrong aristocratic daughter in love with a revolutionary plebeian. He was dubious about Mary's voice, but it turned out her own voice did very well – he was the first person to have heard it for years. She got the part. She had to learn to ride. The film was shot in Somerset, where gentleman John had his country-house.

For weeks she was riding across fields and woods where his grandmother, whose incarnation he had said she was, had won the admiration of a county. But gentleman John had gone abroad with his broken heart, taking the coffin and the manservant with him. Mary did not inquire, for, to tell the truth, she hardly thought of him. As she said in a television interview, when she was emotionally involved in a part, she had no time for anything else. As for him, since he hates films as much as he hates the theatre, he will probably never see this film at all.

But she was observed, while taking a fence, by a local country squire. She married him, briefly but – as she said when it was all over – for long enough. She changed her style, on her way to becoming what every leading actress is doomed to become, a *grande dame* of the British theatre.

Which reminds me of the *grande dame* who was acting in what she critically described as a kitchen-sink play – there were few of the other kind available at that time. Throughout the rehearsals she complained of the disgusting immorality of the words she was forced to speak. At lunch-times in the pub, at the top of a voice trained to carry, she described her views about current morality. At the top of the same voice she told the following story. She was on tour somewhere in the North. To her dressing-room came a man she did feel she had known. This feeling was so strong that she could not bring herself to say she had no idea who he was, and she agreed to go to dinner with him. Dinner over, she was still in the dark although she hadn't been able to enjoy a mouthful for racking her brains for some clue. She at last confessed her predicament. He was rather put out, she said.

She didn't remember the restaurant, at least?

Well, there was something about it . . .

'You don't remember that we came here every night for that marvellous week before I robbed you of your ever-so-precious virginity, darling?'

'They must have redecorated it! Besides, that must have been 1935 – I haven't been here since – I think. And besides, you must know that was *before* I became a Roman Catholic . . .'

Which reminds me of that actress who, playing a nun in a stormily religious play, used to take the habit home with her – with the connivance of the dresser, who understood her feelings. The play, she explained, lacked a true Christian insight. She wore the habit for ironing, washing up, rinsing out her underclothes – tasks which she called 'my little hair shirts'.

An Old Woman and Her Cat

Her name was Hetty, and she was born with the twentieth century. She was seventy when she died of cold and malnutrition. She had been alone for a long time, since her husband had died of pneumonia in a bad winter soon after the Second World War. He had not been more than middle-aged. Her four children were now middle-aged, with grown children. Of these descendants one daughter sent her Christmas cards, but otherwise she did not exist for them. For they were all respectable people, with homes and good jobs and cars. And Hetty was not respectable. She had always been a bit strange, these people said, when mentioning her at all.

When Fred Pennefather, her husband, was alive, and the children just growing up, they all lived much too close and uncomfortable in a Council flat in that part of London which is like an estuary, with tides of people flooding in and out: they were not half a mile from the great stations of Euston, St Pancras and King's Cross. The blocks of flats were pioneers in that area, standing up grim, grey, hideous, among many acres of little houses and gardens, all soon to be demolished so that they could be replaced by more tall grey blocks. The Pennefathers were good tenants, paying their rent, keeping out of debt; he was a building worker, 'steady', and proud of it. There was no evidence then of Hetty's future dislocation from the normal, unless it was that she very often slipped down for an hour or so to the platforms where the locomotives drew in and ground out again. She liked the smell of it all, she said. She liked to see people moving about, 'coming and going from all those foreign places'. She meant Scotland, Ireland, the North of England. These visits into the din, the smoke, the massed swirling people, were for her a drug, like other people's drinking or gambling. Her husband teased her, calling her a gipsy. She was in fact part-gipsy, for her mother had been one, but had chosen to leave her people and marry a man who lived in a house. Fred Pennefather liked his wife for being different from the run of the women he knew, and had married her because of it; but her children were fearful that her gipsy blood might show itself in worse ways than haunting railway stations. She was a tall woman with a lot of glossy black hair, a skin that tanned easily, and dark strong eyes. She wore bright colours, and enjoyed quick tempers and sudden reconciliations. In her prime she attracted attention, was proud and handsome. All this made it inevitable that the people in those streets should refer to her as 'that gipsy woman'. When she heard them, she shouted back that she was none the worse for that.

After her husband died and the children married and left, the Council moved her to a small flat in the same building. She got a job selling food in a local store, but found it boring. There seem to be traditional occupations for middle-aged women living alone, the busy and responsible part of their lives being over. Drink. Gambling. Looking for another husband. A wistful affair or two. That's about it. Hetty went through a period of, as it were, testing out all these, like hobbies, but tired of them. While still earning her small wage as a saleswoman, she began a trade in buying and selling second-hand clothes. She did not have a shop of her own, but bought or begged clothes from householders, and sold these to stalls and the second-hand shops. She adored doing this. It was a passion. She gave up her respectable job and forgot all about her love of trains and travellers. Her room was always full of bright bits of cloth, a dress that had a pattern she fancied and did not want to sell, strips of beading, old furs, embroidery, lace. There were street traders among the people in the flats, but there was something in the way Hetty went about it that lost her friends. Neighbours of twenty or thirty years' standing said she had gone queer, and wished to know her no longer. But she did not mind. She was enjoying herself too much, particularly the moving about the streets with her old perambulator, in which she crammed what she was buying or selling. She liked the gossiping, the bargaining, the wheedling from householders. It was this last which – and she knew this quite well of course – the neighbours objected to. It was the thin edge of the wedge. It was begging. Decent people did not beg. She was no longer decent.

Lonely in her tiny flat, she was there as little as possible, always preferring the lively streets. But she had after all to spend some time in her room, and one day she saw a kitten lost and trembling in a dirty corner, and brought it home to the block of flats. She was on a fifth floor. While the kitten was growing into a large strong tom, he ranged about that conglomeration of staircases and lifts and many dozens of flats, as if the building were a town. Pets were not actively persecuted by the authorities, only forbidden and then tolerated. Hetty's life from the coming of the cat became more sociable, for the beast was always making friends with somebody in the cliff that was the block of flats across the court, or not coming home for nights at a time so that she had to go and look for him and knock on doors and ask, or returning home kicked and limping, or bleeding after a fight with his kind. She made scenes with the kickers, or the owners of the enemy cats, exchanged cat lore with cat-lovers, was always having to bandage and nurse her poor Tibby. The cat was soon a scarred warrior with fleas, a torn ear, and a ragged look to him. He was a multicoloured cat and his eyes were small and yellow. He was a long way down the scale from the delicately coloured, elegantly shaped pedigree cats. But he was independent, and often caught himself pigeons when he could no longer stand the tinned cat food, or the bread and packet gravy Hetty fed him, and he purred and nestled when she grabbed him to her bosom at those times she suffered loneliness. This happened less and less. Once she had realized that her children were hoping that she would leave them alone because the old rag-trader was an embarrassment to them, she accepted it, and a bitterness that always had wild humour in it welled up only at times like Christmas. She sang or chanted to the cat: 'You nasty old beast, filthy old cat, nobody wants you, do they Tibby, no, you're just an alley tom, just an old stealing cat, hey Tibs, Tibs, Tibs.'

The building teemed with cats. There were even a couple of

dogs. They all fought up and down the grey cement corridors. There were sometimes dog and cat messes which someone had to clear up, but which might be left for days and weeks as part of neighbourly wars and feuds. There were many complaints. Finally an official came from the Council to say that the ruling about keeping animals was going to be enforced. Hetty, like the others, would have to have her cat destroyed. This crisis coincided with a time of bad luck for her. She had had flu; had not been able to earn money; had found it hard to get out for her pension; had run into debt. She owed a lot of back rent, too. A television set she had hired and was not paying for attracted the visits of a television representative. The neighbours were gossiping that Hetty had 'gone savage'. This was because the cat had brought up the stairs and along the passageways a pigeon he had caught, shedding feathers and blood all the way; a woman coming in to complain found Hetty plucking the pigeon to stew it, as she had done with others, sharing the meal with Tibby.

'You're filthy,' she would say to him, setting the stew down to cool in his dish. 'Filthy old thing. Eating that dirty old pigeon. What do you think you are, a wild cat? Decent cats don't eat dirty birds. Only those old gipsies eat wild birds.'

One night she begged help from a neighbour who had a car, and put into the car herself, the television set, the cat, bundles of clothes, and the pram. She was driven across London to a room in a street that was a slum because it was waiting to be done up. The neighbour made a second trip to bring her bed and her mattress, which were tied to the roof of the car, a chest of drawers, an old trunk, saucepans. It was in this way that she left the street in which she had lived for thirty years, nearly half her life.

She set up house again in one room. She was frightened to go near 'them' to re-establish pension rights and her identity, because of the arrears of rent she had left behind, and because of the stolen television set. She started trading again, and the little room was soon spread, like her last, with a rainbow of colours and textures and lace and sequins. She cooked on a single gas ring and washed in the sink. There was no hot water unless it was boiled in saucepans. There were several old ladies and a family of five children in the house, which was condemned.

She was in the ground-floor back, with a window which opened on to a derelict garden, and her cat was happy in a hunting ground that was a mile around this house where his mistress was so splendidly living. A canal ran close by, and in the dirty city-water were islands which a cat could reach by leaping from moored boat to boat. On the islands were rats and birds. There were pavements full of fat London pigeons. The cat was a fine hunter. He soon had his place in the hierarchies of the local cat population and did not have to fight much to keep it. He was a strong male cat, and fathered many litters of kittens.

In that place Hetty and he lived five happy years. She was trading well, for there were rich people close by to shed what the poor needed to buy cheaply. She was not lonely for she made a quarrelling but satisfying friendship with a woman on the top floor, a widow like herself who did not see her children either. Hetty was sharp with the five children, complaining about their noise and mess, but she slipped them bits of money and sweets after telling their mother that 'she was a fool to put herself out for them, because they wouldn't appreciate it.' She was living well, even without her pension. She sold the television set and gave herself and her friend upstairs some day-trips to the coast, and bought a small radio. She never read books or magazines. The truth was that she could not write or read, or only so badly it was no pleasure to her. Her cat was all reward and no cost, for he fed himself, and continued to bring in pigeons for her to cook and eat, for which in return he claimed milk.

'Greedy Tibby, you greedy *thing*, don't think I don't know, oh yes I do, you'll get sick eating those old pigeons, I do keep telling you that, don't I?'

At last the street was being done up. No longer a uniform, long, disgraceful slum, houses were being bought by the middle-class people. While this meant more good warm clothes for trading – or begging, for she still could not resist the attraction of getting something for nothing by the use of her plaintive inventive tongue, her still flashing handsome eyes – Hetty knew, like her neighbours, that soon this house with its cargo of poor people would be bought for improvement.

In the week Hetty was seventy years old, came the notice that was the end of this little community. They had four weeks to find somewhere else to live.

Usually, the shortage of housing being what it is in London – and everywhere else in the world, of course – these people would have had to scatter, fending for themselves. But the fate of this particular street was attracting attention, because a municipal election was pending. Homelessness among the poor was finding a focus in this street which was a perfect symbol of the whole area, and indeed the whole city, half of it being fine, converted, tasteful houses, full of people who spent a lot of money, and half being dying houses tenanted by people like Hetty.

As a result of speeches by councillors and churchmen, local authorities found themselves unable to ignore the victims of this redevelopment. The people in the house Hetty was in were visited by a team consisting of an unemployment officer, a social worker and a rehousing officer. Hetty, a strong gaunt old woman wearing a scarlet wool suit she had found among her cast-offs that week, a black knitted tea-cosy on her head, and black buttoned Edwardian boots too big for her, so that she had to shuffle, invited them into her room. But although all were well used to the extremes of poverty, none wished to enter the place, but stood in the doorway and made her this offer: that she should be aided to get her pension – why had she not claimed it long ago? – and that she, together with the four other old ladies in the house should move to a Home run by the Council out in the northern suburbs. All these women were used to, and enjoyed, lively London, and while they had no alternative but to agree, they fell into a sad-dened and sullen state. Hetty agreed too. The last two winters had set her bones aching badly, and a cough was never far away. And while perhaps she was more of an urban soul even than the others, since she had walked up and down so many streets with her old perambulator loaded with rags and laces, and since she knew so intimately London's texture and taste, she minded least of all the idea of a new home 'among green fields'. There were, in fact, no fields near the promised Home, but for some reason all the old ladies had chosen to bring out this old song of a phrase, as if it belonged to their situation, that of old women not far off death. 'It will be nice to be near green fields again,' they said to each other over cups of tea.

The housing officer came to make final arrangements. Hetty Pennefather was to move with the others in two weeks' time. The young man, sitting on the very edge of the only chair in the crammed room, because it was greasy and he suspected it had fleas or worse in it, breathed as lightly as he could because of the appalling stink: there was a lavatory in the house, but it had been out of order for three days, and it was just the other side of a thin wall. The whole house smelled.

The young man, who knew only too well the extent of the misery due to lack of housing, who knew how many old people abandoned by their children did not get the offer to spend their days being looked after by the authorities, could not help feeling that this wreck of a human being could count herself lucky to get a place in his Home, even if it was – and he knew and deplored the fact – an institution in which the old were treated like naughty and dim-witted children until they had the good fortune to die.

But just as he was telling Hetty that a van would be coming to take her effects and those of the other four old ladies, and that she need not take anything more with her than her clothes 'and perhaps a few photographs', he saw what he had thought was a heap of multicoloured rags get up and put its ragged gingery-black paws on the old woman's skirt. Which today was cretonne curtain covered with pink and red roses that Hetty had pinned around her because she liked the pattern.

'You can't take that cat with you,' he said automatically. It was something he had to say often, and knowing what misery the statement caused, he usually softened it down. But he had been taken by surprise.

Tibby now looked like a mass of old wool that has been matting together in dust and rain. One eye was permanently half-closed, because a muscle had been ripped in a fight. One ear was vestigial. And down a flank was a hairless slope with a thick scar on it. A cat-hating man had treated Tibby as he treated all cats, to a pellet from his airgun. The resulting wound had taken two years to heal. And Tibby smelled.

No worse, however, than his mistress, who sat stiffly still, bright-eyed with suspicion, hostile, watching the well-brushed, tidy young man from the Council.

'How old is that beast?'

'Ten years, no, only eight years, he's a young cat about five years old,' said Hetty, desperate.

'It looks as if you'd do him a favour to put him out of his misery,' said the young man.

When the official left, Hetty had agreed to everything. She was the only one of the old women with a cat. The others had budgerigars or nothing. Budgies were allowed in the Home.

She made her plans, confided in the others, and when the van came for them and their clothes and photographs and budgies, she was not there, and they told lies for her. 'Oh, we don't know where she can have gone, dear,' the old women repeated again and again to the indifferent van-driver. 'She was here last night, but she did say something about going to her daughter in Manchester.' And off they went to die in the Home.

Hetty knew that when houses have been emptied for redevelopment they may stay empty for months, even years. She intended to go on living in this one until the builders moved in.

It was a warm autumn. For the first time in her life she lived like her gipsy forbears, and did not go to bed in a room in a house like respectable people. She spent several nights, with Tibby, sitting crouched in a doorway of an empty house two doors from her own. She knew exactly when the police would come around, and where to hide herself in the bushes of the overgrown shrubby garden.

As she had expected, nothing happened in the house, and she moved back in. She smashed a back windowpane so that Tibby could move in and out without her having to unlock the front door for him, and without leaving a window suspiciously open.

She moved to the top back room and left it every morning early, to spend the day in the streets with her pram and her rags. At night she kept a candle glimmering low down on the floor. The lavatory was still out of order, so she used a pail on the first floor instead, and secretly emptied it at night into the canal which in the day was full of pleasure boats and people fishing.

Tibby brought her several pigeons during that time.

'Oh, you are a clever puss, Tibby, Tibby! Oh, you're clever, you are. You know how things are, don't you, you know how to get around and about.'

The weather turned very cold; Christmas came and went. Hetty's cough came back, and she spent most of her time under piles of blankets and old clothes, dozing. At night she watched the shadows of the candle flame on floor and ceiling – the window-frames fitted badly, and there was a draught. Twice tramps spent the night in the bottom of the house and she heard them being moved on by the police. She had to go down to make sure the police had not blocked up the broken window the cat used, but they had not. A blackbird had flown in and had battered itself to death trying to get out. She plucked it, and roasted it over a fire made with bits of floorboard in a baking-pan: the gas of course had been cut off. She had never eaten very much, and was not frightened that some dry bread and a bit of cheese was all that she had eaten during her sojourn under the heap of clothes. She was cold, but did not think about that much. Outside there was slushy brown snow everywhere. She went back to her nest, thinking that soon the cold spell would be over and she could get back to her trading. Tibby sometimes got into the pile with her, and she clutched the warmth of him to her. 'Oh, you clever cat, you clever old thing, looking after yourself, aren't you? That's right, my ducky, that's right, my lovely.'

And then, just as she was moving about again, with snow gone off the ground for a time but winter only just begun, in January, she saw a builder's van draw up outside, a couple of men unloading their gear. They did not come into the house: they were to start work next day. By then Hetty, her cat, her pram piled with clothes and her two blankets, were gone. She also took a box of matches, a candle an old saucepan and a fork and spoon, a tin-opener, a candle and a rat-trap. She had a horror of rats.

About two miles way, among the homes and gardens of amiable Hampstead, where live so many of the rich, the intelligent and the famous, stood three empty, very large houses. She had seen them on an occasion, a couple of years before, when she had taken a bus. This was a rare thing for her, because of the remarks and curious looks provoked by her mad clothes, and by her being able to appear at the same time such a tough battling old thing, and a naughty child. For the older she got, this disreputable tramp, the more there strengthened in her a quality of fierce, demanding childishness. It was all too much of a mixture; she was uncomfortable to have near.

She was afraid that 'they' might have rebuilt the houses, but there they still stood, too tumbledown and dangerous to be of much use to tramps, let alone the armies of London's homeless. There was no glass left anywhere. The flooring at ground level was mostly gone, leaving small platforms and juts of planking over basements full of water. The ceilings were crumbling. The roofs were going. The houses were like bombed buildings.

But in the cold dark of a late afternoon she pulled the pram up the broken stairs and moved cautiously around the frail boards of a second-floor room that had a great hole in it right down to the bottom of the house. Looking into it was like looking into a well. She held a candle to examine the state of the walls, here more or less whole, and saw that rain and wind blowing in from the window would leave one corner dry. Here she made her home. A sycamore tree screened the gaping window from the main road twenty yards away. Tibby, who was cramped after making the journey under the clothes piled in the pram, bounded down and out and vanished into neglected undergrowth to catch his supper. He returned fed and pleased, and seemed happy to stay clutched in her hard thin old arms. She had come to watch for his return after hunting trips, because the warm purring bundle of bones and fur did seem to allay, for a while, the permanent ache of cold in her bones.

Next day she sold her Edwardian boots for a few shillings –

they were fashionable again – and bought a loaf and some bacon scraps. In a corner of the ruins well away from the one she had made her own, she pulled up some floorboards, built a fire, and toasted bread and the bacon scraps. Tibby had brought in a pigeon, and she roasted that, but not very efficiently. She was afraid of the fire catching and the whole mass going up in flames; she was afraid, too, of the smoke showing and attracting the police. She had to keep damping down the fire, and so the bird was bloody and unappetizing, and in the end Tibby got most of it. She felt confused, and discouraged, but thought it was because of the long stretch of winter still ahead of her before spring could come. In fact, she was ill. She made a couple of attempts to trade and earn money to feed herself before she acknowledged she was ill. She knew she was not yet dangerously ill, for she had been that in her life, and would have been able to recognize the cold listless indifference of a real last-ditch illness. But all her bones ached, and her head ached, and she coughed more than she ever had. Yet she still did not think of herself as suffering particularly from the cold, even in that sleety January weather. She had never, in all her life, lived in a properly heated place, had never known a really warm home, not even when she lived in the Council flats. Those flats had electric fires, and the family had never used them, for the sake of economy, except in very bad spells of cold. They piled clothes on to themselves, or went to bed early. But she did know that to keep herself from dying now she could not treat the cold with her usual indifference. She knew she must eat. In the comparatively dry corner of the windy room, away from the gaping window through which snow and sleet were drifting, she made another nest – her last. She had found a piece of polythene sheeting in the rubble, and she laid that down first, so that the damp would not strike up. Then she spread her two blankets over that. Over them were heaped the mass of old clothes. She wished she had another piece of polythene to put on top, but she used sheets of newspaper instead. She heaved herself into the middle of this, with a loaf of bread near to her hand. She dozed, and waited, and nibbled bits of bread, and watched the snow drifting softly in. Tibby sat close to the old blue face that poked out of the pile and put up a paw to touch it. He miaowed and was restless, and then went out into the frosty morning and brought in a pigeon. This the cat put, still struggling and fluttering a little, close to the old woman. But she was afraid to get out of the pile in which the heat was being made and kept with such difficulty. She really could not climb out long enough to pull up more splinters of plank from the floors, to make a fire, to pluck the pigeon, to roast it. She put out a cold hand to stroke the cat.

'Tibby, you old thing, you brought it for me, then, did you? You did, did you? Come here, come in here . . .' But he did not want to get in with her. He miaowed again, pushed the bird closer to her. It was now limp and dead.

'You have it, then. You eat it. I'm not hungry, thank you, Tibby.'

But the carcass did not interest him. He had eaten a pigeon before bringing this one up to Hetty. He fed himself well. In spite of his matted fur, and his scars and his half-closed yellow eye, he was a strong, healthy cat.

At about four the next morning there were steps and voices downstairs. Hetty shot out of the pile and crouched behind a fallen heap of plaster and beams, now covered with snow, at the end of the room near the window. She could see through the hole in the floorboards down to the first floor, which had collapsed entirely, and through it to the ground floor. She saw a man in a thick overcoat and muffler and leather gloves holding a strong torch to illuminate a thin bundle of clothes lying on the floor. She saw that this bundle was a sleeping man or woman. She was indignant – *her* home was being trespassed upon. And she was afraid because she had not been aware of this other tenant of the ruin. Had he, or she, heard her talking to the cat? And where was the cat? If he wasn't careful he would be caught, and that would be the end of him! The man with a torch went off and came back with a second man. In the thick dark far below Hetty, was a small cave of strong light, which was the torchlight. In this space of light two men bent to lift the bundle, which was the corpse of a man or a woman like Hetty. They carried it out across the danger-traps of fallen and rotting boards that made gangplanks over the water-filled basement. One man was holding the torch in the hand that supported the dead person's feet, and the light jogged and lurched over trees and grasses: the corpse was being taken through the shrubberies to a car.

There are men in London who, between the hours of two and five in the morning, when the real citizens are asleep, who should not be disturbed by such unpleasantness as the corpses of the poor, make the rounds of all the empty, rotting houses they know about, to collect the dead, and to warn the living that they ought not to be there at all, inviting them to one of the official Homes or lodgings for the homeless.

Hetty was too frightened to get back into her warm heap. She sat with the blankets pulled around her, and looked through gaps in the fabric of the house, making out shapes and boundaries and holes and puddles and mounds of rubble, as her eyes, like her cat's, became accustomed to the dark.

She heard scuffling sounds and knew they were rats. She had meant to set the trap, but the thought of her friend Tibby, who might catch his paw, had stopped her. She sat up until the morning light came in grey and cold, after nine. Now she did know herself to be very ill and in danger, for she had lost all the warmth she had huddled into her bones under the rags. She shivered violently. She was shaking herself apart with shivering. In between spasms she drooped limp and exhausted. Through the ceiling above her – but it was not a ceiling, only a cobweb of slats and planks – she could see into a dark cave which had been a garret, and through the roof above that, the grey sky, teeming with incipient rain. The cat came back from where he had been hiding, and sat crouched on her knees, keeping her stomach warm, while she thought out her position. These were her last clear thoughts. She told herself that she would not last out until spring unless she allowed 'them' to find her, and take her to hospital. After that, she would be taken to a Home.

But what would happen to Tibby, her poor cat? She rubbed the old beast's scruffy head with the ball of her thumb and muttered: 'Tibby, Tibby, they won't get you, no, you'll be all right, yes, I'll look after you.'

Towards midday, the sun oozed yellow through miles of greasy grey cloud, and she staggered down the rotting stairs, to the shops. Even in those London streets, where the extraordinary has become usual, people turned to stare at a tall gaunt woman, with a white face that had flaming red patches on it, and blue compressed lips, and restless black eyes. She wore a tightly buttoned man's overcoat, torn brown woollen mittens, and an old fur hood. She pushed a pram loaded with old dresses and scraps of embroidery and torn jerseys and shoes, all stirred into a tight tangle, and she kept pushing this pram up against people as they stood in queues, or gossiped, or stared into windows, and she muttered: 'Give me your old clothes, darling, give me your old pretties, give Hetty something, poor Hetty's hungry.' A woman gave her a handful of small change, and Hetty bought a roll filled with tomato and lettuce. She did not dare go into a café, for even in her confused state she knew she would offend, and would probably be asked to leave. But she begged a cup of tea at a street stall, and when the hot sweet liquid flooded through her she felt she might survive the winter. She bought a carton of milk and pushed the pram back through the slushy snowy street to the ruins.

Tibby was not there. She urinated down through the hole in the boards, muttering, 'A nuisance, that old tea,' and wrapped herself in a blanket and waited for the dark to come.

Tibby came in later. He had blood on his foreleg. She had heard scuffling and she knew that he had fought a rat, or several, and had been bitten. She poured the milk into the tilted saucepan and Tibby drank it all.

She spent the night with the animal held against her chilly bosom. They did not sleep, but dozed off and on. Tibby would normally be hunting, the night was his time, but he had stayed with the old woman now for three nights.

Early next morning they again heard the corpse-removers among the rubble on the ground floor, and saw the beams of the torch moving on wet walls and collapsed beams. For a moment the torchlight was almost straight on Hetty, but no one came up: who could believe that a person could be desperate enough to climb those dangerous stairs, to trust those crumbling splintery floors, and in the middle of winter?

Hetty had now stopped thinking of herself as ill, of the degrees of her illness, of her danger – of the impossibility of her surviving. She had cancelled out in her mind the presence of winter and its lethal weather, and it was as if spring were nearly here. She knew that if it had been spring when she had had to leave the other house, she and the cat could have lived here for months and months, quite safely and comfortably. Because it seemed to her an impossible and even a silly thing that her life, or, rather, her death, could depend on something so arbitrary as builders starting work on a house in January rather than in April, she could not believe it: the fact would not stay in her mind. The day before she had been quite clear-headed. But today her thoughts were cloudy, and she talked and laughed aloud. Once she scrambled up and rummaged in her rags for an old Christmas card she had got four years before from her good daughter! In a hard harsh angry grumbling voice she said to her four children that she needed a room of her own now that she was getting on. 'I've been a good mother to you,' she shouted to them before invisible witnesses – former neighbours, welfare workers, a doctor. 'I never let you want for anything, never! When you were little you always had the best of everything! You can ask anybody, go on, ask them then!'

She was restless and made such a noise that Tibby left her and bounded on to the pram and crouched watching her. He was limping, and his foreleg was rusty with blood. The rat had bitten deep. When the daylight came, he left Hetty in a kind of a sleep, and went down into the garden where he saw a pigeon feeding on the edge of the pavement. The cat pounced on the bird, dragged it into the bushes, and ate it all, without taking it up to his mistress. After he had finished eating, he stayed hidden, watching the passing people. He stared at them intently with his blazing yellow eye, as if he were thinking, or planning. He did not go into the old ruin and up the crumbling wet stairs until late – it was as if he knew it was not worth while going at all.

He found Hetty, apparently asleep, wrapped loosely in a

blanket, propped sitting in a corner. Her head had fallen on her chest, and her quantities of white hair had escaped from a scarlet woollen cap, and concealed a face that was flushed a deceptive pink – the flush of coma from cold. She was not yet dead, but she died that night. The rats came up the walls and along the planks and the cat fled down and away from them, limping still, into the bushes.

Hetty was not found for a couple of weeks. The weather changed to warm, and the man whose job it was to look for corpses was led up the dangerous stairs by the smell. There was something left of her, but not much.

As for the cat, he lingered for two or three days in the thick shrubberies, watching the passing people and beyond them, the thundering traffic of the main road. Once a couple stopped to talk on the pavement, and the cat, seeing two pairs of legs, moved out and rubbed himself against one of the legs. A hand came down and he was stroked and patted for a little. Then the people went away.

The cat saw he would not find another home, and he moved off, nosing and feeling his way from one garden to another, through empty houses, finally into an old churchyard. This graveyard already had a couple of stray cats in it, and he joined them. It was the beginning of a community of stray cats going wild. They killed birds, and the field mice that lived among the grasses, and they drank from puddles. Before winter had ended the cats had had a hard time of it from thirst, during the two long spells when the ground froze and there was snow and no puddles and the birds were hard to catch because the cats were so easy to see against the clean white. But on the whole they managed quite well. One of the cats was a female, and soon there were a swarm of wild cats, as wild as if they did not live in the middle of a city surrounded by streets and houses. This was just one of half a dozen communities of wild cats living in that square mile of London.

Then an official came to trap the cats and take them away. Some of them escaped, hiding till it was safe to come back again. But Tibby was caught. Not only was he getting old and stiff – he still limped from the rat's bite – but he was friendly, and did not run away from the man, who had only to pick him up in his arms.

'You're an old soldier, aren't you?' said the man. 'A real tough one, a real old tramp.'

It is possible that the cat even thought that he might be finding another human friend and a home.

But it was not so. The haul of wild cats that week numbered hundreds, and while if Tibby had been younger a home might have been found for him, since he was amiable, and wished to be liked by the human race, he was really too old, and smelly and battered. So they gave him an injection and, as we say, 'put him to sleep'.

Lions, Leaves, Roses ...

As I went towards St Mark's Bridge, where slow water drowned this summer's leaves, she accosted me, grinning, tugging with both hands at the ends of her red-spotted kerchief. 'The sun always follows me,' she said, looking at the midday sun, as brilliant as a sun in Italy, but lower in the sky, it being October and our end of the earth tilting back and towards the cold of the winter which would begin next day or next month. 'Yes,' she said, 'the sun's always after me, yes and the moon too.' She looked for the moon, not visible that day, while the sunlight lit all the sky, the shedding trees, the brilliant grass and us standing on the pavement by the bridge and the canal.

No moon, only one of her familiars present, and her face changed to suspicion. To save the moment from grief I said quickly, 'You're lucky to have the sun for your friend.' Again her face spread in glee, she bent hooting, squeezing out triumphant laughter, and I walked on, envious of her whose cracked mind let the sunlight through. For I was walking that day to catch a fragment of later summer in this clouded year, to catch and have it, and for this purpose it was necessary to walk with emptied mind, and all senses awake, and thoughts, whether dragonflies or blowflies, swatted well away.

The ornate bridge with its white pillars, its six iron lamp-posts, its balustrades, has at its ends flat oblong rectangles like pedestals, but empty. Here I paused to summon and set on watch my own personal lion. The way I see it, a park which has no extensions to or connections with the country, with uncreated wildness, has no rights; it has allowed itself to be enclosed and owned by houses. Already there are wild animals caged there, and right in its centre the roses in their circle are tamed and willing. The lion came off his dry hillside to crouch on St Mark's Bridge, facing inwards, a golden beast, his forepaws tucked under an eternal chest, his eyes green and solid, the eyes of a man, but man much more than any we know. For if I could walk through those eyes, like gates, into the region between them, it would be into a form of understanding that we hear only rumours about. I left him there, as patient under the falling autumn leaves as on his rock on the slopes of (I think) the Hindu Kush, eyes unblinking, with no need to swat away thoughts, words, feelings, for he was everything he saw.

The avenue that runs from St Mark's Bridge Gate to the memorial for Sir Cowasjee Jehangir was silent with warm sun, and full of people walking slowly to feel it, and through their lungs, our lungs, sweetly fanned, sixteen times a minute, the breath of trees whose long exhalation had begun at sunrise that morning. The trees are big here, each one claiming attention, and the air lies heavily, the felt essence of tree. Not only tree, but goat too, a dozen or so white, smelling goats; and when they are passed, the wire paddock, where wolves whose howls will keep good people awake on the winter nights that are coming play charmingly around a tree-trunk.

Almost, almost, I reach that moment when leaves, birds, burn up separately one by one, but I fail, because of the urgency that prompts: quick, this is the last day, probably the very last before the thick cold grey fills the air between me, us, and the sun; the last day when warmth lies about us like the slow support of warm water.

So nearly 'almost' that it was a pain to come back to the pain of not knowing, not being bird, leaf, rose. But here I was, in the outer precincts still, with paths and gates to cross, not even at

> This Fountain
> Erected by the
> Metropolitan Drinking Fountain
> and Cattle Trough Association
> Was the Gift of
> SIR COWASJEE JEHANGIR
> (Companion of the Star of India)

A Wealthy Parsee Gentleman of Bombay
As a Token of Gratitude to the People of England
for the Protection enjoyed by him and his Parsee
Fellow Countrymen Under British Rule in India.
Inaugurated by H.R.H. Princess May, Duchess
of Teck, 1869

Near this, my favourite zany monument, is a green wooden
cross among shining green foliage which was attended by a small
boy who leaned through railings to stick on it some halfpenny
stamps. His earnest tongue protruded, and over it, one after
another, he wiped the orange stamps he then transferred to the
cross.

A hundred yards down the avenue appear the Mappin Terraces, far away on the right in front of tall flats on Primrose Hill,
so juxtaposed it seems that bears might climb from rock shelves
to balconies among potted plants. Suppose I had just this
moment descended from Mars, what could I make of this park,
full of beasts and colours and creatures? What, my eyes just
opening on newness, would I make of a tree? What had I made of
it all those years ago, opening my eyes on the terrace in a dry hot
plain between the snow mountains? Suppose that I, entertaining
this being from Mars, had the task of explanation: Well, sir, *yes* –
I do see ... but not quite. The same general idea, I grant you
(though *we* are smaller), sap runs, limbs branch, but wait a
minute, *they* are fastened to the earth, they can't move ... and
besides, in every spring they suck in leaves from the soil and then
every autumn spit them out again. What for? You do have a
point, it is preposterous, when you think of it, tons and tons and
tons of leaf, just think how many thousands of tons weighing the
trunks and branches of this park alone, and all sucked up the
trunks every year, then dropped again to make their own way
back to the roots. Besides, *we* can think, yes.

In front of me now the chestnut avenue that has, half-way
down it, the cruel white boy who so casually dunks the dolphin's
head, and a few paces away the urn held by four grinning winged
lions most of the year concealed by dripping leaves and petals.
The chestnuts are blazing, are burning, orangey-yellow under

the blue blue sky, and the earth is littered precisely, clearly, with solid, ribbed, curved leaves, green-gold, each one lying defined in its small shell of brown shadow. The long stretch of earth between the chestnut trunks and the sober wooden benches seems embossed with solid shapes of gold, it is all a glitter of blue and gold, and the distractions of the long avenue vanish as the light flares up, just for one moment, for one small moment, into the steady clarity of seeing that I want then fades again, leaving me teeth-gripped, furious on behalf of us all who have so much around us that we cannot take in. I will do it, I swear, I *will* – and turn right between small neat trees whose trunks are marred brown satin, across the road of the Inner Circle, and in. Now I can turn left to the centre of roses (Queen Mary's – she again, metamorphosed now out of Princess- and Duchesshood) or go on past the big knobbed tree that says it is a manna ash, and on past the next which is a weeping elm, to the little hill still fragrant with herbs, although most of them are withering.

The herbs draw me, sniffing, the air being dry and sharp: unlike the slow breath in the avenue, here it is a quick air, a stimulant. And now, despite six stiff-uniformed park attendants sitting side by side on a bench to enjoy the sunlight, it is Italy, with tall aspiring trees around a five-jetted fountain, its white central plume a noble dropping curve. Towards it a path ascends, gently, in measured steps, with generously foliaged urns and sets of red roses and white roses; roses wildfire-coloured, and icy roses bedded in a blue haze.

Again it comes, or becomes: the fountains can never blow in any other shape, each leaf is self-contained, each rose perpetual, the sky blazes blueness into my brain, and as the moment swells up, I begin to exult, feeling that at last I know a hint of what the lion knows always, by nature, but snap! – what I feared happens, words came out of the silence though I had sworn, had promised, that for one day they would be held off.

'No matter how I stare with silent mind . . .'

Oh, quite so, quite so (even though the words do have the stiff lilt proper to a park which, I swear, is native of a century that would understand nothing at all of us), quite so, no matter what I do, it can be guaranteed that clouds of thoughts will come packing my mind, each one better known than the last, and that words will eat up the precious sharpness of feeling like packs of greedy dogs.

'No matter how I stare with silent mind . . .'

Mayakovsky said: 'Not a man, but a cloud in trousers.' Affected, I used to think this; but I don't think so now. Today I choose him, unlikely companion – what would he make of this order, this urbanity? – for the long stroll down the descending path, my back to the plumed fountain, past the six basking attendants, past the working gardeners, past babies in prams and women with reddening necks in hastily that-morning-resumed summer blouses. I walk, shut from the day inside a whirling white or tinted, brownish or rainbow, cloud of thought. Which nothing can dissipate or make silent.

At the foot of this descent are the big gilded gates and a choice: left, past the ponds and the water-flowers and the rose-beds, to the circle of the rose garden; right, past the restaurant, then down under trees so heavy and so huge their weight is a silence, over the little bridge and then curving leftwards again to the boats . . . past the boats, over more bridges and so to the road of the Outer Circle and the long way around to the zoo, where I'll see the four giraffes stretching their astonished heads into the sky, rubbing their necks against a scratching post, four giraffes with hides marked like the cracked mud at the bottom of dried river-beds. Or the elephants, swaying their trunks. Suppose that man from Mars . . .? Or suppose *I* had just that moment jumped into this skin from another planet, what would I think? Well, would a giraffe seem more extraordinary than a tree, if you had never seen either, or elephants than roses?

I'll go back by the rose-garden, to Madame Louis Laperrière, Monique and Rose Gaujat; Soraya and Helen Traubel; Rose Hellène, Pink Parfait, Peace and Malagana. We sit on unobtrusive benches, looking at the coloured roses under this foreign sun, smiling at each other and at ourselves, and a woman sits down and tells us all in confidence: 'I've just seen a squirrel, its tail was all shining, like a girl's hair, it's because of the sun, you know.' A retired gentleman comes to claim his seat, opens a newspaper, but is observed to let it fall again, where it lies gently palpitating on his stomach while his eyes blink slowly and in wonder at the garden before they close.

It is slow here, a drugged place, where voices lower and people walking through put out a finger to *almost* touch a petal. When the shadows from the tall garland-like climbing roses have moved enough to make a different place of it, I leave, and walk out of the great gilded gates to where a tree glitters, each leaf shaking separately, in a million different rhythms. All my resolves for the day have been stolen from me by the sweet delusions of the rose-garden, so I tell myself stolidly that this frantic dance means no more than that the wind is there, and that a tree has no hands or eyes, nor wants them, and so I went retracing paths until towards the north-east exit a man shovelled leaves into a barrow so fast it seemed as if a continuous stream of gold showered from his spade.

The tall houses of the long terraces stood silent, their window-panes on fire.

Since I had entered the park, the earth had spun a tenth of its way around itself and thousands of miles around the sun; and the sun had sped, dragging us with it, in an inconceivable curve towards . . .

As I walked past the shower of gold from the man's shovel, the wind swerved leaves off the barrow, tugged them off the trees, scattered the brilliant grass with copper and with gold.

Leaves, words, people, shadows, whirled together towards autumn and the solstice.

Outside the park, on the pavement, there she was. Still grinning, still tugging at her red-spotted kerchief, apparently brimful of glee, she stood near, or rather under, a huge policeman who looked down at her, quite expressionless, his features determined to make no comment. But 'Is that so?' his pose said, or even 'Fancy that!' to her news of her relationship with the sun, the moon, and this our wet planet.

Spies I Have Known

I don't want you to imagine that I am drawing any sort of comparison between Salisbury, Rhodesia, of thirty years ago, a one-horse town then, if not now, and more august sites. God forbid. But it does no harm to lead into a weighty subject by way of the minuscule.

It was in the middle of the Second World War. A couple of dozen people ran a dozen or so organizations, of varying degrees of left-wingedness. The town, though a capital city, was still in that condition when 'everybody knows everybody else'. The white population was about ten thousand; the number of black people, then as now, only guessed at. There was a Central Post Office, a rather handsome building, and one of the mail sorters attended the meetings of the Left Club. It was he who explained to us the system of censorship operated by the Secret Police. All the incoming mail for the above dozen organizations was first put into a central box marked CENSOR and was read, at their leisure, by certain trusted citizens. Of course all this was to be expected, and what we knew must be happening. But there were other proscribed organizations, like the Watchtower, a religious sect for some reason suspected by governments up and down Africa – perhaps because they prophesied the imminent end of the world? – and some fascist organizations, reasonably enough in a war against fascism. There were organizations of obscure aims, and perhaps five members and a capital of five pounds, and there were individuals whose mail had first to go through the process, so to speak, of decontamination, or defusing. It was this last list of a hundred or so people which was the most baffling. What did they have in common, these sinister ones whose opinions were such a threat to the budding Southern Rhodesian State, then still in the Lord Malvern phase of the Huggins/Lord Malvern/ Welensky/Garfield Todd/Winston Field/Smith succession? After months, indeed years, of trying to understand what could unite them, we had simply to give up. Of course, half were on the Left, kaffir-lovers and so on, but what of the others? It was when a man wrote a letter to the *Rhodesia Herald* in solemn parody of Soviet official style – as heavy then as now – urging the immediate extermination by firing squad of our government, in favour of a team from the Labour Opposition, and we heard from our contact in the post office that his name was now on the Black List, that we began to suspect the truth.

Throughout the war, this convenient arrangement continued. Our Man in the Post Office – by then several men, but it doesn't sound so well – kept us informed of what and who was on the Black List. And if our mail was being held up longer than was considered reasonable, the censors being on holiday, or lazy, authority would be gently prodded to hurry things up a little.

This was my first experience of Espionage.

Next was when I knew someone who knew someone who had told him of how a certain Communist Party Secretary had been approached by the man whose occupation it was to tap communist telephones – we are now in Europe. Of course, the machinery for tapping was much more primitive then. Probably by now they have dispensed with human intervention altogether, and a machine judges the degree of a suspicious person's disaffection by the tones of his voice. Then, and in that country, they simply played back records of conversation. This professional had been in the most intimate contact with communism and communists for years, becoming involved with shopping expeditions, husbands late from the office, love affairs, a divorce or so, children's excursions. He had been sucked into active revolutionary politics through the keyhole.

'I don't think you ought to let little Jackie go at all. He'll be in bed much too late, and you know how bad-tempered he gets when he is over-tired.'

'She said to me No, she said. That's final. If you want to do a thing like that, then you must do it yourself. You shouldn't expect other people to pull your chestnuts out of the fire, she said. If he was rude to you, then it's your place to tell him so.'

He got frustrated, like an intimate friend or lover with paralysis of the tongue. And there was another thing, he was listening to events, emotions, several hours old. Sometimes weeks old, as for instance when he went on leave and had to catch up with a month's dangerous material all in one exhausting twenty-four hours. He found that he was getting possessive about certain of his charges; resented his colleagues listening in to 'my suspects'. Once he had to wrestle with temptation because he longed to seek out a certain woman on the point of leaving her husband for another man. Owing to his advantageous position he knew the other man was not what she believed. He imagined how he would trail her to the café which he knew she frequented, sit near her, then lean over and ask: 'May I join you? I have something of importance to divulge.' He knew she would agree: he knew her character well. She was unconventional, perhaps not as responsible as she ought to be, careless for instance about the regularity of meals, but fundamentally, he was sure, a good girl with the potentiality of good wifehood. He would say to her: 'Don't do it, my dear! No, don't ask me how I know, I can't tell you that. But if you leave your husband for that man, you'll regret it!' He would press her hands in his, looking deeply into her eyes – he was sure they were brown, for her voice was definitely the voice of a brown-eyed blonde – and then stride for ever out of her life. Afterwards he could check on the success of his intervention through the tapes.

To cut short a process that took some years, he at last went secretly to a communist bookshop, bought some pamphlets, attended a meeting or two, and discovered that he would certainly become a Party member if it were not that his job, and a very well-paid one with good prospects, was to spy on the Communist Party. He felt in a false position. What to do? He turned up at the offices of the Communist Party, asked to see the Secretary, and confessed his dilemma. Roars of laughter from the Secretary.

These roars are absolutely obligatory in this convention, which insists on a greater degree of sophisticated understanding between professionals, even if on opposing sides and even if at war – Party officials, government officials, top-ranking soldiers and the like – and the governed, ever a foolish, trusting, and sentimental lot.

First, then, the roar. Then a soupçon of whimsicality: alas for this badly ordered world where men so well equipped to be friends must be enemies. Finally, the hard offer.

Our friend the telephone-tapper was offered a retaining fee by the Communist Party, and their provisional trust, on condition that he stayed where he was, working for the other side. Of course, what else had he expected? Nor should he have felt insulted, for in such ways are the double agents born, those rare men at an altogether higher level than he could ever aspire to reach in the hierarchies of espionage. But his finer feelings had been hurt by the offer of money, and he refused. He went off and suffered for a week or so, deciding that he really did have to leave his job with the Secret Police – an accurate name for what he was working for, though of course the name it went under was much blander. He returned to the Secretary in order to ask for the second time to become just a rank-and-file Communist Party member. This time there was no roar of laughter, not even a chuckle, but the frank (and equally obligatory) I-am-concealing-nothing statement of the position. Which was that he surely must be able to see their view – the Communist Party's. With a toehold in the enemy camp (a delicate way of describing his salary and his way of life) he could be of real use. To stay where he was could be regarded as a real desire to serve the People's Cause. To leave altogether, becoming just honest John Smith, might satisfy his conscience (a subjective and conditioned organ, as he must surely know by now if he had read those pamphlets properly) but would leave behind him an image of the capricious, or even the unreliable. What had he planned to tell his employers? 'I am tired of tapping telephones, it offends me!' Or: 'I regard this as an immoral occupation!' – when he had done nothing else for years? Come, come, he hadn't thought it out. He would certainly be under suspicion for ever more by his ex-employers. And of course he could not be so innocent, after so long spent in that atmosphere of vigilance and watchfulness, as not to expect the communists to keep watch on himself? No, his best course would be to stay exactly where he was, working even harder at tapping telephones. If not, then his frank advice (the Secretary's) could only be that he must become an ordinary citizen, as far from any sort of politics as possible, for his own sake, the sake of the Service he had left, and the sake of the Communist Party – which of *course* they believed he now found his spiritual home.

But the trouble was that he did want to join it. He wanted nothing more than to become part of the world of stern necessities he had followed for so long, but as it were from behind a one-way pane of glass. Integrity had disfranchised him. From now on he could not hope to serve humanity except through the use of the vote.

His life was empty. His resignation cut off his involvement, like turning off the television on a soap opera, with the deathless real-life dramas of the tapes.

He felt that he was useless. He considered suicide but thought better of it. Then having weathered a fairly routine and unremarkable nervous breakdown, became a contemplative monk – high Church of England.

Another spy I met at a cocktail party, in the course of chat about this or that (it was in London, in the late fifties), said that at the outbreak of the Second World War he had been in Greece, or perhaps it was Turkey, where at another cocktail party, over the canapés, an official from the British Embassy invited him to spy for his country.

'But I can't,' said this man. 'You must know that perfectly well.'

'But why ever not?' inquired the official; a Second Secretary I think he was.

'Because, as of course you must know, I am a Communist Party member.'

'Indeed? How interesting? But surely that is not going to stand in the way of your desire to serve your country?' said the official, trumping ferocious honesty with urbanity.

To cut this anecdote short – it comes from a pretty petty level in the affairs of men – this man went home, spent a sleepless night weighing his allegiances, and decided by morning that of course the Second Secretary was right. He would like to serve his country, which was engaged, after all, in a war against fascism. He explained his decision to his superiors in the Communist Party, who agreed with him, and to his wife and his comrades. Then, meeting the Second Secretary at another cocktail party, he informed him of the decision he had taken. He was invited to attach himself to a certain Army unit, in some capacity to do with the Ministry of Information. He was to await orders. In due course they came, and he discovered that it was his task to spy on the Navy, or rather, that portion of it operating near him. Our Navy, of course. He was always unable to work out the ideology of this. That a communist should not be set to spy on, let's say, Russia seemed to him fair and reasonable, but why was he deemed suitable material to spy on his own side? He found it all baffling, and indeed rather lowering. Then, at a cocktail party, he happened to meet a naval officer with whom he proceeded to get drunk, and they both suddenly understood on a hunch that they were engaged in spying on each other, one for the Navy, one for the Army. Both found this work without much uplift; they were simply not able to put their hearts into it, apart from the fact that they had been in the same class at prep school and had many other social ties. Not even the fact that they weren't being paid, since it was assumed by their superiors – quite correctly of course – that they would be happy to serve their countries for nothing, made them feel any better. They developed the habit of meeting regularly in a café where they drank wine and coffee and played chess in a vine-covered arbour overlooking a particularly fine bit of the Mediterranean where, without going through all the tedium of spying on each other, they gave each other relevant information. They were found out. Their excuse that they were fighting the war on the same side was deemed inadequate. They were both given the sack as spies, and transferred to less demanding work. But until D-Day and beyond, the British Army spied on the British Navy, and vice versa. They probably all still do.

The fact that human beings, given half a chance, start seeing each other's points of view seems to me the only ray of hope there is for humanity, but obviously this tendency must be one to cause anguish to seniors in the Diplomatic Corps, and the employers of your common or garden spy – not the high-level spies, but of that in a moment. Diplomats, until they have understood why, always complain that as soon as they understand a country and its language really well, hey presto, off they are whisked to another country. But diplomacy could not continue if the opposing factotums lost a proper sense of national hostility. Some Diplomatic Corps insist that their employees must visit only among each other, and never fraternize with the locals, obviously believing that understanding with others is inculcated by a sort of osmosis. And, of course, any diplomat who shows signs of going native, that is to say really enjoying the manners and morals of a place, must be withdrawn at once.

Not so the masters among the spies: one dedicated to his country's deepest interests must be worse than useless. The rarest spirits must be those able to entertain two or three allegiances at once; the counter-spies, the double and triple agents. Such people are not born. It can't be that they wake up one morning at the age of thirteen, crying: Eureka, I've got it, I was born to be a double agent! Nor can there be a training school for multiple spies, a kind of top class that promising pupils graduate towards. Yet that capacity which might retard a diplomat's career, or mean death to the small fry among spies, must be precisely the one watched out for by the Spymasters who watch and manipulate in the high levels of the world's thriving espionage systems. What probably happens is that a man drifts, even unwillingly, into serving his country as a spy – like my acquaintance of the cocktail party who then found himself spying on the Senior Service of his own side. Then, whether there through a deep sense of vocation or unwillingly, he must begin by making mistakes; is sometimes pleased with himself and sometimes not; goes through a phase of wondering whether he would not have done better to go into the Stock Exchange, or whatever his alternative was – and then suddenly there comes that moment, fatal to punier men but a sign of his own future greatness, when he is invaded by sympathy for the enemy. Long dwelling on what X is doing, likely to be doing, or thinking, or planning, makes X's thought as familiar and as likeable as his own. The points of view of the nation he spends all his time trying to undo, are comfortably at home in a mind once tuned only to those of his own dear Fatherland. He is thinking the thoughts of those he used to call enemies before he understands that he is already psychologically a double agent, and before he guesses that those men who must always be on the watch for such precious material have noticed, perhaps even prognosticated, his condition.

On those levels where the really great spies move, whose names we never hear, but whose existence we have to deduce, what fantastic feats of global understanding must be reached, what metaphysical heights of international brotherhood!

It is of course not possible to do more than take the humblest flights into speculation, while making do with those so frequent and highly publicized spy dramas, for some reason or other so very near to farce, that do leave obscurity for our attention.

It can't be possible that the high reaches of espionage can have anything in common with, for instance, this small happening.

A communist living in a small town in England, who had been openly and undramatically a communist for years, and for whom the state of being a communist had become rather like the practice of an undemanding religion – this man looked out of his window one fine summer afternoon to see standing in the street outside his house a car of such foreignness and such opulence that he was embarrassed, and at once began to work out what excuses he could use to his working-class neighbours whose cars, if any, would be dust in comparison. Out of this monster of a car came two large smiling Russians, carrying a teddy bear the size of a sofa, a bottle of vodka, a long and very heavy roll, which later turned out to be a vast carpet with a picture of the Kremlin on it, and a box of chocolates of British make that had a pretty lady and a pretty dog on it.

Every window in the street already had heads packed behind the curtains.

'Come in,' said he, 'but I don't think I have the pleasure of knowing who . . .'

The roll of carpet was propped in the hall, the three children were sent off to play with the teddy bear in the kitchen, and the box of chocolates was set aside for the lady of the house, who was out doing the week's shopping in the High Street. The vodka was opened at once.

It turned out that it was his wife they wanted: they were interested in him only as a go-between. They wished him to ask his wife, who was an employee of the Town Council, to get hold of the records of the Council's meetings, and to pass these records on to them. Now, this wasn't London, or even Edinburgh. It was a small, unimportant North of England town, in which it would be hard to imagine anything ever happening that could be of interest to anyone outside it, let alone the agents of a Foreign Power. But, said he, these records are open, anyone could go and get copies – you, for instance. 'Comrades, I shall be delighted to take you to the Town Hall myself.'

No, what they had been instructed to do was to ask his wife to procure them minutes and records, nothing less would do.

A long discussion ensued. It was all no use. The Russians could not be made to see that what they asked was unnecessary. Nor could they understand that to arrive in a small suburban street in a small English town in a car the length of a battleship, was to draw the wrong sort of attention.

'But why is that?' they inquired. 'Representatives of the country where the workers hold power should use a good car. Of course, comrade! You have not thought it out from a class position!'

The climax came when, despairing of the effects of rational argument, they said: 'And, comrade, these presents – the bear, the carpet, the chocolates, the vodka – are only a small token in appreciation of your work for our common cause. Of course you will be properly recompensed.'

At which point he was swept by, indeed taken over entirely by, atavistic feelings he had no idea were in him at all. He stood up and pointed a finger shaking with rage at the door: 'How dare you imagine,' he shouted, 'That my wife and I would take money. If I were going to spy, I'd spy for the love of mankind, for duty, and for international socialism. Take those bloody things out of here – wait, I'll get that teddy bear from the kids. And you can take your bloody car out of here too.'

His wife, when she came back from the supermarket and heard the story, was even more insulted than he was.

But emotions like these are surely possible only at the lowest possible levels of spy material – in this case so low they didn't qualify for the first step, entrance into the brotherhood.

Full circle back to Our Man in the Post Office, or, rather, the first of three.

After sedulous attendance at a lot of left-wing meetings, semi-private and public – for above all Tom was a methodical man who, if engaged in a thing, always gave it full value – he put his hand up one evening in the middle of a discussion about Agrarian Reform in Venezuela, and said: 'I must ask permission to ask a question.'

Everyone always laughed at him when he did this, put up his hand to ask permission to speak, or to leave, or to have opinions about something. Little did we realize that we were seeing here not just a surface mannerism, or habit, but his strongest characteristic.

It was late in the meeting, at that stage when the floor is well loaded with empty coffee cups, beer glasses and full ash trays. Some people had already left.

He wanted to know what he ought to do: 'I want to have the benefit of your expert advice.' As it happened he had already taken the decision he was asking about.

After some two years of a life not so much double – the word implies secrecy – as dual, his boss in the Central Post Office called him to ask how he was enjoying his life with the Left. Tom was as doggedly informative with him as he was with us, and said that we were interesting people, well-informed, and full of a high-class brand of idealism which he found inspiring.

'I always feel good after going to one of their meetings,' he reported he had said. 'It takes you right out of yourself and makes you think.'

His chief said that he, for his part, always enjoyed hearing about idealism and forward-looking thought, and invited Tom to turn in reports about our activities, our discussions, and most particularly our plans for the future, as well in advance as possible.

Tom told us that he said to his boss that he didn't like the idea of doing that sort of thing behind our backs because, 'say what you like about the Reds, they are very hospitable'.

The chief had said that it would be for the good of his country.

Tom came to us to say that he had told his boss that he had agreed, because he wanted to be of assistance to the National War Effort.

It was clear to everyone that having told us that he had agreed to spy on us, he would, since that was his nature, most certainly go back to his boss and tell him that he had told us that he had agreed to spy. After which he would come back to us to tell us that he had told his boss that . . . and so on. Indefinitely, if his boss didn't get tired of it. Tom could not see that his chief would shortly find him unsuitable material for espionage, and might even dismiss him from being a sorter in the post office altogether – a nuisance for us. After which he, the chief, would probably look for someone else to give him information.

It was Harry, one of the other two post office employees attending Left Club meetings, who suggested that it would probably be himself who would next be invited to spy on us, now that Tom had 'told'. Tom was upset when everybody began speculating about his probable supersession by Harry or even Dick. The way he saw it was that his complete frankness with both us and his chief was surely deserving of reward. He ought to be left in the job. God knows how he saw the future. Probably that both his boss and ourselves would continue to employ him. We would use him to find out how our letters were slowly moving through the toils of censorship, and to hurry them on, if possible; his chief would use him to spy on us. When I say employ, I don't want anyone to imagine this implies payment. Or, at least, certainly not from our side. Ideology had to be his spur, sincerity his reward.

It will by now have been noticed that our Tom was not as bright as he might have been. But he was a pleasant enough youth. He was rather good-looking too, about twenty-two. His physical characteristic was neatness. His clothes were always just so; he had a small alert dark moustache; he had glossy dark well-brushed hair. His rather small hands were well manicured – this last trait bound to be found offensive by good colonials, whose eye for such anti-masculine evidence (as they were bound to see it), then if not now, was acute. But he was a fairly recent immigrant, from just before the war, and had not yet absorbed the mores.

Tom, in spite of our humorous forecast that he would tell his boss that he had told us, and his stiff and wounded insistence that such a thing was impossible, found himself impelled to do just that. He reported back that his chief had 'lost his rag with him'.

But that was not the end. He was offered the job of learning how to censor letters. He had said to his boss that he felt in honour bound to tell us, and his boss said: 'Oh, for Christ's sake. Tell them anything you damned well like. You won't be choosing what is to be censored.'

As I said, this was an unsophisticated town in those days, and the condition of 'everybody knowing everybody else' was always leading to such warm human situations.

He accepted the offer because: 'My mother always told me that she wanted me to do well for myself, and I'll increase my rating into Schedule Three as soon as I start work on censoring, and that means an increment of fifty pounds a year.'

We congratulated him, and urged him to keep us informed about how people were trained as censors, and he agreed to do this. Shortly after that the war ended, and all the cameraderie of wartime ended as the Cold War began. The ferment of Left activity ended too.

We saw Tom no more, but followed his progress, steady if slow, up the Civil Service. The last I heard he was heading a

Department among whose duties is censorship. I imagine him, a man in his fifties, a husband and no doubt a father, looking down the avenues of lost time to those dizzy days when he was the member of a dangerous revolutionary organization. 'Yes,' he must often say, 'you can't tell me anything about them. They are idealistic, I can grant you so much, but they are dangerous. Dangerous and wrong-headed! I left them as soon as I understood what they really were.'

But of our three post office spies Harry was the one whose career, for a while at least, was the most rewarding for idealistic humanists.

He was a silent, desperately shy schoolboy who came to a public meeting and fell madly in love for a week or so with the speaker, a girl, giving her first public speech and as shy as he was. His father had died and his mother, as the psychiatrists and welfare workers would say, was 'inadequate'. That is to say, she was not good at being a widow, and was frail in health. What little energy she had went into earning enough money for herself and two younger sons to live on. She nagged at Harry for not having ambition, and for not studying for the examinations which would take him up the ladder into the next grade in the Post Office – and for wasting time with the Reds. He longed to be of use. For three years he devoted all his spare time to organization on the Left, putting up exhibitions, hiring halls and rooms, decorating ballrooms for fund-raising dances, getting advertisements for our socialist magazine – circulation two thousand, and laying it out and selling it. He argued principle with Town Councillors – 'But it's not *fair* not to let us have the hall, this is a democratic country, isn't it?' – and spent at least three nights a week discussing world affairs in smoke-filled rooms.

At the time we would have dismissed as beyond redemption anyone who suggested it, but I dare say now that the main function of those gatherings was social. Southern Rhodesia was never exactly a hospitable country for those interested in anything but sport and the sundowner, and the fifty or so people who came to the meetings, whether in the Forces, or refugees from Europe, or simply Rhodesians, were all souls in need of congenial company.

And they were friendly occasions, those meetings, sometimes going on till dawn.

A girl none of us had seen before came to a public meeting. She saw Harry, a handsome, confident, loquacious, energetic, efficient young man. Everyone relied on him.

She fell in love, took him home, and her father, recognizing one of the world's born organizers, made him manager in his hardware shop.

Which leaves the third, Dick. Now there are some people who should not be allowed anywhere near meetings, debates, or similar intellect-fermenting agencies. He came to two meetings. Harry brought him, describing him as 'keen'. It was Harry who was keen. Dick sat on the floor on a cushion. Wild bohemian ways, these, for well-brought-up young whites. His forehead puckered like a puppy's while he tried to follow wild un-Rhodesian thought. He, like Tom, was a neat, well-set-up youth. Perhaps the Post Office, or at least in Rhodesia, is an institution that attracts the well-ordered? I remember he reminded me of a boiled sweet, bland sugar with a chemical tang. Or perhaps he was like a bulldog, all sleek latent ferocity, with its little bulging eyes, its little snarl. Like Tom, he was one for extracting exact information. 'I take it you people believe that human nature can be changed?'

At the second meeting he attended, he sat and listened as before. At the end he inquired whether we thought socialism was a good thing in this country where there was the white man's burden to consider.

He did not come to another meeting. Harry said that he had found us seditious and un-Rhodesian. Also insincere. We asked Harry to go and ask Dick why he thought we were insincere, and to come back and tell us. It turned out that Dick wanted to know why the Left Club did not take over the government of the country and run it, if we thought the place ill run. But we forgot Dick, particularly as Harry, at the zenith of his efficiency and general usefulness, was drifting off with his future wife to become a hardware-store manager. And by then Tom was lost to us.

Suddenly we heard that 'The Party for Democracy, Liberty and Freedom' was about to hold a preliminary mass meeting. One of us was delegated to go along and find out what was happening. This turned out to be me.

The public meeting was in a side room off a ballroom in one of the town's three hotels. It was furnished with a sideboard to hold the extra supplies of beer and sausage rolls and peanuts consumed so plentifully during the weekly dances, a palm in a pot so tall the top fronds were being pressed down by the ceiling, and a dozen stiff dining-room chairs ranged one by one along the walls. When I arrived, there were eleven men and women in the room, including Dick. Unable to understand immediately why this gathering struck me as so different from the ones in which I spent so much of my time, I then saw it was because there were elderly people present. Our gatherings loved only the young.

Dick was wearing his best suit in dark-grey flannel. It was a very hot evening. His face was scarlet with endeavour and covered with sweat, which he kept sweeping off his forehead with impatient fingers. He was reading an impassioned document, in tone rather like the Communist Manifesto, which began: 'Fellow Citizens of Rhodesia! Sincere Men and Women! This is the Time for Action! Arise and look about you and enter into your Inheritance! Put the forces of International Capital to flight!'

He was standing in front of one of the chairs, his well-brushed little head bent over his notes, which were hand-written and in places hard to read, so that these inflammatory sentiments were being stammered and stumbled out, while he kept correcting himself, wiping off sweat, and then stopping with an appealing circular glance around the room at the others. Towards him were lifted ten earnest faces, as if at a saviour or a Party Leader.

The programme of this nascent Party was simple. It was to 'take over by democratic means but as fast as possible' all the land and the industry of the country 'but to cause as little inconvenience as possible' and 'as soon as it was feasible' to institute a regime of true equality and fairness in 'this land of Cecil Rhodes'.

He was intoxicated by the emanations of admiration from his audience. Burning, passionate faces like these (alas, and I saw how far we had lapsed from fervour) were no longer to be seen at our Left Club meetings, which long ago had sailed away on the agreeable tides of debate and intellectual speculation.

The faces belonged to a man of fifty or so, rather grey and beaten, who described himself as a teacher 'planning the total reform of the entire educational system'; a woman of middle age, a widow, badly dressed and smoking incessantly, who looked as if she had long since gone beyond what she was strong enough to bear from life; an old man with an angelic pink face fringed with white tufts who said he was named after Keir Hardie; three schoolboys, the son of the widow and his two friends; the woman attendant from the Ladies' cloakroom who had unlocked this room to set out the chairs and then had stayed out of interest, since it was her afternoon off; two aircraftmen from the R.A.F.; Dick the convenor; and a beautiful young woman no one had ever seen before who, as soon as Dick had finished his manifesto, stood up to make a plea for vegetarianism. She was ruled out of order. 'We have to get power first, and then we'll simply do what the majority wants.' As for me, I was set apart from them by my lack of fervour, and by Dick's suspicion.

This was in the middle of the Second World War, whose aim it was to defeat the hordes of National Socialism. Communist Russia was twenty-five years old. It was more than a hundred and fifty years since the French Revolution, and even more than that since the American Revolution which overthrew the tyrannies of England. The Independence of India would shortly be celebrated. It was nearly twenty years after the death of Lenin. Trotsky had only just been murdered.

One of the schoolboys, a friend of the widow's son, put up his hand to say timidly that he believed 'there might be books which we could read about socialism and that sort of thing'.

'Indeed there are,' said the namesake of Keir Hardie, nodding his white locks, 'but we needn't follow the writ that runs in other old countries when we have got a brand new one here.

(It must be explained that the whites of Rhodesia, then as now, are always referring to 'this new country'.)

'As for books,' said Dick, eyeing me with all the scornful self-command he had acquired since leaving his cushion weeks before on the floor of our living-room, 'books don't seem to do some people any good, so why do we need them? It is all perfectly simple. It isn't right for a few people to own all the wealth of a country. It isn't fair. It should be shared out among everybody, equally, and then that would be a democracy.'

'Well, obviously,' said the beautiful girl.

'Ah yes,' sighed the poor tired woman, emphatically crushing out her cigarette and lighting a new one.

'Perhaps it would be better if I just moved that palm a little,' said the cloakroom attendant, 'it does seem to be a little in your way perhaps.'

'Never mind about the palm,' said Dick magnificently. 'It's not important.'

And this was the point at which someone asked: 'Excuse me, but where do the Natives come in?' (In those days, the black inhabitants of Rhodesia were referred to as the Natives.)

This was felt to be in extremely bad taste.

'I don't really think that is applicable,' said Dick hotly. 'I simply don't see the point of bringing it up at all – unless it is to make trouble.'

'They do live here,' said one of the R.A.F.

'Well, I must withdraw altogether if there's any likelihood of us getting mixed up with kaffir trouble,' said the widow.

'You can be assured that there will be nothing of that,' said Dick, firmly in control, in the saddle, leader of all, after only half an hour of standing up in front of his mass meeting.

'I don't see that,' said the beautiful girl. 'I simply don't see that at all! We must have a policy for the Natives.'

Even twelve people in one small room, whether starting a mass Party or not, mean twelve different, defined, passionately held viewpoints. The meeting at last had to be postponed for a week to allow those who had not had a chance to air their views to have their say. I attended this second meeting. There were fifteen people present. The two R.A.F. were not there, but there were six white trade unionists from the railways, who, hearing of the new Party, had come to get a resolution passed. 'In the opinion of this meeting, the Native is being advanced too fast towards civilization and in his own interests the pace should be slowed.'

This resolution was always being passed in those days, on every possible occasion. It probably still is.

But the nine from the week before were already able to form a solid block against this influx of alien thought – not as champions of the Natives, of course not, but because it was necessary to attend to first things first. 'We have to take over the country first, by democratic methods. That won't take long, because it is obvious our programme is only fair, and after that we can decide what to do about the Natives.' The six railway workers then left, leaving the nine from last week, who proceeded to form their Party for Democracy, Liberty and Freedom. A steering committee of three was appointed to draft a constitution.

And that was the last anyone ever heard of it, except for one cyclostyled pamphlet which was called 'Capitalism is Unfair. Let's Join Together to Abolish it. This means You!'

The war was over. Intellectual ferments of this sort occurred no more. Employees of the post office, all once again good citizens properly employed in sport and similar endeavours, no longer told the citizens in what ways they were being censored and when.

Dick did not stay in the post office. That virus, politics, was in his veins for good. From being a spokesman for socialism for the whites, he became, as a result of gibes that he couldn't have a socialism that excluded most of the population, an exponent of the view that Natives must not be advanced too fast in their own interests, and from there he developed into a Town Councillor, and from there into a Member of Parliament. And that is what he still is, a gentleman of distinguished middle age, an indefatigable server on Parliamentary Committees and Commissions, particularly those to do with the Natives, on whom he is considered an authority.

An elderly bulldog of the bulldog breed he is, every inch of him.

Report on the Threatened City

PRIORITY FLASH ONE

*All coordinates all plans all prints cancelled. As of now con-
dition unforeseen by us obtaining this city. Clear all programmes
all planners all forecasters for new setting on this information.*

PRIORITY

*Base to note well that transmission this channel will probably
be interrupted by material originating locally. Our fuel is low
and this channel therefore only one now operative.*

Summary of Background to Mission

Since our planet discovered that this city was due for destruction
or severe damage, all calculations and plans of our department
have been based on one necessity: how to reach the city to warn
its inhabitants of what is to come. Observing their behaviour,
both through Astroviewers and from our unmanned machines
launched at intervals this past year, their time, our Commissioners for External Affairs decided these people could have
no idea at all of what threatened, that their technology, while so
advanced in some ways, had a vast gap in it, a gap that could be
defined, in fact, precisely by that area of ignorance – not knowing
what was to befall them. This gap seemed impossible. Much time
was spent by our technicians trying to determine what form of
brain these creatures could have that made this contradiction possible – as already stated, a technology so advanced in one area
and blank in another. Our technicians had to shelve the problem,
since their theories became increasingly improbable and since no

species known to us anywhere corresponds even at a long remove with what we believed this one to be. It became, perhaps, the most intriguing of our unsolved problems, challenging and defeating one department after another.

Summary of Objective this Mission

Meanwhile, putting all speculations on one side, attractive though they were, all our resources have been used, at top speed and pressure, to develop a spacecraft that could, in fact, land a team on this planet, since it was our intention, having given the warning, offered the information available to us, but (we thought) not to them, which made the warning necessary, to offer them more: our assistance. We meant to help clear the area, transport the population elsewhere, cushion the shock to the area and then, having done what, after all, we have done for other planets, our particular mental structure being suited to this kind of forecasting and assistance, return to base, taking some suitable specimens of them with us, in order to train them in a way that would overcome the gap in their minds and, therefore, their science. The first part we achieved: that is, we managed, in the time set for it, to develop a spacecraft that could make the journey here, carrying the required number of personnel. It strained our own technology and postponed certain cherished plans of our own. But our craft landed here, on the western shore of the land mass, as planned, and without any trouble, seven days ago.

The Nature of the Problem

You will have wondered why there have been no transmissions before this. There have been two reasons. One: we realized at once that there would be heavier demands on our fuel than we had anticipated and that we would have to conserve it. Two: we were waiting to understand what it was we had to tell you. We did not understand the problem. For it was almost at once clear to us that all our thinking about 'the gap in their mental structure' was off the point. We have never understood the nature of the problem. So improbable is it that we delayed communicating until we were sure. The trouble with this species is not that it is unable to forecast its immediate future; it is that it doesn't seem to care. Yet that is altogether too simple a stating of its condition. If it were so simple – that it knew that within five years its city was to be destroyed, or partly destroyed, and that it was indifferent – we should have to say: This species lacks the first quality necessary to any animal species; it lacks the will to live. Finding out what the mechanism is has caused the delay. Which I now propose partially to remedy by going into an account of what befell us, step by step. This will entail a detailed description of a species and a condition absolutely without precedent in our experience of the inhabited planets.

An Impossible Fact

But, first, there is a fact that you will find hard to believe. We did not find this out at once, but when we did, it was a moment of focus in our investigation, enabling us to see our problem clearly. *This city experienced a disaster, on a fairly large scale, about 65 years ago, their time.*

A thought immediately suggests itself: our experts did not know about this past disaster, only about the one to come. Our thinking is as defective in its way as theirs is. We had decided that they had a gap, that this gap made it impossible for them to see into the immediate future. Having decided this, we never once considered another possibility, the truth – that they had no gap, that they knew about the threatened danger and did not care. Or behaved as if they did not. Since we were unable to conceive of this latter possibility, we did not direct our thoughts and our instruments back in time – their time. We took it absolutely for granted, an assumption so strong that it prevented our effective functioning as much as these creatures' assumptions prevent them from acting – we believed (since we are so built ourselves) that it would be impossible for a disaster to have occurred already, because if we had experienced such a thing, we would have learned from the event and taken steps accordingly. Because of a series of assumptions, then, and an inability to move outside our own mental set, we missed a fact that might have been a clue to their most extraordinary characteristic – the fact that such a very short time ago they experienced a disaster of the sort that threatens again, and soon.

The Landing

Our unmanned craft have been landing on their planet for centuries and have taken various shapes, been of varying substances. These landings were at long intervals until one year ago. These intervals were because, except for its unique destructiveness and belligerence, this species is not the most remarkable or interesting of those made available to our study by our Technological Revolution in its Space Phase. But 12 times recently, each during a period when their planet was at full light potential, we have landed craft, and each time close to the place in question. This was easy, because the terrain is semi-desert and lightly populated. We chose material for the craft that would manifest as their substance light – which is why we always used maximum their planet light as landing times. These craft were visible, if at all, as strong moonlight. The craft we are using on this present mission, the 13th in this series, is of higher concentration, since it is manned.

We landed as planned. The sky was clear, the light of their moon strong. We knew at once that we were visible, because a herd of their young was near, some 50 or 60 of them, engaged in a mating ritual that involved fire, food and strong sound, and as we descended, they dispersed. Tapping their mind streams established that they believed our machine was extraterritorial but that they were indifferent – no, that is not an exact description, but remember, we are trying to describe a mind state that none of us could have believed was possible. It was not that they were indifferent to us but that indifference was generalized throughout their processes, felt by us as a block or a barrier. After the young creatures had gone, we surveyed the terrain and discovered that we were on high land rising to mountains, inland from the water mass on the edge of which stands the city. A group of older specimens arrived. We know now that they live nearby and are all some variety or other of agriculturalist. They stood quite close, watching the craft. An examination of their minds showed a different type of block. Even at that early stage, we were able to establish a difference in texture between their thought streams and those of the young, which we later understood amounted to this: the older ones felt a responsibility or a power to act, as members of society, while the young ones were excluded or had decided to exclude themselves. As this area of the planet turned into the sunlight, it was clear to us that our craft ceased to be visible, for two of these older creatures came so close we were afraid they would actually enter the concentration. But they showed an awareness of our presence by other symptoms – headache and nausea. They were angry because of this damage being done to them – which they could have alleviated by moving farther off; but at the same time, they were feeling pride. This reaction highlighted the difference between them and the young – the pride was because of what they thought we represented; for, unlike the young, they believed we were some kind of weapon, either of their own land mass or of a hostile one, but from their own planet.

War-Making Patterns

Everyone in the System knows that this species is in the process of self-destruction, or part destruction. This is endemic. The largest and most powerful groupings – based on geographical position – are totally governed by their war-making functions. Rather, each grouping *is* a war-making function, since its economies, its individual lives, its movements, are all subservient to the need to prepare for or wage war. This complete domination of a land area by its war-making machinery is not always visible to the inhabitants of that area, as this species is able, while making war or preparing for it, to think of itself as peace-loving – yes, indeed, this is germane to our theme, the essence of it.

Rational Action Impossible

Here we approach the nature of the block, or patterning, of their minds – we state it now, though we did not begin to understand it until later. *It is that they are able to hold in their minds at the same time several contradictory beliefs without noticing it.* Which is why rational action is so hard for them. Now, the war-making function of each geographical area is not controlled by its inhabitants but is controlled by itself. Each is engaged in inventing, bringing to perfection – and keeping secret from its own inhabitants as well as from the 'enemy' – highly evolved war weapons of all sorts, ranging from devices for the manipulation of men's minds to spacecraft.

Subservient Populations

For instance, recent landings on their moon, much publicized by the geographical groupings that made them and followed breathlessly by the inhabitants of the whole planet, were by no means the first achieved by the said groupings. No, the first 'moon landings' were made in secret, in service of one grouping's dominance in war over another, and the slavish populations knew nothing about them. A great many of the devices and machines used by the war departments are continuously under test in all parts of the earth and are always being glimpsed or even seen fully by inhabitants who report them to the authorities. But some of these devices are similar (in appearance, at least) to machines of extraterritorial origin. Citizens reporting 'flying saucers' – to use one of their descriptive phrases – may as well have seen the latest of their own grouping's machines on test as one of our observation craft or observation craft from the Jupiter family. Such a citizen will find that after reaching a certain level in the hierarchies of officialdom, silence will blanket him and his observations – he will in various ways be repulsed, ridiculed or even threatened. As usually happens, a council of highly placed officials was recently ordered to take evidence and report on the by now innumerable sightings of 'unidentified flying objects', but this council finished its deliberations with public words that left the situation exactly as it was before. The official report nowhere stated that there was a minority report by some of its own number. This is the level of behaviour in their public representatives that is tolerated by them. Large numbers, everywhere on the planet, see craft like ours, or like other planets' craft, or war machines from their own or other geographical areas. But such is the atmosphere created by the war departments that dominate everything that these individuals are regarded as mentally inadequate or deluded. Until one of them has actually seen a machine or a spacecraft, he tends to believe that anyone who claims he has is deranged. Knowing this, when he does see something, he often does not say so. But so many individuals now have seen things for themselves that there are everywhere all kinds of dissident or sullen subgroupings. These are of all ages and they cut across the largest and most widespread subculture of them all, that of the young of the species who have grown up in a society of total war-preparedness, who are naturally reluctant to face a future that can only mean early death or maiming and who react in the way mentioned earlier, with a disinclination to take part in the administration of their various societies. The older ones seem much more able to delude themselves, to use words like peace when engaged in warlike behaviour, to identify with their geographical areas. The young ones are clearer-minded, more easily see the planet as a single organism, but are also more passive and hopeless. We put forward the suggestion that the greater, or at least more purposive, energy of the older ones may be because of their comparative narrowness and identification with smaller ideas.

We are now able to explain why the young we met on the night we landed moved away. Some had already had the experience of insisting to the authorities that they had seen strange machines and objects of various kinds and of being discouraged or threatened. They would be prepared to publicize what they had seen in their own news-sheets or to spread it by word of mouth; but, unlike their elders, most of whom seem unable to understand the extent to which they are subjugated to the needs of war, they would never put themselves in a position where their authorities could capture or question them. But the older ones of the area who had seen our previous 12 craft, which had all landed there, had evolved a different attitude. Some had reported what they had seen and had been discouraged. One or two, persisting, had been described as mad and had been threatened with incarceration. But, on the whole, they had taken the attitude of the authorities as a directive to mind their own business. Discussing it among themselves, they had agreed to keep watch on their own account, not saying too much about what they saw. In this group are two spies, who report to the war departments on what is seen and on the reactions of their fellow agriculturalists.

First Attempt at a Warning

Now we come to our first attempt to communicate a warning. Since the 20 or so elders were already on the spot and were unafraid, staying on the site where they believed we might redescend – they did not know it was only the strength of the sun's light that made us invisible – we decided to use them and again made contact with their thought streams, this time in an attempt to project our message. But there was a barrier, or at least something we could not understand, and it was time-consuming for us. We were already aware that we might run short of power.

Incapacity for Fear

Now, of course, we know we made a wrong assessment, for, expecting that the news of the expected disaster would jam their thought machinery in panic, we fed it in very carefully and slowly, taking an entire day and night. When we hit the block, or resistance, we put it down to fear. We were mistaken. This is perhaps the time to state a psychological law we consider basic to them: this is a species immune from fear – but this will be elaborated later, if the power holds. At the end of the day and night, still meeting the same resistance, we allowed ourselves another period of a day and a night to repeat the message, hoping that the fear – as we then saw it – would be overcome. At the end of the second period of transmitting, there was no change in their mental structure. I repeat, none. We know now what was far from our understanding then, that we were telling them something they already knew. As we were not prepared at that time to entertain that hypothesis, we decided that this particular group of individuals was for some reason unsuitable for our purposes and that we must try an altogether different type, and preferably of a different age group. We had tried mature individuals. We had already suspected what we since have confirmed, that in this species the older they get, the less open they are to new thought material. Now, it so happens that the place where our craft descended is in an area much used for the before-mentioned mating rituals. Several times in the two day-and-night periods of our attempt with the older group, youngsters had arrived in various types of metal machines from the city – and had quite soon gone away, sensing our presence, if they did not see us. They all arrived in daylight. But on the third day, as the sunlight went, four young ones arrived in a metal conveyance, got out of it and sat fairly close to us on a small rocky rise.

Second Attempt At A Warning

They looked like healthy, strong specimens, and we began to transmit our information, but in greater concentration than we had used with the older individuals. But in spite of the increased power these four absorbed what we fed into them and reacted in exactly the same way as their elders. We did not understand this and, taking the chance of setting them into a panic flight, concentrated our entire message (which had taken two entire days and nights with the mature group) into the space of time between the sunlight's going and its return. Their minds did not reject what we said nor jam up in fear. They were voicing to one another, in a mechanical way, what we were feeding into them. It sounded like his, over and over again – with variations:

'They say we have only five years.'

'That's bad.'

'Yeah, it's going to be real bad.'

'When it comes, it's going to be the worst yet.'

'Half the city might be killed.'

'They say it might be as bad as that.'

'Any time in the next five years, they say.'

It was like pouring a liquid into a container that has a hole in it. The group of older ones had sat around for two days and nights repeating that the city was due for destruction, as if they were saying that they could expect a headache, and now these four were doing the same. At one point they stopped the monotone exchanges and one, a young female, accompanying herself on a stringed musical instrument, began what they call a song; that is, the vocalizations cease to be an exchange between two or more individuals, but an individual, or a group, very much enlarging the range of tones used in ordinary exchange, makes a statement. The information we fed into these four emerged in these words, from the young female:

> We know the earth we live upon
> Is due to fall.
> We know the ground we walk upon
> Must shake.
> We know, and so . . .
> We eat and drink and love,
> Keep high,
> Keep love,
> For we must die.

Phase I Abandoned

And they continued with their mating rituals. We then discontinued the emission of thought material, if for no other reason than that we had already used up a fourth of our power supply with no result. This, then, was the end of Phase I, which was the attempt to transfer the warning material into the brains of selected members of the species for automatic telepathic transmission to others. We set about Phase II, which was to take possession of the minds of suitable individuals in a planned campaign to use

them as mouthpieces for the warnings. We decided to abandon
the first phase in the belief that the material was running straight
through their mental apparatus like water through sieves because
it was so foreign to the existing mental furniture of their minds
that they were not able to recognize what we were saying. In
other words, we still had no idea that the reason they did not
react was that the idea was a commonplace.

Phase II Attempted

Three of us therefore accompanied the four youngsters in their
machine when they returned to the city, because we thought that
in their company we would most quickly find suitable individuals to take over – we had decided the young were more likely
to be useful than the mature. The way they handled this machine
was a shock to us. It was suicidal. Their methods of transport are
lethal. In the time it took to reach the suburbs of the city –
between the lightening of the dark and the sun's appearance –
there were four near collisions with other, equally recklessly
driven vehicles. Yet the four youngsters showed no fear and reacted with the mechanism called laughter; that is, with repeated
violent contractions of the lungs, causing noisy emission of air.
This journey, their recklessness, their indifference to death or
pain, made us conclude that this group of four, like the group of
20 older ones, was perhaps atypical. We were playing with the
idea that there are large numbers of defective animals in this
species and that we had been unlucky in our choices. The machine was stopped to refuel and the four got out and walked
about. Three more youngsters were sitting on a bench huddled
against one another, in a stupor. Like all the young, they wore a
wide variety of clothing and had long head fur. They had several
musical instruments. Our four attempted to rouse them and
partly succeeded: the responses of the three were slow and, it
seemed to us, even more clumsy and inadequate. They either did
not understand what was being said or could not communicate
what they understood. We then saw that they were in the power
of some kind of drug. They had quantities of it, and the four

wished also to put themselves in its power. It was a drug that sharpens sensitivity while it inhibits ordinary response: the three were more sensitive to our presence than the four had been – they had not been aware of our presence in the vehicle at all. The three, once roused from their semi-consciousness, seemed to see, or at least to feel, us and directed towards us muttered sounds of approval or welcome. They seemed to associate us with the sun's appearance over the roof of the refuelling station. The four, having persuaded the three to give them some of the drug, went to their vehicle. We decided to stay with the three, believing that their sensitivity to our presence was a good sign. Testing their thought streams, we found them quite free and loose, without the resistances and tensions of the others we had tested. We then took possession of their minds – this was the only moment of real danger during the whole mission. Your envoys might very well have been lost then, dissolving into a confusion and violence that we find hard to describe. For one thing, at that time we did not know how to differentiate between the effects of the drug and the effects of their senses. We now do know and will attempt a short description. The drug causes the the mechanisms dealing with functions such as walking, talking, eating, and so on, to become slowed or dislocated. Meanwhile, the receptors for sound, scent, sight, touch, are opened and sensitized. But, for us, to enter their minds is in any case an assault, because of the phenomenon they call beauty, which is a description of their sense intake in an ordinary condition. For us, this is like entering an explosion of colour; for it is this that is the most startling difference between our mode of perceiving and theirs: the physical structure of their level appears in vibrations of brilliant colour. To enter an un-drugged mind is hard enough for one of us; to keep one's balance is difficult. As it was, it might easily have happened that we were swept away in contemplation of vivid colour.

Necessity to Condense Report, Power Failing

Although the temptation to dwell on this is great, we must condense this report if we wish to keep any use of this channel: the pressure of local material is getting very strong. In brief, then, the three youngsters, reeling with pleasure because of this dimension of brilliance which we of course all know about through deduction but which, I assure you, we have never approached even in imagination, shouting and singing that the city was doomed, stood on the side of the road until one of the plentiful machines stopped for us. We were conveyed rapidly into the city. There were two individuals in the vehicle, both young, and neither reacted in any way to the warnings we were giving them through the minds or, rather, voices of our hosts. At the end of the rapid movement, we arrived in the city, which is large, populous and built around a wide indentation of the shore of the water mass. It is all extremely vivid, colourful, powerfully affecting the judgement, and it heightened the assault on our balance. We made a tentative decision that it is impracticable for our species to make use of this method: of actually possessing selected minds for the purpose of passing on information. It is too violent a transformation for us. However, since we were there, and succeeding in not being swept away into a highly tinted confusion of pleasure, we agreed to stay where we were, and the three we were possessing left the vehicle and walked out into the streets, shouting out the facts as we thought them: that there was little doubt that at some moment between now and five years from now, there would be a strong vibration of the planet at this point and that the greater part of the city might be destroyed, with severe loss of life. It was early in the day, but many of them were about. We were waiting for some sort of reaction to what we were saying, interest at the very least; queries; some sort of response to which we could respond ourselves with advice or offers of help. But of the very many we met in that brief progress through the streets, *no one took any notice at all*, except for a glance or a short indifferent stare.

Capture by the Authorities

Soon there was a screeching and a wailing, which we at first took to be the reaction of these creatures to what we were saying, some sort of warning, perhaps, to the inhabitants, or statements that measures towards self-preservation must be taken; but it was another vehicle, of a military sort, and the three (we) were taken up from the streets and to a prison because of the disturbance we were making. This is how we understood it afterwards. At the time, we thought that the authorities had gathered us in to question us as to the revelations we had to make. In the hands of the guards, in the street and the military vehicle and the prison, we kept up a continuous shouting and crying-out of the facts and did not stop until a doctor injected our three hosts with some other drug, which caused them instantly to become unconscious. It was when we heard the doctor talking to the guards that we first heard the fact of the previous catastrophe. This was such a shock to us that we could not then take in its implications. But we decided at once to leave our hosts, who, being in any case unconscious, would not be any use to us for some time, even if this method of conveying warnings had turned out to be efficacious – and it obviously was not – and make different plans. The doctor was also saying that he had to treat large numbers of people, particularly the young ones, for 'paranoia'. This was what our three hosts were judged to be suffering from. Apparently, it is a condition when people show fear of forthcoming danger and try to warn others about it and then show anger when stopped by authority. This diagnosis, together with the fact that the doctor and the authorities knew of the coming danger and of the past catastrophe – in other words, that they consider it an illness or a faulty mental condition to be aware of what threatens and to try to take steps to avoid or soften it – was something so extraordinary that we did not then have time to evaluate it in depth, nor have we had time since to do so, because —— ...

AND FINALLY, TO END THIS NEWS FLASH, A REAL HEART-WARMER. FIVE ORDINARY PEOPLE, NOT RICH FOLKS, NO, BUT PEOPLE LIKE YOU AND ME, HAVE GIVEN UP A MONTH'S PAY TO SEND LITTLE JANICE WANAMAKER, THE CHILD WITH THE HOLE IN THE HEART, TO THE WORLD-FAMED HEART CENTRE IN

FLORIDA. LITTLE JANICE, WHO IS TWO YEARS OLD,
COULD HAVE EXPECTED A LONG LIFE OF INVALIDISM;
BUT NOW THE FAIRY WAND OF LOVE HAS CHANGED ALL
THAT AND SHE WILL BE FLYING TOMORROW MORNING
TO HAVE HER OPERATION, ALL THANKS TO THE FIVE
GOOD NEIGHBOURS OF ARTESIA STREET ——— ... The
expected interruptions of this wavelength; but, as we have no
way of knowing at which point the interruption began, to
recapitulate, we left the doctor and the guards in discussion of
the past catastrophe, in which 200 miles of ground were ripped
open, hundreds of people were killed and the whole city was
shaken down in fragments. This was succeeded by a raging fire.

Humour as a Mechanism

The doctor was recalling *humorously* (note previous remarks
about laughter, a possible device for release of tension to ward off
or relieve fear and, therefore, possibly one of the mechanisms
that keep these animals passive in the face of possible extinction)
that for some years after the previous catastrophe, this entire
geographical grouping referred to the great fire, rather than to
the earth vibration. This circumlocution is still quite common.
In other words, a fire being a smaller, more manageable
phenomenon, they preferred, and sometimes still prefer, to use
that word, instead of the word for the uncontrollable shaking of
the earth itself. A pitiable device, showing helplessness and
even fear. But we emphasize here again that everywhere else
in the System, fear is a mechanism to protect or to warn, and in
these creatures, the function is faulty. As for helplessness, this
is tragic anywhere, even among these murderous brutes, but
there is no apparent need for them to be helpless, since they
have every means to evacuate the city altogether and to ——— ...
THE NEW SUBURB PLANNED TO THE WEST. THIS WILL
HOUSE 100,000 PEOPLE AND WILL BE OPEN IN THE
AUTUMN OF NEXT YEAR FULLY EQUIPPED WITH SHOPS,
CINEMAS, A CHURCH, SCHOOLS AND A NEW MOTORWAY.
THE RAPID EXPANSION OF OUR BEAUTIFUL CITY, WITH

ITS UNIQUE CLIMATE, ITS SETTING, ITS SHORE LINE,
CONTINUES. THIS NEW SUBURB WILL DO SOMETHING TO
COMBAT THE OVERCROWDING AND ——

The Jettisoning of Phases I, II and III

In view of the failure of Phases I and II, we decided to abandon
Phase III, which was planned to be a combination of I and II –
inhabiting suitable hosts to use them as loud-speakers and, at the
same time, putting material into available thought streams for
retransmission. Before making further attempts to communicate,
we needed more information. To summarize the results of Phase
II, when we inhabited the three drugged young, we understood
we must be careful to assume the shapes of older animals, and
those of a technically trained kind, as it was clear from our experience in the prison that the authorities disliked the young of
their species. We did not yet know whether they were capable of
listening to the older ones, who are shaped in the image of their
society.

Inability to Assess Truth

While at that stage we were still very confused about what we
were finding, we had at least grasped this: that this species, on
being told something, has no means of judging whether or not it
is true. We on our planet assume, because it is our mental structure and that of all the species we have examined, that if a new
fact is made evident by material progress, or by a new and hitherto unexpected juxtaposition of ideas, then it is accepted as a
fact, a truth – until an evolutionary development by-passes it.
Not so with this species. It is not able to accept information, new
material, unless it is from a source it is not suspicious about. This
is a handicap to its development that it is not possible to exagger-
ate. We choose this moment to suggest, though of necessity
briefly, that in future visits to this planet, with information of use
to this species (if it survives), infinite care must be taken to pre-
pare plenipotentiaries who resemble in every respect the most
orthodox and harmless members of the society. For it is as if the

mechanism fear has been misplaced from where it would be useful – preventing or softening calamity – to an area of their minds that makes them suspicious of anything but the familiar. As a small example, in the prison, because the three young animals were drugged and partly incoherent, and because (as it has become clear to us) the older animals who run the society despise those who are not similar to the norms they have established, it would not have mattered what they said. If they had said (or shouted or sung) that they had actually observed visitors from another planet (they had, in fact, sensed us, felt us) as structures of finer substance manifesting as light – if they had stated they had seen three roughly man-sized creatures shaped in light – no notice at all would have been taken of them. But if an individual from that secion of their society which is especially trained for that class of work (it is an infinitely subdivided society) had said that he had observed *with his instruments* (they have become so dependent on machinery that they have lost confidence in their own powers of observation) three rapidly vibrating light structures, he would at least have been credited with good faith. Similarly, great care has to be taken with verbal formulation. An unfamiliar fact described in one set of words may be acceptable. Present it in a pattern of words outside what they are used to and they may react with all the signs of panic – horror, scorn, fear.

Adaptation to their Norm for their Dominant Animals

We incarnated as two males of mature age. We dressed ourselves with the attention to detail they find reassuring. An item of clothing cut differently from what is usual for older animals will arouse disapproval or suspicion. Sober tones of colour are acceptable; bright tones, except in small patches, are not. We assure you that if we had dressed even slightly outside their norm, we could have done nothing at all. It is the dominant males who have to restrict their choice of clothing. Women's garb is infinitely variable, but always changing, suddenly and dramatically, from one norm or pattern to another. The young can wear what they please as long as they are not part of the machinery of government. The cutting and arranging of their head fur is also important. Women and the young enjoy latitude in this, too, but we had to see that our head fur was cut short and kept flattened. We also assumed a gait indicating soberness and control, and facial expressions that we had noted they found reassuring. For instance, they have a way of stretching the lips sideways and exposing the teeth in a sort of facial arrangement they call a smile that indicates that they are not hostile, will not attack, that their intentions are to keep the peace.

Thus disguised, we walked about the city engaged in observation, on the whole astounded that so little notice was taken of us. For while we were fair copies, we were not perfect, and a close scrutiny would have shown us up. But one of their characteristics is that they, in fact, notice very little about one another; it is a remarkably unnoticing species. Without arousing suspicion, we discovered that everybody we talked to knew that a disturbance of the earth was expected in the next five years, that while they 'knew' this, they did not really believe it, or seemed not to, since their plans to live as if nothing whatsoever was going to happen were unaltered and that a laboratory or institute existed to study the past upheaval and make plans for the forthcoming one —— ... AT THE BASEBALL GAME THIS AFTERNOON, A PORTION OF THE SCAFFOLDING GAVE WAY AND 60 PEOPLE WERE KILLED. THERE HAVE BEEN MESSAGES OF SYMPATHY FROM THE PRESIDENT, HER MAJESTY THE QUEEN OF GREAT BRITAIN AND THE POPE. THE MANAGER OF THE SPORTS STADIUM WAS IN TEARS AS HE SAID: 'THIS IS THE MOST TERRIBLE THING THAT I HAVE EVER SEEN. I KEEP SEEING THOSE DEAD FACES BEFORE MY EYES.' THE CAUSE OF THE ACCIDENT IS THAT THE BUILDING OF THE STANDS AND THEIR MAINTENANCE, AND THE PROVISION OF CRUSH BARRIERS, ARE SUBJECT TO MAXIMUM PROFIT BEING EARNED BY THE OWNERS. THE FUND SET UP AS THE CORPSES WERE CARRIED FROM THE STADIUM HAS ALREADY REACHED $200,000, AND MORE KEEPS POURING ——

The Institute

We entered the Institute for Prognosis and Prevention of Earth Disturbance as visitors from Geographical Area 2 – one allied at this time with this area and, therefore, welcome to observe its work.

A short description of this organization may be of use. There are 50 of their most highly skilled technicians in it, all at work on some of the most advanced (as advanced as ours in this field) equipment for the diagnosis of vibrations, tremors, quakes. The very existence of this institute is because of the knowledge that the city cannot survive another five years – or is unlikely to do so. All these technicians live in the city, spend their free time in it – and the institute itself is in the danger area. They are all likely to be present when the event occurs. Yet they are all cheerful, unconcerned and – it is easy to think – of extreme bravery. But after a short time in their company, discussing their devices for predicting the upheaval, it is difficult to resist the conclusion that like the youngsters in the machine for transportation, who steer it in such a way that they are bound to kill or maim themselves or others, they are in some way set not to believe what they say – that they are in danger and will most certainly be killed or maimed together with the rest of the population —— ... THE FIRE BROKE OUT AT DAWN, WHEN FEW PEOPLE WERE IN THE STREETS, AND WAS SO POWERFUL THAT IT REACHED THE FOURTH STORY FROM THE BASEMENT IN MINUTES. THE SCORES OF PEOPLE IN THE BUILDING WERE DRIVEN UPWARD BY THE FIRE, A FEW MANAGING TO NEGOTIATE THE FIRE ESCAPES, WHICH WERE MOSTLY ENGULFED IN FLAMES, AN UN-KNOWN MAN IN THE STREET PENETRATED THE BUILDING, IN SPITE OF THE SMOKE AND THE FLAMES, AND RES-CUED TWO SMALL CHILDREN LEFT CRYING ON THE SECOND FLOOR. ANOTHER TWO MINUTES AND IT WOULD HAVE BEEN TOO LATE. HE INSTANTLY PLUNGED BACK INTO THE INFERNO AND BROUGHT OUT AN OLD WOMAN ON HIS BACK. IN SPITE OF PROTESTS FROM THE BY

NOW LARGE CROWD, HE INSISTED ON RE-ENTERING
THE FLAMING BUILDING AND WAS LAST SEEN AT A
SECOND-FLOOR WINDOW FROM WHICH HE THREW DOWN
A BABY TO THE PEOPLE BELOW. THE BABY WILL SUR-
VIVE, BUT THE UNKNOWN HERO FELL BACK INTO THE
FLAMES AND ——

A Basic Mechanism

We believe we have established one of their mechanisms for
maintaining themselves in impotence and indecision. It is
precisely this: that they do continuously discuss and analyse.
For instance, the technicians of this institute are always issuing
warnings to the city's officials and to the populace. Their
prognoses, one after another, come true – that minor vibrations
are likely to occur in this or that area – yet warnings continue to
be issued, discussion goes on. So accustomed have they become
to this state of affairs that we found it was not possible to discuss
active means for prevention with them. They would have become suspicious that we were some sort of trouble-makers. In
short, they do not find frightening discussion about the timing,
the nature, the power of probable earth convulsions, but they are
hostile to suggestions about the possible transfer of population
or rebuilding of the city elsewhere. We have said that this is an
infinitely subdivided society: it is the institute's task to warn, to
forecast, not its responsibility to suggest solutions. But this
mechanism – the role of talk – is merely part of a much deeper
one. We now suspect that a great many of the activities that they
themselves see as methods of furthering change, saving life, im-
proving society, are in fact methods of preventing change. It is
almost as if they were afflicted with a powerful lassitude, a lack
of vital energy, which must resist change, because it is so easily
exhausted. Their infinite number of varieties of oral, verbal
activity are expenditures of vital energy. They are soothed and
relieved by stating a problem, but, having done this, seldom have
the energy left to act on their verbal formulations. We have even
concluded that they feel that by stating a problem, it becomes in

some way nearer solution —— ... PROTESTS THAT THE THREE SKYSCRAPERS ON THIRD STREET ARE TO BE PULLED DOWN IN ORDER TO BUILD THREE MUCH HIGHER BUILDINGS, INSTEAD OF PUTTING THE MONEY INTO PROVIDING LOW-RATE ACCOMMODATION FOR THE CITY'S POOR, OF WHICH RECENT SURVEYS REVEAL THERE ARE 1,000,000 OR MORE, NEARLY A QUARTER OF THE TOTAL POPULATION, AND ALL IN ACCOMMODATIONS SO INADEQUATE THAT —— ... for instance, debates, discussions, verbal contests of all sorts, public and private, continue all the time. All their activities, public and private, are defined in talk, public or private. It is possible that they are so constituted that, for them, an event has not occurred at all unless it has been discussed, presented in words —— ... 35 CONVENTIONS IN THE MONTH OF MAY ALONE, TOTALLING 75,000 DELEGATES FROM EVERY PART OF THE CONTINENT, WHILE AT THE SAME TIME THE TOURIST FIGURES FOR MAY TOPPED THOSE FOR ANY PREVIOUS MAY. THIS YEAR IS ALREADY A RECORD FOR CONVENTIONS AND TOURISM GENERALLY, PROVING THAT THE ATTRACTIONS OF OUR CITY, ITS SITUATION, ITS CLIMATE, ITS AMENITIES, ITS REPUTATION FOR HOSPITALITY, EVER INCREASE IN EVERY PART OF THE CIVILIZED GLOBE. IT IS ESSENTIAL TO STEP UP THE BUILDING OF NEW HOTELS, MOTELS AND RESTAURANTS AND TO —— ... the one thing they do not seem able to contemplate is the solution that has seemed to us obvious ever since we observed their probable future and decided to devote so much of our own planet's resources to trying to help our sister planet – to evacuate the city altogether. This is incredible, we know. Of course, you will find it so.

Indifference to Loss of Life

We can only report what we find – that at no point have the inhabitants of this city even considered the possibility of abandoning it and moving to an area that is not absolutely certain to be destroyed. Their attitude towards life is that it is unimportant. They are indifferent to their own suffering, assume that their species must continuously lose numbers and strength and health by natural disasters, famine, constant war. That this attitude goes side by side with infinite care and devotion to individuals or to small groups seems to us to indicate —— ... THE DONATED SUM IS TO BE USED TO BUILD A MEMORIAL, TO BE ERECTED IN THE SQUARE. IT WILL BE IN THE SHAPE OF A COLUMN, WITH THE HEAD OF WILLIAM UNDERSCRIBE, THE DECEASED, IN RELIEF ON ONE SIDE.

LAID TO REST
UPON THE BREAST
OF NATURE
GONE BUT NOT FORGOTTEN

WILL BE CARVED ON THE OTHER. JOAN UNDERSCRIBE, WHO LOST HER HUSBAND FIVE YEARS AGO, HAS WORKED SEVEN DAYS A WEEK FROM SIX IN THE MORNING UNTIL TEN AT NIGHT AT THE AVENUE MOTEL TO EARN THE SUM NECESSARY FOR THIS SIMPLE BUT MOVING MEMORIAL. SHE HAS JEOPARDIZED HER HEALTH, SHE CLAIMS. THE FIVE YEARS OF UNREMITTING TOIL HAVE TAKEN THEIR TOLL. BUT SHE HAS NO REGRETS. HE WAS THE BEST HUSBAND A WOMAN EVER HAD, SHE TOLD OUR REPORTER —— ... on the point of deciding there was nothing we could do against such total indifference to their condition; but since they are at least prepared to talk about situations, we devised a plan —— ... THE BIGGEST ENTERTAINMENT EVER, COMBINING THE WORLD'S TOP CIRCUSES, ICE SHOWS, NON-STOP POP CONCERTS FOR THE ENTIRE WEEK, DAY AND NIGHT, NOT TO MENTION THREE OPERAS FROM THE WORLD'S GREATEST, THE BRITISH NATIONAL THEATRE COMPANY IN THAT PERENNIAL ATTRACTION, THE INTERNATIONAL CULTURAL STAR ACE, 'THE THREE SISTERS', WHICH WILL BE ATTENDED BY OUR OWN FIRST LADY AND HER CHARMING DAUGHTERS AND A GLITTERING ARRAY OF STARS, INCLUDING BOB HOPE

—— ... 'calling a conference' is to gather a large number of individuals in one place, in order to exchange verbal formulations. This is probably their main anxiety-calming mechanism; they certainly resort to it on every occasion, whether under that name, called by governments, administrative bodies, authorities of all kinds, or under other names, for very often this procedure is social. For instance, a conference can be called a party and be for pleasure, but discussion on a theme or themes will be, in fact, the chief activity. The essential factor is that many of the creatures assemble in one place, to exchange word patterns with others, afterwards telling others not present what has occurred —— ... THE CITY'S CONSERVATION YEAR IS OVER AND MUST BE COUNTED A REMARKABLE SUCCESS. IT BURNED AN AWARENESS OF WHAT WE CAN EXPECT SO DEEPLY INTO ALL OUR MINDS AND HEARTS THAT INTEREST IS NOW NOT LIKELY TO FADE. A CONFERENCE TO —— ... opinions.

Their Education

The ability to define these, and to differentiate them from those of other people, forms a large part of their education. When two of these creatures meet for the first time, they will set about finding out what opinions the other holds and will tolerate each other accordingly. Non-stimulating, easily tolerated opinions can also be called 'received ideas'. This means that an idea or a fact has been stamped with approval by some form of authority. The phrase is used like this: 'That is a received idea.' 'Those are all received ideas.' This does not necessarily mean that the idea or fact has been acted on or that behaviour has been changed. Essentially, a received idea is one that has become familiar, whether effective or not, and no longer arouses hostility or fear. The mark of an educated individual is this: that he has spent years absorbing received ideas and is able readily to repeat them. People who have absorbed opinions counter to the current standard of ideas are distrusted and may be called opinionated. This description is earned most easily by women and young people.

By that time, we were well known to everyone in the institute as Herbert Bond, 35 years old, male, and John Hunter, 40 years old, male. We had learned enough to avoid the direct 'Why don't you take such and such steps?' since we had learned that this approach caused some sort of block or fault in their functioning, but approached like this: 'Let us discuss the factors militating against the taking of such and such a step'; for instance, making sure that new buildings were not erected close to the areas where tremors or vibrations must occur.

This formulation was initially successful, evoking the maximum amount of animated talk without arousing hostility. But, very shortly, a strong emotion was aroused by phrases and words of which we list a few here: profit motive, conflicting commercial interests, vested interests, capitalism, socialism, democracy – there are many such emotive words. We were not able to determine, or not in a way that our economic experts would recognize as satisfactory, the significance of these phrases, since the emotions became too violent to allow the conference to continue. The animals would certainly have begun to attack one another physically. In other words, the range of opinion (see above) was too wide to be accommodated. Opinion, that is, on matters to do with disposal and planning of population. Opinion concerning earth disturbance was virtually unanimous.

Barbaric Method of Town Planning Unique in Our System, but see Histories of Planets 2 and 4

It appears that their population disposal, their city planning, is not determined by the needs of the people who live in an area but is the result of a balance come to by many conflicting bodies and individuals whose reason for participating in such schemes is self-interest. For instance: before the violence engendered by this subject closed the conference, we had gathered that the reason a particularly large and expensive group of buildings was built directly in the line of maximum earth disturbance was that that part of the city commands high 'rents' – that is, people are prepared to pay more to live and work in that area than elsewhere. Nor can the willingness of the builders and planners to erect buildings in the maximum danger area be put down to callousness, since in many cases the individuals concerned themselves live and work there —— ... THE EMERGENCY UNIT AT THE HOSPITAL IN WHICH A TEAM OF TEN DOCTORS AND NURSES WORKS AROUND THE CLOCK TO SAVE LIVES THAT WOULD HAVE BEEN LOST AS RECENTLY AS FIVE YEARS AGO – AND ARE STILL LOST IN HOSPITALS NOT EQUIPPED WITH EMERGENCY UNITS. THE PATIENTS ARE USUALLY THE VICTIMS OF CAR ACCIDENTS OR STREET FIGHTS AND ARRIVE AT THE UNIT IN A STATE OF SEVERE SHOCK. SINCE AS SHORT A DELAY AS FIVE MINUTES CAN MAKE THE DIFFERENCE BETWEEN LIFE AND DEATH, TREATMENT IS STARTED AS THE PATIENT IS LIFTED OUT OF THE AMBULANCE —— ... as a good deal of the anger was directed against their own young, we left the institute and returned to the centre of the city, where we again made contact with the young.

The Institute Found Not Useful

The young ones working at the institute in menial and assistive positions were all of a different subculture, patterned on the older animals in clothing and behaviour. The young animals we met in the city were in herds, or smaller groups, and not easily contacted by Herbert Bond and John Hunter, who, being older and dressed in the uniform of the dominant males, were suspected of being spies of some sort. We therefore reincarnated ourselves as two youngsters, male and female, having decided to spend a fourth of what was left of our supply of power in trying to persuade them to agree on one issue and to act on it. For, like their elders, they discuss and talk and sing endlessly, enjoying pleasurable sensations of satisfaction and agreement with others, making these an end in themselves. We suggested that in view of what was going to happen to the city, they, the young ones, might try to persuade all those of their age to leave and live elsewhere, to make for themselves some sort of encampment, if to build a new city was beyond their resources, at any rate a place in which refugees would be welcomed and cared for.

Failure with the Young

All that happened was that a number of new songs were sung, all of a melancholy nature, all on the theme of unavoidable tragedy. Our encounter with these young ones was taking place on the beach and at the time of the fading of the sunlight. This is a time that has a powerfully saddening effect on all the animals. But it was not until afterwards that we understood we should have chosen any time of the day but that one. There were large numbers of young, many with musical instruments. Half a dozen of them converted the occasion into a conference (see above) by addressing the mass not as their elders do, through talking, but through singing – the heightened and emotional sound. The emotion was of a different kind from that at the conference at the institute. That had been violent and aggressive and nearly resulted in physical attack. This was heavy, sad, passive. Having failed to get them to discuss, either by talking or by singing, a mass exodus from the city, we then attempted discussing how to prevent individuals from massing in the most threatened areas (we were in one at the time) and how, when the shock occurred, to prevent mass deaths and injuries and how to treat the injured, and so forth.

Despair of the Young

All these attempts failed. We might have taken a clue from the drugged condition of the three whose minds we at first occupied and from the indifference to death of the four in the metal conveyance. We have concluded that the young are in a state of disabling despair. While more clear-minded, in some ways, than their elders – that is, more able to voice and maintain criticism of wrongs and faults – they are not able to believe in their own effectiveness. Again and again, on the beach, as the air darkened, versions of this exchange took place:

'But you say you believe it must happen, and within five years.'

'So they say.'

'But you don't think it will?'

'If it happens, it happens.'

'But it isn't *if* – it will happen.'

'They are all corrupt, what can we do? They want to kill us all.'

'Who are corrupt?'

'The old ones. They run everything.'

'But why don't you challenge them?'

'You can't challenge them. They are too strong. We have to evade. We must be fluid. We must be like water.'

'But you are still here, where it is going to happen.'

'So they say.'

A song swept the whole gathering. It was now quite dark. There were many thousands massed near the water.

> It will happen soon,
> So they say,
> We will not live to fight
> Another day.
> They are blind.
> They have blown our mind.
> We shall not live to fight,
> We live to die.

Mass Suicides

And hundreds of them committed suicide – by swimming out into the water in the dark, while those who stood on higher ledges by the water threw themselves in —— ... A DONATION OF $500,000 TO BUILD A BIRD SANCTUARY IN THE PARK. THIS WILL HAVE SPECIMENS OF EVERY KNOWN SPECIES IN THE WORLD. IT IS HOPED THAT SPECIES THREATENED WITH EXTINCTION DUE TO MAN'S CRUELTY AND UNCONCERN WILL FIND THIS SANCTUARY A USE-FUL BANK FROM WHICH THEY CAN REPLENISH AND STRENGTHEN VARIETIES UNDER THREAT —— ... very low stock of power. We decided to make one last attempt, to concentrate our material in a single place. We decided to leave the herds of young and to return to the older animals, since these were in authority. Not to the institute, since we had proved their emotional instability. It was essential to choose a set of words that would not cause emotion – a received idea.

Now, the idea that the behaviour of an individual or a group can be very different from its, or their, self-description is already part of their mental furniture and is enshrined in many time-worn word sets. For instance, 'Don't judge by what he says but by what he does.'

We decided to reinforce this soothing received idea with another of their anxiety-reducing devices. We have already noted that a conference is such a device. A variety of this is to put ideas into heightened or emotional sound, as was done by the young on the beach. We decided that neither of these was suitable for our last attempt. We considered and discarded a third that we have not yet mentioned. This is when disturbing or unpalatable ideas are put into ritual form and acted out in public to small groups or relayed by a technical device, 'television', which enables visual images to be transmitted simultaneously to millions of people. A sequence of events that may fall outside their formal code of morality, or be on its border line, will be acted out, causing violent approval or disapproval – it is a form of catharsis. After a time, these sequences of acted-out events become familiar and are constantly performed. This way of trying out, of acclimatizing unfamiliar ideas, goes on all the time, side by side with ritual acting-out of situations that are familiar and banal – thus making them appear more interesting. This is a way of making a life situation that an individual may find intolerably tedious and repetitive more stimulating and enable him to suffer it without rebelling. These dramas, of both the first and the second kind, can be of any degree of sophistication. But we decided on a fourth mechanism or method: a verbal game. One of their games is when sets of words are discussed by one, two or more individuals, and these are most often transmitted through the above-mentioned device.

We had reassumed our identities as Herbert Bond and John Hunter, since we were again contacting authority, and approached a television centre with forged credentials from a geographical area called Britain, recently a powerful and combative subspecies, which enjoys a sort of prestige because of past aggressiveness and military prowess.

Laughter, Functions Of, See Above

We proposed a game of words, on the theme 'Don't judge by words but by actions'. The debate took place last night. To begin with, there was a good deal of laughter, a sign that should have warned us. This was not antagonistic, 'laughing at', which is found disagreeable but which, in fact, is much safer a reaction than 'laughing with', which is laughter of agreement, of feeling flattered. This second type is evoked by ideas that are minority ideas, when the minority consider they are in advance of the mass. The aggressive and hostile laughter is a safer reaction because it reassures onlookers that a balance is being kept, where as the sympathetic laughter arouses feelings of anxiety in those watching, if the ideas put forward are challenging to norms accepted by them. Our thesis was simple and as already outlined: that this society is indifferent to death and to suffering. Fear is not experienced, or not in a way that is useful for protecting society or the individual. No one sees these facts, because all the sets of words that describe behaviour are in contrast to the facts. The official sets of words are all to do with protection of oneself and others, caution about the future, pity and compassion for others. Throughout all this – that is, while we developed our thesis – we were greeted by laughter.

These games have audiences invited to the places where they are played, so that the makers of the ritual can judge the probable reaction of the individuals outside, all over the city, in front of their television. The laughter was loud and prolonged. Opposing Herbert Bond and John Hunter, professors of words from Britain, were two professors of words from the local university. They have rules of debate, the essence of which is that each statement must have the same weight or importance as the preceding. The opposing professors' statements, of equal length to ours, stated the opposite view and were light and humorous in tone. Our turn coming again, we proved our point by stating the facts about this city's behaviour in the face of a certain disaster – but we did not get very far. As soon as we switched from the theoretical, the general, to the particular, the laughter died away and violent hostility was shown. There is a custom that if people watching a ritual dislike it, they send hostile messages to the relay point. What Herbert Bond and John Hunter said caused so much violent emotion that the technical equipment used for listening to these messages broke down. While the two local professors maintained the calmness of manner expected during these games, they were nervous and, the ritual over, they said they thought they would lose their employment. They were hostile to us, as being responsible. They complained that, as 'foreigners', we did not realize that these rituals must be kept light in tone and general in theme.

When we two got to the door of the building, there was a mob outside, mostly of older animals, very hostile. The managers of the ritual game pulled us back and took us up to the top of the building and set guards on us, as apparently the mob was angered to the point of wishing to kill us – again, the focus of their anger was that we were foreign. We complied, since there was no point in creating further disorder and ——— ... BRING YOUR DECEASED TO US, WHO ARE FRIENDS OF YOUR FAMILY, FRIENDS IN YOUR DISTRESS. TREATED WITH ALL REVERENCE, CARED FOR AS YOU CARED WHEN MOTHER, FATHER, HUSBAND, WIFE, BROTHER OR LITTLE SISTER WAS STILL WITH YOU, THE SLEEPING ONE WILL BE BORNE TO THE LAST HOME, LAID GENTLY TO REST IN A PLOT WHERE FLOWERS AND BIRDS WILL ALWAYS PLAY AND WHERE YOU CAN VISIT AND MUSE ... IN YOUR LEISURE HOURS, YOU WILL ALWAYS HAVE A HAVEN WHERE YOUR THOUGHTS CAN DWELL IN LOVING HAPPINESS ON YOUR DEPARTED FRIENDS, WHO ——— ... We are running very short of power. There is nothing more we can do. This mission must be regarded as a failure. We have been able to achieve nothing. We have also failed to understand what is the cause of their defectiveness. There is no species like this one on any other planet known to us.

As the guards on our place of detention relaxed their vigilance, we simply dematerialized and returned to the craft. They will think we escaped or perhaps were the subjects of kidnapping by the still-hostile crowd that we could see from the top of the building where —— ... SHOCKING AND DISGUSTING PROGRAMME THAT OFFENDED IN A WAY NO OTHER PRO-GRAMME HAS IN THIS COMMENTATOR'S MEMORY. IT IS NOT WHAT WAS SAID BY OUR TWO VISITORS, IT WAS THE WAY IT WAS SAID. AFTER ALL, WE ALL HAVE TO LIVE WITH 'THE FACTS' THAT THEY SO NAIVELY SEEM TO IMAGINE ARE A REVELATION TO US. FOR SHEER BAD TASTE, CRUDITY OF TONE, UGLINESS OF MANNER AND INSENSITIVITY TO THE DEEPER FEELINGS OF THE VIEW-ERS, NOTHING CAN BE COMPARED WITH PROFESSORS BOND AND HUNTER LAST NIGHT.

Departure from the Planet

We are now reassembled as our original six and will shortly be returning. We have a tentative conclusion. It is this: that a society that is doomed to catastrophe, and that is unable to pre-pare for it, can expect that few people will survive except those already keyed to chaos and disaster. The civil, the ordered, the conforming, the well-tempered, can expect to fall victim at first exposure. But the vagabonds, criminals, mad, extremely poor, will have the means to survive. We conclude therefore, that when, within the next five years, the eruption occurs, no one will be left but those types the present managers of society consider undesirable, for the present society is too inflexible to adapt – as we have already said, we have no idea why this should be so, what is wrong with them. But perhaps concealed in this city are groups of individuals we did not contact, who saw no reason to contact us, who not only foresee the future even but who are taking steps to –

*

THE WEST COAST EXAMINER

Sam Baker, a farmer from Long Ridge, said he saw a 'shining round thing' take off one hundred yards away from his fence yesterday evening as the sun went down. Says Sam: 'It rose into the air at such a rate it was almost impossible to follow it with my eyes. Then it disappeared.' Others from the same area claim to have seen 'unusual sights' during the past few days. The official explanation is that the unusually vivid sunsets of the past month have caused strong reflections and mirages off rocks and stretches of sand.

Military Sector III to H.Q.
(Top Confidential)

The U.F.O. that landed some time in the night of the 14th, and was viewed as it landed, remained stationary for the entire period of seven days. No one was seen to leave the U.F.O. This is exactly in line with the previous 12 landings in the same spot. This was the 13th U.F.O. of this series. But this was rather larger and more powerful than the previous 12. The difference registered by Sonoscope 15 was considerable. This U.F.O., like the previous 12, was only just visible to ordinary vision. Our observer, farmer Jansen H. Blackson, recruited by us after the first landing a year ago, volunteered that this one was much more easily seen. 'You had to stare hard to see the others, but I saw this one coming down, also lifting off, but it went up so fast I lost it at once.' The suggestion from M 8 is that all 13 are observation craft from the Chinese. The view of this section is that they are from our Naval Department 15, and it is our contention that as they have no right to access to this terrain, which is under the aegis of War Department 4, we should blast them to hell and gone next time they try it on.

Air Force 14 to Centre

The alightings continue – Number 13 last week. This was also unmanned. Confirm belief Russian origin. Must report also two further landings to the south of the city, both in the same place and separated by an interval of three weeks. These two craft identical with the series of 55 alighting to north of city last year. The two southern landings coincided with the disappearance of 11 people, five the first time, six the second. This makes 450 people gone without trace during the past two years. We suggest it is no longer possible to dismiss the fact that the landings of these craft always mean the disappearance of two to ten people with the word 'coincidence'. We must face the possibility that all or some are manned, but by individuals so dissimilar in structure to ourselves that we cannot see them. We would point out that Sonoscope 4 is only just able to bring these types of craft within vision and that, therefore, the levels of density that might indicate the presence of 'people' might escape the machine. We further suggest that the facetiousness of the phrase 'little green men' might mask an atttiude of mind that is inimical to a sober evaluation or assessment of this possibility.

Confirm at earliest if we are to continue policy of minimizing these disappearances. We can still find no common denominator in the *type* of person taken off. The only thing they all have in common is that they were, for a variety of reasons, somewhere in the areas in which these craft choose to descend.

THE WEST COAST EXAMINER

Our observer at filling station Lost Pine reports that groups of people are driving south out of the city to the area where the latest U.F.O.s are known to descend and take off. Last night they numbered over 50,000

Air Force 14 to Centre

In spite of Total Policy 19, rumours are out. We consider it advisable to cordon off the area, although this might precipitate extreme panic situation. But we see no alternative. The cult called Be Ready for the Day is already thousands strong and sweeping the city and environs. Suggest an announcement that the area is contaminated with a chance leak of radio-activity.

Not a Very Nice Story

This story is difficult to tell. Where to put the emphasis? Whose perspective to use? For to tell it from the point of view of the lovers (but that was certainly not their word for themselves – from the viewpoint, then, of the guilty couple) – is as if a life were to be described through the eyes of some person who scarcely appeared in it; as if a cousin from Canada had visited, let's say, a farmer in Cornwall half a dozen unimportant times, and then wrote as if these meetings had been the history of the farm and the family. Or it is as if a stretch of years were to be understood in terms of the extra day in Leap Year.

To put it conventionally is simple: two marriages, both as happy as marriages are, both exemplary from society's point of view, contained a shocking flaw, a secret cancer, a hidden vice.

But this hidden horror did not rot the marriages, and seemed hardly to matter at all: the story can't be told as the two betrayed ones saw it; they didn't see it. They saw nothing. There would be nothing to tell.

Now, all this was true for something like twenty years; then something happened which changed the situation. To be precise, what happened was the death of one of the four people concerned. But at any moment during those twenty years, what has been said would have been true: conventional morality would judge these marriages to have a secret face all lies and lust; from the adulterers' point of view, what they did was not much more important that sharing a taste for eating chocolate after the doctor has said no.

After that death, however, the shift of emphasis: the long unimportance of the twenty years of chocolate-eating could be seen as a prelude to something very different; could be seen as heartless frivolity or callousness redeemed providentially by responsibility? But suppose the death had not occurred?

It is hard to avoid the thought that all these various ways of looking at the thing are nonsense . . .

Frederick Jones married Althea, Henry Smith married Muriel, at the same time, that is in 1947. Both men, both women, had been much involved in the war, sometimes dangerously. But now it was over, they knew that it had been the way it had gone on and on that had affected them most. It had been endless.

There is no need to say much about their emotions when they married. Frederick and Althea, Henry and Muriel, felt exactly as they might be expected to feel, being their sort of people – middle-class, liberal, rather literary – and in their circumstances, which emotionally consisted of hungers of all kinds, but particularly for security, affection, warmth, these hungers having been heightened beyond normal during the long war. They were all four aware of their condition, were able to see themselves with the wryly tolerant eye of their kind. For they at all times knew to a fraction of a degree the state of their emotional pulse, and were much given to intelligent discussion of their individual psychologies.

Yet in spite of views about themselves which their own parents would have regarded as intolerable to live with, their plans and aims for themselves were similar to those of their parents at the same age. Both couples wished and expected that their marriages would be the bedrock of their lives, that they would have children and bring them up well. And it turned out as they wanted. They also expected that they would be faithful to each other.

At the time these marriages took place, the couples had not met. Both Dr Smith and Dr Jones, separately, had had the idea of going into partnership and possibly founding a clinic in a poor area. Both had been made idealists by the war, even socialists of a non–ideological sort. They advertised, made contact by letter, liked each other, and bought a practice in a country town in the West of England where there would be many poor people to look after, as well as the rich.

Houses were bought, not far from each other. While the two

men were already friends, with confidence in being able to work together, the wives had not met. It was agreed that it was high time this event should take place. An occasion was to be made of it. The four were to meet for dinner in a pub five miles outside the little town. That they should all get on well was known by them to be important. In fact both women had made small humorous complaints that if their 'getting on' was really considered so important, then why had their meeting been left so late?

As the two cars drove up to the country inn, the same state of affairs prevailed in each. There was bad humour. The women felt they were being patronized, the men felt that the women were probably right but were being unreasonable in making a fuss when after all the main thing was to get settled in work and in their homes. All four were looking forward to that dinner – the inn was known for its food – while for their different reasons they resented being there at all. They arrived in each other's presence vivid with variegated emotions. The women at once knew they liked each other – but, after all, they might very well have not liked each other! – and made common cause about the men. The four went into the bar, where they were an animated and combative group.

By the time they moved into the dining-room ill-humour had vanished. There they sat, with their wine and good food. They were attracting attention, because they were obviously dressed up for a special occasion, but chiefly because of their own consciousness of well-being. This was the peak of their lives; the long tedium of the war was over; the men were still in their early thirties, the women in their twenties. They were feeling as if at last their real lives were starting. They were all good-looking. The men were of the same type: jokes had been made about that already. They were both dark, largely built, with the authority of doctors, 'comfortable' as the wives said. And the women were pretty. They soon established (like showing each other their passports, or references of decency and reliability) that they shared views on life – tough, but rewarding; God – dead; children – to be brought up with the right blend of permissiveness and discipline; society – to be cured by common sense and mild firmness but without extremes of any sort.

Everything was well for them; everything would get better.

They sat a long time over their food, their wine, and their happiness, and left only when the pub closed, passing into a cold clear night, frost on the ground. It happened that conversations between Frederick Jones and Muriel Smith, Althea Jones and Henry Smith, were in progress, and the couples, so arranged, stood by their respective cars.

'Come back to us for a nightcap,' said Henry, assisting his colleague's wife in beside him, and drove off home.

Frederick and Muriel, not one word having been said, watched them go, then turned to each other and embraced. This embrace can best be described as being the inevitable continuation of their conversation. Frederick then drove a few hundred yards into a small wood, where the frost shone on the grass, stopped the car, flung down his coat, and then he and Muriel made love – no, that's not right, had sex, with vigour and relish and enjoyment, while nothing lay between them and their nakedness and some degrees of frost but a layer of tweed. They then dressed, got back into the car, and went back to town, where Frederick drove Muriel to her own home, came in with her for the promised nightcap, and took his own wife home.

Both married couples made extensive love that night, as the atmosphere all evening had promised they would.

Muriel and Frederick did not examine their behaviour as much as such compulsive examiners of behaviour might have been expected to do. The point was, the incident was out of character, unlike them, so very much *not* what they believed in, that they didn't know what to think about it, let alone what to feel. Muriel had always set her face against the one-night stand. Trivial, she had said it was – the word 'sordid' was over-moral. Frederick, both professionally and personally, had a lot to say about the unsatisfactory nature of casual sexual relationships. In his consulting room he would show carefully measured disapproval for the results – venereal disease or pregnancy – of such relations. It was not a moral judgement he was making, he always said; no, it was a hygienic one. He had been heard to use the word 'messy'. Both these people had gone in, one could say on principle, for the serious affair, the deep involvement. Even in wartime, neither had had casual sex.

So while it was hardly possible that such extraordinary behaviour could be forgotten, neither thought about it: the incident could not be included in their view of themselves.

And besides, there was so much to do, starting the new practice, arranging the new homes.

Besides too, both couples were so pleased with each other, and had such a lot of love to make.

About six weeks after that evening at the pub, Frederick had to drop in to Henry and Muriel's to pick up something, and found Muriel alone. Again, not one word having been said, they went to the bedroom and – but I think the appropriate word here is screwed. Thoroughly and at length.

They parted; and again unable to understand themselves, let the opportunity to think about what had happened slide away.

The thing was too absurd! They could not say, for instance, that during that famous evening at the pub, when they first met, that they had eyed each other with incipient desire, or had sent out messages of need or intent. They had not done more than to say to themselves, as one does: I'd like to make love with this man, this woman, if I wasn't well-suited already. They certainly could not have said that during the intervening six weeks they had dreamed of each other, finding their actual partners unsatisfactory. Far from it.

For if these, Muriel and Frederick, were natural sexual partners, then so were Frederick and Althea, Henry and Muriel.

If we now move on ten years and look back, as the guilty couple, Frederick and Muriel, then did – or, rather, as both couples did, ten years being a natural time or place for such compulsive self-examiners to make profit-and-loss accounts – it is only in an effort to give the right emphasis to the thing.

For it is really hard to get the perspective right. Suppose that I had, in fact, described the emotions of the two very emotional courtships, the emotional and satisfying affairs that preceded marriage, the exciting discoveries of marriage and the depths and harmonies both couples found, and had then said, simply: on many occasions two of these four people committed adultery, without forethought or afterthought, and these adulterous episodes, though extremely enjoyable, had no effect whatever on the marriages – thus making them sound something like small bits of grit in mouthfuls of honey. Well, but even the best of marriages can hardly be described as honey. Perhaps it is that word adultery – too weighty? redolent of divorces and French farce? Yet it is still in use, very much so: it is a word that people think, and not only in the law courts.

Perhaps, to get the right emphasis, in so far as those sexual episodes were having an effect on the marriages, one might as well not mention them at all? But not to mention them is just as impossible – apart from what happened in the end, the end of the story. For surely it is absolutely outside what we all know to be psychologically possible for the partners of happy marriages, both of them founded on truth and love and total commitment, to have casual sex with close mutual friends – thus betraying their marriages, their relationships, themselves and for these betrayals to have no effect on them at all?

No guilt? No private disquiet? What was felt when, gazing into their loving partners' eyes, with everything open and frank between them, Frederick, Muriel, had to think: How can I treat my trusting partner like this?

They had no such thoughts. For ten years the marriages had prospered side by side. The Joneses had produced three children, the Smiths two. The young doctors worked hard, as doctors do. In the two comfortable gardened houses, the two attractive young wives worked as hard as wives and mothers do. And all that time the marriages were being assessed by very different standards, which had nothing to do with those trivial and inelegant acts of sex – which continued whenever circumstances allowed, quite often, though neither guilty partner searched for occasions – all that time the four people continued to take their emotional pulses, as was their training: the marriages were satisfactory; no, not so satisfactory; yes, very good again. It was better in the second year than in the first, but less good in the third than in the fourth. The children brought the couples closer together in some ways, but not in others – and so on. Frederick was glad he had married delightful and sexy little Althea; and she was glad she had married Frederick, whose calm strength was her admirable complement. And Henry was pleased with Muriel, so vivacious, fearless and self-sufficing; and Muriel was similarly glad she had chosen Henry, whose quietly humorous mode of dealing with life always absorbed any temporary disquiets she might be suffering.

All four, of course, would sometimes wonder if they should have married at all, in the way everyone does; and all four would discuss with themselves and with each other, or as a foursome, the ghastliness of marriage as an institution and how it should be abolished and something else put in its place. Sometimes, in the grip of a passing attraction for someone else, all four might regret that their choices were now narrowed down to one. (At such times neither Frederick nor Muriel thought of each other; they took each other for granted, since they were always available, like marriage partners.) In short, and to be done with it, at the end of ten years, and during the soul-searching and book-keeping that went on then, both couples could look back on marriages that had in every way fulfilled what they had expected, even in the way of 'taking the rough with the smooth'. For where is the pleasure in sweet-without-sour? In spite of, because of, sexually exciting times and chilly times, of temporary hostilities and harmonies, of absences or illnesses, of yearning, briefly, for others – because of all this they had enjoyed a decade of profoundly emotional experience. In joy or in pain, they could not complain about flatness, or absence of sensation. And after all, emotion is the thing, we can none of us get enough of it.

What transports the couples had suffered! What tears the two women had wept! What long delicious nights spent on prolonged sexual pleasure! What quarrels and crises and dramas! What depth of experience everywhere! And now the five children, each one an emotion in itself, each one an extension of emotion, claiming the future for similar pleasurable or at least sensational rivers of feeling.

It was round about the eleventh year that there came a moment of danger to them all. Althea fell in love with a young doctor who had come to help in the practice while the two senior doctors took leave. The two families usually took holidays together, but this time the men went off tramping in Scotland leaving the women and children.

Althea confided in Muriel. It was not a question of leaving her Frederick: certainly not. She could bear to hurt neither him nor the children. But she was suffering horribly, from desire and all kinds of suddenly discovered deprivations, for the sake of the young man with whom she had slept half a dozen times furtively – horrible word! – when the children were playing in the garden or were asleep at night. Her whole life seemed a desert of dust and ashes. She could not bear the future. What was the point of living?

The two young women sat talking in Althea's kitchen.

They were at either end of the breakfast table around which so many jolly occasions had been shared by them all. Althea was weeping.

Perhaps this is the place to describe these two women. Althea was a small round dark creature, who always smelled delightful, and who was described by her husband as the most eminently satisfactory blend of femininity and common sense. As for Muriel, she was a strong large-boned woman, fair, with the kind of skin that tans quickly, so that she always looked very healthy. Her clothes were of the kind called casual, and she took a lot of trouble over them. Both women of course often yearned to be like the other.

These two different women sat stirring coffee-cups as they had done a hundred times, while the five children shouted, competed and loved in the garden, and Althea wept, because she said this was a watershed in her marriage, like eating the apple in Eden. If she told her beloved husband that she was – temporarily, she did so hope and believe – besottedly in love with this young doctor, then it must be the end of everything between them. But if she didn't tell him, then it was betrayal. Whatever she did would have terrible results. *Not* telling Frederick seemed to her worse even than the infidelity itself. She had never, ever, concealed anything from him. Perfect frankness and sincerity had been their rule – no, not a rule, they had never had to lay down rules for behaviour that came so excellently and simply out of their love and trust. She could not imagine keeping anything from Frederick. And she was sure he told her everything. She could not bear it, would certainly leave him at once, if she knew that he had ever lied to her. No, she would not mind infidelity of a certain kind – how could she mind? – now that she forfeited any rights in the matter! But lies, deceptions, furtiveness – no, that would be the end, the end of everything.

Althea and Muriel stayed together, while one woman wept and talked and the other listened, stopping only when the children came in, for all that day, and all the next, and for several after that. For Muriel was understanding that it was the words and tears that were the point, not what was said: soon the energy of suffering, the tension of conflict, would have spent itself, making it all seem less important. But Muriel was determined not to listen for one minute more than was necessary. And soon she was able to advise Althea, the tears having abated, not to tell her Fred anything at all, she would just have to learn to live with a lie.

And now of course she had to think, really to think, whether she liked it or not, about the way she had been making love – or sex – in a frivolous, and some people might say sordid, way with her best friend's husband. She was being made to think. Most definitely she did not want to think it was extraordinary, the strength of her instinct *not* to examine that area of her life.

However, examining it, or, rather, touching lightly on it, she was able to congratulate herself, or, rather, both herself and dear Fred, that never had they in the presence of their spouses enjoyed that most awful of betrayals, enjoyment of their complicity while their said spouses remained oblivious. She could not remember ever, when together, their so much as looking at each other in an invitation to make love, or sex; she was positive they had never once allowed their eyes to signal: These poor fools don't know our secret. For certainly they had never felt like this. They had not ever, not once, made plans to meet alone. They might have fallen into each other's arms the moment the opportunity offered, as if no other behaviour was possible to them, but they did not engineer opportunities. And, having arrived in each other's arms, all laughter and pleasure, there was never a feeling of having gone one better than Althea and Henry, of doing them down in any way. And having separated, they did not think about what had happened, or consider their partners; it was as if these occasions belonged to another plane altogether – that trivial, sordid and unimportant, that friendly, good-natured and entirely enjoyable plane that lay beside, or above, or within, these two so satisfactory marriages.

It occurred to Muriel that its nature, its essence, was lack of emotion. Her feeling for Frederick, what Frederick felt for her, was all calm sense and pleasure, with not so much as a twinge of that yearning anguish we call being in love.

And, thinking about it all, as these long sessions with weeping and miserable (enjoyably miserable?) Althea had made her do, she understood, and became determined to hold on to, her belief that her instinct, or compulsion, never to examine, brood or make emotional profit-and-loss accounts about the sex she had with Frederick was healthy. For as soon as she did put weight on that area, start to measure and weigh, all sorts of sensations hitherto foreign to this relationship began to gabble and gobble, insist and demand. Guilt, for one.

She came to a conclusion. It was so seditious of any idea held in common by these four and their kind that she had to look at it, as it were, sideways. It was this: that very likely the falling-in-love with the young doctor was not at all as Althea was seeing it (as anyone was likely to see it); the point was not the periods of making love – love, not sex! – which of course had been all rapture, though muted, inevitably, with their particular brand of wry and civilized understanding, but it was the spilling of emotion afterwards, the anguish, the guilt. Emotion was the point. Great emotion had been felt, had been suffered. Althea had suffered, was suffering abominably. Everyone had got it wrong:

the real motive for such affairs was the need to suffer the pain
and the yearning afterwards.

The two marriages continued to grow like trees, sheltering the
children who flourished beneath them.

Soon, they had been married fifteen years.

There occurred another crisis, much worse.

Its prelude was this. Owing to a set of circumstances not important – Althea had to visit a sick mother and took the children;
the Smith children went to visit a grandmother – Frederick and
Muriel spent two weeks alone with each other. Ostensibly they
were in their separate homes, but they were five minutes' drive
from each other, and not even in a gossipy inbred little English
town could neighbours see anything wrong in two people being
together a lot who were with each other constantly year in and
out.

It was a time of relaxation. Of enjoyment. Of quiet. They
spent nights in the same bed – for the first time. They took long
intimate meals together alone, for the first time. They had seldom
been alone together, when they came to think of it. It was extraordinary how communal it was, the life of the Joneses and the
Smiths.

Their relationship, instead of being the fleeting, or flighty,
thing it had been – rolls in the hay (literally), or in the snow, an
hour on the drawing-room carpet, a quick touch-up in a telephone booth – was suddenly all dignity, privacy and leisure.

And now Frederick showed a disposition to responsible feeling
– love was the word he insisted on using – while Muriel ner-
vously implored him not to be solemn. He pointed out that he
was betraying his beloved Althea, that she was betraying her darling Henry, and that this was what they had been doing for years
and years, and without a twinge of guilt or a moment's reluctance.

And without, Muriel pointed out, *feeling*.

Ah yes, she was right, how awful, he was really beginnig to
feel that . . .

For God's sake, she cried, stop it, don't spoil everything, can't
you see the dogs of destruction are sniffing at our door? Stop it,

darling Fred, I won't have you using words like love, no, no, that is our redeeming point, our strength – we haven't been in love, we have never agonized over each other, desired each other, missed each other, wanted each other; we have not ever 'felt' anything for each other ...

Frederick allowed it to be seen that he found this view of them too cool, if not heartless.

But, she pointed out, what they had done was to help each other in every way, to be strong pillars in a foursome, to rejoice at the birth of each other's children, to share ideas and read books recommended by the other. They had enjoyed random and delightful and irresponsible sex without a twang of conscience when they could – had, in short, lived for fifteen years in close harmony.

Fred called her an intelligent woman.

During that fortnight love was imminent on at least a dozen occasions. She resisted.

But there was no doubt, and Muriel saw this with an irritation made strong by self-knowledge – for of course she would have adored to be 'in love' with Frederick, to anguish and weep and lie awake – that Frederick, by the time his wife came back, was feeling thoroughly deprived. His Muriel had deprived him. Of emotional experience.

Ah emotion, emotion, let us bathe in thee!

For instance, the television, that mirror of us all:

A man has crashed his car, and his wife and three children have burned to death.

'And what did you feel when this happened?' asks the bland, but humanly concerned, young interviewer. 'Tell us, what did you *feel*?'

Or, two astronauts have just survived thirty-six hours when every second might have meant their deaths.

'What did you feel? Please tell us, what did you feel?'

Or, a woman's two children have spent all night exposed on a mountain-top but were rescued alive.

'What did you feel?' cries the interviewer. 'What did you feel while you were waiting?'

An old woman has been rescued from a burning building by a passer-by, but for some minutes had every reason to think that her end had come.

'What did you feel? You thought your number was up, you said that, didn't you? What did you feel when you thought that?'

What do you think I felt, you silly nit, what would you have felt in my place? What does everybody watching this programme know perfectly well that I felt? So why ask me when you know already?

Why, madam? – of course it is because feeling is our substitute for tortured slaves and dying gladiators. We have to feel sad, anxious, worried, joyful, agonized, delighted. I feel. You feel. They felt. I felt. We were feeling . . . If we don't feel, then how can we believe that anything is happening to us at all?

And since none of us feel as much as we have been trained to believe that we ought to feel in order to prove ourselves profound and sincere people, then luckily here is the television where we can see other people feeling for us. So tell me, madam, what did you *feel* while you stood there believing that you were going to be burned to death? Meanwhile the viewers will be chanting our creed: We feel, therefore we are.

Althea came back, the children came back, life went on, and Frederick almost at once fell violently in love with a girl of twenty who had applied to be a receptionist in the surgery. And Muriel felt exactly the same, but on the emotional plane, as a virtuously frigid wife felt – so we are told – when her husband went to a prostitute: If I had only given him what he wanted, he wouldn't have gone to *her*!

For she knew that her Frederick would not have fallen in love with the girl if she had allowed him to be in love with her. He had had an allowance of 'love' to be used up, because he had not understood – he had only said that he did – that he was wanting to fall in love: he needed the condition of being in love, needed to feel all that. Or, as Muriel muttered (but only very privately, and to herself), he needed to suffer. She should have allowed him to suffer. It is clear that everybody needs it.

And now there was the crisis, a nasty one, which rocked all four of them. Althea was unhappy, because her marriage was at stake; Frederick was talking of a divorce. And of course she was remembering her lapse with the young doctor four years before, and the living lie she had so ably maintained since. And Frederick was suicidal, because he was not so stupid as not to know that to leave a wife he adored, and was happy with, for the sake of a girl of twenty was – stupid. He was past forty-five. But he had never loved before, he said. He actually said this, and to Henry, who told Muriel.

Henry, who so far had not contributed a crisis, now revealed that he had suffered similarly some years before, but 'it had not seemed important'. He confessed this to Muriel, who felt some irritation. For one thing, she felt she had never really appreciated Henry as he deserved, because the way he said 'it had not seemed important' surely should commend itself to her? Yet it did not; she felt in some ridiculous way belittled because he made light of what had been – surely? – a deep experience? And if it had not, why not? And then, she felt she had been betrayed; that she was able to say to herself she was being absurd did not help. In short, suddenly Muriel was in a bad way. More about Frederick than about Henry. Deprived in a flash of years of sanity, she submerged under waves of jealousy of the young girl, of deprivation – but of what? what? she was in fact deprived of nothing! – of sexual longing, and of emotional loneliness. Her Henry, she had always known, was a cold fish. Their happiness had been a half-thing. Her own potential had always been in cold storage. And so she raged and suffered, for the sake of Frederick, her real love – so she felt now. Her only love. How could she have been so mad as not to enjoy being really in love, two weeks of love. How could she not have seen, all those years, where the truth lay. How could she . . .

That was what she felt. What she *thought*, and knew, was that she was mad. Everything she felt now had nothing, but nothing, to do with her long relationship with Frederick, which was as pleasant as a good healthy diet and as unremarkable, and nothing to do with her marriage with Henry, whom she loved deeply, and who made her happy, and whose humorous and civilized company she enjoyed more than anyone's.

Frederick brought his great love to an end. Or, to put it accurately, it was brought to an end: the girl married. For a while he sulked; he could not forgive life for his being nearly fifty. Althea helped him come back to himself, and to their life together.

Muriel and Henry re-established their loving equilibrium.

Muriel and Frederick for a long time did not, when they found themselves together, make sex. That phase had ended, so they told each other when they had a discussion: they had never had a discussion of this sort before, and the fact that they were having one seemed proof indeed that they had finished with each other. It happened that this talk was taking place in his car, he having picked her up from some fête given to raise funds for the local hospital. Althea had not been able to attend. The children, once enjoyers of such affairs, were getting too old for them. Muriel was attending on behalf of them all, and Frederick was giving her a lift home. Frederick stopped the car on the edge of a small wood, which was now damp and brown with winter: this desolation seemed a mirror of their own dimmed and ageing state. Suddenly, no word having been spoken, they were in an embrace – and, shortly thereafter, on top of his coat and under hers in a clump of young birches whose shining winter branches dropped large tingling lively drops tasting of wet bark on to their naked cheeks and arms.

But, the psychologically oriented reader will be demanding, what about those children? Adolescent by now, surely?

Quite right. The four had become background figures for the dramas of the young ones' adolescence; their passions were reflections of their children's; and part of their self-knowledge had to be that Frederick's need to be in love and the associated traumas were sparked off by the adults being continually stimulated by their five attractive offspring, all of whom were of course perpetually in love or in hate.

It goes without saying, too, that the parents felt even more guilty and inadequate because they worried that their lapses, past, present and imaginary, might have contributed to the stormy miseries of the children. Which we all know too well to have to go through again. But what violence! what quarrels! what anguish! Adolescence is like this, we all know, and so do the children. The Jones and Smith youngsters behaved exactly as they were expected to. Oh the dramas and the rebellions, the leavings-of-home and the sullen returns; oh the threats of drug-taking, then the drug-taking and the return to caution; the near-pregnancies, the droppings out and in, the ups and downs at schools, the screamed accusations at the parents for their total stupidity, backwardness, thickheadedness and responsibility for all the ills in the world.

But just as the script prescribes crisis, so it prescribes the end of crisis. Those five attractive young people, with benefits of a sound middle-class background and its institutions, with their good education, with their intelligent and concerned parents – what could go wrong? Nothing did. They did well enough at school and were soon to go to university. Could they have any other future beyond being variations on the theme of their parents?

Twenty years had passed.

There came an opportunity for the two doctors to join a large doctors' combine in London. It was in a working-class area, but the senior doctors had consulting rooms in Harley Street. Doctors Smith and Jones had continued idealistic, conditionally socialist, and were shocked by the thought that they might also succumb to what they thought of as a Jekyll and Hyde existence.

The two families decided to buy a very large house in North London, and to divide it. That way they would all have much more space than if they each had a house. And the children were more like brothers and sisters and should not be separated by anything as arbitrary as a move to a new home.

Soon after the move to London Henry died. There was no sense in him dying in his fifties. He had thought of himself as healthy, almost as immortal. But he had always smoked heavily, he was rather plump, and he worked very hard. These were reasons enough, it was thought, for him to have a stroke and for Muriel to be a widow in her forties.

Muriel stayed in the shared house with her two children, a boy of eighteen and a girl of fourteen. After discussing it thoroughly with Althea, Frederick made arrangements to help support Muriel, to be a father to the children, to support this other family as he was sure Henry would have done for Althea and the three children if it had been Frederick who had had the stroke. As it might have been: Frederick's habits and constitution were similar to Henry's. Frederick was secretly frightened, made resolutions to eat less, smoke less, work less, worry less: but he was doing more of everything because Henry had gone.

In order to support his greater responsibilities, Frederick attended two days a week and a morning in Harley Street – Muriel acted as his receptionist there, and for the two other doctors who shared his set of rooms. He also worked hard in the combine's clinics, making up by evening sessions and night visiting for time spent in Moneyland. So Frederick and Muriel were now working together, as well as seeing each other constantly in the much-shared family life. Muriel was more with Frederick than Althea was.

And now that Muriel was a widow, and the opportunities were more, the sex life of the two had become as stable as good married sex.

Muriel, thinking about it, had decided that it was probable Frederick had deliberately 'stepped up' his sexual life with her because he knew she must be feeling sexually deprived. This was very likely the kind of sexually friendly consideration that would happen in a polygamous marriage? What made her come to this conclusion was that now they would often cuddle as married people do, for instance staying an hour or so after time in the Harley Street rooms, their arms around each other, discussing the day's problems, or perhaps driving off on to Hampstead Heath to discuss the children, sharing warmth and affection – like married people.

For Fred could hardly be missing this sort of affection, far from it, and that he was giving it to her must be the result of a conscious decision, of kindness.

They sometimes did say to each other that what they all had

together – but only they two knew it – was a polygamous marriage.

When in company, and people were discussing marriage, the marriage problems of Western man, the problems caused by the emancipation of women, monogamy, fidelity, whether one should 'tell' or not, these two tended to remain silent or to make indifferent remarks that sounded in spite of themselves impatient – as people do when entertaining inadmissible thoughts.

Both of them, the man and the woman, had found themselves thinking, had even heard themselves exclaiming aloud as the result of such thoughts, 'What a lot of rubbish, what lies!' – meaning, no less, these intelligent and sensible ideas we all do have about the famous Western problematical marriage.

Muriel had only understood that she was married to Frederick when she started to think about marrying again: but it was not likely that anyone would want to marry a 45-year-old woman with children at their most demanding and difficult time. She could not imagine marrying again: for it would mean the end of her marriage with Frederick. This was probably how they would all go on, into their old age, or until one of them died.

This was Muriel's thinking on the situation.

Frederick: Muriel was right, he had indeed thought carefully about his old friend's loneliness. She would probably not marry again: she was not after all of the generation where there were more men than women. And there was something too independent and touch-me-not about her. Her silences were challenging. Her green eyes were outspoken. A tall rangy woman with bronze hair (she dyed it), people noticed her, and called her beautiful or striking: of her, people used the strong adjectives. The older she got, the dryer and cooler became her way of talking. Enemies called her unkind, or masculine; friends, witty. *He* enjoyed these qualities, but would he if they were not the other half, as it were, of Althea? Whom people tended to call 'little'. So did he. Dear little Althea.

He would give Muriel as much warmth, as much sex, as he could, without of course giving any less to his wife. For years his relations with Muriel had been all jam, nothing to pay, a bonus.

Now he felt her as part of his sudden increase in responsibility when Henry died, part of what he must give to the two children. He was fond of Muriel – indeed, he was sure he loved her. He knew he loved the children almost as well as his own. It was an ungrudging giving of himself – but there was something else in him, another worm was at work. For what was strongest in Frederick now neither his wife nor Muriel knew anything about. It was his longing for the girl Frances – married with children. Neither of his women had understood how deep that had gone. He had not understood it himself at the time.

Now, years later, it seemed to him that his life was divided between dark, or perhaps a clear flat grey, and light – Frances. Between everything heavy, plodding, difficult, and everything delicious – Frances. Nothing in his actual life fed delight or sprang from it: somewhere else was a sweetness and ease which he had known once, when he had loved Frances.

By now he did know that Frances, a lovely but quite ordinary girl, must be a stand-in for something else. It must be so. No small human being could possibly support the weight of such a force and a fierceness of longing, of want, of need. From time to time, when he straightened himself morally, and physically, for it was like a physical anguish, from a pain that swept all through him, or when he woke up in the morning out of a dream that was all pain of loss to see Althea's sleeping face a few inches away on the other pillow, he had to tell himself this: It is not possible that I am suffering all this, year after year, because of a girl I was in love with for a few crazy months.

Yet that was how it felt. On one side was the life he actually led; on the other, 'Frances'.

His intelligence told him everything it ought, such as that if he had been fool enough to leave Althea for Frances, or if Frances had been fool enough to marry him, in a very short time Frances would have been a dear known face on a shared pillow, and what Frances had represented would have moved its quarters elsewhere.

But that was not what he felt. Although he worked so hard – it was virtually two jobs that he had now, one with the poor and the ignorant, for whom he remained concerned, and one with the rich; although he maintained with the most tender love and consideration the emotional and physical needs of the two women; although he was a good and tactful father for five children – he felt he had nothing, lacked everything.

Althea ... we move into the shoes, or behind the eyes, of the innocent party.

These three people had all taken on loads with the death of Henry. With Muriel working, Althea's was to run all the large house, to do the shopping, to cook, to be always available for the children. She did not mind it, she had never wanted a career. But it was hard work, and soon she felt herself to be all drudgery and domesticity, and just at the time when, with the children older, she had looked forward to less. But this strain was nothing compared to the real one, which was that she had cared very much about being so attractive, and cherished for it. Cherished no less, she demanded even more of her vanishing looks. She could not bear to think that soon she would be elderly, soon Frederick would not want her. Comparing her tragic sessions in front of her mirror, and her feelings of inadequacy, with her husband's affection, she knew that she was unreasonable. Well, it was probably the 'change'.

She read many medical books and consulted another doctor – not one her husband knew – and got pills and came to regard her emotional state, all of it, everything she thought and felt, as a symptom without validity.

For she knew that her relationship with her husband was warm, good – wonderful. While other people's marriages frayed and cracked and fell apart, hers, she knew, was solid.

But when she looked at her life, when she looked back, she too divided what she saw into two. For her, the sunlit time lay on the other side of the affair with the young doctor. It was not the physical thing she regretted, no; it was that she had not told her husband. Time had done nothing at all to soften her guilt about it. Frederick and she had known a time of perfection, of complete trust and belief. Then she, Althea, had chosen to destroy it. It was her fault that he had fallen so much in love with the girl

Frances. Oh, he was likely to fall in love with someone at some point: of course, everyone did – hadn't she? But so violently? That could only have been because of some deep lack between them. And she knew what it was: she had told him lies, had not trusted him.

She was left now with much more than she deserved. If she had to share him now – a little, with Muriel – then it was what she deserved. Besides, if she, Althea, had been left a widow, then she would have leaned as heavily on Henry. On whom else?

Sometimes Althea had wild moments when she decided to tell Frederick about the young doctor; but that would be absurd, out of proportion. To talk about it now, would surely be to destroy what they still had? To say: For more than a decade now I have been lying to you – she could not imagine herself actually doing it.

Sometimes she listened to other people talking about their marriages, and it seemed to her that they were able to take infidelities much more lightly. Lies, too. Althea kept telling herself that there must be something very wrong in her that she had to keep brooding about it, worrying, grieving.

For instance, there were these people who went in for wife-swopping. They thought nothing of making love in heaps and in bunches, all together. Some of them said their marriages were strengthened – perhaps they were. Perhaps if she and her Fred had shared each other with other couples ... Who, Muriel and Henry? – no, surely that could be too dangerous, too close? Surely they – the wife-swoppers – made a rule not to get involved too close to home? But that was not the point at all, the point was, the lying, the deception.

The fact was, the only person in the world who knew all the truth about her was Muriel! Muriel had known about the young doctor, and knew about the years of lying. How odd that was, for your woman friend to be closer than your own husband! It was *intolerable.* Unbearable. Althea found it horrible to say to herself: I trust Muriel more than I do Frederick; my behaviour has proved that I do.

Of course she had sometimes had her thoughts about Frederick and Muriel. She had recently been jealous – a little, not much. This was because Muriel was working with Frederick now.

Often, when the three of them were together, Althea would look at those two, her husband, her closest friend, and think: Of course, if I died, they would marry. This was not envious; but her way of coming to terms with it. She even thought – though this was the sort of thing Muriel said, the kind of thing people expected from Muriel: This is a sort of group marriage, I suppose.

But Althea did not suspect a sexual tie. Not that he hadn't often said he found Muriel attractive. But one always could sense that sort of thing. Of course in all those years there must have been something: a kiss or two? A little more perhaps after a party or something like that? But not much more, these two would never deceive her. She could trust Muriel with anything; her old friend was a well into which confidences vanished and were forgotten; Muriel never gossiped, never condemned. She was the soul – if one could use that old-fashioned word – of honour. As for Frederick, when he had fallen in love, not only his wife, but the whole world had known of it: he was not a man who could, or who wanted to, conceal his feelings. But the real thing was this: the three of them had made, and now lived inside, an edifice of kindliness and responsibility and decency; it was simply not possible that it could harbour deception. It was inconceivable. So much so that Althea did not think about it: it was not sexual jealousy that she felt.

But she felt something else that she was ashamed of, that she had to wrestle with, in silence and in secrecy. She could not stop herself thinking that if Henry could die without warning, apparently in full health, then why not Frederick?

Althea was by nature a fussy and attentive wife, but Frederick did not like this in her. She longed to say: Take it easy, work less, worry less – relax. She knew he believed that he ought to be doing all this: duty ordained otherwise.

Often she would wake in the night out of dreams full of terror: if Frederick was on call, she would see the bed empty beside her, and think that this was what she could expect from the future. Then she would go to the stairs to see if Muriel's light was still on; it often was, and then Althea would decend the stairs to Muriel's kitchen, where they would drink tea or cocoa until Frederick came back. Muriel did not ask what drove Althea down the stairs so often at night, but she was always gay and consoling – kind. She was kind. Well, they were all kind people.

Sometimes, on those rare evenings when they could all be together, without pressures from Frederick's work, Althea, having cleared the table and come to join those two people – her husband, a large, worried-looking man in spectacles, sitting by a lamp and piles of medical magazines, engaged on his futile task of keeping up with new discovery; and a lean, restless woman who was probably helping one of the youngsters with homework, or a psychological problem – sometimes Althea would see that room without its centre, without Frederick. She and Muriel were alone in the room with the children. Yes, that is how it would all end, two ageing women, with the children – who would soon have grown up and gone.

Between one blink of an eye and another, a man could vanish, as Henry had done.

In the long evenings when Frederick was at the clinic, or on call, and it was as if the whole house and its occupants waited for him to come back, then Althea could not stop herself from looking across the living-room at Muriel in the thought: *Coming events cast their shadow before. Can't you feel it?*

But Muriel would look up, smile, laugh, offer to make tea for them all, or would say that she heard Frederick's car and she was tired and would take herself to bed – for she was tactful, and never stayed on in the evenings past the time she was wanted.

But this is our future, Althea would think. Their future, hers and Muriel's, was each other.

She knew it. But it was neurotic to think like this and she must try to suppress it.

The Other Garden

There were rumours another garden was hidden among trees.

Before finding it you speculate, make pictures of it in your mind. Perhaps it is hidden because it is so unlike everything else in the park that it would strike people as discordant? And if it is unlike, or out of key, then in what ways? The park already holds so much variety. The world's birds and animals are there. A tree will turn out to be an immigrant from Lebanon, another from Canada. Gulls come from the sea, migrating birds plane down to the many water-surfaces on their way from one continent to another. There is wilderness near the canal where blackberries may be picked, there are fields of rough grass for lying on, or rolling on, or loving on, or running the dog or playing football and cricket. There are parts like Italy and parts that could not be anything but England. An island full of docketed plants for gardeners to bend over is reached by a little bridge that must have been copied from a teacup. Roses, miniature waterfalls, poplars, lakes, fountains, a theatre ... What could possibly not be appropriate, be considered bizarre? A sand garden, as they have them in the East? But surely that would be hard to keep free of blown leaves. A garden of pebbles, coloured and matched? A sculpture garden, with metal and stone among gravel?

There is nothing you can't imagine the park accommodating, with no more of a jar than you get now, turning your eyes from oaks and beeches to bears on their rocky ledges or the head of a giraffe staring over a flowering bush, then to a small boy racing under a kite shaped like a yellow dish with a face on it.

Small children will take from their mother's kitchen a sprouting onion and a couple of carrots and, finding a few inches of bare soil in a corner, will plant them. Mother offers packets of seed and a garden fork and expertise, but the children fiercely guard their own conception: in the night the onion will make many, the carrots multiply. 'No, no, this way, we want it this way, we don't want your old seeds. You say *a few weeks* But that's for ever ... we want them to grow *now*!' Perhaps this was man's first attempt to manipulate nature? No, you can't imagine that garden, but the houses of the gardeners and keepers are tucked away all over the park and around these, probably, are samples of these embryo gardens. In a bombed building, rebuilt years ago now, a small girl used to dawdle on her way to school. She had made herself a house of a dozen bricks and some mortar rubble. Around the house she had a garden, spikes of wilting forsythia and blades of grass. Each morning she ran in with a new plant, a crocus pulled from her mother's garden, then a twig of cherry when it appeared in the spring. Everywhere was flowering growth, and the child came in daily in her purpose to make her own garden: a few square inches of dust with some withering fragments of plant. She scattered water on them from branches that had been rain-soaked in the night, she shaded them with a plank pulled from the debris of the building. Nothing helped, they had to die. So she brought shells, bits of glass and china, pebbles, beads, and made a pattern that said to her *garden*, one that would not die or dry out and vanish away.

Well then, if the other garden is not concealed because it is exotic, perhaps it is the quintessence of the park, a concentrated statement of it? And so, at last, it turns out to be. Strolling in the park, looking at trees and shrubs, you turn your head and see it. There it is.

It was a January day I saw it first. The night had been cold, the sky was chilly blue, full of racing cloud.

I was looking at a wide oblong of formal grass, with a deep border on either side. At the other end, shallow steps, almost the width of the grass, lifted the garden to its next level. The width of the steps, enough for a dozen or so to go up abreast, gives this reticent and secret place a look of welcome, as if it were waiting for guests. Yet there is no one in sight.

Of course, to see it in January means that you are imagining it in June; the dislocation you have suffered by seeing the garden there, where you didn't expect it, is sharpened by seeing two gardens at once, summer superimposed on this winter scene: easy, that morning, because of the sunlight everywhere, and the noise of the birds, bathing in it.

The grass of the lower garden, on its west side, and in shade, was filmed with ice that would not melt that day. The winter-flowering viburnum, pink crumb-like buds, shed a faint sharp scent, like wind off snow.

The sound of footsteps is absorbed in grass, you walk in silence.

The steps are shallow and curved, and on either side are low pillars, and on them scrolls of stone, like frozen water-chutes. Above each scroll are shells, like those in Salamanca on that wall where people come to stand and watch the shadows move on dulled pink stone, the same colour as the stone that is used in the Cotswolds.

The green oblong of the pool of grass now lies behind, with its borders where the plants are all cut back. In spring, what will they be? And in summer? Of course, lavender and pinks, rue and rosemary, origanum, thyme, catmint and peony. They will be scented, butterfly-filled, bee-visited, and people will stand hanging their noses over them, as drunk as the insects. The grass will be warm. Behind the borders now are stark bushes and trees, but when the leaves come this lower part will be enclosed twice, first by hedge, and then by a shimmer of green.

Even now, when you are well into the garden, on the steps, it is not possible to see the shape of the whole.

The second level has a fountain, as a centre to many roses – and grass, grass again, the roses will bloom over grass, not tarmac, and no footsteps will ever intrude here. A glossy black boy with a mermaid echoes the statue of the chestnut avenue, boy-with-dolphin, and also the spouting fishes of the poplar fountain. The water is frozen, but the ice has been broken for the birds. The thick water holds glassy plates that balance and slide, and on the coldly sunny edge a thrush and a blackbird wait for me to go so that they can drink.

Everywhere are birds. A blackbird uses his yellow beak in the soil under the roses. A fat pigeon holds his chest into the sun. Sparrows are quarrelling as if it were spring. Crows are making a fuss in some trees. And a squirrel, who surely ought to be hibernating, is watching what I shall do next.

At the edge of this round garden is another statue, of a girl holding a kid, its horns still in bud.

It is the kind of statue that can only arouse thoughts of the kind that true artists despise, such as: How the sculptor must have loved that girl! She is beautiful, with a strong-boned face. Her hair looks wet. It is impossible not to imagine the sculptor saying: 'Now wet your head. I'm going to do your hair today.' And the owner of that face will surely have said at some point during the sitting, with the controlled common sense that sounds like dry humour: 'For goodness' sake, this statue is going to look as if the goat keeps turning its head to have a quick swig.' But of course the artist went sternly on, ignoring her. The kid is tucked under one arm, very high, and close to her bare breasts.

It is the gentlest, most charming of statues, and it is

To all the Protectors of the Defenceless

It is in darkened bronze. The girl looks at the little animal, which is looking across to the shining black of the boy and mermaid rising out of the frozen water.

Some weeks later, on a day when the skies were low and dark, everything soaked and dismal, there was a wreath around the baby goats neck. It was of daphne, fragrant pinkish-mauve on pale-brown naked wool. Someone had reached up to garland the goat, and recently, for the flowers were fresh.

Soundlessly over grass into the next circle of this delicate garden, which is like a series of bubbles one above another. But you still can't make out the plan of the place; you can never see all of it at once. This 'bubble' is smaller than the first. The person who said that this other garden was here, said, too, that it was laid out in the shape of a man. The second bubble would be the chest.

It is like Queen Mary's Rose Garden, but an exquisite copy, segments of earth filled with roses in grass: these round gardens are like garlands laid on grass. It is enclosed by an espalier of limes, a lacing of black knobby branches that are horizontal and stiff on either side of the central stems. The black wood glistens and drips, the sunlight makes crystals of the scattering water. Each knob is already sprouting the yellowy shoots that when spring comes will make wands of green: the theme of garland will be repeated again.

A variety of birds sit on the cold wood, waiting for spring to start. The sky churns and tumbles.

At the very end of this series of grassy shapes is a very small circle or bubble – the head. Roses again. It is an intimate, gay little place, and in summer it must be like being caught in a bunch of flowers and greenery. You look up into blue, past black twigs, and out into the next bubble through the elegant bareness of the spread-eagled limes.

The design is still not evident, though you know it now: you are holding it in your mind, a tiny circle, a large one, a larger one still, then the grassy oblong bordered and hedged on either side.

A small breeze lifts a dozen of last autumn's frozen leaves and clatters them on the icy film where the shadow is. In summer they will be butterflies and rose petals.

Silently back, over grass, with the blackbird hopping behind: you might be a gardener, and a gardener means turned soil. There is nobody else here, no one at all.

Back through one circle after another, then across the grass that lies beyond the steps. As you leave, the place draws itself in behind you, is gathered into itself, like water settling after a stone has disturbed it. There it is, whole, between its hedges, its bare trees, repeating and echoing like a descant, using every theme that is used in the great park outside, but used there roughly, in crude form.

A long way off now, the pigeon holds out its shining chest, and the blackbirds and thrushes probe the earth.

But the squirrel comes fast to the gate, and holds up its paws, as if it were begging; then it rakes my legs with its front paws like a cat wanting to be attended to, or to be fed.

Turn your back, turn a corner – it is all gone.

The Story of a Non-Marrying Man

I met Johnny Blakeworthy at the end of his life. I was at the beginning of mine, about ten or twelve years old. This was in the early thirties, when the Slump had spread from America even to us, in the middle of Africa. The very first sign of the Slump was the increase in the number of people who lived by their wits, or as vagrants.

Our house was on a hill, the highest point of our farm. Through the farm went the only road, a dirt track, from the railway station seven miles away, our shopping and mail centre, to the farms farther on. Our nearest neighbours were three, four and seven miles away. We could see their roofs flash in the sunlight, or gleam in the moonlight across all those trees, ridges and valleys.

From the hill we could see the clouds of dust that marked the passage of cars or wagons along the tracks. We would say: 'That must be so-and-so going in to fetch his mail.' Or: 'Cyril said he had to get a spare part for his plough, his broke down, that must be him now.'

If the cloud of dust turned off the main road and moved up through the trees towards us, we had time to build up the fire and put on the kettle. At busy times for the farmers, this happened seldom. Even at slack times, there might be no more than three or four cars a week, and as many wagons. It was mostly a white man's road, for the Africans moving on foot used their own quicker, short-cutting paths. White men coming to the house on foot were rare, though less rare as the Slump set in. More often now, coming through the trees up the hill, we saw walking towards us a man with a bundle of blankets over his shoulder, a rifle swinging in his hand. In the blanket-roll was always a frying-pan and a can of water, sometimes a couple of tins of bully beef, or a Bible, matches, a twist of dried meat. Sometimes this man had an African servant walking with him. These men always called themselves Prospectors, for that was a respectable occupation. Many did prospect, and nearly always for gold.

One evening, as the sun was going down, up the track to our house came a tall stooped man in shabby khaki with a rifle and a bundle over one shoulder. We knew we had company for the night. The rules of hospitality were that no one coming to our homes in the bush could be refused; every man was fed, and asked to stay as long as he wanted.

Johnny Blakeworthy was burned by the suns of Africa to a dark brown, and his eyes in a dried wrinkled face were grey, the whites much inflamed by the glare. He kept screwing up his eyes, as if in sunlight, and then, in a remembered effort of will, letting loose his muscles, so that his face kept clenching and unclenching like a fist. He was thin: he spoke of having had malaria recently. He was old: it was not only the sun that had so deeply lined his face. In his blanket-roll he had, as well as the inevitable frying-pan, an enamel one-pint saucepan, a pound of tea, some dried milk, and a change of clothing. He wore long, heavy khaki trousers for protection against lashing grasses and grass-seeds, and a khaki bush-shirt. He also owned a washed-out grey sweater for frosty nights. Among these items was a corner of a sack full of maize meal. The presence of the maize flour was a statement, and probably unambiguous, for the Africans ate maize-meal porridge as their staple food. It was cheap, easily obtainable, quickly cooked, nourishing, but white men did not eat it, at least not as the basis of their diet, because they did not wish to be put on the same level as Africans. The fact that this man carried it was why my father, discussing him later with my mother, said: 'He's probably gone native.'

This was not a criticism. Or rather, while with one part of the collective ethos the white men might say, 'He's gone native!' – and in anger – with a different part of their minds, or at different times, it could be said in bitter envy. But that is another story . . .

Johnny Blakeworthy was of course asked to stay for supper

and for the night. At the lamplit table, which was covered with every sort of food, he kept saying how good it was to see so much real food again, but it was in a vaguely polite way, as if he was having to remind himself that this was how he should feel. His plate was loaded with food, and he ate, but kept forgetting to eat, so that my mother had to remind him, putting a little bit more of nice undercut, a splash of gravy, helpings of carrots and spinach from the garden. But by the end he had eaten very little, and hadn't spoken much either, though the meal gave an impression of much conversation and interest and eating, like a feast, so great was our hunger for company, so many were our questions. Particularly the two children questioned and demanded, for the life of such a man, walking quietly by himself through the bush, sometimes twenty miles or more a day, sleeping by himself under the stars, or the moon, or whatever weather the seasons sent him, prospecting when he wished, stopping to rest when he needed – such a life, it goes without saying, set us restlessly dreaming of lives different from those we were set towards by school and by parents.

We did learn that he had been on the road for 'some time, yes, some time now, yes'. That he was sixty. That he had been born in England, in the south, near Canterbury. That he had been adventuring up and down and around southern Africa all his life – but adventure was not the word he used, it was the word we children repeated until we saw that it made him uncomfortable. He had mined: had indeed owned his own mine. Had farmed, but had not done well. Had done all kinds of work, but 'I like to be my own master.' He had owned a store, but 'I get restless, and I must be on the move.'

Now there was nothing in this we hadn't heard before – every time, indeed, that such a wanderer came to our door. There was nothing out of the ordinary in his extraordinariness. Except, perhaps, as we remembered later, sucking all the stimulation we could out of the visit, discussing if for days, he did not have a prospector's pan, nor had he asked my father for permission to prospect on this farm. We could not remember a prospector who had failed to become excited by the farm, for it was full of chipped rocks and reefs, trenches and shafts, which some people said went back to the Phoenicians. You couldn't walk a hundred yards without seeing signs ancient and modern of the search for gold. The district was called 'Banket' because it had running through it reefs of the same formation as reefs called Banket on the Rand. The name alone was like a signpost.

But Johnny said he liked to be on his way by the time the sun was up.

I saw him leave, down the track that was sun-flushed, the trees all rosy on one side. He shambled away out of sight, a tall, much too thin, rather stooping man in washed-out khaki and soft hide shoes.

Some months later, another man out of work and occupying himself with prospecting, was asked if he had ever met up with Johnny Blakeworthy, and he said yes, he had indeed! He went on with indignation to say that 'he had gone native' in the Valley. The indignation was false, and we assumed that this man too might have 'gone native', or that he wished he had, or could. But Johnny's lack of a prospecting-pan, his maize meal, his look at the supper table of being out of place and unfamiliar – all was explained. 'Going native' implied that a man would have a 'bush wife', but it seemed Johnny did not.

'He said he's had enough of the womenfolk, he's gone to get out of their way,' said this visitor.

I did not describe, in its place, the thing about Johnny's visit that struck us most, because at the time it did not strike us as more than agreeably quaint. It was only much later that the letter he wrote us matched up with others, and made a pattern.

Three days after Johnny's visit to us, a letter arrived from him. I remember my father expected to find that it would ask, after all, for permission to prospect. But any sort of letter was odd. Letter-writing equipment did not form part of a tramp's gear. The letter was on blue Croxley writing-paper, and in a blue Croxley envelope, and the writing was as neat as a child's. It was a 'bread-and-butter letter'. He said that he had very much enjoyed our kind hospitality, and the fine cooking of the lady of the house. He was grateful for the opportunity of making our acquaintance.

'With my best wishes, yours very truly, Johnny Blakeworthy.'

Once he had been a well-brought-up little boy from a small English country town. 'You must always write and say thank-you after enjoying hospitality, Johnny.'

We talked about the letter for a long time. He must have dropped in at the nearest store after leaving our farm to go north. It was twenty miles away. He probably bought a single sheet of paper and a lone envelope. This meant that he had got them from the African part of the store, where such small retailing went on – at vast profit, of course, to the storekeeper. He must have bought one stamp, and walked across to the post office to hand the letter over the counter. Then, due having been paid to his upbringing, he moved back to the African tribe where he lived – beyond post offices, letter-writing, and the other impedimenta that went with being a white man.

The next glimpse I had of the man, I still have no idea where to fit into the pattern I was at last able to make.

It was years later. I was a young woman at a morning tea-party. This one, like all others of its kind, was an excuse for gossip, and most of that was – of course, since we were young married women – about men and marriage. A girl, married not more than a year, much in love, and unwilling to sacrifice her husband to the collective, talked instead about her aunt from the Orange Free State. 'She was married for years to a real bad one, and then up he got and walked out. All she heard from him was a nice letter, you know, like a letter after a party or something. It said, "Thank you very much for the nice time." Can you beat that? And later still she found she had never been married to him because all the time he was married to someone else.'

'Was she happy?' one of us asked, and the girl said, 'She was nuts all right, she said it was the best time of her life.'

'Then what was she complaining about?'

'What got her was, having to say Spinster, when she was as good as married all those years. And that letter got her goat, "I feel I must write and thank you for . . ." something like that.'

'What was his name?' I asked, suddenly understanding what was itching at the back of my mind.

'I don't remember. Johnny something-or-other.'

That was all that came out of that most typical of South African scenes, the morning tea-party on the deep shady veranda, the trays covered with every kind of cake and biscuit, the gossiping young women watching their offspring at play under the trees, filling in a morning of their lazy lives before going back to their respective homes where they would find their meals cooked for them, the tables laid, and their husbands waiting. That tea-party was thirty years ago, and still that town has not grown so wide that the men can't drive home to take their midday meals with their families. I am talking of white families, of course.

The next bit of the puzzle came in the shape of a story which I read in a local paper, of the kind that gets itself printed in the spare hours of presses responsible for much more renowned newspapers. This one was called the *Valley Advertiser*, and its circulation might have been ten thousand. The story was headed: OUR PRIZE-WINNING STORY, 'THE FRAGRANT BLACK ALOE'. BY OUR NEW DISCOVERY, ALAN McGINNERY.

When I have nothing better to do, I like to stroll down Main Street, to see the day's news being created, to catch fragments of talk, and to make up stories about what I hear. Most people enjoy coincidences, it gives them something to talk about. But when there are too many, it makes an unpleasant feeling that the long arm of coincidence is pointing to a region where a rational person is likely to feel uncomfortable. This morning was like that. It began in a flower shop. There a woman with a shopping list was saying to the salesman: 'Do you sell black aloes?' It sounded like something to eat.

'Never heard of them,' said he. 'But I have a fine range of succulents. I can sell you a miniature rock-garden on a tray.'

'No, no, no. I don't want the ordinary aloes. I've got all those. I want the Scented Black Aloe.'

Ten minutes later, waiting to buy a toothbrush at the cosmetic counter at our chemist, Harry's Farmacy, I heard a woman ask for a bottle of Black Aloe.

Hello, I thought, black aloes have suddenly come into my life!

'We don't stock anything like that,' said the salesgirl, offering rose, honeysuckle, lilac, white violets and jasmine, while obviously reflecting that black aloes must make a bitter kind of perfume.

Half an hour later I was in a seed shop, and when I heard a petulant female voice ask, 'Do you stock succulents?' then I knew what was coming. This had happened to me before, but I couldn't remember where or when. Never before had I heard of the Scented Black Aloe, and here it was, three times in an hour.

When she had gone I asked the salesman, 'Tell me, is there such a thing as the Scented Black Aloe?'

'Your guess is as good as mine,' he said. 'But people always want what's difficult to find.'

And at that moment I remembered where I had heard that querulous, sad, insistent, hungry note in a voice before (voices, as it turned out!) – the note that means that the Scented Black Aloe represents, for that time, all the heart's desire.

It was before the war. I was in the Cape and I had to get to Nairobi. I had driven the route before, and I wanted to get it over. Every couple of hours or so you pass through some little dorp, and they are all the same. They are hot, and dusty. In the tea-room there is a crowd eating ice-cream and talking about motor cycles and film stars. In the bars men stand drinking beer. The restaurant, if there is one, is bad, or pretentious. The waitress longs only for the day when she can get to the big city, and she says the name of the city as if it was Paris, or London, but when you reach it, two hundred or five hundred miles on, it is a slightly larger dorp, with the same dusty trees, the same tea-room, the same bar, and five thousand people instead of a hundred.

On the evening of the third day I was in the northern Transvaal, and when I wanted to stop for the night, the sun was blood-red through a haze of dust, and the main street was full of cattle and people. There was the yearly Farmers' Show in progress, and the hotel was full. The proprietor said there was a woman who took in people in emergencies.

The house was by itself at the end of a straggling dusty street, under a large jacaranda tree. It was small, with chocolate-coloured trelliswork along the veranda, and the roof was sagging under scarlet bougainvillaea. The woman who came to the door was a plump, dark-haired creature in a pink apron, her hands floury with cooking.

She said the room was not ready. I said that I had come all the way from Bloemfontein that morning, and she said, 'Come in, my second husband was from there when he came here in the beginning.'

Outside the house was all dust, and the glare was bad, but inside it was cosy, with flowers and ribbons and cushions and china behind glass. In every conceivable place were pictures of the same man. You couldn't get away from them. He smiled down from the bathroom wall, and if you opened a cupboard door, there he was, stuck up among the dishes.

She spent two hours cooking a meal, said over and over again how a woman has to spend all her day cooking a meal that is eaten in five minutes, inquired after my tastes in food, offered second helpings. In between, she talked about her husband. It seemed that four years ago a man had arrived in the week of the Show, asking for a bed. She never liked taking in single men, for she was a widow living alone, but she did like the look of him, and a week later they were married. For eleven months they lived in a dream of happiness. Then he walked out and she hadn't heard of him since, except for one letter, thanking her for all her kindness. That letter was like a slap in the face, she said. You don't thank a wife for being kind, like a hostess, do you ? Nor do you send her Christmas cards. But he had sent her one the Christmas after he left, and there it was, on the mantelpiece, With Best Wishes for a Happy Christmas. But he was so good to me, she said. He gave me every penny he ever earned, and I didn't need it, because my first hubby left me provided for. He got a job as a ganger on the railways. She could never look at another man after him. No woman who knew anything about life would. He had his faults of course, like everyone. He was restless and moody, but he loved her honestly, she could see that, and underneath it all, he was a family man.

That went on until the cocks began to crow and my face ached with yawning.

Next morning I continued my drive north, and that night, in Southern Rhodesia, I drove into a small town full of dust and people standing about in their best clothes among milling cattle. The hotel was full. It was Show time.

When I saw the house, I thought time had turned back twenty-four hours, for there were the creepers weighing down the roof, and the trellised veranda, and the red dust heaped all around it. The attractive woman who came to the door was fair-haired. Behind her, through the door, I saw a picture on the wall of the same handsome, blond young man with his hard grey eyes that had sun-marks raying out from around them into the sunburn. On the floor was playing a small child, obviously his.

I said where I had come from that morning, and she said wistfully that her hubby had come from there three years before. It was all just the same. Even the inside of the house was like the other, comfortable and frilly and full. But it needed a man's attention. All kinds of things needed attention. We had supper and she talked about her 'husband' – he had lasted until the birth of the baby and a few weeks beyond it – in the same impatient, yearning, bitter, urgent voice of her sister of the evening before. As I sat there listening, I had the ridiculous feeling that in hearing her out so sympathetically I was being disloyal to the other deserted 'wife' four hundred miles south. Of course he had his faults, she said. He drank too much sometimes, but men couldn't help being men. And sometimes he went into a daydream for weeks at a stretch and didn't hear what you said. But he was a good husband, for all that. He had got a job in the Sales Department of the Agricultural Machinery Store, and he had worked hard. When the little boy was born he was so pleased ... and then he left. Yes, he did write once, he wrote a long letter saying he would never forget her 'affectionate kindness'. That letter really had upset her. It was a funny thing to say, wasn't it?

Long after midnight I went to sleep under such a large tinted picture of the man that it made me uncomfortable. It was like having someone watching you sleep.

Next evening, when I was about to drive out of Southern Rhodesia into Northern Rhodesia, I was half looking for a little town full of clouds of reddish dust, and crowding cattle, the small house, the waiting woman. There seemed no reason why this shouldn't go on all the way to Nairobi.

But it was not until the day after that, on the Copper Belt in Northern Rhodesia, that I came to a town full of cars and people. There was going to be a dance that evening. The big hotels were full. The lady whose house I was directed to was plump, red-haired, voluble. She said she loved putting people up for the night, though there was no need for her to do it since while her husband might have his faults (she said this with what seemed like hatred) he made good money at the garage where he was a mechanic. Before she was married, she had earned her living by letting rooms to travellers, which was how she had met her husband. She talked about him while we waited for him to come in to supper. 'He does this every night, every night of my life! You'd think it wasn't much to ask, to come in for meals at the right time, instead of letting everything spoil, but once he gets into the bar with the men, there is no getting him out.'

There wasn't a hint in her voice of what I had heard in the voices of the other two women. And I have often wondered since if in her case, too, absence would make the heart grow fonder. She sighed often and deeply, and said that when you were single you wanted to be married, and when you were married you wanted to be single, but what got her was, she had been married before, and she ought to have known better. Not that this one wasn't a big improvement on the last, whom she had divorced.

He didn't come in until the bar closed, after ten. He was not as good-looking as in his photographs, but that was because his overalls were stiff with grease, and there was oil on his face. She scolded him for being late, and for not having washed, but all he said was: 'Don't try to house-train me.' At the end of the meal she wondered aloud why she spent her life cooking and slaving for a man who didn't notice what he ate, and he said she shouldn't bother, because it was true, he didn't care what he ate. He nodded at me, and went out again. It was after midnight when he came back, with a star-dazed look, bringing a cold draught of night air into the hot lamplit room.

'So you've decided to come in?' she complained.

'I walked out into the veld a bit. The moon is strong enough to read by. There's rain on the wind.' He put his arm around her waist and smiled at her. She smiled back, her bitterness forgotten. The wanderer had come home.

I wrote to Alan McGinnery and asked him if there had been a model for his story. I told him why I wanted to know, told him of the old man who had walked up to our house through the bush, fifteen years before. There was no reason to think it was the same man, except for that one detail, the letters he wrote, like 'bread-and-butter' letters after a party or a visit.

I got this reply: 'I am indeed indebted to you for your interesting and informative letter. You are right in thinking my little story had its start in real life. But in most ways it is far from fact. I took liberties with the time of the story, moving it forward by years, no decades, and placing it in a more modern setting. For the time when Johnny Blakeworthy was loving and leaving so many young women – I'm afraid he was a very bad lot! – is now out of the memory of all but the elderly among us. Everything is so soft and easy now. "Civilization" so-called has overtaken us. But I was afraid if I put my "hero" into his real setting, it would seem so exotic to present-day readers that they would read my little tale for the sake of the background, finding that more interesting than my "hero".

'It was just after the Boer War. I had volunteered for it, as a young man does, for the excitement, not knowing what sort of a war it really was. Afterwards I decided not to return to England. I thought I would try the mines, so I went to Johannesburg, and there I met my wife, Lena. She was the cook and housekeeper in a men's boarding-house, a rough job, in rough days. She had a child by Johnny, and believed herself to be married to him. So did I. When I made inquiries, I found she had never been married, the papers he had produced at the office were all false. This made things easy for us in the practical sense, but made them worse in some ways. For she was bitter and I am afraid never really got over the wrong done to her. But we married, and I became the child's father. She was the original of the second woman in my story. I describe her as home-loving, and dainty in her ways. Even when she was cooking for all those miners, and keeping herself and the boy on bad wages, living in a room not much larger than a dog's kennel, it was all so neat and pretty. That was what took my fancy first. I dare say it was what took Johnny's too, to begin with, at any rate.

'Much later – very much later, the child was almost grown, so it was after the Great War, I happened to hear someone speak of Johnny Blakeworthy. It was a woman who had been "married" to him. It never crossed our minds to think – Lena and me – that he had betrayed more than one woman. After careful thought, I decided never to tell her. But *I* had to know. By then I had done some careful field-work. The trail began, or at least began for me, in Cape Province, with a woman I had heard spoken of, and had then tracked down. She was the first woman in my story, a little plump pretty thing. At the time Johnny married her, she was the daughter of a Boer farmer, a rich one. I don't have to tell you that this marriage was unpopular. It took place just before the Boer War, that nasty time was to come, but she was a brave girl to marry an Englishman, a *roinek*. Her parents were angry, but later they did the right thing and took her back when he left her. He did really marry her, in church, everything correct and legal. I believe that she was his first love. Later she divorced him. It was a terrible thing, a divorce for those simple people. Now things have changed so much, and people wouldn't believe how narrow and church-bound they were then. That divorce hurt her whole life. She did not marry again. It was not because she did not want to! She had fought with her parents, saying she must get a divorce, because she wanted to be married. But no one married her. In that old fashioned rural community, in those days, she was a Scarlet Woman. A sad thing, for she was a really nice woman. What struck me was that she spoke of Johnny with no bitterness at all. Even twenty years later, she loved him.

'From her, I followed up other clues. With my own wife, I found four women in all. I made it three in my little story: life is always much more lavish with coincidence and drama than any fiction writer dares to be. The red-headed woman I described was a barmaid in a hotel. She hated Johnny. But there was little doubt in my mind what would happen if he walked in through that door.

'I told my wife that I had been big-game hunting. I did not want to stir up old unhappiness. After she died I wrote the story of the journey from one woman to another, all now of middle age, all of whom had been "married" to Johnny. But I had to alter the settings of the story. How fast everything has changed! I would have had to describe the Boer family on their farm, such simple and old-fashioned, good and bigoted people. And their eldest daughter – the "bad" one. There are no girls like that now, not even in convents. Where in the world now would you find girls brought up as strictly and as narrowly as those on those Boer farms, fifty years ago? And *still* she had the courage to marry her Englishman, that is the marvellous thing. Then I would have had to describe the mining camps of Johannesburg. Then the life of a woman married to a storekeeper in the bush. Her nearest neighbour was fifty miles away and they didn't have cars in those days. Finally, the early days of Bulawayo, when it was more like a shanty town than a city. No, it was Johnny that interested me, so I decided to make the story modern, and in that way the reader would not be distracted by what is past and gone.'

It was from an African friend who had known the village in which Johnny died that I heard of his last years. Johnny walked into the village, asked to see the Chief and, when the Chief assembled with the Elders, asked formally for permission to live in the village, as an African, not as a white man. All this was quite correct, and polite, but the Elders did not like it. This village was a long way from the centres of white power, up towards the Zambesi. The traditional life was still comparatively unchanged, unlike the tribes near the white cities, whose structure had been smashed for ever. The people of this tribe cherished their distance from the white man, and feared his influence. At least, the older ones did. While they had nothing against this white man as a man – on the contrary, he seemed more human than most – they did not want a white man in their life. But what could they do? Their traditions of hospitality were strong: strangers, visitors, travellers, must be sheltered and fed. And they were democratic: a man was as good as his behaviour; it was against their beliefs to throw a person out for a collective fault. And perhaps they were, too, a little curious. The white men these people had seen were the tax-collecters, the policemen, the Native Commissioners, all coldly official or arbitrary. This white man behaved like a suppliant, sitting quietly on the outskirts of the village, beyond the huts, under a tree, waiting for the Council to make up its mind. Finally they let him stay, on condition that he shared the life of the village in every way. This proviso they probably thought would soon get rid of him. But he lived there until he died, six years, with short trips away to remind himself, perhaps, of the strident life he had left. It was on such a trip that he had walked up to our house and stayed the night.

The Africans called him Angry Face. This name implied that it was only the face which was angry. It was because of his habit of screwing up and then letting loose his facial muscles. They also called him Man Without a Home, and The Man Who Has No Woman.

The women found him intriguing, in spite of his sixty years. They hung about his hut, gossiped about him, brought him presents. Several made offers, even young girls.

The Chief and his Elders conferred again, under the great tree in the centre of the village, and then called him to hear their verdict.

'You need a woman,' they said, and in spite of all his protests, made it a condition of his staying with them, for the sake of the tribe's harmony.

They chose for him a woman of middle age whose husband had died of the blackwater fever, and who had had no children. They said that a man of his age could not be expected to give the patience and attention that small children need. According to my friend, who as a small boy had heard much talk of this white man who had preferred their way of life to his own, Johnny and his new woman 'lived together in kindness'.

It was while I was writing this story that I remembered something else.

When I was at school in Salisbury there was a girl called Alicia Blakeworthy. She was fifteen, a 'big girl' to me. She lived with her mother on the fringe of the town. Her stepfather had left them. He had walked out.

Her mother had a small house, in a large garden, and she took in paying guests. One of these guests had been Johnny. He had been working as a game warden up towards the Zambesi river, and had had malaria badly. She nursed him. He married her and took a job as a counter-hand in the local grocery store. He was a bad husband to Mom, said Alicia. Terrible. Yes, he brought in money, it wasn't that. But he was a cold, hard-hearted man. He was no company for them. He would just sit and read, or listen to the radio, or walk around by himself all night. And he never appreciated what was done for him.

Oh, how we schoolgirls all hated this monster! What a heartless beast he was!

But the way *he* saw it, he had stayed for four long years in a suffocating town-house surrounded by a domesticated garden. He had worked from eight to four selling groceries to lazy women. When he came home, this money, the gold he had earned by his slavery, was spent on chocolates, magazines, dresses, hair-ribbons, for his townified step-daughter. He was invited, three times a day, to sit down at a table crammed with roast beef and chickens and puddings and cakes and biscuits.

He used to try and share his philosophy of living.

'I used to feed myself for ten shillings a week!'

'But why? What for? What's the point?'

'Because I was free, that's the point! If you don't spend a lot of money, then you don't have to earn it and you are free. Why do you have to spend money on all this rubbish? You can buy a piece of rolled brisket for three shillings, and you boil it with an onion and you can live off it for four days! You can live off mealie-meal well enough. I often did, in the bush.'

'Mealie-meal! I'm not going to eat native food!'

'Why not? What's wrong with it?'

'If you can't see why not, then I'm afraid I can't help you.'

Perhaps it was here, with Alicia's mother, that the idea of 'going native' had first come into his head.

'For crying out aloud, why cake all the time, why all these new dresses, why do you have to have new curtains, why do we have to have curtains at all, what's wrong with the sunlight? What's wrong with the starlight? Why do you want to shut them out? Why?'

That 'marriage' lasted four years, a fight all the way.

Then he drifted his way north, out of the white man's towns, and up into those parts that had not been 'opened up to white settlement', and where the Africans were still living, though not for long, in their traditional ways. And there at last he found a life that suited him, and a woman with whom he lived in kindness.

The Temptation of Jack Orkney

His father was dying. It was a telegram, saying also: YOU UNOBTAINABLE TELEPHONE. He had been on the telephone since seven that morning. It was the house keeper who had sent the telegram. Did Mrs Markham not know that she could have asked the telephone authorities to interrupt his conversations for an urgent message? The irritation of the organizer who is manipulating intractable people and events now focused on Mrs Markham, but he tried to alleviate it by reminding himself that Mrs Markham was housekeeper not only to his father but to a dozen other old people.

It had been a long time since he had actually organized something political; others had been happy to organize *him* – his name, his presence, his approval. But an emotional telephone call from an old friend, Walter Kenting, before seven that morning, appealing that they 'all' should make a demonstration of some sort about the refugees – the nine million refugees of Bangladesh this time – and the information that he was the only person available to do the organizing, had returned him to a politically active past. Telephoning, he soon discovered that even the small demonstration they envisaged would be circumscribed, because people were saying they could see no point in a demonstration when television, radio and every newspaper did little else but tell the world about these millions of sufferers. What was the point of a dozen or twenty people 'sitting down' or 'marching' or even being hungry for twenty-four hours in some prominent place? Surely the point of these actions in the past had been to draw public attention to a wrong?

Now the strength of his reaction to Mrs Markham's inadequacy made him understand that his enthusiastic response to

Walter so early that morning had been mostly because of weeks, months, of inactivity. He could not be so exaggerating details if he were not under-employed. He had been making occupation for himself, calling it stocktaking. He had been reading old diaries, articles of his own, twenty or more years old, letters of people he had not seen, sometimes for as long. Immersing himself in his own past had of course been uncomfortable; this is what it had been really like in Korea, Israel, Pretoria, during such and such an event; memory had falsified. One knew that it did, but he had believed himself exempt from this law. Every new day of this deliberate evocation of the past had made his own part in it seem less worth while, had diminished his purposes and strengths. It was not that he now lacked offers of work, but that he could not make himself respond with the enthusiastic willingness which he believed every job of work needed. Of his many possibilities the one that attracted him most was to teach journalism in a small college in Nigeria, but he could not make up his mind to accept: his wife didn't want to go. Did he want to leave her in England for two years? No; but at one time this certainly would not have been his reaction!

Nor did he want to write another adventure book: in such empty times in the past he had written, under *noms de plume*, novels whose attraction was the descriptions of the countries he had set them in. He had travelled a great deal in his life, often dangerously, in the course of this war or that, as a soldier and as a journalist.

He might also write a serious book of social or political analysis: he had several to his credit.

He could do television work, or return to active journalism.

The thing was that now the three children were through university he did not need to earn so much money.

Leisure, leisure at last! he had cried, as so many of his friends were doing, finding themselves similarly placed.

But half a morning's energetic organizing was enough to tell him – exactly as his mother had been used to tell him when he was adolescent – 'Your trouble is, you haven't got enough to do!'

He sent a telegram to Mrs Markham: ARRIVING TRAIN
EARLY EVENING. Flying would save him an hour; proper
feeling would no doubt choose the air; but he needed the train's
pace to adjust him for what was ahead. He rang Walter Kenting
to say that with the organizing still undone, urgent family
matters were claiming him. Walter was silent at this, so he said:
'Actually, my old man is going to die in the next couple of days.
It has been on the cards for some time.'

'I am sorry,' said Walter. 'I'll try Bill or Mona. I've got to go to
Dublin in fifteen minutes. Are you going to be back by Saturday?
– oh, of course, you don't know.' Realizing that he was sounding
careless or callous, he said: 'I do hope things will be all right.'
This was worse and he gave up: 'You think that a twenty-four-
hour fast meets the bill better than the other possibilities? Is that
what most people feel, do you think?'

'Yes. But I don't think they are as keen as usual.'

'Well, of course not, there's too much of bloody everything,
that's why. You could be demonstrating twenty-four hours a
day. Anyway, I've got to get to my plane.'

While Jack packed, which he knew so well how to do, in ten
minutes, he remembered that he had a family. Should everyone
be at the deathbed? Oh, surely not! He looked for his wife: she
was out. Of course! The children off her hands, she too had
made many exclamations about the attractions of leisure, but
almost at once she signed up for a psychology course as part of a
plan to become a Family Counsellor. She had left a note for him:
'Darling, there's some cold lamb and salad.' He now left a note
for her: 'Old man on his way out. See you whenever. Tell girls
and Joseph. All my love. Jack.'

On the train he thought of what he was in for. A family
reunion, no less. His brother wasn't so bad, but the last time he
had seen Ellen, she had called him a Boy Scout, and he had
called her a Daughter of the British Empire. Considering it a
compliment, she had been left with the advantage. A really
dreadful woman, and as for her husband – surely he wouldn't be
there too? He would have to be, as a man? Where would they all
fit in? Certainly not in that tiny flat. He should have put in his

note to Rosemary that she should telephone hotels in S——. Would the other grandchildren be there? Well, Cedric and Ellen would be certain to do the right thing, whatever that was: as for himself he could telephone home when he had found what the protocol was. But, good God, surely it was bad enough that three of them, grown-up and intelligent people – grown-up, anyway – were going to have to sit about waiting, in a deathbed scene, because of – superstition. Yes, that was what it was. Certainly no more than outdated social custom. And it all might go on for days. But perhaps the old man would be pleased? At the approach of a phrase similar to those suitable for deaths and funerals, he felt irritation again: this would lead, unless he watched himself, to self-mockery, the spirit of farce. Farce was implicit, anyway, in a situation which had himself, Ellen and Cedric in one room.

Probably the old man wasn't even conscious. He should have telephoned Mrs Markham before rushing off like – well, like a journalist, with two pairs of socks, a spare shirt and a sweater. He should have bought a black tie? Would the old man have wished it? (Jack noted the arrival of an indubitably 'suitable' phrase, and feared worse for the immediate future.)

The old man had not worn black or altered his cheerfulness when his wife died.

His wife, Jack's mother.

The depression that he had suspected was in wait for him, now descended. He understood that he had been depressed for some time: this was like dark coming down into a fog. He had not admitted that he was depressed, but he ought to have known it by the fact that what he had woken up to each morning was not his own expectation of usefulness or accomplishment, but his wife's.

Now if Rosemary died . . . but he would not think about that, it would be morbid.

When his mother died, his father had made the simplest of funerals for her – religious, of course. All the family, the grand-children too, had stayed in the old house, together for the first time in years. The old man had behaved like a man who knew that his grief ought not to be inflicted on others. Jack had not been close to his mother: he had not liked her. He was close to no member of the family. He now knew that he loved his wife, but that had not been true until recently. There were his beautiful daughters. There was his son Joseph, who was a chip off the old block – so everyone insisted on saying, though it infuriated Joseph. But they could not meet without quarrelling. That was closeness of a kind?

He ought to have been more attentive when the mother died, to the old man, who had probably been concealing a good deal behind his mild dignity. Of course! And, looking back ten years, Jack knew that he had known what his father was feeling, had been sympathetic, but had also been embarrassed and unable to give anything of himself – out of fear that more would be asked? – had pretended obtuseness.

The old house was Church property, divided into units for old people who had been good parishioners. None had been friends before going to live there, but now it seemed that they were all close friends, or at least kept each other company in a variety of ways under the eye of Mrs Markham who also lived there, looked after the house, after them. She put flowers in the church and mended surplices and garments of that sort – she was fifty, poor old thing. Jack now told himself that he was over fifty, although the 'baby of the family', and that his sister Ellen with whom he was to spend an unknown number of days was fifty-five, while his boring brother Cedric was older still.

This train was not full and moved pleasantly through England's green and pleasant land. There were two other people in the compartment. Second class. Jack travelled second class when he could: this was one of the ways he used to check up on himself that he was not getting soft with success – if you could call what he had success. His brother and sister did, but that was the way they looked at life.

One fellow-passenger was a middle-aged woman, and one a girl of about twenty-three or -four who leaned an elbow on the window-ledge and stared at Buckinghamshire, then Berkshire, then Wiltshire, all green and soft on this summery day. Her face was hidden behind glittering yellow hair. Jack classed her as a London secretary on her way home for a family visit, and as the kind of young person he would get on with – that is, like his daughters rather than his son.

He was finding the company of his girls all pleasure and healing. It seemed to him that everything he had looked for in women now flowed generously towards him from Carrie and Elizabeth. It was not that they always approved him, far from it; it was the quality of their beauty that caressed and dandled him. The silk of their hair flattered, their smiles, even when for somebody else, gave him answers to questions that he had been asking of women – so it seemed to him now – all his life.

Though of course he did not see much of them: while living in the same house, upstairs, they led their own lives.

The woman, whom he disliked because she was not young and beautiful – he was aware that he should be ashamed of this reaction, but put this shame on to an agenda for the future – got off the train, and now the girl at the window turned towards him and the rest of the journey was bound to be delightful. He had been right – of course, he was always right about people. She worked in an office in Great Portland Street, and she was going for a visit to her parents – no, she 'got on' with them all right, but she was always pleased to be back in her flat with her friends. She was not a stranger to Jack's world; that is, she was familiar with the names of people whose lives expressed concern for public affairs, public wrong and suffering, and she used the names of his friends with a proprietary air – she had, as it were, eaten them up to form herself, as he, Jack, had in his time swallowed Keir Hardie, Marx, Freud, Morris and the rest. She, those like her, now possessed 'the Old Guard', their history, their opinions, their claims. To her, Walter Kenting, Bill, Mona, were like statues on plinths, each representing a degree of opinion. When the time came to give her his own name, he said it was Jack Sebastian, not Jack Orkney, for he knew he would join the pantheon of people who were her parents-in-opinion, and, as he had understood, were to be criticized, like parents.

The last time he had been Jack Sebastian was to get himself out of a tight spot in Ecuador, during a small revolution: he had escaped prison and possible death by this means.

If he told this girl about that, he knew that as he sat opposite her, she would gaze in judiciously measured admiration at a man retreating from her into history. He listened to her talk about herself, and knew that if things had been otherwise – he meant, not his father's dying, but his recently good relations with his wife – he could easily have got off the train with the girl, and persuaded her to spend the rest of her holiday with him, having made excuses to her family. Or he could have met her in London. But all he wanted now was to hear her voice, and to let himself be stimulated by the light from her eyes and her hair.

She got off the train, with a small laughing look that made his heart beat, and she strode off across the platform with her banners of yellow hair streaming behind her, leaving him alone in the brown compartment full of brown air.

At the station he was looking for a taxi when he saw his brother Cedric. A brown suit that discreetly confined a small stomach came towards him. That suit could only clothe a member of the professional classes, it had to be taken into account before the face, which was, as it happened, a mild pale face that had a look on it of duty willingly performed.

Cedric said, in his way of dealing all at once with every possible contingency: 'Mrs Markham said it had to be this train. I came because Ellen has only just come herself: I arrived first.'

He had a Rover, dark blue, not new. He and Jack, defined by this car and particularly accurately in this country town, drove through soothingly ancient streets.

The brothers drove more or less in silence to the church precincts. As they passed in under a thirteenth-century stone archway, Cedric said: 'Ellen booked a room for you. It is the Royal Arms, and she and I are there too. It is only five minutes from Father.'

They walked in silence over grass to the back door of this solid brick house which the Church devoted to the old. Not as a charity of course. These were the old whose own saved money or whose children could pay for their rooms and for Mrs Markham. The poor old were elsewhere.

Mrs Markham came forward from her sitting-room and said,

'How do you do, Mr Orkney?' to Jack, smiling like a hostess at Cedric. 'I am sure you would all like some tea now,' she directed. 'I'll bring you some up.' She was like the woman on the train. And like Ellen.

He followed his brother up old wooden stairs that gleamed, and smelled of lavender and wax polish. As always happened, the age of the town, and of the habits of the people who lived in it, the smell of tradition, enveloped Jack in well-being: he had to remind himself that he was here for an unpleasant occasion. At the top of the stairs various unmarked doors were the entrances to the lives of four old people. Cedric opened one without knocking, and Jack followed him into a room he had been in twice before on duty visits. It was a smallish, but pleasant, room with windows overlooking the lawns that surrounded the church.

Sister Ellen, in thick grey tweed, sat knitting. She said: 'Oh Jack, there you are, we are all here at last.'

Jack sat. Cedric sat. They had to arrange their feet so as not to entangle in the middle of the small floor. They all exchanged news. The main thing that had happened to the three of them was that the children had all grown up.

The grandchildren, eight of them, knew each other, and had complicated relationships: they were a family, unlike their parents.

Mrs Markham brought tea, of the kind appropriate to this room, this town: scones, butter, jam, comb honey, fruit buns, cherry cake, fruit cake. Also cream. She left, giving the three a glance that said: At last it is all as it should be.

Jack asked: 'Have you seen him?'

'No,' said Cedric a fraction of a second before Ellen did. It was clear that here was competition for the perfect disposition of this death. Jack was remembering how these two had fought for domination over each other, and over, of course, himself.

'That is to say,' said Ellen, 'we have seen him, but he was not conscious.'

'Another stroke?' asked Jack.

'He had another before Christmas,' said Cedric, 'but he didn't tell us, he didn't want to worry us.'

'I heard about it through Jilly,' said Ellen. Jilly was her daughter.

'And I through Ann,' said Cedric. Ann was his.

Jack had now to remind himself that these names represented persons, not samples of pretty infancy.

'He is very close to Ann,' said Cedric.

'He is fond of Jilly too,' said Ellen.

'I suppose there is a nurse in there?' asked Jack. 'Oh of course, there must be.'

'There is a day nurse and a night nurse, and they change places at dawn and dusk,' said Ellen. 'I must say, I am glad of this tea. There was no restaurant on the train.'

'I wonder if I could see him?' asked Jack, and then corrected it: 'I shall go in to see him.' He knew, as he spoke, that all the way on the train he had in fact been waiting for the moment when he could walk into the little bedroom, and his father would smile at him and say – he had not been able to imagine what, but it must be something that he had been waiting to hear from him, or from somebody, for years. This surely was the real purpose of coming here? That what he had in fact been expecting was something like a 'deathbed scene', with vital advice and mutual comfort, embarrassed him, and he felt that he was stupid. Now he understood that embarrassment was the air of this room: the combat between elder brother and sister was nominal; they skirmished from habit to cover what they felt. Which was that they were in a position not allowed for by their habits of living. Jack had a vision of rapidly running trains – their lives; but they had had to stop the trains, had had to pull the emergency cords, and at great inconvenience to everyone, because of this ill-timed death. Death had to be ill-timed? It was its nature? Why was it felt to be? There was something ridiculous about this scene in which he was trapped: three middle-aged children sitting about in one room, idle, thinking of their real lives which stagnated, while in another room an old man lay dying, attended by a strange woman.

'I'm going in,' he said, and this time got up, instinctively careful of his head: he was tall in this low-ceilinged room.

'Go in without knocking,' said Ellen.

'Yes,' Cedric confirmed.

Jack stooped under the door-frame. An inappropriate picture had come into his mind. It was of his sister in a scarlet pinafore and bright-blue-checked sleeves tugging a wooden horse which was held by a pale plump boy. Jack had been scared that when Ellen got the horse a real fight would start. But Cedric held on, lips tight, being jerked by Ellen's tugs as a dog is tugged by the other dog who has fastened his teeth into the bit of meat or the stick. This scene had taken place in the old garden, for it had been enclosed by pink hydrangeas, while gravel had crunched underfoot. They must all have been very young, because Ellen had still been the classic golden-haired beauty: later she became large and ordinary.

What he was really seeing was his father sitting up against high pillows. A young woman in white sat with her hands folded, watching the dying man. But he looked asleep. It was only when he saw the healthy young woman that Jack understood that his father had become a small old man: he had definitely shrunk. The room was dark, and it was not until Jack stood immediately above his father that he saw the mouth was open. But what was unexpected was that the eyelids had swelled and were blue, as if decomposition had set in there already. Those bruised lids affected Jack like something in bad taste, like a fart at a formal meal, or when making love of a romantic sort. He looked in appeal at the nurse, who said in a natural voice which she did not lower at all: 'He did stir a moment ago, but he didn't really come to himself.'

Jack nodded, not wanting to break the hush of time that surrounded the bed, and bent lower, trying not to see the dying lids, but remembering what he could of his father's cool, shrewd, judging look. It seemed to him as if the bruised puffs of flesh were trembling, might lift. But this stare did not have the power to rouse his father, and soon Jack straightened himself – cautiously. Where did the Church put its tall old people, he wondered, and backed out of the room, keeping his eyes on the small old man in his striped pyjamas which showed very clean under a dark grey cardigan that was fastened under the collar with a gold tie-pin, giving him a formal, dressed-up look.

'How does he seem?' asked Ellen. She had resumed her knitting.

'Asleep.'

'Unconscious,' said Cedric.

Jack asserted himself – quite easily, he saw with relief. 'He doesn't look unconscious to me. On the contrary, I thought he nearly woke up.'

They knew the evening was wearing on: their watches told them so. It remained light; an interminable summer evening filled the sky above the church tower. A young woman came through the room, a coat over her white uniform, and in a moment the other nurse came past them, on her way out.

'I think we might as well have dinner,' said Ellen, already folding her knitting.

'Should one of us stay perhaps?' corrected Cedric. He stayed, and Jack had hotel dinner and a bottle of wine with his sister; he didn't dislike being with her as much as he had expected. He was even remembering times when he had been fond of Ellen.

They returned to keep watch, while Cedric took his turn for dinner. At about eleven the doctor came in, disappeared for five minutes into the bedroom, and came out saying that he had given Mr Orkney an injection. By the time they had thought to ask what the injection was, he had said that his advice was that they should all get a good night's sleep, and had gone. Each hesitated before saying that they intended to take the doctor's advice: this situation, traditionally productive of guilt, was doing its work well.

Before they had reached the bottom of the stairs, the nurse came after them: 'Mr Orkney, Mr Orkney . . .' Both men turned, but she said: 'Jack? He was asking for Jack.'

Jack ran up the stairs, through one room, into the other. But it seemed as if the old man had not moved since he had last seen him. The nurse had drawn the curtains, shutting out the sky so full of light, of summer, and had arranged the lamp so that it made a bright space in the dark room. In this was a wooden chair with a green cushion on it, and on the cushion a magazine. The lit space was like the detail of a picture much magnified. The nurse said: 'Really, with that injection, he ought not to wake now.' She took her place again with the magazine on her lap, inside the circle of light.

Yet he had woken, he had asked for himself, Jack, and for nobody else. Jack was alert, vibrating with his nearness to what his father might say. But he stood helpless, trying to make out the bruises above the eyes, which the shadows were hiding. 'I'll stay here the night,' he declared, all energy, and strode out, only just remembering to lower his head in time, to tell his sister and his brother, who had come back up the stairs.

'The nurse thinks he is unlikely to wake, but I am sure it would be what he would wish if one of us were to stay.'

That he had used another of the obligatory phrases struck Jack with more than amusement: now the fact that the prescribed phrases made their appearance one after the other was like a guarantee that he was behaving appropriately, that everything would go smoothly and without embarrassment, and that he could expect his father's eyes to appear from behind the corrupted lids – that he would speak the words Jack needed to hear. Cedric and Ellen quite understood, but demanded to be called at once if . . . They went off together across the bright grass towards the hotel.

Jack sat up all night; but there was no night, midsummer swallowed the dark; at midnight the church was still glimmering and people strolled talking softly over the lawns. He had skimmed through Trollope's *The Small House at Allington,* and had dipped into a book of his own called *With the Guerrillas in Guatemala.* The name on the spine was Jack Henge, and now he wondered if he had ever told his father that this was one of his *noms de plume,* and he thought that if so, it showed a touching interest on his father's part, but if not, that there must have been some special hidden sympathy shown in the choice or chance that led to its sitting here on the old man's shelves side by side with the Complete Works of Trollope and George Eliot and

Walter Scott. But, of course, it was unlikely now that he would ever know ... his father had not woken, had not stirred, all night. Once he had tiptoed in and the nurse had lifted her head and smiled; clearly, though the old man had gone past the divisions of day and night, the living must still adhere to them, for the day nurse had spoken aloud, but now it was night, the nurse whispered: 'The injection is working well. You try to rest, Mr Orkney.' Her solicitude for him, beaming out from the bright cave hollowed from the dark of the room, enclosed them together in the night's vigil, and when the day nurse came, and the night nurse went yawning, looking pale, and tucking dark strands of hair as if tidying up after a night's sleep, her smile at Jack was that of a comrade after a shared ordeal.

Almost at once the day nurse came back into the living-room and said: 'Is there someone called Ann?'

'Yes, a granddaughter, he was asking for her?'

'Yes. Now, he was awake for a moment.'

Jack suppressed: 'He didn't ask for me?' – and ran back into the bedroom which was now filled with a stuffy light that presented the bruised lids to the nurse and to Jack.

'I'll tell my brother that Ann has been asked for.'

Jack walked through fresh morning air that had already brought a few people on to the grass around the church, to the hotel, where he found Cedric and Ellen at breakfast.

He said that no, he had not been wanted, but that Ann was wanted now. Ellen and Cedric conferred and agreed that Ann 'could reasonably be expected' never to forgive them if she was not called. Jack saw that these words soothed them both; they were comforting himself. He was now suddenly tired. He drank coffee, refused breakfast, and decided on an hour's sleep. Ellen went to telephone greetings and the news that nothing had changed to her family; Cedric to summon Ann, while Jack wondered if he should telephone Rosemary. But there was nothing to say.

He fell on his bed and dreamed, woke, dreamed again, woke, forced himself back to sleep but was driven up out of it to stand in the middle of his hotel room, full of horror. His dreams had been landscapes of dark menacing shapes that were of man's making – metallic, like machines, steeped in a cold grey light, and scattered about on a plain where cold water lay spilled about, gleaming. This water reflected, he knew, death, or news, or information about death, but he stood too far away on the plain to see what pictures lay on its surfaces.

Now Jack was one of those who do not dream. He prided himself on never dreaming. Of course he had read the 'new' information that everyone dreamed every night, but he distrusted this information. For one thing he shared in the general distrust of science, of its emphatic pronouncements; for another, travelling around the world as he had, he had long ago come to terms with the fact that certain cultures were close to aspects of life which he, Jack, had quite simply forbidden. He had locked a door on them. He knew that some people claimed to see ghosts, feared their dead ancestors, consulted witch-doctors, dreamed dreams. How could he not know? He had lived with them. But he, Jack, did not consult the bones or allow himself to be afraid of the dark. Or dream. He did not dream.

He felt groggy, more than tired: the cold of the dream was undermining him, making him shiver. He got back into bed, for he had slept only an hour, and continued with the same dream. Now he and Walter Kenting were interlopers on that death-filled plain, and they were to be shot, one bullet each, on account of non-specific crimes. He woke again: it was ten minutes later. He decided to stay awake. He bathed, changed his shirt and his socks, washed the shirt and socks he had taken off, and hung them over the bath to drip. Restored by these small ritual acts which he had performed in so many hotel rooms and in so many countries, he ordered fresh coffee, drank it in the spirit of one drinking a tonic or prescribed medicine, and walked back across sunlit grass to the old people's house.

He entered on the scene he had left. Ellen and Cedric sat with their feet almost touching, one knitting and one reading the *Daily Telegraph*. Ellen said: 'You haven't slept long.' Cedric said: 'He has asked for you again.'

'*What!*' While he had slept, his energies draining into that debilitating dream, he might have heard, at last, what his father wanted to say. 'I think I'll sit with him a little.'

'That might not be a bad idea,' said his sister. She was annoyed that she had not been 'asked for'? If so, she showed no signs of it.

The little sitting-room was full of light; sunshine lay on the old wood sills. But the bedroom was dark, warm, and smelled of many drugs.

The nurse had the only chair – today just a piece of furniture among many. He made her keep it, and sat down slowly on the bed, as if this slow subsidence could make his weight less.

He kept his eyes on his father's face. Since yesterday the bruises had spread beyond the lids: the flesh all around the eyes and as far down as the cheek-bones was stained.

'He has been restless,' said the nurse, 'but the doctor should be here soon.' She spoke as if the doctor could answer any question that could possibly ever be asked; and Jack, directed by her as he had been by his sister and his brother, now listened for the doctor's coming. The morning went past. His sister came to ask if he would go with her to luncheon. She was hungry, but Cedric was not. Jack said he would stay, and while she was gone the doctor came.

He sat on the bed – Jack had risen from it, retreating to the window. The doctor took the old man's wrist in his and seemed to commune with the darkened eyelids. 'I rather think that perhaps . . .' He took out a plastic box from his case, that held the ingredients of miracle-making: syringe, capsules, methylated spirits.

Jack asked: 'What effect does that have?' He wanted to ask: Are you keeping him alive when he should be dead?

The doctor said: 'Sedative and pain-killer.'

'A heart stimulant?'

Now the doctor said: 'I have known your father for thirty years.' He was saying: I have more right than you have to say what he would have wanted.

Jack had to agree; he had no idea if his father would want to be allowed to die, as nature directed, or whether he would like to be kept alive as long as possible.

The doctor administered an injection, as light and as swift as the strike of a snake, rubbed the puncture with one gentle finger, and said: 'Your father looked after himself. He has plenty of life in him yet.'

He went out. Jack looked in protest at the nurse: what on earth had been meant? Was his father not dying? The nurse smiled, timidly, and from that smile Jack gathered that the words had been spoken for his father's sake, in case he was able to hear them, understand them, and be fortified by them.

He saw the nurse's face change: she bent over the old man, and Jack took a long step and was beside her. In the bruised flesh the eyes were open and stared straight up. This was not the human gaze he had been wanting to meet, but a dull glare from chinks in damaged flesh.

'Ann,' said the old man. 'Is Ann here?'

From the owner of those sullen eyes Jack might expect nothing; as an excuse to leave the room, he said to the nurse, 'I'll tell Ann's father.'

In the living-room sunlight had left the sills. Cedric was not there. 'It's Ann he wants,' Jack said. 'He has asked again.'

'She is coming. She has to come from Edinburgh. She is with Maureen.'

Ellen said this as if he was bound to know who Maureen was. She was probably one of Cedric's ghastly wife's ghastly relations. Thinking of the awfulness of Cedric's wife made him feel kindly towards Ellen. Ellen wasn't really so bad. There she sat, knitting, tired and sad but not showing it. When you came down to it she didn't look all that different from Rosemary – unbelievably also a middle-aged woman. But at this thought Jack's loyalty to the past rebelled. Rosemary, though a large, fresh-faced, greying woman, would never wear a suit which looked as if its edges might cut, or have her hair set in a helmet of ridges and frills. She wore soft pretty clothes, and her hair was combed straight and long, as she had always worn it: he had begged her to keep it like that. But if you came to think of it, probably the lives the two women led were similar. Probably they were all more alike than

229 The Temptation of Jack Orkney

any one of them would care to admit. Including Cedric's awful wife.

He looked at Ellen's lids, lowered while she counted stitches. They were her father's eyes and lids. When she lay dying probably her lids would bruise and puff.

Cedric came in. He was very like the old man – more like than any of them. He, Jack, was more like their mother, but when he was dying perhaps his own lids ... Ellen looked up, smiled at Cedric, then at Jack. They were all smiling at each other. Ellen laid down her knitting, and lit herself a cigarette. The brothers could see that this was the point when she might cry. But Mrs Markham came in, followed by a well-brushed man all white cuffs and collar and pink fresh skin.

'The Dean,' she breathed, with the smile of a girl.

The Dean said: 'No, don't get up. I dropped in. I am an old friend of your father's, you know. Many and many a game of chess have we played in this room ...' and he had followed Mrs Markham into the bedroom.

'He had Extreme Unction yesterday,' said Ellen.

'Oh,' said Jack. 'I didn't realize that Extreme Unction was part of his ...' He stopped, not wanting to hurt feelings. He believed both Ellen and Cedric to be religious.

'He got very High in the end,' said Cedric.

Ellen giggled. Jack and Cedric looked inquiry. 'It sounded funny,' she said. 'You know, the young ones talk about getting high.'

Cedric's smile was wry; and Jack remembered there had been talk about his elder son, who had threatened to become addicted. What to? Jack could not remember: he would have to ask the girls.

'I suppose he wants a church service and to be buried?' asked Jack.

'Oh yes,' said Cedric. 'I have got his will.'

'Of course, you would have.'

'Well, we'll just have to get through it all,' said Ellen. It occurred to Jack that this was what she probably said, or thought, about her own life: Well, I've just got to get through it. The thought surprised him: Ellen was pleasantly surprising him. Now he heard her say: 'Well, I suppose some people have to have religion.'

And now Jack looked at her in disbelief.

'Yes,' said Cedric, equally improbably, 'it must be a comfort for them, one can see that.' He laid small strong hands around his crossed knees and made the knuckles crack.

'Oh Cedric,' complained Ellen, as she had as a girl: this knuckle-cracking had been Cedric's way of expressing tension since he had been a small boy.

'Sorry,' said Cedric. He went on, letting his hands fall to his sides, and swing there, in a conscious effort towards relaxing himself. 'From time to time I take my pulse – as it were. Now that I am getting on for sixty one can expect the symptoms. Am I getting God? Am I still myself? Yes, no, doubtful? But so far, I can report an even keel, I am happy to say.'

'Oh, one can understand it,' said Ellen. 'God knows, one can understand it only too well. But I really would be ashamed . . .'

Both Ellen and Cedric were looking at him, to add his agreement – of which they were sure, of course. But he could not speak. He had made precisely the same joke a month ago, in a group of 'the Old Guard', about taking his pulse to find out if he had caught religion. And everyone had confessed to the same practice. To get God, after a lifetime of enlightened rationalism, would be the most shameful of capitulations.

Now his feelings were the same as those of members of a particularly exclusive Club on being forced to admit the lower classes; or the same as that Victorian bishop's who, travelling to some cannibal-land to baptize the converted, had been heard to say that he could wish that his Church admitted degrees of excellence in its material: he could not believe that his lifetime of impeccable service would weigh the same as that of these so recently benighted ones.

Besides, Jack was shocked: to hear these sentiments from Ellen, looking as she did, leading the life she did – she had no right to them! She sounded vulgar.

She was saying: 'Of course I do go to church sometimes to

please Freddy.' Her husband. 'But he seems to be losing fervour rather than gaining it, I am glad to say.'

'Yes,' said Cedric. 'I am afraid I have rather the same thing with Muriel. We have compromised on Christmas and Easter. She says it is bad for my image not to be a church-goer. Petersbank is a small place, you know, and the good people do like their lawyers and doctors to be pillars of society. But I find that sort of trimming repulsive and I tell her so.'

Again they waited for Jack; again he had to be silent. But surely by now they would take his opinions for granted? Why should they? If they could become atheist, then what might he not become? The next thing, they'll turn out to be socialists, he thought. Surely all this godlessness must be a new development? He could have sworn that Ellen had been devout and Cedric correct towards a Church which – as far as Jack had been concerned – had been irritation, humiliation, tedium, throughout his childhood. Even now he could not think of the meaningless services, the Sunday school, the fatuity of the parsons, the social conformity that was associated with the Church, without feeling as if he had escaped from a sticky trap.

Ellen was saying: 'As for me, I am afraid I find it harder to believe as I get older. I mean, God, in this terrible world, with new horrors every minute. No, I am afraid it is all too much.'

'I quite agree,' said Cedric. 'The devil's more like it.'

'Yes,' said Jack, able to speak at last. 'Yes, that's about it, I'm afraid.' It was the best he could do. The room was now full of good feeling, and they would have begun to talk about their childhood if the bedroom door had not opened, and the Dean come out. The smile he had shed on the nurse was still on his healthy lips, and he now let it benefit the three, while he raised his hand in what looked like a benediction. 'No, don't get up!' He was almost at once out of the other door, followed close by Mrs Markham.

The look the three now shared repudiated the Dean and all his works. Ellen smiled at her brother exactly as – he realized in capitulation to a totally unforeseen situation – his own wife would have done. Cedric nodded private comment on the stupidities of mankind.

Soon Cedric went to the bedroom, to return with the report that the old man looked pretty deep in. Then Ellen went, and came back saying that she didn't know how the nurse could bear it in that hot dark room. But as she sat down, she said: 'In the old days, one of us would have been in there all the time?'

'Yes,' said Cedric. 'All of us.'

'Not just a nurse,' said Ellen. 'Not a stranger.'

Jack was thinking that if he had stuck it out, then he would have been there when his father called for him; but he said: 'I'm glad it is a nurse. I don't think there is very much left of *him*.'

Ann arrived. What Jack saw first was a decided, neat little face, and that she wore a green jacket and trousers that were not jeans but 'good' as her aunt Ellen used the word. Ellen always had 'good' clothes that lasted a long time. Ann's style was not, for instance, like Jack's daughters', who wore rags and rubbish and cast-offs and who looked enchanting, like princesses in disguise. She kissed her father, because he was waiting for her to do this. She stood examining them with care. Her father could be seen in her during that leisurely, unembarrassed examination: it was both her right and her duty to do this. Now Jack saw that she was small, with a white skin that looked greenish where it was shaded, and hair as pale as her father's had been. Her eyes, like her father's, were green.

She said: 'Is he still alive?'

The voice was her father's, and it took her aunt and her uncle back, back – she did not know the reason for their strained, reluctant smiles as they gazed at her.

They were suffering that diminution, that assault on individuality which is the worst of families: some invisible dealer had shuffled noses, hands, shoulders, hair and reassembled them to make – little Ann, for instance. The dealer made out of parts a unit that the owner would feed, maintain, wash, medicate for a lifetime, thinking of it as 'mine', except at moments like these, when knowledge was forced home that everyone was put together out of stock.

'Well,' said Ann, 'you all look dismal enough. Why do you?'

She went into the bedroom, leaving the door open. Jack understood that Ann had principles about attitudes towards death: like his own daughters.

The three crowded into the room.

Ann sat on the bed, high up near the pillow, in a way that hid the old man's face from them. She was leaning forward, the nurse – whom Ann had ignored – ready to intervene.

'Grandad!' she said. 'Grandad! It's me!'

Silence. Then it came home to them that she had called up Lazarus. They heard the old man's voice, quite as they remembered it: 'It's you, is it? It is little Ann?'

'Yes, Grandad, it's Ann.'

They crowded forward, to see over her shoulder. They saw their father, smiling normally. He looked like a tired old man, that was all. His eyes, surrounded by the puffy bruises, had light in them.

'Who are these people?' he asked. 'Who are all these tall people?'

The three retreated, leaving the door open.

Silence from the bedroom, then singing. Ann was singing in a small clear voice: 'All things bright and beautiful.'

Jack looked at Cedric. Ellen looked at Cedric. He deprecated: 'Yes, I am afraid that she is. That's the bond, you see.'

'Oh,' said Ellen, 'I see, that explains it.'

The singing went on:

> 'All things bright and beautiful,
> All creatures great and small,
> All things wise and wonderful,
> The Lord God made them all.'

The singing went on, verse after verse like a lullaby.

'She came to stay with him,' said Cedric. 'At Easter, I think it was. She slept here, on the floor.'

Jack said: 'My girls are religious. But not my son of course.'

They looked blankly sympathetic: it occurred to Jack that his son's fame was after all circumscribed to a pretty small circle.

'He takes after me,' said Jack.

'Ah,' said Cedric.

'A lot of them are religious,' said Ellen, brisk.

'It's the *kind* of religion that sticks in one's craw,' said Jack. 'Simple faith and Celtic crosses.'

'I agree,' said Cedric. 'Pretty low-level stuff.'

'Does the level matter?' asked Ellen. 'Surely *c'est le premier pas qui coûte*?'

At which Jack looked at his sister in a disbelief that was meant to be noticed. Cedric, however, did not seem surprised: of course, he saw Ellen more often. He said mildly: 'I don't agree. One wouldn't mind if they went on to something a bit more elevated. It's this servants' hall village green mothers' meeting sort of thing. You spend a fortune trying to educate them decently and then it ends up in . . . My eldest was a Jesus freak for a few months, for example. After Winchester, Balliol, the lot.'

'What is a Jesus freak?' inquired Ellen.

'What it sounds like.'

Normally Jack would have cut out emotionally and mentally at the words 'servants' hall', but he was still with them. He said: 'What gets me is that they spout it all out, so pat and pretty, you know, and you get the feeling it might be anything, anything they had picked up or lay to hand – *pour épater le bourgeois,* you know.'

At this he had to think that the other two must be thinking, but were too polite to say, that his own socialism, a degree or two off full communism when he was in his teens, had had no deeper cause. This unspoken comment brought the conversation to a stop.

The singing had stopped too. It was getting dark.

'Well,' said Ellen, 'I tell you what I'm going to do, I am going to have a bath and then dinner and then a good night's sleep. I think Ann is meeting father's requirements better than we could.'

'Yes,' said Cedric.

He went to the door, and communicated this news to his daughter, who said she would be fine, she would be super, she would stay with her grandad, and if she got tired she could sleep on the floor.

Over the dinner table at the hotel, it was a reunion of people who had not met for a long time. They drank some wine and they were sentimental.

But the little time of warmth died with the coffee, served in the hall, which let in draughts from the street every time somebody came in.

Jack said: 'I'll turn in, I didn't sleep last night.'

'Nor I.'

'Nor I.'

They nodded at each other; to kiss would have been exaggerated. Jack went upstairs, while Cedric and Ellen went to telephone their families.

In the bedroom he stood by the window and watched how the light filled the lime outside. Breaths of tree-air came to his face. He was full of variegated emotions, none, he was afraid, to do with his father: they were about his brother and his sister, his childhood, that past of his which everything that happened to him these days seemed to evoke, seemed to present to him, sharp, clear, and for the most part painful: he did not feel he could sleep, he was over-stimulated. He would lie on his bed for a rest. Waking much later, to a silence that said the night had deepened all around him, with the heaviness of everybody's sleeping, he started up into a welter of feeling that he could not face, and so burrowed back into sleep again, there to be met by – but it was hard to say what.

Terror was not the word. Nor fear. Yet there were no other words that he knew for the state he found himself in. It was more like a state of acute attention, as if his whole being – memory, body, present and past chemistries – had been assaulted by a warning, so that he had to attend to it. He was standing, as it were, at the alert, listening to something which said: Time is passing, be quick, listen, attend.

It was the knowledge of passing time that was associated with the terror, so that he found himself standing upright in the dark room, crying out: 'Oh, no, no, no, I understand, I am sorry, I . . .' He was whimpering like a puppy. The dark was solid around him, and he didn't know where he was. He believed himself to be in a grave, and he rushed to the window, throwing it open as if he were heaving a weight off himself. The window was hard to open. At last he forced it, leaning out to let the tree-air come to his face, but it was not air that came in, but a stench, and this smell was confirmation of a failure which had taken place long ago, in some choice of his, that he had now forgotten. The feeling of urgency woke him: he was lying on his bed. Now he really did shoot into the centre of the room, while the smell that had been the air of the dream was fading around him. He was terrified. But that was not the word . . . he feared that the terror would fade, he would forget what he had dreamed; the knowledge that there was something that had to be done, done soon, would fade, and he would forget even that he had dreamed.

What *had* he dreamed? Something of immense importance.

But as he stood there, with the feeling of urgency draining away and his daytime self coming back, even while he knew, as powerfully as he had ever known anything, that the dream was the most important statement ever made to him, the other half of him was asserting old patterns of thought, which said that to dream was neurotic and to think of death morbid.

He turned on the light, out of habit, a child chasing away night-fears, and then at once switched it off again, since the light was doing its job too well: the dream was dwindling into a small feeling that remarked in a tiny nagging voice that he should be attending to something. And Jack was chasing after the dream: No, no, don't go . . .

But the feeling of the dream had gone, and he was standing near the window, telling himself – but it was an intellectual statement now, without force – that he had had a warning. A warning? Was it that? By whom? To whom? He must do something . . . but what? *He had been terrified of dying:* he had been forced to be afraid of that. For the first time in his life he had been made to feel the fear of death. He knew that this is what he would feel when he was in his father's position, lying propped on pillows, with people around him waiting for him to die. (If the state of the world would allow his death such a degree of civilization!)

All his life he had said lightly: Oh, death, I'm not afraid of death, it will be like a candle going out, that's all. On these occasions when, just like his brother Cedric, he checked up on himself for internal weakness, he had said to himself: I shall die, just like a cat or a dog, and too bad, when I die, that's that. He had known the fear of fear of course: he had been a soldier in two wars. He had known what it was to rehearse in his mind all the possible deaths that were available to him, removing pain and horror by making them familiar, and choosing suitable ways of responding – words, postures, silences, stoicisms – that would be a credit to him, to humanity. He knew very well the thought that to be hit over the head like an ox, stunned before the throat was cut, was the highest that he could hope for: annihilation was what he had elected.

But his dream had been horror of annihilation, the threat of nothingness ... it already seemed far away. He stretched his arms up behind his head, feeling the strength of his body. *His* body, that was made of fragments of his mother and his father, and of their mothers and their fathers, and shared with little Ann, with his daughters, and of course with his son – exactly like him, his copy. Yes, his, his body, strong, and pulsing with energy – he pushed away the warning from the dream, and switched on the light again, feeling that *that* was over. It was one in the morning, hardly the hour, in an English country hotel, to ask for tea, for coffee. He knew he would not dare to lie again on that bed, so he went down, to let himself out. He was going to his father.

Ann was wrapped in blankets, lying on the floor of the living-room. He knelt by her and gazed at the young face, the perfect eyelids that sealed her eyes shut like a baby's, incisive but delicate, shining, whole.

He sat on his father's bed where Ann had sat, and saw that the old man was slipping away. Jack could not have said why he knew, but he did know the death would be this day: it occurred to him that if he had not had that dream, he would not have known; he would not have been equipped to know, without the dream.

He walked the rest of the night away, standing to watch the

bulk of the old church dwindling down under a sky lightening with dawn. When the birds began, he returned to the hotel, bathed and with confidence woke his sister and brother, saying that yes, they could have breakfast but should not take too much time over it.

At eight-thirty they arrived to find Ann again crouched up on the bed near the old man, crooning to him bits of hymn, old tunes, nursery rhymes. He died without opening his eyes again.

Cedric said he would deal with all the arrangements, and that he would notify them of the funeral, which would probably be on Monday. The three children of the old man separated in good feeling and with kisses saying that they really ought to see more of each other. And Jack said to Ann that she must come and visit. She said yes, it would be super, she could see Elizabeth and Carrie again, how about next week-end? There was to be a Pray-in for Bangladesh.

Jack returned to his home, or rather, to his wife. She was out. He suppressed grievance that there was no note from her: after all, he had not telephoned. She was at another class, he supposed.

He went to see if anybody was in the girls' flat. Carrie and Elizabeth had made rooms for themselves on the top floor, and paid rent for them. They both had good jobs. There was an attic room used occasionally by Joseph.

Hearing sounds, he knocked, with a sense of intruding, and was bidden to come in by Carrie, who seemed in conflict at the sight of him. This was because she, like the others, had been waiting for his coming, waiting for the news of the death. She had prepared the appropriate responses, but had just finished cooking a meal, and was putting dishes on to the table. A young man whose face he did not know was coming towards the table, ready to eat.

Carrie was flushed, her long dark hair fell about, and she was wearing something like a white sack, bordered with deep white lace.

'My father died,' he said.

'Oh, poor you,' said Carrie.

'I don't know,' said Jack.

'This is Bob,' said Carrie. 'My father. Dad, would you like to eat with us? It is a business lunch, actually.'

'No, no,' said Jack. 'I'll see you later.' She called after him: 'Dad, Dad, I'm sorry about Grandad.'

'Oh, he was due to go,' Jack called back.

He cut himself bread and cheese, and rang Walter's office. Walter was back from Dublin, but had to fly to Glasgow that afternoon: he was to appear on television in a debate on the Common Market. He would be back by midday Saturday: the Twenty-Four-Hour Fast would start at two o'clock Saturday. Thirty people were expected to take part. It was a good thing Jack was back: he could take over again.

But what was there to be done?

Nothing much really; he should keep a tag on the names. Some might decide to drop out again. Considering the scale of the horror at that moment taking place in India, the mass misery, it would be a surprisingly small turn-out – he was sorry, he had to leave, a car was waiting.

It is normal to feel, on returning to the place one lives in, after having been away, that one has not left at all: this is not what Jack was feeling now. Whether it was because he was so tired, or because he was more upset by his father's death than he knew, he felt at a distance from his commonplace self, and particularly at a distance from the Jack Orkney who knew so well how to organize a sit-down, or a march, or how to produce such occasions properly for the Press or television.

Walter's contrasting the numbers of the people involved in the Bangladesh tragedy with the numbers who were prepared not to eat, publicly, for twenty-four hours in London had struck him as bathos, as absurdity, but he knew that normally that was how he would be reacting himself.

Now he tried to restore himself by summoning well-tried thoughts. Every time the radio or television was turned on, every time you saw a newspaper, the figure *nine million* was used, with the information that these refugees had no future, or none of a normal kind. (India's short, sharp, efficient war that reprieved these same nine million was of course months in the future.) But there was nothing to be done; this catastrophe had the same feeling as the last, which had been Nigeria: a large number of people would die of starvation or would be murdered, but there was no power strong enough to stop this.

It was this feeling of helplessness that seemed to be the new factor; each time there was something of the kind, the numbers of people grew larger, and the general helplessness augmented. Yet all that had happened was that great catastrophes were being brought to general attention more forcefully than in the past. Not long ago, as recently as thirty years ago, it had been a commonplace for small paragraphs in newspapers to say that six, seven, eight million people had died, were dying of starvation, in China: communism had put an end to famine, or to the world's hearing about it. A very short time ago, a decade, several million might die in a bad season in India: the green revolution had (possibly temporarily) checked that. In Russia millions had died in the course of some great scheme or other: the collectivization of the peasants, for instance.

The most shocking thing that had happened to his generation was the event summed up by the phrase 'six million Jews'. Although so many millions of people had been killed or had died in that war, and in a thousand awful ways, it was that one thing, the *six million*, which seemed worst. Because, of course, as everyone knew, it had been willed and deliberate murder . . . Was it really any more deliberate than the *nine million* of Stalin's forcible collectivization? And how about that *nine*, or *ninety*, million – the never-to-be-known figure for the deaths of black men in Africa caused by white men in the course of bringing civilization to that continent? (This figure, whatever it was, never could accumulate about it the quality of senseless horror that had the figure for the death camps and gas chambers under Hitler. Why not?) During the next twelve months, between *twelve* and *twenty-four* million would die of starvation in the world (the figure depended on the source of calculation). The twelve months after, this figure would double – by the end of a decade, the numbers of people expected to die annually of hunger was beyond calculation … These figures, and many more, clicked through his well-stocked journalist's head, and against them he heard Walter's voice rather tetchy, critical, saying that there would only be thirty people for the Twenty-Four-Hour Fast.

Yes, of course it was ridiculous to think on these lines and particularly when you were tired; he had been thrown off balance worse than he knew. He would sleep for a little – no, no, better not, he would rather not, he would not go to his bed unless Rosemary could be with him. Well, there were things that he ought to be doing, he was sure: for one thing, he had not read the newspapers for three days, or listened to the news. He regarded it as his responsibility to read all the newspapers every day, as if knowing what was bad could prevent worse. He did not want to read the papers; he wanted to sit down and wait quietly for his wife. This made him guilty, and he was associating his reluctance to plunge into the misery and threat of the newspapers with the brutalizing of everybody, everyone's acceptance of horror as normal. Well, it was – when had storms of blood and destruction *not* swept continuously over the globe?

His will was being attacked: he had no will. This was why he needed to see Rosemary. This thought, he knew, had put a small whimsical grimace on to his face; the grimace was for the benefit of an observer. The observer was himself: it was there for the sake of his pride – a very odd thing had happened between him and his wife. For a long time, in fact for most of the marriage, they would have said that they were unhappily married. It had been a war marriage of course, like those of most of their contemporaries. It had begun in passion, separation, dislocation. They had felt, on beginning to live together for the first time, when they had been married for nearly six years, that their good times had been stolen from them. Then three children: they had turned Rosemary into an obsessed, complaining woman; so he had seen her, and so she now saw herself during that period. He was most often out of England, and had many affairs, some of them serious. He knew she had been in love with someone else: she, like himself, had refused to consider a divorce because of the effect on the children. There was of course nothing remarkable in this history: but some of the men he knew had divorced, leaving first wives to bring up children. He knew that many of his friends' wives, like Rosemary, had been obsessed with grievance at their lot, yet had been dutiful mothers.

Various unhappy balances had been achieved by himself and Rosemary, always regarded as second-best. Best was in fantasy, or what other people had. Then the children grew up, and were no longer there to be cooked for, worried about, shopped for, nursed – suddenly these two people who had been married thirty years discovered they were enjoying each other. They could not use the words 'a second honeymoon' because they had never had a first. Jack remembered that at the other end of what now seemed like a long tunnel of responsibility, worry, guilt – relieved by frequent exile whose enjoyability caused more guilt – had been a young woman with whom he had been more in love than with anybody since. He relaxed into the pleasures of his home, pleasure with Rosemary, who, appreciated at last, took on energy and poise, lost her listlessness, her reproach, her patience under neglect.

It had been the completeness of her revival that was the only thing disturbing about their being in love again: Jack lived marvelling that so little a thing as his own attention should be enough to nourish this creature, to burnish her with joy. He could not help being guilty anew that so little an effort towards self-discipline would have produced the kindness which could have made this woman's life happy, instead of a martyrdom. Yet he knew he had not been capable of even so small an effort: he had found her intolerable, and the marriage a burden, and that was the truth. But the thought he could not come to terms with was this: what sort of a creature was she, to be fed and made happy by the love of a creature like himself?

And Rosemary was not the only woman he observed enjoying a new lease of life. At parties of 'the Old Guard' it was enough simply to look around at the wives of the same age as his own wife, the women recently released from nursery and kitchen, to see many in the same condition, without having to ask if a second honeymoon was in progress – and here was another source of unease. He was not able to ask, to discuss frankly, or even to raise the matter at all, and yet these were friends, he had been with them, worked with them, faced a hundred emergencies with them – but they did not have with each other the friendship of the kind that would enable them to talk about their relationships with each other, with their wives, their wives with them. Yet this was friendship, or at least it was as close to friendship as he was likely to get. Intimacy he had known, but with women with whom he was having affairs. Intimacy, frankness, trust, had, as it were, been carried inside him, to be bestowed on loved women, and withdrawn when that love had ended because he was married. So it was not that he had not known perfect intimacy; it was that he had known it with several people, one after another. What was left now of these relationships was a simplicity of understanding when he met these women again – those that he did meet, for, after all, many of these affairs had taken place in other countries. But even now he had to admit that this state had never been achieved with his wife, as good as their relation now was: for what he could not share with her was a feeling he could not control that he had to value her less for being so satisfied – more, fulfilled – with so little. Himself.

Yet, for all these reservations, the last two years had been better than anything he had expected with a woman, except in the expectations of his dreams about marriage so long ago. They went for holidays together, for week-ends to old friends, to the theatre, for special meals at restaurants, and for long walks. They made little treats for each other, gave each other presents, had developed the private language of lovers. And all the time her gaiety and energy grew, while she could not prevent herself watching him – not knowing that she did it, and this humbled him and made him wretched – for the return of the old tyrant, the boor. Always he was aware that their happiness lacked a foundation.

But what foundation ought there to be?

Now he wanted to tell his wife the dream he had had about death. This is why he had been longing to see her. But he had not allowed himself to understand the truth, which was that he couldn't tell her. She dreaded change in him; she would feel the dream as a threat. And it was. For another thing, this new easy affection they had would not admit the words he would have to use. What words? None he knew could convey the quality of the dream. The habits of their life together made it inevitable that if he said: Rosemary, I had a terrible dream, well no, that was not it, its terribleness is not the point, wait, I must tell you – she would reply: Oh Jack, you must have eaten something. Are you well? – And she would run off to get him a glass of medicine of some sort. Her smile at him, while she handed it to him, would say that she knew, they both knew, that he didn't really need it, but she enjoyed looking after him when at last he was enjoying being looked after.

Tea-time came. Jack watched the young man from upstairs walk away under the summer's load of leaf. The telephone rang twice, both times for Rosemary. He took messages. He saw Elizabeth come up the path to the side door, nearly called to her, but decided not. He sat on into the summer afternoon, feeling that it was appropriate to be melancholy: it was what was expected of him. But that was not it! It was as if he had no substance at all, there was nothing to him, no purpose, no worth . . . something was draining quietly away from him, had been, for a long time.

Elizabeth came running in, saying: 'Oh Father, I am so sorry, you must be feeling low.' Caroline came after her. Carrie was now dressed in a purple shawl over tight red cotton trousers. Elizabeth, still in what she had worn to work, had on a dark-green trouser suit, but her own personality had been asserted since she came home: she had tied her hair back with an exotic-looking piece of red material, and it was making a froth of gold curls around her face. His cold heart began to stir and to warm, and they sat themselves down opposite, ready to share his grief.

Rosemary now came in, a large, tall woman, smiling and shedding energy everywhere.

'Oh darling,' said she, 'you didn't telephone. I am so sorry. You have had tea, I hope?'

'He's dead,' said Elizabeth to her mother.

'He died this morning,' said Jack, not believing that it had been that morning.

Rosemary slowed her movements about the room, and when she turned to him, her face, like the faces of her daughters, was not smiling.

'When is the funeral?'

'I don't know yet.'

'I'll come with you,' said Elizabeth.

'I won't,' said Carrie. 'I don't like funerals. Not our kind of funeral.'

'And I won't either if you don't mind,' said Rosemary. 'That is, not unless you want me there.' A glass and decanter had appeared beside him, and Rosemary was causing whisky to descend into the glass in a gold stream.

The whisky was not the point, the women's serious faces not the point, the funeral and who was at it, not the point.

'There is no need for any of you to come,' he said. And added, as he had been afraid he might: 'It wouldn't be expected of you.'

All three showed relief, even Elizabeth.

Rosemary hated funerals: they were morbid. Carrie being sort of Buddhist, believed, apparently, in putting corpses out for the vultures. Elizabeth's Christianity, like Ann's, was without benefit of church services.

'Oh no, I want to come with you,' said Elizabeth.

'Well, we'll see.'

He told them about the death – a mild and well-ordered affair. He said that Ellen and Cedric had been there, and watched for his wife's humorous glance so that he could return it: she wanted to convey sympathy for having to be with his family even for two days. Then he began speaking about the Twenty-Four-Hour Fast. He did not ask if they would join him, but he was hoping they would.

Now, while Rosemary had early on been inculcated with his left-wing opinions, during all the years of their unhappiness his activities had been seen by her as being in some subtle way directed against her, or, at any rate, as depriving her of something.

But recently she had several times gone with him to a meeting or a demonstration. Looking guilty, she said that she couldn't join the Fast, because she had a lecture Saturday night, on Stress in the Family. She made it sound funny, in her way of appearing like an intelligent child submitting to official pedantry; but there was no doubt she would be at the lecture. Carrie said nothing: she thought any kind of politics silly. Elizabeth said she would have joined the Fast, but she had a demonstration of her own on Saturday.

Jack now remembered Ann's programme, said that Ann was coming at the week-end for a Pray-in. It turned out that this was the same as Elizabeth's. Both girls were pleased that Ann was coming, and starting talking about her and her relations with her parents. These were not very good: Ann found them materialistic, conventional, bourgeois. Jack was not able to be much amused; he found himself in sympathy with Cedric, possibly even with his sister-in-law. Probably Elizabeth and Carrie said to their friends that their parents were materialistic and bourgeois. He knew that his son Joseph did.

The girls had been going out for the evening, but because of the death, and wanting to cheer their father up, they stayed in to supper. Rosemary's new practice, now that the decades of compulsive cooking, buying, fussing, were done with, was to keep food to its simplest. She offered them soup, toast and fruit. The girls protested: the parents could see that this was because they needed to do something to show their sympathy. Rosemary and Jack sat hand in hand on the sofa, while the girls made a long and delicious meal for them all.

They went to bed early: it was still not quite dark outside. But he needed to make love with his wife, feeling that here at least the cold which threatened him would be held at bay.

But the shell of himself loved, the shell of himself held Rosemary while she fell asleep and turned away from him. He was awake, listening to the tides of blood moving in his body.

He crept downstairs again. He read the newspapers – making himself do so, like a penance for callousness. He listened to the radio, avoiding news bulletins. He did not go to bed again until it was fully light, and was woken an hour later by Cedric: practical reasons had set the funeral for tomorrow, Saturday, at eleven.

Friday he spent in the activities that the journalist was so good at. Saturday was not a good day for train and air services: to reach S— in time for the funeral, and to be back by two, would need luck and ingenuity. He checked the weather forecast: rain and mist were expected. Having made the arrangements, he rang Mona, since Walter was still in Glasgow. Mona was not only the wife of an 'Old Guard', but one in her own right. It had been agreed that he, Jack, would be on the steps of the church at ten, to welcome the fasters as they arrived, and to see that the posters proclaiming the event were in place. He now asked Mona to do all this, explaining why.

'Oh dear,' she said, 'I am so sorry about your father. Yes, luckily I can do it. Who is coming? – wait, I'll get a pencil.'

He gave her the names over the telephone, while she wrote them down.

They were the names of people with whom he had been associated in a dozen different ways, ever since the war ended: it seemed now as if the war had been an instrument to shake out patterns of people who would work and act together – or against each other, for the rest of their lives. They had not known about this process while it was happening, but that was when 'the Old Guard' had been formed. The phrase was a joke of course, and for family use: he certainly would never use it to Walter, Bill, Mona and the rest – they would be hurt by it. Carrie had said one day, reporting a telephone call: 'I didn't get his name, but it sounded like one of the Old Guard.'

These names appeared continually together on dozens, hundreds, of letterheads, appeals, protests, petitions: if you saw one name, you could assume the others. Yet their backgrounds had been very different, of all classes, countries, even races. Some had been communists, some had fought communism. They were Labour and Liberal, vegetarian and pacifist, feeders of orphaned children, builders of villages in Africa and India, rescuers of refugees and survivors of natural and man-made calamities.

They were journalists and editors, actors and writers, film-makers and trade unionists. They wrote books on subjects like Unemployment in the Highlands and The Future of Technology. They sat on councils and committees and the boards of semi-charitable organizations, they were Town Councillors, Members of Parliament, creators of documentary film programmes. They had taken the same stands on Korea and Kenya, on Cyprus and Suez, on Hungary and the Congo, on Nigeria, the Deep South and Brazil, on South Africa and Rhodesia and Ireland and Vietnam and ... and now they were sharing opinions and emotions on the nine million refugees from Bangladesh.

Once, when they had come together to express a view, it had been a minority view, and to get what they believed publicized had sometimes been difficult or impossible. Now something had happened which not all of them had understood: when they expressed themselves about this or that, it was happening more and more often that their views were identical with conventional views put forward freely by majorities everywhere. Once they had been armed with aggressive optimistic views about society, about how to change it; now they were on the defensive. Once they had forecast utopias; now they forecast calamity, failed to prevent calamity, and then worked to minimize calamity.

This view of the Old Guard had been presented to Jack by his son, the chip off the old block.

When Jack had finished the list of names, Mona said: 'Surely we can do better than that?' and he said, apologetically (why, when it was not his fault?): 'I think a lot of people are feeling that the media are doing it for us.'

Then he decided to ring his son, who had not yet heard about his grandfather. To reach Joseph was not easy, since he worked for a variety of 'underground' organizations, slept in many places, might even be out of the country.

At last Jack rang Elizabeth, who was already at her place of work, heard where Joseph was likely to be, and finally reached his son. On hearing that his grandfather was dead, Joseph said: 'Oh that's bad, I am sorry.' On being asked if he and his friends 'with nothing better to do' would like to join the Twenty-Four-Hour Fast, he said: 'But haven't you been reading the newspapers?' Jack did not want to say that he had not read them enough to know what his son's programme was likely to be, but it turned out that 'all of us' were organizing a Protest March for that Sunday.

In his son's briskness, modified because of the death, Jack heard his own youth speaking, and a sense of justice made him sound apologetic towards his son. He felt, too, the start of exhaustion. This was because his effort to be fair made it necessary to resurrect his own youth as he talked to Joseph, and it took the energy that in fantasy he would be using to bring Joseph around to see his point of view: he had recently been indulging fantasies of confronting Joseph with: 'Look, I have something of great importance to say, can you let me have an hour or two?' He was on the point of saying this now, but Joseph said: 'I have to rush off, I'm sorry, see you, give my love to everyone.'

He knew exactly what he wanted to say, not only to his son – to his own youthful self – but to the entire generation, or, rather, to that part of it which was political, the political youth. What he felt was, he knew, paradoxical: it was because his son was so much like him that he felt he had no son, no heir. What he wanted was for his son to carry on from himself, from where he, Jack, stood now: to be his continuation.

It was not that his youthful self had been, was, conceited, crude, inexperienced, intolerant: he knew very well that his own middle-aged capacities of tact, and the rest, were not much more than the oil these same qualities – not much changed – used to get their own way; he wasn't one to admire middle-aged blandness, expertise.

What he could not endure was that his son, all of them, would have to make the identical journey he and his contemporaries had made, to learn lessons exactly as if they had never been learned before.

Here, at precisely this point, was the famous 'generation gap'; here it had always been. It was not that the young were unlike their parents, that they blazed new trails, thought new thoughts, displayed new forms of courage: on the contrary, they behaved exactly like their parents, thought as they had – and, exactly like their parents, could not listen to this simple message: that it had all been done before.

It was this that was so depressing, and which caused the dryness of only just achieved tolerance on the part of the middle-aged towards 'the youth' – who, as they themselves had done, behaved as if youth and the freedom they had to 'experiment' were the only good they had, or could expect, in their lives.

But this time the 'gap' was much worse because a new kind of despair had entered into the consciousness of mankind: things were too desperate, the future of humanity depended on humanity being able to achieve new forms of intelligence, of being able to learn from experience. That humanity was unable to learn from experience was written there for everyone to see, since the new generation of the intelligent and consciously active youth behaved identically with every generation before them.

This endless cycle, of young people able to come to maturity only in making themselves into a caste which had to despise and dismiss their parents, insisting pointlessly on making their own discoveries – it was, quite simply, uneconomic. The world could not afford it.

Every middle-aged person (exactly as his or her parents had done) swallowed the disappointment of looking at all the intelligence and bravery of their children being absorbed in – repetition, which would end, inevitably in them turning into the Old Guard. Would, that is, if Calamity did not strike first. Which everybody knew now it was going to.

Watching his son and his friends was like watching laboratory animals unable to behave in any way other than that to which they had been trained – as he had done, as the Old Guard had done ... At this point in the fantasy, his son having accepted or at least listened to all this, Jack went on to what was really his main point. What was worst of all was that 'the youth' had not learned, were repeating, the old story of socialist recrimination and division. Looking back over his time – and, after all, recently he had had plenty of time to do just this, and was not that important, that a man had reached quiet water after such a buffeting and a racing and could think and reflect? – he could see one main message. This was that the reason for the failure of socialism to achieve what it could was obvious: that some process, some mechanism, was at work which made it inevitable that every political movement had to splinter and divide, then divide again and again, into smaller groups, sects, parties, each one dominated, at least temporarily, by some strong figure, some hero, or father, or guru figure, each abusing and insulting the others. If there had been a united socialist movement, not only in his time – which he saw as that since the Second World War – but in the time before that, and the epoch before that, and before that, there would have been a socialist Britain long ago.

But as night followed day, the same automatic process went on ... But if it *was* automatic, he imagined his son saying, then why talk to me like this? – Ah, Jack would reply, but you have to be better, don't you see? You have to, otherwise it's all at an end, it's finished, can't you see that? Can't you see that this process where one generation springs, virginal and guiltless – or so it sees itself – out of its debased predecessors, with everything new to learn, makes it inevitable that there must soon be division, and self-righteousness, and vituperation? Can't you see that that has happened to your lot? There are a dozen small newspapers, a dozen because of their differences. But suppose there had been one or two? There are a dozen little groups, each jealously defending their differences of dogma on policy, sex, history. Suppose there had been just one?

But of course there could not be only one, history showed there could not – history showed this, clearly, to those who were prepared to study history. But the young did not study history, because history began with them. Exactly as history had begun with Jack and his friends.

But the world could no longer afford this ... The fantasy did not culminate in satisfactory emotion, in an embrace, for instance, between father and son; it ended in a muddle of dull thoughts. Because the fantasy had become increasingly painful, Jack had recently developed it in a way which was less personal –

less challenging, less real? He had been thinking that he could discuss all these thoughts with the Old Guard and afterwards there could perhaps be a conference? Yes, there might be a confrontation, or something of that kind, between the Old Guard and the New Young. Things could be said publicly which never seemed to get themselves said privately? It could all be thrashed out and then ... meanwhile there was the funeral to get through.

That night, Friday, the one before the funeral, no sooner had he gone to sleep than he dreamed. It was not the same dream, that of the night in the hotel room, but it came as it were out of the same area. A corridor, long, dark, narrow, led to the place of the first dream, but at its entrance stood a female figure which at first he believed was his mother as a young woman. He believed this because of what he felt, which was an angry shame and inadequacy: these emotions were associated for him with some childhood experience which he supposed he must have suppressed; sometimes he thought he was on the point of remembering it. The figure wore a straight white dress with loose lacy sleeves. It had been his mother's dress, but both Elizabeth and Carrie had worn it 'for fun'. This monitor was at the same time his mother and his daughters, and she was directing him forward into the darkness of the tunnel.

His wife was switching on lights and looking at him with concern. He soothed her back to sleep, and for the second night running left his bed soon after he had got into it to read the night away and to listen to radio stations from all over the world.

Next morning he travelled to the airport in light fog, to find the flight delayed. He had left himself half an hour's free play, and in half an hour the flight was called and he was airborne, floating west inside grey cloud that was his inner state. He who had flown unmoved through the skies of most countries of the world, and in every kind of weather, was feeling claustrophic, and had to suppress wanting to batter his way out of the plane and run away across the mists and fogs of this upper country. He made himself think of something else: returned to the fantasy about the Conference. He imagined the scene, the hall packed to the doors, the platform manned by the well-known among the various generations of socialist. He saw himself there, with Walter on one side and his son on the other. He imagined how he, or Walter, would speak, explaining to the young that the survival of the world depended on them, that they had the chance to break this cycle of having to repeat and repeat experience: they could be the first generation consciously to take a decision to look at history, to absorb it, and in one bound to transcend it. It would be like a willed mutation.

He imagined the enthusiasm of the Conference – a sober and intelligent enthusiasm of course. He imagined the ending of the Conference when ... and here his experience took hold of him, and told him what would happen. In the first place, only some of the various socialist groups would be at the Conference. Rare people, indeed, would be prepared to give up the hegemony of their little groups to something designed to end little groups. The Conference would throw up some strong personalities, who would energize and lead: but very soon these would disagree and become enemies and form rival movements. In no time at all, this movement to end schism would have added to it. As always happened. So, if this was what Jack knew was bound to happen, why did he ... They were descending through heavy cloud. There was heavy rain in S——. The taxi crawled through slow traffic. By now he knew he would not be in time to reach the cemetery. If he had really wanted to make sure of being at the funeral he would have come down last night. Why hadn't he? He might as well go back now for all the good he was doing; but he went on. At the cemetery the funeral was over. Two young men were shovelling earth into the hole at the bottom of which lay his father: like the men in the street who continually dig up and rebury drains and pipes and wires. He took the same taxi back to the house in the church precincts, where he found Mrs Markham tidying the rooms ready to hold the last years of another man or woman, and his brother Cedric sorting out the old man's papers. Cedric was crisp: he quite understood the delay; he too would have been late for the funeral if he had not taken the precaution of booking rooms in the Royal Arms. But both he and Ellen had been there, with his wife and Ellen's husband. Also Ann. It would have been nice if Jack had been there, but it didn't matter.

It was now a warm day, all fog forgotten. Jack found a suitable flight back to London. High in sunlight he wondered if his father had felt as if he had no heir? He had been a lawyer: Cedric had succeeded him. In his youth he had defended labour agitators, conscientious objectors, taken on that kind of case: from religious conviction, not from social feeling. Well, did it make any difference why a thing was done, if it was done? This thought, seditious of everything Jack believed, lodged in his head – and did not show signs of leaving. It occurred to Jack that perhaps the old man had seen himself as his heir, and not Cedric, who had always been so cautious and respectable? Well, he would not now know what his father had thought: he had missed his chance to find out.

Perhaps he could talk to Ann and find out what the old man had been thinking? The feebleness of this deepened the inadequacy which was undermining him – an inadequacy which seemed to come from the dream of the female in a white dress? Why had that dream fitted his two lovely daughters into that stern unforgiving figure? He dozed, but kept waking himself for fear of dreaming. That he was now in brilliant sunshine over a floor of shining white cloud so soon after the flight through fog, dislocated his sense of time, of continuity even more: it was four days ago that he had had that telegram from Mrs Markham?

They ran into fog again above Heathrow, and had to crawl around in the air for half an hour before they could land. It was now four, and the Twenty-Four-Hour Fast had begun at two. He decided he would not join them, but he would drop in and explain why not.

He took the Underground to Trafalgar Square.

Twenty people, all well known to him and to the public, were grouped on the steps and porch of St Martin's. Some sat on cushions, some on stools. A large professionally made banner said: THIS IS A TWENTY-FOUR-HOUR FAST FOR THE STARVING MILLIONS OF BANGLADESH. Each faster had flasks of water, blankets and coats for the night ahead. Meanwhile it was a warm misty afternoon. Walter had a thick black sweater tied around his neck by the sleeves. Walter was the centre of the thing: the others related to him. Jack stood on the other side of the road thinking that his idea of talking with these his old friends about a joint conference with 'the youth' was absurd, impractical: now that he was again in the atmosphere of ordinary partisan politics he could see that it was.

He was longing to join them, but this was because he wanted to be enclosed in a group of like-minded people, to be supported by them, to be safe and shielded from doubts and fears. And dreams.

By Walter was his wife Norah, a small pretty woman whom he had always thought of as Walter's doormat. He had done, that is, until he had understood how afraid Rosemary had been of himself. Norah had once said to him after a meeting: 'If Walter had been an ordinary man I might have resented giving up my career, but when you are married to someone like Walter, then of course you are glad to submerge yourself. I feel as if this has been my contribution to the Movement.' Norah had been a journalist.

Walter's face, usually a fist of intention and power, was beaming, expansive: they all looked as if they were at a picnic, Jack thought. Smug, too. That he should think this astounded him, for he knew that he loved and admired them. Yet now, looking at Walter's handsome face, so well known to everyone from newspaper and television, it had over it a mask of vanity. This was so extraordinary a metamorphosis of Jack's view of his friend that he felt as if an alien was inhabiting him: a film had come over his eyes, distorting the faces of everyone he looked at. He was looking at masks of vanity, complacency, stupidity or, in the case of Walter's Norah, a foolish admiration. Then Jack's sense of what was happening changed: it was not that he was looking through distorting film, but that a film had been stripped off what he looked at. He was staring at faces that horrified him because of their naked self-centredness; he searched faces that must be like his own, for something he could admire, or need. And hastily he wiped his hand down over his own face, for he knew that on it was fastened a mask of vanity; he could feel it there. Under it, under an integument that was growing inwards into his flesh, he could feel something small, formless, blind – something pitiful and unborn.

Now, disgusted with his treachery, but still unable to take his hand down from his face, unable to prevent himself from trying to tug off that mask fastened there, he walked over to his friends who, seeing him come, smiled and looked about them for a place where he could sit. He said: 'I can't join you I am afraid. Transport trouble,' he added ridiculously, as first surprise, then incomprehension, showed on their faces. Now he saw that Walter had already registered: *His father!* – and saw that this born commander was framing the words he would use as soon as Jack turned his back: 'His father has died, he has just come from the funeral.' But this was no reason why he shouldn't be with them: he agreed, absolutely. Now he moved away, but glanced back with a wave and a smile: they were all gazing after the small drama embodied in: His father has just died. They looked as if they were hungry for the sensation of it – he was disliking himself for criticizing people whom he knew to be decent and courageous, who, ever since he had known them, had taken risks, given up opportunities, devoted themselves to what they believed to be right. To what *he* believed was right . . . He was also a bit frightened. Thoughts that he would never have believed he was capable of accommodating were taking root in him: he felt as if armies of others waited to invade.

He decided to walk down to the river, perhaps even to take a trip to Greenwich, if he could get on to a boat at all on a warm Saturday afternoon. He saw coming towards him a little procession under banners of: JESUS IS YOUR SAVIOUR and JESUS LIVES! All the faces under the banners were young; these young people were in no way distinguished by their clothes from the young ones he had watched marching, with whom he had marched, for the last fifteen years or more. Their clothes were gay and imaginative, their hair long, their faces all promise. He was smiling at Ann, who carried a square of cardboard that said: JESUS CARES ABOUT BANGLADESH. A voice said, 'Hello, Dad!' and he saw his Elizabeth, her golden hair in heavy pigtails over either shoulder. Hands, Ann's and Elizabeth's, pulled him in beside them. In this way one of the most prominent members of the Old Guard found himself marching under a poster which said: CHRIST CAME TO FEED THE HUNGRY. REMEMBER BANGLADESH! Ann's little face beamed with happiness and the results of the exercise. 'It was a nice funeral,' she said. 'I was telling Liz about it. It had a good feeling. Grandad liked it, I am sure.'

To this Jack found himself unable to reply, but he smiled and, with a couple of hundred Jesus-lovers, negotiated the Square, aided by some indulgent policemen. In a few moments he would pass his friends on the steps of the church.

'I shouldn't be here,' he said. 'False pretences.'

'Oh why?' inquired his daughter, really disappointed in him. 'I don't see that at all!'

Ann's look was affectionate and forgiving.

Around him they were singing 'Onward, Christian soldiers'. They sang and marched, or, rather, shuffled and ambled, and he modified his pace to theirs, and allowed his depression to think for him that whether the banners were secular and atheist on principle, or under the aegis of Jesus, twenty-four million people would die in the world this year of starvation, and that he would not give a new penny for the chances of anybody in this square living another ten years without encountering disaster.

He was now aware that Mona was staring at him: in her decisive face, in her unequivocal blue eyes, was not a trace of what he usually saw there – the reminder of their brief but pleasurable affair. She turned to tug at Walter's sleeve, in a way that betrayed panic – more than ordinary shock, anyway. Now they all turned to look at him: they were all blank, they could not take it in. He had a need to wave his arms and shout: Nonsense, can't you see that I am with my daughter and my niece? He felt he should apologize. He could not stand being condemned by them, his side, his family, but even as he nodded and smiled embarrassed greeting, he saw that Walter, whose mouth at first had really dropped open, had seen Elizabeth, whom of course he had known all her life. All was explainable! For the second time in half an hour Jack watched Walter framing words with which to exculpate him: Jack was with his daughter, that was it! After all, Jack was not the only one among them whose offspring had caught God in various extraordinary forms!

Jack entered the Square with the children, was informed that they would come to visit him later, and he left them singing energetic hymns by a fountain.

He took buses home. He was looking forward to letting the false positions of the day dissolve themselves into unimportance while he laughed over them with his wife; but now he remembered that she would not be there, nor expect him to be.

There was a note, not to him but to Carrie, saying: 'Please feed the cat, shall be very late, might stay at Judy Miller's please lock all doors much love.'

It was seven: it seemed like mid-afternoon. He drew the curtains to make a night, and sat in it with a glass of whisky. Later Ann came in to tell him about the funeral, about Jesus. He moved his position in his chair so that he could look at her shining eyelids. Carrie came in, and he looked at her, but her eyes were a woman's. He knew about her love-life, because she talked freely to her parents about it, but if she had never said a word he would have known from her knowledgeable breasts, from the way the flesh was moulded to her eyeballs by kisses. She breathed tenderness and care for him, he was happy she was there, but it was Ann he wanted to look at.

They discussed their respective faiths. Ann did not need to join a Church because she had a direct relationship with Jesus, who loved her as she loved Him. Carrie defined her religion as 'sort of Eastern, she supposed'. No, she didn't think it was Buddhist so much as Hindu. She believed in reincarnation but could not see the point of cow-worship, though anything that made people be nice to animals was worth it, she thought. Had Ann read the Upanishads? That was what she believed in. She was taking it for granted that her father had not, and would not. She would like to be a vegetarian, but after all she shared a kitchen with Elizabeth, who would object ... Here Elizabeth came in, having bathed and put on an ancient peacock-blue lace dinner dress that had holes in the sleeves: Jack remembered Rosemary in it, twenty years before. Elizabeth was indignant, and said she would not at all mind Carrie turning vegetarian, she was ready to be one herself. But what would they feed the cat on? Were human beings going to kill all the cats and dogs in the world because they weren't vegetarian? Carrie got angry at this, and said, There you are: I told you, I knew you didn't want to be vegetarian! Ann restored good feeling by laughing at them both.

They went on discussing the exact nuances of their beliefs, *I* believe that, no I don't agree with that, no I think it is more that ... surely not, oh no, how can you believe that? An hour or so went by. Jack lifted the drawn curtain: there was a heavy golden light everywhere, thunder in the evening sky, the trees had damp yellow aureoles. He dropped the curtain, and they were in a small low lamplight, and the three girls were discussing Women's Liberation. Jack hated women talking about this, not because he disagreed with any of it, but because he had never been able to cope with it, it was all too much for him. He felt increasingly that he had reason to feel guilty about practically every relationship he had ever had with a woman except for two or three special love affairs, which were outside ordinary categorization, but did not know how to change himself — if, indeed, he wanted to. These three young women had different, but precisely defined, opinions about the roles of women, with Carrie representing an extreme of femininity, and Ann, surprisingly, militant. Elizabeth talked about the lot of working women and had no time for what she called 'futile psychologizing'. This phrase made them quarrel, and for the first time Jack saw Ann strident. The quarrel went on, and then they saw that Jack was silent, and they remembered that his father was just dead, and they cooked for him, handing him many dishes, each as if it were a poultice for some wound he had suffered. Then, with an effort towards being reasonable, they went on discussing their ideological positions about Women's Liberation. Jack was again in the condition he had been in in the Square, when he had looked across traffic at his old friends. All he had been able to see there was a variety of discreditable emotions; all he could see in these charming faces was self-importance. What mattered to them was the moment when they said: I think so and so, no I don't think that. He knew that what they believed was not as important to them as that they had come to an opinion and the reasons why they had reached that opinion. They possessed their beliefs or opinions; they owned them.

Now they were back to religion again: the other two attacked Ann for being Christian when Christianity's history in relation to women was so retrogressive. To which Ann said to Carrie: 'You can talk, how about women in India?'

'Yes,' said Carrie, 'but then I don't believe in women being the same as men.'

This started the quarrel again, and their voices rose.

He had to stop himself saying that they sounded like a Conference of World Churches debating doctrinal differences, because he knew that if it came to dogmas, and disagreements about historical personalities, then his faith, socialism, beat them all. He looked at, listened to, his daughters, his brother's daughter, and knew that in two, three, ten years (if they were all allowed to live so long) they would be laying claim, with exactly the same possessiveness, to other creeds, faiths, attitudes.

Again he felt like a threatened building, the demolition teams at work on its base. He was seeing, like a nightmare, the world like a little ball covered over with minuscule creatures all vociferously and viciously arguing and killing each other over beliefs which they had come to hold by accident of environment, of geography.

He told the girls he had not been sleeping well, must go to bed: he could no longer stand listening while they staked precise claims in fields of doctrine. They went off, kissing him fondly: he knew from the warmth of the kisses that they had talked about his reactions to Grandad's death; everything was bound to be much worse for him, of course, because he was an atheist and did not believe in survival after death.

They each had a different version of their futures. Ann, for instance, believed that she would sit up after her death, exactly as she was now, but better, and would recognize her friends and family, and Jesus would be there too.

Jack was thinking that his own attitude to life after death had been collected quite casually: when he was young and forming (or acquiring) his opinions, the people and writers he admired wore atheism like a robe of honour. Not to believe in an after-life was like a certificate of bravery and, above all, clarity of thinking. If he had been young now, he might have collected, according to the chances of his experience, and just as lightly, any one of a variety of opinions. Reincarnation? Why not? After all, as Carrie said, it was an optimistic and forward-looking creed. But when he was young he couldn't have taken to a belief in reincarnation, if for no other reason than that he never met anyone who had it. He had known that a few cranks believed in it, and people in India, but that was about it.

Now he made a ritual of going to bed. The sky was still full of light, so he made the room black. He drank hot milk. He wooed sleep, which he had never done in his life, and soon lay awake, hands behind his head. But he could not spend a third night reading and listening to the radio. Then lights crashed on and his wife was in the room. She was apologetic, and quite understood that he hadn't felt like joining the Fast. Her mind, he could see, was on her lecture and the friends she had met afterwards. He watched her dimming her vitality, damping her good mood, because she was afraid of it disturbing him. She lay in bed smiling, bright-eyed. She asked about the funeral, was sorry she had not gone, sorry he had not reached it. Poor Jack! Smiling, she offered her arms, and grateful, he went into them. He would have gone on making love all night, but she went to sleep. In the close protective dark he lay beside his wife and in imagination saw the sky fill with dawn.

He fell asleep, he fell into a dream. In the dream he was thinking of what he had kept out of his consciousness all day, for to think of it was morbid. His father lay in a tight box under feet of wet soil. He, Jack, lay with him. He stifled and panicked, and the weight on him was as if he had been buried alive, in wet cement. He woke, and finding that although a cool damp light lay everywhere, and birds were at work on the lawn, it was only half past four. He turned on the radio, and made pictures in his head of the towns the stations were in, and lists of the people he had known in these towns, and then divided these into friends and enemies, and then, by a different classification, into the dead and the living, and so he returned in memory to the wars he had fought in or had reported, and relived, in a half-sleep, crisis-points, moments of danger, when he might have been killed, that now made him sweat and tremble but which then he had simply lived through. When it seemed to him as if hours of a new day had already passed, he went back upstairs and got into bed beside his wife.

But at breakfast she betrayed that she had known he had not been beside her: she started to talk about the job in Nigeria. He knew that she did not want to go away for two years, leaving all her new interests, new friends, new freedom. There, she would be back inside duties she had escaped from. There would be entertaining of a formal kind, there would be much social life. Yet it sounded as if she was trying to bring herself to believe she wanted to go if he did: she was worried about him.

He said, instead of replying about Nigeria, that he would like to go to church, just to see what it was like these days. She took in a puzzled but patient breath, let it sigh out of her, and looked at him with loving and respectful eyes – just like, he thought, the way Norah looked at Walter. She said: 'Oh, I can understand why. You mean, you missed the funeral service?'

Perhaps it was because he had missed the funeral service. He put on a suit and she a dress, and they went to church together, for the first time, except for weddings. Carrie and Elizabeth went with them, Carrie because God was everywhere, Elizabeth because he was particularly in churches. Ann would not come; she had Jesus by the hand as she sat on the floor reading the Sunday newspapers.

He sat through the service in a rage; perhaps it was a retrospective rage; certainly this was what he had felt throughout years of compulsory attendance at Evensong and Matins, and Services Early and Late, at his public school. He did not mind that it was mumbo-jumbo: it was bound to be! What he minded was that people voluntarily submitted themselves to the ministry of men palpably no better than themselves, men whose characters were written on their faces. This was perhaps what had first directed him towards socialism? He had not been able to stand that people submitted to being lied to, cheated, dominated, by their equals? He was again afflicted by yesterday's disability: a film had rolled away from what he looked at. That man, wearing black with white lace and embroidery, and dangling strips of this and that colour – the sort of attractive nonsense that Carrie and Liz might wear – that man intoning and dancing and posturing through the service, had a face like Walter's. They were both public men, performers. Their features were permanently twisted by vanity and self-importance. Jack kept passing his hand across his own face, feeling the ugliness of the love of power on it. And Rosemary put her arm in his, asking if he felt well, if he had toothache? He replied with violence that he must have been mad to want to come: he apologized for inflicting it on her.

'Oh, it doesn't matter for once,' she said, with mildness, but glanced over her shoulder to see if Carrie and Elizabeth had heard: it was extraordinary how they all kowtowed to their children, as if they feared to offend them.

After the midday meal he felt as if he could sleep at last, and did so.

The dream pulled him down into itself as he rolled on to his bed in the sultry yellow afternoon light – and passed out. This time, as he sank down beside his father, who was very cold – he could feel the cold coming out and claiming him – the weight pressed them both down, right through the earth that was below the tight box. His father disappeared and he, Jack, quite alone, was rocking on a light-blue sea. This too dissolved into air, but not before he had been pierced through and through with an extraordinary pain that was also a sweetness. He had not known anything like this before; in the dream he was saying to himself: That's a new thing, this sweetness. It was quickly gone, but astonishing, so that he woke up, pleased to wake up, as if out of a nightmare, yet what he had been happy to wake from was that high, piercing sweetness. Unhealthy, he judged it. It was not yet tea-time; he had slept an hour and not been refreshed. He went down to be told as a joke by his wife that a journalist had rung that morning to find out his views on the Twenty-Four-Hour Fast: did his not having been there mean that he was against it? Ann had answered, and had said that Mr Orkney was at church. The journalist had seemed surprised, Ann said. She had had to repeat it more than once. Had she meant that Jack Orkney was at a wedding? At a christening? No, no, at church, at Sunday morning service.

Jack knew the journalist; they had been in several foreign fields together. Jack was now seriously worried, as a man is when faced with the loss of reputation. He said to himself: I was not worried what people thought of me when I was young. He was answered: You mean, you were not worried by what people said who were not *your side*. He said: Well, but now it is not a personal thing, criticism of me is a criticism of my side; surely it is right to worry about letting my own side down?

There was no answer to this, except a knowledge he was dishonest.

Rosemary suggested a long walk. He could see she had been thinking how to make him whole again – how to protect her own happiness, he could not prevent himself thinking. He was more than ready to walk as many miles away as they could before dark: when they had first met, before they married, one of their things had been to walk miles, sometimes for days on end. Now they walked until it was dark, at eleven o'clock: they worked out it was over fifteen miles, and were pleased that this was still so easy for them, at their age, and in the middle of their undemanding life. But the night now confronted Jack, a narrow tunnel at the end of which waited a white-robed figure, pointing him into annihilation.

That night he did not sleep. The windows were open, the curtains drawn back, the room full of light from the sky. He pretended to sleep, so as to protect his wife from anxiety, but she lay alert beside him, also pretending sleep.

Next morning it was a week since Mrs Markham's wire, and he

became concerned for his health. He knew that not to sleep for night after night, as he was doing, was simply not possible. During the following days he went further into this heightened, over-sensitized state, like a country of which he had heard rumours but had not believed in. On its edges his wife and daughters smiled and were worried about him. He slept little, and when he did he was monitored by the female figure in white, now a composite of his mother, his wife and his daughters, but quite impersonal: she used their features but was an impostor. This figure had become like an angel on a wedding cake, or on a tomb, full of false sentiment; its appearance was accompanied, like a strain of particularly nauseating and banal music, by the sweetly piercing emotion, only it was much worse now; it was the essence of banality, of mawkishness, like being rolled in powdered sugar and swallowed into an insipid smile. The horror of this clinging sickliness was worse even than the nightmare – he could no longer remember the quality of that, only that it had occurred – of the night in the hotel. His bed, the bedroom, soon the entire house, was tainted by this emotion, which was more a sensation, even like nausea, as if he could never rid himself of the taste of a concentration of saccharine which he had accidentally swallowed. He was all day in a state of astonishment, and self-distrust: he made excuses not to go to bed.

Walter came to see him. Unannounced. As soon as Jack saw him getting out of his car, he remembered something which told him why Walter had come. About four years before, Mona had reviewed a religious book, the memoirs of some sort of mystic, in a way which surprised them all. They would have expected a certain tone – light, carefully non-solemn, for it did not do to give importance to something which did not deserve it – not mocking of course, which would have had the same result, but the tone you use to indicate to children that while you may be talking about, let's say, ghosts, or telling a story about a witch, the subject is not one to be taken seriously. But Mona had not used this subtly denigrating tone. Various of the Old Guard had commented on this. Then she had reviewed a book of religious poetry, which of course could not be dismissed in the light disin-

fecting tone, since poetry was obviously in a different category –
but the point was that none of them would have reviewed it at all.
For one thing no editor would think of asking them to. It was all
very upsetting. There had been a party at Bill's house and Mona
was not there. She had been discussed: she was at the age when
women 'get' religion. Jack, fond of Mona, offered to go and see
her. His visit was to find out, as he put it to himself, if she was
'still with us'. He had found her amiable, and her usual self,
helping to organize a conference for the coming week. He had
probed – oh, tactfully, of course. He mentioned an article in one
of the Sundays about a certain well-known religious figure, and
said he found the man a nauseating self-seeker. Mona had said
that she wàs inclined to agree. He had said casually, 'Of course I
am only too ready to forgive somebody who can't face old age
and all that without being cushioned by God.' Mona had remarked that for her part she could not believe in personal survival after death. Well, of course not, but for years that she could
not would have been taken for granted. He remembered feeling
protective affection for her: as if he were helping to save her from
a danger. Seeing Walter at a meeting to do with the Crisis in Our
Communications a week later, he had said that he had made a
point of visiting Mona and that she had seemed quite sound to
him.

He knew now what to expect from Walter.

Walter was looking furtive. Of course Jack knew that this
furtiveness was not anything he would have noticed normally:
this state he was in exaggerated every emotion on other people's
faces into caricatures. But Walter was playing a double part,
almost that of a spy (as he had with Mona of course, now he
came to think of it), and Furtiveness was written large on him.

Walter mentioned the Fast – a success – and then made a
clumsy sort of transition which Jack missed, and was talking
about Lourdes. Jack wondered why Lourdes? And then he
laughed: it was a short laugh, of astonishment, and Walter did
not notice it. Or, rather, had not expected a laugh in this place,
found it discordant, and therefore discounted it, as if it had not
happened. Walter was trying to find out if Jack's religious con-

version – the rumour had spread that he went to church on Sundays – included a belief in miracles, such as took place, they said, at Lourdes. Jack said he had been to Lourdes once for the *Daily* —— over some so-called miracles some years ago. Walter nodded, as if to say: That's right. He was already feeling relieved, because Jack had used the right tone. But he was still showing the anxiety of a priest who knew his beliefs to be the correct ones and was afraid of a lamb straying from the flock. He mentioned that Mona was suspected of having become a Roman Catholic. 'Good God, no,' said Jack, 'she can't have.' He sounded shocked. This was because his reaction was that she had been deceiving him, had lied. He sat silent, trying to remember the exact tones of her voice, how she had looked. If she was a Catholic, could she have said she did not believe in a personal survival? But he knew nothing at all of what Catholics thought, except that they did not believe in birth control, but did believe in the Pope.

Remembering that Walter was still there, and silent, he looked up to see him smiling with relief. The smile seemed to him extraordinary in its vulgarity, yet he knew that what he was seeing was the pleasure of a good comrade: Walter was happy that nothing was going to spoil their long friendship. The spontaneity of his reply over Mona had reassured him; now, mission accomplished, Walter was already thinking about the various obligations he had to get back to. But he stayed a little, to discuss some committee on pollution he was helping to set up.

He talked: Jack listened, wondering if this was the right time to raise the question of 'the young'. Walter's two sons were both classic revolutionaries and they despised their father for his success, his position in the socialist world, for 'his compromises with the ruling class'. Jack was thinking that of all the people in the world it was Walter, so like himself in experience, position and – he was afraid – character, with whom he should be able to talk about his preoccupation. But he was beginning to realize that there was a difference, and it was obviously an important one, between them. Jack was more on the outskirts of politics. He was more of a freelance, but Walter was always in the thick of every political struggle, always involved with the actual details of organization. He never did anything else. And this was why he was so far from Jack's present vision of things, which saw them all – the people like them – continually planning and arranging and organizing towards great goals, but fated to see these plans fail, or become so diluted by pressures of necessity that the results resembled nothing of what had been envisaged at the start. Sitting there, looking at his old friend's forceful and energetic face, it was in a double vision. On the one hand he thought that this was the one man he knew whom he would trust to see them all through any public or private tight spot; but at the same time he wanted to howl out, in a protest of agonized laughter, that if the skies fell (as they might very well do), if the seas rolled in, if all the water became undrinkable and the air poisoned and the food so short everyone was scratching for it in the dust like animals, Walter, Bill, Mona, himself, and all those like them, would be organizing Committees, Conferences, Sit-downs, Fasts, Marches, Protests and Petitions, and writing to the authorities about the undemocratic behaviour of the police.

Walter was talking about some negotiation with the Conservatives. Normally Jack would be listening to an admirably concise and intelligent account of human beings in conflict. Now Jack could see only that on his friend's face was a look which said: *I am Power.* Jack suddenly got up with a gesture of repulsion. Walter rose automatically, still talking, not noticing Jack's condition. Jack reminded himself that in criticizing Walter he had forgotten that he must be careful about himself: he had again, and suddenly, become conscious of the expressions that were fitting themselves down over his face, reflecting from Walter's, horrifying him in their complacency or their cruelty. And his limbs, his body, kept falling into postures of self-esteem and self-approval.

Walter was moving to the door, still talking. Jack, trying to keep his face blank, to prevent his limbs from expressing emotions which seemed to him appropriate for a monster, moved cautiously after him. Walter stood in the door – talking. Jack wanted him to go. It tired him, this self-observation he could not stop: there was his image at the door, oblivious to anything in the world but his own analysis of events. Yet at last, as Walter said good-bye and he saw Jack again – which he had not done for some minutes, being too self-absorbed – a worried look came into his face, and because of this look Jack knew that what Walter saw was a man standing in a rigid, unnatural position who had his hands at his lower cheeks, fretfully fingering the jaw-bone, as if it were out of place.

Walter said, in a simple and awkward voice: 'It's a bit of a shock when your old man goes. I know when mine died it took me quite a time to get back to normal.'

He left, like a health visitor, and Jack thought that Walter had had to get back to normal when his father died. He was thinking, too, that the cure for his condition was activity. Walter was more sensible than himself: he filled every moment of his time.

He decided to go to the family doctor for sleeping pills. This was a house that self-consciously did not go in for pills of any kind. Or did not now: Rosemary, during what she now called 'my silly time' – which after all had gone on for some years – had taken sleeping pills a lot. But that, even while she did it, had seemed to her a betrayal of her real nature. The girls went in for health in various ways – diets, yoga, home-made bread. His son was too strong – of course! – to need medicine. He smoked pot, Jack believed, and on principle – well, so would Jack have done at his age, the law on marihuana was absurd.

He told the doctor he was not sleeping well. The doctor asked for how long. He had to think. Well, for about a month, perhaps six weeeks.

The doctor said: 'That's not going to kill you, Jack!'

'All right, but before I get into the habit of not sleeping I'd like something – and *not* a placebo, please.' The glance the doctor gave him at this told him that he had in fact been deciding to prescribe a placebo, but there had been something in Jack's voice to make him change his mind.

'Is there anything else worrying you?'

'Nothing. Or everything.'

'I see,' said the doctor, and prescribed sleeping pills and anti-depressants.

Jack had the prescriptions made up, then changed his mind: if he started taking these pills, it would be some sort of capitulation. To what, he did not know. Besides, he was thinking: Perhaps they might make it worse? 'It' was not only the sweet mawkishness which threatened him at every turn, in a jingle of a tune for an advertisement on television, a shaft of light from behind cloud at sunrise, a kitten playing in the next garden, but the feeling, getting worse, that he was transparent, an automaton of unlikeable and predictable reactions. He was like a spy in his own home, noticing the slightest reactions of thought or emotion in his wife and daughters, seeing them as robots. If they knew how he was seeing them, how loathsome they were in their predictability, their banality, they would turn and kill him. And quite rightly. For he was not human. He was outside humanity. He even found himself walking abruptly out of rooms where he was sitting with Rosemary, or one or other of the girls; he could not stand his own horror and pity because of them, himself, everybody.

Yet they were treating him with perfect kindness. He knew that this was what it really was: even if he had to see it all as falsity, mere habits of kindness, sympathy, consideration, tact, which none of them really felt, wanting him to get back to normal, so that life could go on without stress.

His wife particularly longed for this. While he took care that he did not betray the horror he was immersed in, she knew well enough their time was over – the gaiety and charm of it, the irresponsibility. Probably for good. Being what she was, thoughtful, considerate (taught by society to show thoughtfulness and sympathy when she wasn't really feeling it, he could not stop himself thinking), she was trying to decide what to do for the best. Sometimes she asked if he didn't think he should write another book – even if he would like to make a trip abroad without her; she talked about Nigeria. Each time Nigeria was mentioned, his response to it was strong: it was the idea of forgetting himself entirely in an active and tightly planned life.

But he did not want to commit himself. He felt he would be losing an opportunity – but of what? And besides, how could he?

He believed he was seriously ill, in some inconceivable, unprecedented way; how could he take a job when his energies had to go into presenting a bland and harmless surface to those around him, into preventing his hand rising furtively up to his face, to see if the masks of greed or power were fastened there, into watching the postures his body assumed, which must betray his vices to anyone looking his way – or would betray them, if everybody wasn't blind and deaf, absorbed in their 'kindness', their awful, automatic, meaningless 'sympathy'.

One night his son arrived upstairs. Joseph used sometimes to come, unannounced, and went up through the girls' rooms to the attic to sleep. He took food from his sisters' kitchen. Sometimes he brought friends.

About a year ago there had been a row over the friends. Feeling one evening as if the top part of his house had been invaded by a stealthy army, Jack had gone up and found a dozen or so young men, and a couple of girls, all lying about on sleeping bags and blankets under the rafters. They had moved in. A girl was cooking sausages in a frying-pan that was on a camping stove; about a foot away was a drum that had written on it: PARAFFIN. INFLAMMABLE. The flame from the stove was turned too high, and showed around the edges of the frying-pan. Jack jumped forward, turned it down, removed the pan, and stood up, facing them, the pan in his hand. His usual responses to his son – apology, or the exhaustion due to the effort to be fair – had been cut, and he asked: 'What's the matter with you lot? What's wrong? You aren't stupid!'

Coming up the stairs he had been preparing a 'humorous' remark – which he was afraid would sound pompous, to the effect: How about introducing me to my guests? Now he stared at them, and the young faces stared back. There was a half-scared smile in the face of the girl who had been cooking, but no one said anything. 'I think you had better get out,' said Jack at last and went downstairs. Soon after he had watched the whole lot cross the garden like a tribe on the move, with their stove, their cartons, their paper-carriers, their guitars, their sleeping bags.

Now he came to think of it, this incident had been the beginning of his inadmissible depression. He had spent days, weeks, months, thinking about it. He felt there was a contempt there, in the carelessness, that went beyond anything he knew how to cope with: he did not understand it, them – his son. Who, meanwhile, had resumed his habits, and continued to drop in for a night or two when he had nowhere better to sleep. So it was not, Jack reasoned, that Joseph despised a roof over his head, as such? They had all been so stoned they had not known what they were doing? No, it hadn't seemed like it. They had not bothered to look at the drum, had not known it was full? But that was scarcely an excuse – no, it was all too much, not understandable . . . He had not talked to his son since, only seen him go past.

The telephone rang from upstairs: Carrie said that Joseph would be down to see him in a few moments, if Jack 'had nothing better to do'.

Instantly Jack was on the defensive: he knew that Joseph criticized him for having been away so much when the three children were growing up. This message was a reference to that – *again?* If it was simply careless, what had come into his head, then that made it even worse, in a way . . . Joseph came running lightly down the stairs and into the living-room. A muscular young man, he wore skin-tight blue jeans, a tight blue sweatshirt, and a small red scarf at his throat tied like a pirate's. The clothes were old, but as much care had gone into their choosing, preparation and presentation as a model getting ready for a photograph . . . While Jack knew he had already begun the process of comparison that always left him exhausted, he could not stop, and he was wondering: Was it that we were as obsessed with what we wore but I've forgotten it? No, it's not that: our convention was that it was bourgeois to spend time and money on clothes, that was it, but their convention is different, that's all it is and it is not important.

Joseph had a strong blue gaze, and a strong straight mouth. The mouth was hidden under a wiry golden beard. A mane of wiry yellow hair fell to his shoulders. Jack thought that the beard and the long hair were there because they were fashionable, and would be dropped the moment they were not . . . *Well, why not? He wished very much he could have swaggered about in beard and mane – that was the truth.*

This aggressively vivid young man sat on a chair opposite Jack, put his palms down on his thighs with his fingers pointing towards each other, and the elbows out. In this considering, alert position he looked at his father.

Jack, a faded, larger, softer version of what he was seeing, waited.

Joseph said: 'I hear you have got religion.'

'The opium,' said Jack, in a formal considering way, 'of the people. Yes. If that's what it is, I have got it.'

Jack felt particularly transparent, because of his son's forceful presence. He knew that his posture, the smile on his face, were expressing apology. He already knew the meeting was doomed to end unpleasantly. Yet he was looking for the words to appeal to his son, to begin the 'real' talk that they should be having.

Joseph said: 'Well, that's your business.' He sounded impatient: having raised the subject, or at least used it as an opener, now he was saying that his father's processes were of no interest or importance. 'You've been following the Robinson affair?'

Jack could not remember for a moment which affair that was but did not like to say so.

'We have to pay the defence lawyer. And there's the bail. We need at least three thousand pounds.'

Jack did not say anything. It was not from policy, but inadequacy, yet he saw his son beginning to make the irritable movements of power, of confidence, checked and thwarted. It crossed his mind that of course his son saw him as powerful and confident, and this it was that accounted for the aggression, the hostility, the callousness. Into Jack's mind now came sets of words framed rhetorically: since this was not how he was feeling, he was surprised. 'Why does it have to be like this, that more hate is used on people of the same side, thus preventing us ever from uniting in a common front, preventing us from bringing down the enemy?' These were words from the imaginary conversation with Joseph that he so often indulged in: only now did it strike him that he never had fantasies of a personal relationship – of their going for a holiday together for instance, or just spending an evening, or walking for an hour or so. 'Can't you see,' the inner rhetoric-maker was continuing, 'that the vigour of your criticism, your inconoclasm, your need to condemn the past without learning from it, will take you relentlessly to stand exactly where your despised elders stand now?'

It suddenly occurred to Jack, and for the first time, that he had repudiated his past. This so frightened him, leaving him, as it must, by himself out in the air somewhere, without comrades and allies – *without a family* – that he almost forgot Joseph's presence. He was thinking: For weeks now, ever since the old man's death – before, even? – I've been thinking as if I have abandoned socialism.

Joseph was saying: 'I don't have to tell you what the conditions are like in that prison, how they are being treated.'

Jack saw that the 'I don't have to tell you' was in fact an admission that in spite of everything he said, Joseph saw him as an ally. 'You've come to me for money?' he asked, as if there could be another reason.

'Yeah. Yeah. That's about it, I suppose.'

'Why do you have to be American?' Jack asked in sudden real irritation. 'You're not American. Why do you all have to?'

Joseph said, with a conscious smile: 'It's a mannerism, that's all.' Then he looked stern again, in command.

Jack said: 'I'm one of the old rich lefties you were publicly despising not long ago. You didn't want to have anything to do with us, you said.'

Joseph frowned and made irritable movements which said that he felt that the sort of polemic which abused people not standing exactly where he stood was rather like breathing, a tradition, and he genuinely felt his father was being unreasonable in taking such remarks personally. Then he said, as if nothing better could be expected: 'Then I take it it is not?'

'No,' said Jack. 'I am sorry.'

Joseph got up; but he looked hesitant, and even now could sit down — if Jack said the right things. If he could push aside the rhetorical sentences that kept coming to his tongue: how should they not? — he had spent many hours of fantasy ensuring that they would!

Jack suddenly heard himself saying, in a low, shaking, emotional voice: 'I am so sick of it all. It all just goes on and on. Over and over again.'

'Well,' said Joseph, 'they say it is what always happens, so I suppose that ought to make us feel better.' His smile was his own, not forced, or arranged.

Jack saw that Joseph had taken what he had said as an appeal for understanding between them personally: he had believed that his father was saying he was sick of their bad relations.

Had that been what he was saying? He had imagined he was talking about the political cycle. Jack now understood that if in fact he made enough effort, Joseph would respond, and then . . . He heard himself saying: 'Like bloody automatons. Over and over again. Can't you see that it is going to take something like twenty years for you lot to become old rich lefties?'

'Or would if we aren't all dead first,' said Joseph, ending the thing as Jack would, and with a calm, almost jolly smile. He left, saying: 'The Robinson brothers are likely to get fifteen years if we don't do something.'

Jack, as if a button had been pushed, was filled with guilt about the Robinson brothers and almost got up to write a cheque there and then. But he did not: it had been an entirely automatic reaction.

He spent a few days apparently in the state he had been in for weeks; but he knew himself to have reached the end of some long inner process that had proved too much for him. This interview with his son had been its end, as, very likely, the scene in the attic had been its beginning? Who knew? Who could know! Not Jack. He was worn out, as at the end of a long vigil. He found himself one morning standing in the middle of his living-room saying over and over again: 'I can't stand any more of this. I can't. I won't.'

He found the pills and took them with the same miserable

determination that he would have had to use to kill something that had to be killed. Almost at once he began to sleep and the tension eased. He no longer felt as if he was carrying around, embodied in himself, a question as urgent as a wound that needed dressing, but that he had no idea what the language was in which he might find an answer. He ceased to experience the cloying sweetness that caused a mental nausea, a hundred times worse than the physical. In a few days he had already stopped seeing his wife and daughters as great dolls who supplied warmth, charm, sympathy, when the buttons of duty or habit were pressed. Above all, he did not have to be on guard against his own abhorrence: his fingers did not explore masks on his face, nor was he always conscious of the statements made by his body and his limbs.

He was thinking that he was probably already known throughout the Left as a renegade; yet, examining the furniture in his mind, he found it not much changed.

It occurred to him, and he went on to consider it in a brisk judicious way, that it was an extraordinary thing that whereas he could have sat for an examination at a moment's notice on the history, the ideas and the contemporary situation of socialism, communism and associated movements, with confidence that he would know the answers even to questions on the details of some unimportant sect in some remote country, he was so ignorant of religious history and thought that he could not have answered any questions at all. His condition, in relation to religious questions, was like that of a person hearing of socialism for the first time and saying: 'Oh yes, I've often thought it wasn't fair that some people should have more than others. You agree, do you?'

He decided to go to the British Museum Reading Room. He had written many of his books there. His wife was delighted, knowing that this meant he was over the crisis.

He sent in his card for books on the history of the religions, on comparative religion, and on the relation of religion to anthropology.

For the first few days it seemed that he was still under the spell of his recent experience: he could not keep his attention from wandering from the page, and the men and women all around him bending over books seemed to him insane: this habit of solving all questions by imbibing information through the eyes off the printed page was a form of self-hypnotism. He was seeing them and himself as a species that could not function unless it took in information in this way.

But this soon passed and he was able to apply himself.

As he read, he conscientiously examined what he thought: was this changing at all? No, his distaste for the whole business could be summed up by an old idea of his, which was that if he had been bred, let us say, in Pakistan, that would have been enough for him to kill other people in the name of Mohammed, and if he had been born in India, to kill Moslems without a qualm. That had he been born in Italy, he would have been one brand of Christian, and if he had stuck with his family's faith, he would be bound to suspect Roman Catholicism. But above all what he felt was that this was an outdated situation. What was he doing sitting here surrounded by histories and concordances and expositions and exegetics? He would be better occupied doing almost anything else – a hundred years ago, yes, well, that had been different. The struggle for a Victorian inside the Church had meant something; for a man or a woman then to say, 'If I had been born an Arab I would be praying five times a day looking at Mecca, but had I been a Tibetan I would have believed in the Dalai Lama' – that kind of statement had needed courage then, and the effort to make it had been worth while.

There were, of course, the mystics. But the word was associated for him with the tainted sweetness that had so recently afflicted him, with self-indulgence, and posturing, and exaggerated behaviour. He read, however, Simone Weil and Teilhard de Chardin; these were the names he knew.

He sat, carefully checking his responses: he was more in sympathy with Simone Weil, because of her relations with the poor, less with Teilhard de Chardin who seemed to him not very different from any sort of intellectual: he could have been a useful sort of politician for instance? It occurred to him that he was in the process of choosing a degree or class of belief, like a pipe from a display of pipes, or a jacket in a shop, that would be on easy terms with the ideas he was already committed to, and, above all, would not disturb his associates. He could imagine himself saying to Walter: Well, yes, it is true that I am religious in a way – I can see the point of Simone Weil, she took poverty into account. She was a socialist of a kind, really.'

He bought more books by both Simone Weil and Teilhard, and took them home, but did not read them: he had lost interest, and besides an old mechanism had come into force. He realized that sitting in the Reading Room he had been thinking of writing a book describing, but entirely as a tourist, the varieties of religious behaviour he had actually witnessed: a festival in Ceylon involving sacred elephants for instance. The shape of this book was easy to find: he would describe what he had seen. The tone of it, the style – well, there might be a difficulty. There should not of course be the slightest tone of contempt; a light affectionate amusement would be appropriate. He found himself thinking that when the Old Guard read it they would be relieved as to the health of his state of mind.

Abandoning the Reading Room, he found that Carrie was becoming seriously interested in a young man met through her brother: he was one of the best known of the new young revolutionaries, brave, forthright, everything a young revolutionary should be. Carrie was in the process of marrying her father? A difficulty was that this young man and Joseph had recently quarrelled. They had disagreed so violently over some policy that Joseph had left his particular group, and had formed another. Rosemary thought the real reason for the quarrel was that Joseph resented his sister loving his friend but did not realize it. Jack took his wife to task over this, saying that to discredit socialist action because it had, or might have, psychological springs, was one of the oldest of Reaction's tricks. But, said Rosemary, every action had a psychological base, didn't it, so why shouldn't one describe what it was? Jack surprised himself by his vehemence in this discussion – it was, in fact, a quarrel. For he believed, with Rosemary, that probably Joseph was reacting emotionally: he had always been jealous of his sisters. Whatever the truth of it was, Carrie was certainly forgetting her 'Eastern thing'. She was already talking about it as of a youthful and outgrown phase. Rosemary, in telling Jack this, kept glancing apologetically at him: the last thing she wanted to do, she said, was to disparage any experience which he might be going through himself. Or had gone through.

Had gone through.

There was a conference on the theme of Saving Earth from Man, and he had been afraid he wasn't going to be asked. He was, and Mona rang up to say she would like to go with him. She made some remarks that could be openings to his joining her in a position that combined belief in God with progressive action: he could see that she was willing to lay before him this position, which she had verbalized in detail. He closed that door, hoping it did not sound like a snub. He was again thinking of something called 'religion' as an area coloured pink or green on a map, and in terms of a belief in an after-life, like a sweetened dummy for adults. In addition to this, he had two sets of ideas, or feelings, in his mind: one, these he had always held, or held since his early maturity; the other, not so much a set of ideas as a feeling of unease, disquiet, guilt, which amounted to a recognition that he had missed an opportunity of some sort, but that the failure had taken place long before his recent experience. Which he now summarized to himself in Walter's words as: It's a shock when your old man dies. His life had been set in one current, long ago; a fresh current, or at least a different one, had run into it from another source; but, unlike the springs and rivers of myth and fairy tale, it had been muddied and unclear.

He could see that his old friends were particularly delighted to see him at the Conference, ready to take an active part. He was on the platform, and he spoke several times, rather well. By the time the Conference was over, there was no doubt he was again confirmed as one of the Old Guard, trusted and reliable.

Because of the attention the Conference got, he was offered a rather good job on television, and he nearly took it. But what he needed was to get out of England for a bit. Again Rosemary mentioned Nigeria. Her case was a good one. He would enjoy it, it was work he would do well, he would be contributing valuably. She would enjoy it too, she added loyally. As of course she would, in many ways. After all, it was only for two years, and when she came back it would be easy for her to pick up what she had dropped. And Family Counsellors would still be needed, after all! Something that had seemed difficult, now seemed easy, not much more than a long trip to Europe. They were making it easy of course because of that refusal to look at the consequences of a thing that comes from wanting to leave options open. Spending two years in Africa would change them both, and they did not want to admit that they had become reluctant to change.

On the night after he had formally agreed to go to Nigeria he had the dream again – the worst. If worst was the word? – in this region of himself different laws applied. He was dropping into nothingness, the void: he was fighting his way to a window and there he battered in panes to let in air, and as he hit with his fists and shouted for help the air around him thinned and became exhausted – and he ceased to exist.

He had forgotten how terrible – or how powerful – that dream had been.

He paced his house, wearing the night away. It was too late: he was going to Nigeria because he had not known what else it was he could do.

During that night he could feel his face falling into the lines and folds of his father's face – at the time, that is, when his father had been an elderly, rather than an old, man. His father's old man's face had been open and sweet, but before achieving that goodness – like the inn at the end of a road which you have no alternative but to use? – he had had the face of a Roman, heavy-lidded, sceptical, obdurate, facing into the dark: the man whose pride and strength has to come from a conscious ability to suffer, in silence, the journey into negation.

During the days that followed, when the household was all plans and packing and arranging and people running in and out, Jack was thinking that there was only one difference between himself now and himself as he had been before 'the bit of a shock.' He had once been a man whose sleep had been – nothing, non-existent, he had slept like a small child. Now, in spite of everything, although he knew that fear could lie in wait there, his sleep had become another country, lying just behind his daytime one. Into that country he went nightly, with an alert, even if ironical, interest: the irony was due to his habits of obedience to his past – for a gift had been made to him. Behind the face of the sceptical world was another, which no conscious decision of his could stop him exploring.

Doris Lessing

THE SUMMER BEFORE THE DARK

Kate Brown, 45-year-old mother of four grown-up children, embarks on a summer of exploration, freedom and self-discovery, during which she rejects the stereotypes of femininity – which, like her conventional clothes, do not fit any longer.

'A summer journey of self-discovery which ends amazingly, in an act of self-definition so searching, so acute and total, one puts down the book shaken, enlarged, in awe' – *Sunday Times*

'Painfully, poignantly authentic' – *New Statesman*

'It should not be missed' – Robert Nye in the *Guardian*

THE GRASS IS SINGING

The Grass is Singing was Doris Lessing's first novel and brought her immediate recognition. A story of white people in Rhodesia, it is both an accurate picture of Africa as it appears to the average settler and a subtle story of a doomed marriage.

'Original and striking ... full of those terrifying touches of truth, seldom mentioned but instantly recognized. By any standards, this book shows remarkable power and imagination' – *New Statesman*

Margaret Drabble

A SUMMER BIRD-CAGE

Two sisters. Bright, attractive Sarah, newly down from Oxford and now bed-sittering in London; and beautiful Louise, who has just made a brilliant marriage to the rich but unlikeable novelist Stephen Halifax. Despite a promising start things seem to be going badly and as the situation builds up to its bizarre climax, Louise and Sarah have to discover whether they can really forgive each other for existing.

THE MILLSTONE

Rosamund – independent, sophisticated, enviably clever – is terrified of true maturity. Then, ironically, her first sexual experience leaves her pregnant ... Margaret Drabble shows how Rosamund faces up to a failed abortion and the trials of unmarried motherhood.

THE GARRICK YEAR

This novel takes the lid off a theatrical marriage; inside we find Emma, married to an egocentric actor playing a year's season at a provincial theatre festival, David, her husband – and Wyndham the producer. The mixture turns rapidly to acid.

JERUSALEM THE GOLDEN

The girl from Northam was grateful to find herself accepted in London intellectual circles. To Clara the London life seemed so much more real than the world of her home town. She could become the golden girl and have real affairs with married men, just like in the novels.

also published

The Waterfall
The Needle's Eye
Realms of Gold

The Ice Age
The Middle Ground

and a biography

Arnold Bennett

A CHOICE OF PENGUINS

☐ *The Englishman's Daughter* **Peter Evans** £1.95

From London and Venice to Moscow, Peter Evans's brilliant, surprising thriller traces a grey landscape of treason and sexual duplicity. 'Stunningly plotted' – *Guardian*. 'As fast-moving as *Gorky Park*' – Len Deighton

☐ *A Dark and Distant Shore* **Reay Tannahill** £3.50

Vilia is the unforgettable heroine, Kinveil Castle is her destiny, in this full-blooded saga spanning a century of Victoriana, empire, hatreds and love affairs. 'A marvellous blend of *Gone with the Wind* and *The Thorn Birds*. You will enjoy every page' – *Daily Mirror*

☐ *Death in Zanzibar* **M. M. Kaye** £1.95

Holidaying on the beautiful 'Isle of Cloves', Dany Ashton is caught up in a plot whirling round buried gold, blossoming romance, and murder . . . 'I recommend it wholeheartedly to those who fancy the idea of Agatha Christie with a touch of romantic suspense' – *Standard*

☐ *Running Time* **Gavin Lambert** £1.95

From child starlet to screen goddess, this is the story of the meteoric rise of Baby Jewel, propelled through the star system by her glamorous, calculating mother. A Hollywood bestseller, and 'a funny, dazzling showstopper' – *Good Housekeeping*

☐ *The Best of Roald Dahl* £4.95

Twenty ingenious and blood-curdling tales chosen from Dahl's bestselling volumes – *Over to You, Someone Like You, Kiss Kiss* and *Switch Bitch*.

A CHOICE OF PENGUINS

☐ *Lace* **Shirley Conran** £2.95

Lace is, quite simply, a publishing sensation: the story of Judy, Kate, Pagan and Maxine; the bestselling novel that teaches men about women – and women about themselves. 'Riches, bitches, sex and jetsetters' locations – they're all there' – *Sunday Express*

☐ *Castaway* **Lucy Irvine** £2.50

'Writer seeks "wife" for a year on tropical island.' This is the extra-ordinary, candid, sometimes shocking account of what happened when Lucy Irvine answered the advertisement and went off to discover for herself the realities of such a 'marriage' – and all our desert island dreams. 'Fascinating' – *Daily Mail*

These books should be available at all good bookshops or news-agents, but if you live in the UK or the Republic of Ireland and have difficulty in getting to a bookshop, they can be ordered by post. Please indicate the titles required and fill in the form below.

NAME _____ BLOCK CAPITALS

ADDRESS _____

_____

_____

Enclose a cheque or postal order payable to The Penguin Bookshop to cover the total price of books ordered, plus 50p for postage. Readers in the Republic of Ireland should send £IR equivalent to the sterling prices, plus 67p for postage. Send to: The Penguin Book-shop, 54/56 Bridlesmith Gate, Nottingham, NG1 2GP.

You can also order by phoning (0602) 599295, and quoting your Barclaycard or Access number.

Every effort is made to ensure the accuracy of the price and availability of books at the time of going to press, but it is sometimes necessary to increase prices and in these circumstances retail prices may be shown on the covers of books which may differ from the prices shown in this list or elsewhere. This list is not an offer to supply any book.

This order service is only available to residents in the UK and the Republic of Ireland.